The Science Fiction of L. E. Modesitt, Jr.

The Parafaith War

"Modesitt has created a meticulously detailed military-sf adventure that confronts the ethical reasons behind war but maintains a strong focus on the warrior-of-tomorrow's daily life."

—*Library Journal*

Of Tangible Ghosts

"Meticulously extrapolated . . . Alternate world tales and espionage thrillers both demand an abundance of intricate detail to be convincing and Modesitt doesn't stint for either thread of his narrative."

—*The Washington Post Book World*

"*Of Tangible Ghosts* succeeds in original fashion on many fronts."

—*The Denver Post*

"A comprehensively imagined alternate world with surprises at both global and personal levels. Alternate history with rigor, inventiveness, mystery, suspense, and flair—what more could you ask for?"

—David Alexander Smith

"The alternate universe novel is, to my mind, one of the most engaging forms science fiction can take, and *Of Tangible Ghosts* is as fine an example as one is apt to encounter anytime soon. . . . There is excitement and tantalizing near-familiarity on every page. *Of Tangible Ghosts* is a delightful read."

—Alfred Coppel

TOR BOOKS BY L. E. MODESITT, JR.

THE
PARAFAITH
WAR

L. E. MODESITT, JR.

A Tom Doherty Associates Book
New York

This is a work of fiction. All of the characters, organizations, and events portrayed in this novel are either products of the author's imagination or are used fictitiously.

THE PARAFAITH WAR

Copyright © 1996 by L. E. Modesitt, Jr.

All rights reserved.

Edited by David G. Hartwell

A Tor Book
Published by Tom Doherty Associates
175 Fifth Avenue
New York, NY 10010

www.tor-forge.com

Tor® is a registered trademark of Macmillan Publishing Group, LLC.

ISBN 978-0-7653-9790-4

Our books may be purchased in bulk for promotional, educational, or business use. Please contact your local bookseller or the Macmillan Corporate and Premium Sales Department at 1-800-221-7945, extension 5442, or by e-mail at MacmillanSpecialMarkets@macmillan.com.

First Edition: February 1996
Second Mass Market Edition: November 2017

Printed in the United States of America

0 9 8 7 6 5 4 3 2 1

To and for Carol Ann

1

Trystin Desoll shifted in the control seat of East Red Three and tried to ignore the acrid smell of plastic decaying under the corrosive assault of Mara's atmosphere and the faint hint of ammonia that lurked in the corners of the perimeter station. Both odors mingled with the false citrus of too many glasses of Sustain mixed in the small galley behind the duty screens, and with the staleness of air recycled and reprocessed too many times.

At 13:02.51, his implant-enhanced senses seared alert-red, and Trystin stiffened, fingers reaching, implant clicking in. As his direct-feed commands flared through the station net, he could sense the shields dropping into place even before the faint vibrations through the station confirmed the electroneural signals.

"Revs at zero nine two—"

Before Ryla's words had reached his ears, Trystin triggered the direct-feed for the eastern sector, splitting his mental screen into the four all-too-familiar images. In the upper right were the forward reclamation towers, still well behind the eastern perimeter; in the upper left the line of brown-suited attackers; in the lower right the computer enhancement showing the various hidden defense emplacements, the attackers, and the probability figures for each system, the numbers changing as the revs moved toward the towers. The lower left simply showed the entire sector as if from a satellite plot, with a colored dot showing the location of the downed—and since destroyed—paraglider, a reconstruction of the probable revvie tracks, East Red Three itself, and the hazy spot where another storm was forming over the badlands to the northeast.

Trystin scanned the revvie communications band, ran the comps, realizing that the revs had almost reached the perimeter before the sensors had discovered them. He triggered the line of antisuit bomblets, checking the display that seemed to scroll before his eyes against each clickback, finally nodding as the mental images indicated that all the bomblets had vaporized. Immediately, the lower left display showed the slowing of the revs' advance.

Nearly simultaneously, he fired off a standard attack report to Perimeter Control, to keep them informed, not that they could help him now, but PerCon would be all over him if he reported the attack after the fact. That was one reason for the implant and standard format—it took less than an instant.

To take out the revs, Trystin could have gone with the gattlings, or with the laser, but the input from the scanners indicated new reflectives on the revvie suits. Besides, he preferred giving some of the revs a chance to survive, a preference that some of the other perimeter officers, especially Quentar, who was one of the duty officers in East Red Two immediately to the north, suggested might be Trystin's undoing.

According to the net's computations, there was a ninety-percent probability that the revvie assault had originated from the downed paraglider that had hit the badlands less than a day earlier. The radar-transparent paraglider had come from the revvie troid ship that had gotten through the SysCon DefNet before being neutralized by the backups. How many assault wings had gotten free before the neutralization was another question. So was how much equipment the revs had pulled out of the glider before the patrol wing had lobbed in rockets and scorched it out of existence.

Trystin needed to find out. So some of the revs would survive, not that they'd necessarily enjoy the experience.

"Ryla. Get the wagon ready for revvie pickup." Voice was slower than direct-feed, but the noncoms weren't equipped to handle direct-feed.

"Yes, ser. We need info, ser?"

"That's affirmative. Looks like a follow-up from that troid ship. The sensors didn't register. Run a sampling on the suit fabric of a deader. If it's new, let HQ know."

"Stet, ser."

"There's at least one deader . . . the bomblets impacted a rev. The others are in shock, mostly milling around."

"We can use the organics. I won't be taking the wagon until they're almost stiffed."

"That's fine, so long as you get a couple. Use Block B. No double-celling, and if there are more than ten alive, use the end cells in A."

"Stet, ser."

Trystin refocused on the close-up of a dozen figures—probably men, given the revvie ratios—in outside combat suits, the solid brown with the white lightnings of the Prophet running up the sleeves. The respirator hoods and low backpacks gave them a hulking appearance, even as the synthfab coveralls began to shred.

"Pretty new suits, ser," added Ryla.

"Only twenty years old," snorted Trystin.

"Still don't feel sorry for 'em, ser."

"No. You don't have to. Out." Trystin went back to the overhead view, clicking in the enhancers and trying to see if another squad of revs had surfaced anywhere in the red-brown hills beyond the perimeter.

With the ambient heat and the gusting winds, only motion analysis had much chance of picking up revs at any distance. The satellite feed didn't have tight enough discrimination for something as small as a trooper, not one in camouflage brown, and the high-intensity scanners on the perimeter towers lost discrimination beyond five kays—or the nearest hilltop.

Besides the revs, the near scanners were now showing the storm buildup, and that bothered Trystin. The revs, if there were any more in his sector, could almost walk to the perimeter behind the storm front, if it drifted westward—except the revs already had arrived almost unnoticed, and they shouldn't have been able to do that.

He flicked into the meteorological module. "Interrogative storm, badlands, outsector."

"Not projected to intersect perimeter line at this time." The words, and the supporting data, seemed to scroll across his mental screen before he clicked back into surveillance.

The screens showed no other revs, no sign of anything besides the badlands, the growing storm, and the normal backdrop. He took a deep swallow of Sustain from the cup in the holder, then swallowed before he clicked on-net, direct-feed priority to Ulteena, the sector watch to the south, and to Quentar, who was now on duty at East Red Two to the north.

"Trystin in East Red Three. Just had a revvie thrust from that paraglider. Single squad. Sensors didn't pick up revs until late. Might be something new."

"Thanks, Trystin. Nothing on the screens here. We'll keep a watch." Ulteena projected almost a cuddly feel through the net. Trystin snorted to himself. Her neutralization ratio was the highest on the eastern perimeter.

"Stet, buddy," came back from Quentar. "Clear here. We'll up-scan, though. Remember. The only safe rev's a dead rev."

"Just wanted you to know."

"Stet."

Trystin wiped his forehead, damp despite the cooling system. He sniffed. The station still smelled of Sustain, ammonia, and a bit of the floral incense Gerfel had burned to mask the acridness of the station's odors.

"Ser?" called Ryla. "They're all down. I'm taking the wagon."

"Stet. Ryla?"

"Yes, ser?"

"If it moves, nail it."

"Yes, ser."

Trystin wiped his forehead again. He didn't need a noncom being wiped out by a deader play. Thanos knew when the station would get a permanent replacement if that happened, and he was already dead on his feet. The last thing he wanted to do was break in another tech.

He refocused on the split screens, but there was no discernible motion on any screen—either revs or local wildlife. Then, the last of the local hyenas had disappeared when the scumpers had. Trystin hadn't ever seen a scumper, but the system files showed them as oblong rough rocks with big extrudable feet, just the sort of thing to fascinate Salya. His ecoscientist sister had voiced more than a few doubts about the ethics of planoforming a planet with advanced life-forms, and for her a scumper was advanced.

Trystin half frowned and shifted his weight in the command seat, then scanned the power screen. The shrouded turbine fans were swiveled into the wind and holding at thirty percent of load, the balance coming from the fuel-cell banks in the plastcrete bunker beneath the station. After checking the fuel status, he triggered a request for resupply. The organonutrient glop was low, and tankers didn't run the perimeter lines when the revs were out.

The winds had been low lately, and that meant the station was drawing more from the fuel cells. He shook his head as he realized that he hadn't deployed the fan shields. There was too damned much to think about and too little time when the revs appeared without any warning. At least, he'd had the power, but that wouldn't have counted for much if one of the revs had punched holes through the blades or jammed the bearings with shrapnel. Neither Ryla nor PerCon would have been too happy.

Hhhstttt . . . cracccckkkk!!! The storm that had begun to form above the badlands discharged into the dry wash five kays east of the tower.

He almost screamed with the intensity of the static before the overload breakers cut in. His hands trembled, and his eyes watered.

"Shit . . . shit . . . shit . . ."

"Ser? You all right?"

"Friggin' stormlash . . . that's all." Trystin shook his head, angry that he'd actually broadcast. His implant cutoffs should have dropped him off-line more quickly. Idiot, he thought.

"Times, ser, I'm real glad I'm just a noncom."

"Thanks, Ryla."

"Anytime, ser."

Hhhsttt . . . craccckkkk!!! The second static flash wasn't as bad as the first, but his system still twitched. He kept his mouth shut, idly wishing that the station could tap the storm's power, as he watched Ryla guide the pickup wagon along the line beyond the perimeter, checking the area beyond the bomblet line. As the big-tired wagon passed, designed to keep from sinking into the too-fine soil, Ryla placed a replacement bomblet in each of the holders, and triggered their retraction into the artificial cacti. In one way, the revs were lucky. The antisuit bomblets were only installed around the stations. If they'd attacked the towers, it would have been gattlings or rockets, neither of which left much—except a crude form of fertilizer.

The wagon scooped the inert figures into the numbered bins.

"Pickup and replacement complete, ser. Looks like about five live, and seven for organics."

"Stet."

Trystin continued to scan the perimeter at high intensity until the telltales showed the wagon inside the station and the five captives in their cells in Block B.

"They're in, ser. Five are breathing."

"Stet. Mangrin will be pleased."

"So will Yressa. She likes making those revvie boys work."

Trystin pursed his lips, then steeled himself as his visuals picked up the lightning stroke.

Hsssttt!

After the shiver passed, he listened.

"She says they'll make that island bloom yet," Ryla continued.

"Maybe. She'll have to convince them that it's the will of the Prophet. You ready to go back on the board?"

"Yes, ser. Just a minute. Got to get the wagon in the stall."

Trystin waited, still scanning the screens, but there were no signs of the other revvie squads, although he and Ryla knew the paragliders carried more than a single squad, usually a lot more. Where those squads might be in the twisted hills of the badlands was another question, although Trystin would have liked to have known. Then, so would PerCon.

"Set, ser."

"Stet. Going down to see our visitors. Let me know about the suit stuff after I get back."

"Luck, ser. Don't be too nice."

As the storm rose, Trystin checked the fans—carrying half the load. Maybe that would slow down organonutrient use in the fuel cells. With a deep breath, he slipped out of the command seat and walked down the narrow steps to the lower level, to the right and through the permaplast door into Block B.

After ensuring the block door was closed behind him, he triggered the combat reflex biofeedback, unarmed module, and slipped through the sliding grate into the cell of the first rev—blond-haired and blue-eyed, like most of them, and probably in his early twenties, T-time.

The young military missionary launched himself right at Trystin, seemingly in slow motion, as Trystin stepped aside and his hands moved through two short arcs. The rev lay gasping on the stone floor for a minute, then lurched toward the Coalition officer. Trystin's knee snapped across the revvie soldier's shoulder, and threw the man against the stone wall.

"Oooffff . . ."

"Are you finished?" Trystin asked conversationally.

"Golem! Infidel!"

"That's not the question. I'd prefer not to hurt you." Trystin watched, saw the tensing muscles and stepped inside the rush, using his elbow and stiffened fingers to drop the rev back onto the stone.

"Oooo . . ."

"We could keep this up all day, but sooner or later, I'm going to miscalculate and really hurt you. Not that it matters to you. You're perfectly willing to die for the Prophet." Trystin paused, watching the rev and his eyes. "Have you considered that, since you're alive, He might have some use for you besides fertilizer?"

"Fert—" The soldier snapped his mouth shut.

"All the stories are true. We can't afford to waste anything here. Who knows? If you keep this up until I have to kill you, you just might end up as fertilizer or as nutrients for the pork industry. We keep the pigs in tunnels," Trystin lied.

"Golem! Infidel? Why should I believe anything you say?"

"Because I could have killed you and didn't. Because what happens to you depends on me." Trystin's eyes fixed on the other, triggering the superacute hearing. "How many squads came in on that glider?"

"Four" came through the subvocalization even as the rev snapped, "None but ours."

"Four," mused Trystin, direct-feeding the information to Ryla's console.

"Four? Shit, Lieutenant," responded Ryla through the link. "We got nothing on the screens."

"Did you get all your equipment out of the glider?"

"Yes . . ." "I don't know."

"Did the other squads have back-strapped heavy weapons?"

"I don't know."

"How long are the others supposed to stay under cover?"

"Days . . ." came the subvocalization, followed by the spoken words, "I don't know."

"How many glider wings were there on the mother troid?"

"Twenty . . ." subvocalized, followed by the spoken, "I don't know."

"How many gliders came off the mother troid?"

"I don't know." Subvocalization revealed nothing. A

line soldier who wasn't much more than the Prophet's gatt-ling feed wouldn't know, but Trystin had hoped.

"Was your troid one of the new ones with twenty in-system scouts?"

"Thirty . . . golem . . ." followed by, "I don't know."

Hsssttt! Despite the static burst from the storm and the headache, Trystin forced himself to remain calm.

"Was your Sword a Cherubim?"

"Seraphim." "I don't know."

"A Seraphim? My goodness. And did your troid bring in an EMP-Slam?"

". . . 'course . . ." covered by the inevitable question, "What's that?"

"Is it hot in those new suits?"

"Yes." "I don't know."

"How many of the other squads were angels?"

"One." "I don't know what you're talking about, golem."

"Any of you have fun with the angels?"

The rev lurched at Trystin, who blurred aside and let him crash into the wall.

"It's nice to know that you do have some remotely human drives," Trystin found himself saying conversa-tionally. Careful . . . you're not supposed to bait them. Careful—the warning seared through him from some-where. He took a deep breath.

"You going to kill me now? Turn me into fertilizer?" The blue eyes were bleak, and Trystin almost felt sorry for him. Almost.

"No." Not yet, thought Trystin. Not that I care. After triggering the door, he slipped outside and let the door seal the rev inside.

Outside, Trystin dropped a physiological overlay in place to call up some reserves for a few minutes, then took a series of deep breaths, letting the strength flow back into him. He'd pay for it later.

Even after months of sporadic interrogations, he still wasn't used to the mindless hatred the revs had been in-doctrinated with or the fact that they saw Coalition offi-cers as golems, more machines than human. Trystin didn't appear different from any other human, and looked, unfortunately, more like a rev than an Eco-Tech. He wasn't wired with metal—his implant was totally organic and invisible.

After a last deep breath, he triggered the second door and stepped around the moving grate and into the next cell, link-closing it behind him.

"You creatures really are part of the machinery." Another blond-haired blue-eyed rev, older than the first, studied him. "Indoc or interrogation?"

"Interrogation." Trystin noted the muscular tightening. "I wouldn't."

"Golems, aren't you? All machine, no soul." The muscles relaxed, but not totally. "Worse than the Immortals. You even look like a son of the Prophet. Did they re-create you in that image?"

"Hardly. I was born this way." Trystin continued to monitor the rev's muscular tension. "Did you really expect that a glider with only four squads could do much?"

"Hoped" was the subvocalization. "That wasn't my duty, ser."

Trystin tried not to frown. The "ser" bothered him. "Did you really want to throw away a squad of angels?"

"No." There was no conflict between the answer and the subvocal message.

The man was clearly an officer who'd been thoroughly briefed on Coalition officers' capabilities. Trystin pushed. "Why are you hiding that you're an officer?"

"I'm not hiding anything. You never asked."

"Why were you in the first attack?"

"Why not?"

Trystin wanted to shake his head. All the subvocalization detection wouldn't help in the slightest if he couldn't keep the other man off balance.

"What's your rank?"

"Assistant Force Leader."

"What squad was the Force Leader with?"

"Second" was followed by the verbal, "He stayed with the other squads."

"What do you really hope to get from these attacks?" Trystin let his voice become more conversational.

"Officially, that would be for others to say, ser."

"What do *you* want?"

"To wipe that mechanically superior grin off your young face."

"Do you want to live?"

The subvocalized *"Yes"* was followed by, "I'm not that certain survival is an option. You people don't seem to believe in the sacredness of life."

"Do you?" snapped Trystin.

"Yes."

"Then why are you out here trying to kill us?" Trystin wished he had bitten back the words. The man was getting to him. How could anyone who belonged to a faith, a system, that sent thousands of young troopers out to die, just to wear the Eco-Tech systems down for conquest—how could he claim that life was sacred?

". . . abominations . . . not real life . . ." "You surrendered your souls."

"Is that why the troid ship was carrying an EMP-Slam?"

"Yes." "I wasn't aware of that."

"How many more troid ships followed yours?"

"Three . . . think." "That's certainly none of my business."

"How many wings cleared the troid before you?"

"None." "I don't know."

"How many come after you?"

". . . three . . . more . . ." "I'm not a pilot, ser."

"How many troids are scheduled to attack Mara in the next year?"

"I don't know. Until the land belongs to the Lord."

"Are all your troops—"

"They aren't troops. They're missionaries."

"Excuse me. Are all your armed missionaries wearing the new suits?"

"Of course."

"When will you start bringing in heavier weapons?"

"Soon." "When the Lord wills."

Trystin looked at the composed man who stood there in what amounted to a white shipsuit. All the telltales and scans indicated, prisoner or not, that the rev was indeed as composed as he looked. "Won't you ever stop?"

"No. Not while we're about the Lord's business."

"Why does the Lord's business just involve our real estate? Why don't you go after the Hyndjis or the Argentis?"

". . . go after abominations . . ." "We follow the Lord's will."

Trystin shook his head, and stepped back.

"While I believe, nothing you say, golem, can shake me."

As the cell door shut, Trystin was certainly aware of the truth of the rev officer's convictions, and that nothing any outsider could say would shake his faith. Outside in the corridor, Trystin gathered himself together before entering the third cell, trying to ignore the more prevalent odor of ammonia and the ultrafine grit that seemed to settle everywhere in the blocks.

Trystin triggered the grate and stepped into the third cell.

The cold green eyes of the third rev looked at Trystin impassively, then his body lurched upward and toward the tech officer, almost as though independent of the rev himself.

Red seared through Trystin's system, more quickly than the mentally scripted alert system, or the report of electromuscular generation, and the door was opening as he kicked the rev back and threw himself out the door, triggering its emergency closure before he was quite clear of the cell.

His boots scraped the door, and some of the force of the explosion skidded him along the smooth stones of Block B, but he scrambled to his feet and looked back toward the bulging grate-door to the third cell. Wisps of greasy smoke curled through the bent frame of the door.

Blood dripped from the side of his jaw as Trystin scanned the corridor, then shook his head, and called his implant into the maintenance level. Only the single cell was damaged.

Now the smell of explosives, smoke, and charred meat joined the fainter odor of ammonia. Trystin swallowed hard.

"Ser!"

"We've got a new wrinkle, Ryla. Put this on-line, for all perimeter stations—no . . . I'll do it." Trystin took another deep breath and walked slowly back up toward the control center. After the heavy door to Block B closed behind him, he off-lined the unarmed combat step-up and the acute hearing and slogged toward the console seat, where he slumped as he coded the transmission. He took a long swallow of Sustain and walked to the galley to mix more as he direct-fed the message through his implant.

"PerCon, from East Red Three. New rev tactic. Bioelectric detonation of organic explosives . . ." After checking the data picked up by the scanners, he went on to summarize the use of biologically generated electric fields to detonate pseudomuscle or bone mass that was actually a form of plasex. ". . . thus, scanners pick up no electronic components. The electric generation is apparently triggered by a crude form of biofeedback. Could be dangerous for interrogators or others in direct rev contact."

He poured the Sustain powder into the glass and stirred, taking the glass back to the console seat with him.

Almost as the report went direct-feed, Ulteena clicked in.

"Sounds nasty. How are you, machman?"

"Sore. Few cuts. Angry. Why don't they leave us alone?"

" 'Cause the Prophet says we're the ungodly and golems. Or worse—descendants of the cursed immortals."

"Shit, we both fought the immortals. That's why old Earth and Newton are charred cinders."

"They've got a selective memory for history. You know that. So get some rest, and snap clean."

"I will. I will. After I download the interrogations and the info."

"Always the one to do it proper." Her voice—direct-fed or not—gentled.

"I try."

"I know." The last transmission was even softer before she off-lined.

He wondered what Ulteena looked like, since they'd never synced off duty. He shrugged. Probably not at all cuddly, but with shoulders broader than his and a nose sharper than a skimmer prow.

With another deep breath, he clicked into the log and began to itemize the results of the interrogation, including the facts that there might be as many as another sixty paragliders swirling into Mara's atmosphere, if they weren't already, not to mention that the troid ships were now carrying thirty in-system scouts, and that three more squads from the downed glider had yet to show up. He added the business about the insulation and the continued determination of the revs that Mara would fall to the Prophet.

"Ser?"

"Yes, Ryla?"

"You were right about the fabric on the revvie suits. Something new, and it's not only heat-shielding, but wave-transparent. I direct-lined the results to HQ, and they asked me to send a sample on the shuttle. It'll be ready for the afternoon pickup."

"Stet."

When the log-out report was in-lined and out on the DistribNet, Trystin sat back in the command seat. Then he sat up and refocused on the scanners in the two cells holding the revs he hadn't interrogated.

They scanned clean, right down to muscle density.

"Trystin?"

He looked up.

Gerfel stood beside him, stocky, dark-skinned, and dark-haired. "You ought to be careful. Could have been a rev."

"Shit . . . good luck. Revs up to some new stuff. In-feed the log before you scan."

"Before?"

"I mean it. They got new suit shields and new tricks."

"Praise their friggin' prophet."

"I wouldn't." He paused. "We pulled in five—in Block B. I only got through three of them. One of them exploded—suicide-type. There are two left. Can you handle them?"

"Can I handle them? I've been doing this longer than you have."

"I know. But B three is a mess. Rev was a live bomb. Bioorganic explosives. I did scans on the last two. They look clean, but be careful. Bastards really explode in your face."

"So that's why you look like that."

"Yeah. Be careful."

"I will. Especially now." Gerfel paused and offered a slight smile. "One thing I like about you, Trystin. You're lucky, and that counts for a lot."

"Can't always afford to count on it." Trystin climbed out of the command seat.

"No. But it helps."

"You ready?"

"I've got it."

Trystin logged out and off-lined, sensing Gerfel's aura on the net as she slipped in. He cleared his throat. "The incense helps. Thanks."

"Not enough, pretty boy, but I'm glad it takes some of the edge off."

He forced a smile before turning. His legs felt watery as he walked toward his cubicle.

"Off-line, Ryla. Gerfel's on. Call her if another batch of revs pops up before you're relieved." It wasn't likely, not with the noncom relief a half a stan after the duty officer, but Trystin didn't know what else to say.

"Stet, ser."

He trudged onward, thinking that he really should be going to the exercise room. He really should, but his feet carried him toward his cubicle, and his bunk.

He managed to lie down and close his eyes before the wave of blackness washed over him. Eight and a half hours on-line with an hour of step-up—too much, far too much.

2

✴ "And He will love thee and bless thee and multiply thee; He will also bless the fruit of thy womb, and the fruit of thy land, thy corn, thy wine, and thine oil and all the works of thy forges and the works of the tools of thy tools, and the increase of all that He hath given thee in the worlds to which His Prophet hath brought thee, as He swore unto thy fathers and their fathers.

"Ye shall be blessed above all people, in all the worlds and mansions of thy Father, so long as ye shall follow the words of His Prophet.

"Ye shall consume all the people which the Lord thy God shall deliver unto thee; thine eyes shall have no pity upon them; neither shall ye serve their gods, nor the gods of the land, nor the gods of the forge nor the gods of the coin, for those will be a snare unto ye.

"Do not say in thine hearts, those worlds are more than I; how are we to dispossess them?

"Be not afraid of the heathen, nor those that follow the false gods, nor those that would counsel unto thee, let us reason together; for well-crafted words are but a snare, and cannot stand before faith in thy Father the Lord.

"Listen to thy Father, and the words of the Prophet, and ye shall remember what the Lord God did unto Pharaoh, and unto those who surrendered their souls to the god of gold and precious metals, and unto those who saw not the many mansions in thy Father's house, and despaired in the dust of ancient Sodom, or those who despaired and perished upon the ashes of ancient Earth.

"The graven images of other gods ye shall burn with the fires of the heavens and the depths; ye shalt not take those technologies and those beliefs that are on them, nor take them into thee lest ye be snared therein, for such are an abomination to the Lord thy God, as spoken by His Prophet.

"Ye shall not be afrighted by them, for the Lord thy God is among thee, a mighty god and terrible. And He shall deliver their kings unto thine hand, and thou shalt destroy their names from under heaven. There shall be no man or woman to stand against thee, not even those who once would have lived forever, and ye shall render them unto dust and raise on that dust new mansions in thy Father's house, as it is His will. . . ."

Book of Toren
Original Edition

3

 At 0650 Trystin, a mug of Sustain in hand, crossed the space between the small galley and the control center, conscious that Voren had been watching from the command chair. The incense odor had died down, but the ammonia remained, as did the citrus-bitter smell of Sustain. Sustain with him.

"You're looking cheerful." Voren straightened. "Glad that incense smell is gone."

"Don't feel that cheerful."

Voren's eyes glazed as he clicked out of the system. Then he stood up. "Hate the swing watch. That extra half hour is murder."

"Anything happen?"

"No. Been watching for something more from the stupid paraglider—but nothing. Damned revs'll show up before long, though. Bet on that. But it's your baby. I'm going to get some sleep." Voren stood and yawned, then turned and trudged down toward the bunking cubicles, running his hand through his dark brown hair.

After settling into the command seat, Trystin scanned the messages waiting for him. Most were routine, except for three.

"Trystin Desoll, LT, SecWatch, East Red Three, from Perimeter Control. Re yours of 1651 13/10/788 concerning new rev tactic. Appreciate datadump and parameters. Will advise you further."

Advise him further? About what? What else wasn't PerCon telling him?

The second one, from Quentar, was shorter.

"Trystin, Weslyn didn't get your warning in time. Terrible mess. The second squad from the last paraglider dump hit East Red Six about the same time they hit you. Damned revs."

He hadn't really known Weslyn—just vaguely remembered him as short and squarish, darker even than the Eco-Tech norm, and one of the newest Service officers on Mara.

The third message was puzzling.

"Trystin Desoll, LT, SecWatch, East Red Three. Report MedCen, Klyseen, Mara, 0900, 10/21/788, for screening as per Farhkan f/up study. Considered duty day."

Farhkan follow-up study? What the frig was that? He on-lined his own file for a key-word search, while he went four-screen. The screens showed all defense equipment functioning and ready; no movement along the hundred kays of his perimeter; and no storms building over the badlands, although those didn't usually appear until midday or later.

Cling. The mental chime alerted him that the system had located the Farhkan references. Trystin scanned through them, nodding as he remembered. When he had just been finishing his Service officer training, he, and all the other trainees about to be commissioned, had received an invitation to take part in a study sponsored by the Farhkan cultural mission. The study involved periodic in-depth physicals and occasional interviews. Participation also provided an annual bonus of nearly three percent of his base pay. He'd signed up, taken the physical, and forgotten about the requirement for follow-ups.

Trystin shrugged. If the physical made it a duty day off the perimeter line, that was an added bonus. He could probably even count on spending part of the day with Ezildya.

Dropping his attention back to full four-screen, he squared himself in the command chair.

"Anything new, ser?" Ryla's voice snapped through the link.

"Nothing yet. Could be we'll have a quiet day. They happen sometimes."

"Sometimes, ser." Ryla sounded less than certain.

"Did the shuttle get our prisoners? And . . . raw materials?" Trystin could have checked himself, but he was making conversation.

"Yes, ser. Packed away on the 0440, rear section. Authenticated by Brysan. Mangrin flicked receipt already."

"Hope Yressa makes the survivors sweat."

"Me, too." Ryla paused. "The crackers are down to eighty-five percent. We'll need an overhaul on the ones in towers four and fourteen in the next month. Could be sooner. I'll copy you on the report."

"Stet."

As the noncom began his daily business of checking, scheduling, and troubleshooting the forward reclamation equipment, Trystin flicked the satellite plot into high resolution and tried to study the hills, but all he really got were blurs and an incipient headache.

In some ways, the perimeter setup didn't make the best military sense, because the installations were too close to the perimeter, but the reclamation equipment was there because its job was to change deadland and badland into something more receptive to the cross-gene engineered plantings that were laid down in patterns following the initial soil cracking.

So . . . the perimeter defense installations were set, and periodically moved forward, to protect the most expensive and critical equipment from the revvie attacks. And the greenery followed, kays and kays behind.

Trystin's principal duty was to protect the equipment, and the installation, just like every other Service officer's job on the Maran perimeter was. Or in the Helconyan satellite stations. Or in the Sasktoon perimeter lines, or the Safryan Belt installations, now that Safrya was basically habitable.

With the thought of Helconya, he wondered how Salya's biologicals were going. She'd always had that kind of bent, enjoying their father's gardens from the time she could reach out to the flowers. Trystin smiled. His older sister had talent, talent beyond screen-watching and neutralizing revs.

At 09:06.51, his senses seared alert-red, and Trystin overlined the four-split with the command options.

What looked to be another squad of revs had poured from over the steepest hill, sliding through the local equivalent of a cross between a cactus and scrub brush. They carried long objects larger than the standard assault rifles. Trystin could count nearly two full squads of the lightning-streaked suits, their new heat-shielding clearly effective against the sensors.

"Revs at zero eight nine—" Ryla's observation came late.

Ping! Ping! Crumpt!

The three-screen identified the heavy penetrating shells and the boosted rocket pryers as they impacted the composite armor of the sector building. Trystin belatedly shielded the fans, then dumped the attack report on-line.

Both the weapons and the revs were aimed, not at the rear, and main, reclamation towers, but toward the sector building housing Trystin, the sector maintenance-equipment center, and the sector perimeter-defense center.

Ping! Crumpt! Crumpt!

The explosions sent vibrations through the building.

"Heavy shells, ser!"

The revs surged forward.

Crumpt! Crumpt! The sector building shook with the impact of the shells and pryers, and Trystin could feel the damage-assessment reports building in the backfile. He triggered the antipersonnel gattlings. After the day before, he had no desire to risk more revvie booby traps, and this was the most heavily armed group of revs he'd personally seen. Osberyl-tipped, depleted uranium shells fragmented across the revvie line.

CRUUMPTTT!!!!

The entire sector control building rocked with the explosion, and Trystin dropped from four-screen into status, flashing through the maintenance lines, finding minor damage, jammed internal portals, but a ninety-two-plus status. While atmospheric integrity remained, his hand touched the emergency respirator pak in his belt for reassurance, long after his mind had returned to four-screen to survey the area to the east of the sector building.

He shook his head and went on-line to send a follow-up report to PerCon.

"Perimeter Control, from East Red Three, station under attack by single squad. Have neutralized revs. Will follow up with analysis."

The reddish sands showed only fragments of synthfab and a spray of brownish lumps—that and a superficial fusing of the soil's silicon, a fusing that pointed like an antique arrow toward the command center.

"What was that, ser?"

"Something new, Ryla. Still analyzing."

"They just exploded, ser."

Trystin had already called up the visuals and frozen them. The explosion had taken place faster than the scanner speed, but from what Trystin could tell, the gattlings' antipersonnel shrapnel had triggered something.

He froze the attack visuals and went back to four-scan for another sweep of East Red Three, but the visuals and the heat sensors showed a three-kay clearance, not that the sensors were all that accurate if the revs came in with insulation—like the last two waves had.

He flicked back to the visuals and full sensor screens of the attack, trying not to shake his head as he did. At least two of the revs had literally turned into the human equivalent of shaped charges with the impact of the heavy gattling shrapnel. He studied the suit shapes again and frowned.

"Ryla?"

"Yes, ser?"

"You filed that report on the new revvie suit fabric, didn't you?"

"Yesterday."

"Take a look at the attack visuals and the energy flows. They'll be in your screens in a moment. It looks like the fabric has something like one-way energy reflection that works with explosives." From what Trystin could tell from the screen recordings, the fabric—at least the part in front of the back-carried respirator paks—had turned the bioelectric explosion forward and toward the sector building. If the revs had been much closer . . .

He did shake his head.

Better heat-sensor insulation, more scout coverage, more glider wings, bioelectric suicide traps, hand-carried heavy weapons, and now this.

"Bastards . . . you mean they're turning their troops into shaped charges?"

"I don't know that it's quite that bad—just the ones who are captured or killed by high-impact charges."

"That's most of them, isn't it?" asked the noncom. "What about the ones you sent to Yressa?"

"Shit . . . talk to you later."

He remembered to unshield the fans—he worried about the power drain, since the promised organonutrient tanker hadn't shown yet. A fusactor would have been more practical in some ways, but the Eco-Tech compact kept nuclear power in orbit and deep-space ships. He kept checking the sensors and the satellite plot, even as he direct-fed his third urgent report to PerCon in as many days—and then copied both reports to the South Ocean reclamation station where Yressa directed the rev captives.

He wiped his forehead. What did the revs want? For

every one of their troops to be killed? Was Quentar right in claiming the only safe rev was a dead rev?

He took another scan of the maintenance status of the station before linking to Ryla's console.

"Yes, ser?"

"Most of it can wait, but that side door on the lower level is leaking, and it's getting worse."

"I'd already flagged that, ser, and I'll try to get it sealed."

"How about the other doors?"

"I might be able to handle it later, and maybe tonight . . ."

"Thanks."

Trystin went back to a full-concentration scan of the four screens before leaning back in the command seat and letting the systems work for him.

If the information he'd gotten from the captured revs had been correct, there couldn't be too many more squads from the downed paraglider. On the other hand, there could be as many as sixty gliders on their way down to Mara, although Trystin doubted that the DefNet had been *that* lax.

HHsstttt . . . ssss . . . The long, low crackle hiss-burned through the implant, and Trystin checked the metplot, noting that wind shift had apparently resulted in a storm buildup earlier than usual.

He shook his head, not really wanting to damp the system's sensitivity. Instead he continued to study the four screens, wincing at each burst of static. Still, the rising winds were good for the power system.

The mental *cling!* alerted Trystin to the incoming, and he called it up on his internal screen.

"Trystin Desoll, LT, SecWatch, East Red Three, from Perimeter Control. Re yours of 0926 14/10/788. Send full datadump to PerCon and to RESCOM."

With a deep breath Trystin began compiling the data-dump requested by PerCon, although it took little enough time, objectively. It just *seemed* like forever. He tagged the dump with a cover transmittal and pulsed it out.

"Perimeter Control/RESCOM [Klyseen], from Trystin

Desoll, LT, SecWatch, East Red Three. As per request, datadump follows."

Was it only 1100? He hoped Yressa and the research people could check on the latest rev captives and that he hadn't sent them troyens. He wiped his forehead. How could anyone know that the revs were getting even sneakier?

He scanned the screens with full concentration, but nothing showed to the east besides the red sandy soil, the hills, the ammonia cacti, the weedgrass clumps, and the gathering clouds that promised headaches later in the day.

After standing and stretching, Trystin walked around the command seat. He really didn't need to stay that close to the main console. The direct neural input was faster, but the rules were there in case the implant-based systems went, and he had to run the defenses manually—not that he wanted to. Not being able to react fast enough was a good way to get killed, and manual operation was far slower. But using a defective net was also a quick way to overloading his implant—and to neural burnout.

Finally, he walked back to the galley to refill the cup of Sustain, and then trotted back up to the command seat.

Outside, in the thin atmosphere, the precrackers turned soil, and the crackers cracked it. To the west, the planters dropped the cross-gene plantings in patterns. To the south, the latest water comet melted, and the water-vapor content of the atmosphere climbed marginally, and bit by bit the amount of oxygen rose.

Beyond the red-blue haze that was the sky, more troid ships were flung out of the revvie systems, and more para-gliders and troops were on their way toward Mara, and Trystin. Why did the revs beat on the Coalition, rather than the Hyndji systems or the Argenti plutocracy? Was it because ecologic technology was the closest thing to the genetic manipulation that had created the immortals? Or because the Coalition was closer and had more potentially habitable real estate? And why did all the revs seem so certain about the rectitude of their ways?

He took another sip of Sustain and studied the screens,

waiting for Gerfel. Tonight, no matter how he felt, no matter how bad the exercise room smelled, he was going through his workout. Tonight.

He studied the screens and sipped Sustain.

4

Two days passed, and no more revs attacked East Red Three. That didn't lessen the problems, Trystin reflected, including the ones that hadn't arrived, like the fuzzy EDI tracks beyond the Belt that probably meant another troid attack. Or the general alert for more paraglider descents. Was that based on Trystin's interrogations? Or on something more?

Trystin wished he knew, but junior first lieutenants didn't rate need-to-know on the basis of alerts. At least, the quieter days had left him with enough energy to use the workout room.

He scanned the four screens with greater attention, then concentrated on the satellite plot. Nothing—nothing, as was usually the case. He checked the power screen. The organonutrient supply was down to twenty percent, but the fans were carrying nearly sixty percent of the ambient load.

He coughed, once, then again, finally taking a deep breath, which just triggered more coughs. Despite Ryla's efforts, the atmospheric leakage was worse than before the repairs, according to the on-line telltales. There was definitely more than the normal faint acridness of ammonia.

Had the repairs even been done? He went on-line and scanned the entries. No repairs. No deliveries of replacements or spares.

"Ryla?"

"Yes, ser?"

"The syslog shows maintenance hasn't fixed our leaks yet. I'm still smelling outside glunk."

"It's worse down here, ser."

Trystin supposed it was. Ryla was closer to the bent frames.

"I'll buy that. What's with maintenance?"

"East Red Six. Most of the lower section wiped out. Then, the big attack on the western line."

"A lot of damage there?"

"Noncom scuttle is that the revs got three stations."

That would certainly explain it.

"Thanks. See what I can run down."

"I'd appreciate it, ser."

Trystin went into the deep-net, only to find a block across the maintenance levels. He grinned. More than one way to find out. The sector feed lines weren't blocked, and he just sent pulses through the DistribNet.

Of the twenty west-perimeter stations, five came up null. He nodded, but before he could link to Ryla's console, a mental *cling!* alerted him to a direct-feed from HQ.

"Desoll, East Red Three."

"Lieutenant, Major Sperto, HQ Ops. We have enough trouble on the west perimeter at the moment without having to worry about line-pulse tracers from the curious. Since you were the first hit with the new revvie weapon, it's understandable. Once we sort it out, you'll know. Now keep off the net unless it's official. And keep your speculations to yourself."

"Yes, ser."

"We'll post it when it's time."

"Yes, ser."

Trystin swallowed, then linked to Ryla's console.

"Yes, ser."

"They were hit hard, but HQ zapped me for prying. I'll let you know when the details come in. Could be as many as five stations, but that could also be system overload. Keep it to yourself until it's official."

"Five . . . bastards! . . . Thanks, ser."

"I didn't tell you. Understand?"

"Yes, ser."

"I'll let you know when I've got something official. Do we have anything that we could use to caulk around that bent mainframe?"

"I've been trying, ser, but . . ."

"I know." The trace gases in the Maran atmosphere, some the said-to-be-temporary results from the reatmosphering efforts, had a tendency to be corrosive. From Trystin's point of view, they scarcely seemed temporary.

Another hour of scanning, in between routine checks of equipment status, left Trystin with nothing new on the revs.

Thhrrrrummmmm . . . Trystin stiffened at the distant rumbling, even before the searing wave of white noise flashed through his implant, and the stars flickered across his internal four-screen display.

His eyes watered, and his head ached, although the atmospheric transit of the water comet headed for the new south sea hadn't been close enough to actually vibrate the station's walls. After Trystin straightened and rubbed his forehead, he wondered what the revs would think as the water slowly rose around their island prison. Would they think? Were they really human? And had Yressa found out anything about the revs? Maybe all those he'd transhipped had been fine.

"Lieutenant?"

"Yes, Ryla?"

"One of the turners is dropping off, down from ninety to a shade over eighty-five. Diagnostics don't show anything. I'm taking the scooter out."

"Stet. I'll keep a track."

"Thanks, ser."

Trystin watched the scooter go out, scanned the perimeter and the satellite plot, checked the maintenance board that Ryla couldn't while he was on the scooter, and waited. And waited. Then he had more Sustain, and wished he hadn't as it hit his guts with a jolt.

Cling! The fainter "sound" of the message signal indicated it wasn't urgent, but he called it up and mentally scrolled through it.

"Trystin Desoll, LT, SecWatch, East Red Three, from SOUSEAREC. Re yours of 1452 14/10/788 concerning new rev biologicals. Status check confirmed your data on bio-electric and organic explosion potentials. Three revs neutralized and transferred to RESCOM FFS."

He nodded. At least he'd gotten the word to Yressa in time. He stood and walked back to the galley for synthetic cheese and less synthetic algae crackers. Any more Sustain, and he'd be floating in the command seat.

In the small cooler was something wrapped in foil. Trystin edged it open, and then closed it. Real cheese. His mouth watered, but he left the package there. It was probably Gerfel's, and represented who knew how many creds of translation costs alone. Mara wasn't ready for any form of milk animals—not yet anyway, or not out of the tunnels and domes.

Finally, he took a few algae crackers and chewed them slowly.

The scooter blip in the three-screen had turned and was heading back to the station. Trystin held his breath as fine dust churned, but Ryla managed to right the scooter without digging it into the soil. Once the second-stage creepers were established, the soil got firmer as the biosphere got more complex. But the second-stage work hadn't gotten more than a hundred kays from Klyseen so far, and that meant that handling vehicles along the perimeter remained tricky. It was all too easy to bury a scooter in the fine soil.

As the scooter neared the station, Trystin called the tech. "Ryla? Find anything?"

"No, ser. I think the turner's whole mainboard is cooking, but I can't tell for sure. Going to have to put in a requisition for a replacement, but nothing will happen until it blows. Don't believe us techs until the electronics roast into silicon junk."

"All right. Let me know when the scooter's in and everything's secure."

The telltales would show that Ryla was back and that

the doors were closed, but not his condition. Trystin
waited.

"Lieutenant. Back on maintenance board."

"You got it."

"Anything new on the revs, ser?"

"RESCOM says they're working on it."

"They'll work till endday at the end of time." The noncom snorted.

Trystin shifted his weight, then stood and paced around
the command area, his eyes straying to the armaglass window that offered a far less accurate view than the two-
screen inside his mind.

Another *cling!*—not so faint, this time. Trystin moistened his lips with his tongue and scrolled up the message.

"All PerCon Stations, from RESCOM and PerCon. Be
alert to possibility that rev captives may contain biological-
based organic explosives not detectable by current first-
level scan systems. Until further notice, take no captives.
Take no captives. See DistribNet data RSC–1410–2."

While Trystin wasn't that fond of the revs, the "take no
captives" directive bothered him. Yet what could PerCon
do? Any rev could be booby-trapped to take out a station
or worse. Why did the revs do it? He shook his head as he
sat back down in the command seat.

After taking another complete four-screen scan, Trystin
called up the Research Command data bulletin and
scrolled through it, noting that it was a more scientific
presentation of what he had discovered.

"Ryla? How are the crackers doing?"

"They're hovering around eighty percent, ser."

"How about that turner?"

"It's hanging in there, but it doesn't feel right. Anything
new?"

"Not about the western stations. PerCon has ordered a
no-captives directive because of their organic traps."

"Bastards. How can they do that to their own?"

"I don't know. Something about their faith, I guess."
Trystin paused. "I'll let you know if there's a new status."

"Thanks, ser."

Trystin went back to checking the perimeter, checking the badlands, checking the power flow, and, in between four-screen scans, calling up rev backgrounders from the databanks. None of it was helpful, except to refresh his knowledge. The revs—Revenants of the Prophet—were a messianic, xenophobic, evangelistic culture whose members seemed universally to believe their mission was to claim the universe for the sons and daughters of the Prophet in the name of God.

Trystin shook his head. Was there a God? If so, what human could presume to know his mind? And how could such a god be good if he or she or it allowed followers to destroy any race or culture that opposed the expansion of the revs? He shrugged. If there were no god, then such claims were merely an excuse for destruction and expansion. Of course, that kind of rationalization was all too human. He snorted.

Cling! At the in-feed alert, he called up the message.

"All PerCon Stations. DefCom visual plot indicates three paragliders on entry envelopes. Probably landfall coordinates follow. Full alert on perimeter stations. DefCon Two. DefCon Two . . ."

Trystin plugged the coordinates into his system and cross-checked, but the indicators were that the revvie drop was aimed at the western perimeter stations—just what they needed with as many as twenty percent of the western stations either destroyed or marginally functional.

Over the next standard hour, he watched, but nothing came up anywhere within his screens, or within the satellite plot covering the eastern line.

He got more Sustain, noting the increasing odor of ammonia. Or was it the decreasing effect of Gerfel's incense? He did manage to keep his hands off the cheese, and tried not to drool when he thought about it.

Then it was back to the screens, more watching, more scanning—but nothing, as usual, until the in-feed alert— *cling!*

"All East Perimeter PerCon Stations. DefCon visual plot indicates three paragliders have impacted beyond west perimeter. DefCon Two stand down. DefCon Two stand down."

Trystin stood and stretched, then walked over to the small galley and began to rummage in the cooler. He deserved something, even if it were only synthetic cheese on algae crackers.

5

 The whole building stank, not only with ammonia, but with weedgrass, and the combined stench had overwhelmed Gerfel's latest incense-burning.

As Trystin entered the command center, he wanted to claw at his nose. The invisible grit from the sandy soil was so fine that it drifted through all but the tightest seals, and the station's seals were less than perfectly tight.

"I'm taking the midday shuttle," Voren said. "I don't care if I have to sleep sitting up coming and going. I've got to get out of this stench." He rubbed a nose that was noticeably red.

"Lucky you." Trystin coughed, then sneezed.

"You could go to Klyseen tonight and get back on the 0440. Otherwise, you won't sleep."

"I just might. I just might." Trystin wrinkled his nose, trying not to sneeze again.

"Oh, Gerfel's off-night's tonight. Hirachi's rotating duty now, but he won't be here until the late shuttle. He never is." Voren's eyes glazed as he logged off duty. "Also, Jynstin is coming with me. Think you two can handle it for a while?"

"We should be able to."

"It's all yours."

"I've got it." Trystin linked with the system and logged in.

Voren walked toward the stairs, then turned. "That cheese of Gerfel's?"

Trystin nodded.

"She said I could finish it. I couldn't. It's too rich. You can have the last of it. She told me it was better to share."

Trystin had often wondered what else the two had shared. "Thanks. I did drool over it when I was eating algae crackers."

"So did I, except I asked Gerfel. You've got to ask, young fellow."

Trystin shook his head at Voren's directness. Voren was less than a year older and Trystin's senior by only six months, even if the combination of shadowed heavy whiskers and hair over every centimeter of his body conveyed the impression of greater age.

"Ask and you shall receive." Voren headed for the steps down to the showers and his cubicle.

At times, Trystin wished he had the other's directness. Then again, he really didn't want to be that kind of person. Or was he just deceiving himself? He settled into the command chair and began his checks, but Voren had left everything clean. The fans were contributing ten percent of the power load with the light winds, and the organonutrient tanks were down to fifteen percent. He shook his head and pulsed through a follow-up order for the nutrients, citing the low fuel level.

Then he went through the messages. Nothing new, but the earlier general warning about possible additional revvie paraglider assaults remained current. If even a third of the wings had gotten clear of the troid, there would be far too many revs running around Mara. Although most survived low metabolic state through high-temp planetary entry, Trystin shivered, thinking about what the rev troopers—or missionaries—went through and how few ever returned.

He coughed again, then, noting that Ryla had finally come on, linked to the noncom console.

"Ryla?"

"Yes, ser?"

"I take it that maintenance has far more to deal with than our bent frame and leaky seals?"

"Yes, ser. I've been using that quick-caulk stuff, but it only lasts a few stans before the air pressure and everything eats through it."

"Isn't there anything better?"

"Sure. Inert stabilized fluorocarbons—except they aren't exactly stabilized here . . ."

"Yeah . . . no thanks. Tell me again why we're trying to reclaim this place."

"The word is that someone thought it was a good idea at the time."

"And the revs want to take it from us."

"That makes more sense. They've all got eight kids a family."

"How about five per sister, with five or six sisters per patriarch?" asked Trystin.

"Wouldn't mind being a patriarch."

"You want the odds on that? Only the ones that survive their missions get to be patriarchs. And I don't care much for their missions." Not when they come as living weapons, thought Trystin.

"Me, neither."

"Here comes first light. Time to see the beautiful badlands of Mara in full color."

"I'll be a lot happier someplace farther along, ser, like Safrya."

"Maybe your next tour will be there."

"Maybe."

With that, Trystin let Ryla get on with the business of repairs and technical checkups, while he ran through the four screens one at a time before dropping into simultaneous four-screen.

Nearly a stan later, Ryla up-linked. "Lieutenant Desoll, ser?"

"Yes, Ryla."

"Number three cracker's down to fifty percent and overheating. The datalinks are burned out."

"You're cleared out. I'll watch the rest of the maintenance board."

"Be a bit before I get the scooter clear. I'll need a bunch of stuff, ser."

"That's fine. Let me know when you clear the bay."

"Stet."

The noncoms did most of the physical maintenance work, but they didn't have to worry about burning out their neural systems, either. Trystin rubbed his forehead and shifted his weight, then stood and walked to the armaglass window. The scratched pane showed him far less than his screens, but at times the view through his eyes and the grit-scarred armaglass seemed more real.

"Clearing the bay now, ser."

"Stet." Trystin walked back and forth, his consciousness more on the screens than on the gray plastic walls that surrounded him.

Kkcchewww!! The itching got worse, and the odor of ammonia was stronger. He forced himself to stop rubbing his nose.

After running through the maintenance screens, Trystin plopped back into his chair and continued scanning, even though the screens and detectors showed nothing beyond the badlands, the building storms, and the reclamation towers and equipment. At least the winds had increased the power from the fans to nearly thirty percent.

Cling! Trystin swallowed the algae cracker, and washed it down with Sustain even as he called up the message.

"All PerCon Stations. DefCom visual plot indicates two paragliders on entry envelopes. Probable landfall coordinates follow. Full alert on perimeter stations. DefCon Two. DefCon Two . . ."

Trystin plugged the coordinates into his system and cross-checked.

"Shit . . ." This time the indicators suggested that revvie drop was aimed at the midsection of the eastern perimeter stations—a bit south of East Red Three—but that could change, and probably would. The revs were good enough atmospheric pilots that the gliders never came down quite where DefCom said they would. By the time the DefCom and satellite plots had them located and the rockets were away, the gliders were usually empty shells, and the revs were clear and headed for perimeter stations.

He pulsed the scooter and got the relay to Ryla's suit unit.

"Ryla? How are you coming?"

"Damned cracker's a mess, ser, but they wouldn't listen. Mainboard's pretty much melted solid. Don't know how it's working as well as it is."

"Can you wind it up in a stan?"

"Be done in less than half that. Not much I can do."

"We got a rev drop in entry."

"I'll make that even quicker, ser."

"Stet."

Trystin waited and watched, but even with the satellite plot he couldn't see any sign of the revvie paragliders. He fixed and drank another cup of Sustain, and wished he hadn't as his stomach roiled.

"Ser, I'm back, and we're buttoned up. Heard anything?"

"Not yet."

Trystin studied the screens, but could only see the few native cacti bending in the wind and grit scudding along the hillsides. Above the higher sections of the badlands, clouds had begun to form.

Cling!

"All PerCon Stations. DefCom has confirmed two paraglider landfall near eastern perimeter. Both gliders have been neutralized. Landfall coordinates and estimated time of landfall follow. Full alert on eastern perimeter stations. DefCon One. DefCon One . . ."

The coordinates were east and slightly south of East Red Three, almost where predicted, surprisingly—and less than five kays right down the wash. The landfall had been nearly three quarters of a standard hour earlier.

Trystin pursed his lips and took another full scan. With the coordinates, and by straining the resolution capabilities of the system, he thought he could make out a ·badlands valley containing discolored soil and a few long objects that might have been glider components. Why didn't the system have better resolution? The capabilities had been there for centuries. Was it the cost?

He linked to Ryla's console. "Ryla, we could have company anytime."

"I was afraid you'd say that."

"Sorry."

"Damned revs."

Having no answer to that sentiment, Trystin took another full screen-by-screen scan before dropping into balanced four-screen.

At 14:16.13, alert-red spilled through the system, although Trystin had already called up the command options when a flicker of dust appeared on the farthest hill.

Ping! Ping! Crumpt! Without a rev in sight, the first round of shells impacted the station's composite armor.

Trystin triggered the shields, both for the station entries and the fans. A single red signal flashed—the shield for the main vehicle-entry door on the south side of the station had jammed, not that there was a thing Trystin could do about it.

"Revs!"

"Got 'em, Ryla." Except that he didn't directly, only through the impacts of their weapons. Visual shielding? Trystin checked the impact angles of the incomings with a visual replay, then reset one of his rockets into a high-arc trajectory toward the dust puff on the far hill.

Crumpt! Crumpt! The building shivered again under the revvie rockets.

Using full scan, Trystin watched his rocket, noting the detonation on his screen. Outside of the gout of red soil, there were no additional explosions, but there were also no more shells impacting on the command center.

The lieutenant nodded. His calculations had been good enough to silence the revs, but only momentarily. He recalculated, assuming forward or sideways motion to keep the revs out of the direct line of the gattlings.

Crumpt! Crumpt! Crumpt!

"The maintenance-door shield's jammed, ser."

"Stet. Happened when I dropped the shields, but I figured I couldn't do much in the middle of an attack. You all right there?"

"I'd better be, ser. No place else to go that's any safer—except the bolthole, and I'm not one for burying myself." There was a pause before the noncom asked, "What they got there?"

"Something that screens them, and a lot of rockets." As he spoke, Trystin released another spread of rockets, then simultaneously sent an attack report to PerCon.

Crumpt! Crumpt! The next round of revvie rockets slammed into the station, and Trystin winced as he watched for the impact of his own rockets.

Not only was there a gout of dirt, but a secondary explosion on the flatter slope of one of the hills beyond the perimeter.

Crumpt! Another rocket slammed the station.

Clearly, not enough of a secondary explosion. Trystin recalculated and released another spread of rockets.

Crumpt! Ping!

Some of the revs were close enough for rifle fire, and Trystin didn't like that at all, not when he couldn't see much and when the revs had some form of new heat-shielding clearly effective against the sensors.

Ping! Ping! Crumpt!

Finally, the three-screen identified the source of the shells and the boosted rocket pryers and reverse-tracked them to the backside of the nearest hill to the northeast. As usual, the revs had their weapons aimed at the station building itself, rather than at the heavy reclamation equipment.

Still wondering why that seemed to be so, Trystin used a spread of rockets to reply, since the revs were out of gattling range.

Ping! Crumpt! Crumpt!

Another series of explosions, these visible on the short-range direct scanners, dotted the hillside—and one small secondary explosion followed.

A series of distortions seemed to flow downhill toward the station, and Trystin flicked through scanning frequencies until he found one that gave him what amounted to flickering outlines.

Even with the use of all screens and sensors, Trystin couldn't seem to get a hard count on the revs, as if the sensors and the optical scanners were facing some sort of interference. He could see that, again, some of the flickering figures carried the longer assault rifles.

Crumpt! Crumpt! Crumpt! The entire station building shivered.

Now that the revs were in range, Trystin triggered the antipersonnel gattlings and the antisuit bomblets, but the revs seemed to have avoided the artificial cacti with the bomblets, except for a few stragglers on one side.

After the earlier attacks, Trystin had no desire to risk more revvie booby traps, and this was the most heavily armed group of revs he'd personally seen. The exterior sensors relayed the sprayed fragmenting of the osberyl-tipped depleted uranium shells across the revvie line.

CRUUMPTTT!!!!

The entire sector control building rocked with the explosion, and Trystin dropped from four-screen into status, flashing through the maintenance lines.

Crumpt! Crumpt!

So many subsystems reported overload or damage that the backfile flared red. Trystin couldn't even have counted the impaired systems.

AIR SYSTEM INTEGRITY LOST!!

Some atmospheric integrity remained, but not enough for breathing. Trystin shoved the emergency respirator over his face, and jammed the tube into the seat pak.

Crumpt!

"Ryla! Air system's down. Get into your respak!"

No response, and a check-pulse indicated that the noncom's system was off-line. There was nothing Trystin could do, not in the middle of an attack. If he didn't stop the revs, then it wouldn't matter what shape Ryla was in.

Jumping from the command center, Trystin yanked the

combat suit from the locker and stuffed himself into it, automatically disconnecting the respirator tube and holding his breath as he dropped the helmet in place and made the seals. He hated the damned armor, both for the restriction in his net access, and even more for the price he'd pay in using it, but the revs, or some of them, were in the station—or they would be before long.

He kicked his reflexes up, ignoring the buzzing sensation that the boost gave him, and pulled the heavy-duty slug thrower out of its rack, along with several clips. Then he headed for the steps to the station's lower level.

As he neared the staircase, the vibrations warned him, and he eased to the side, then dropped flat, waiting.

Two ghostlike and wavering figures, faintly brownish, charged up the stairs. Only slightly more clear were the outlines of the assault rifles that each carried.

Trystin squeezed the trigger on his own rifle just twice.

Both figures tumbled backward, and seemed to disappear at the bottom of the stairway. No movement—or flickering images. Even before they had disappeared, Trystin moved toward the maintenance chute with the ladder, designed for emergency access to the station's half-buried lower level.

As he moved, he scanned the net wide-band to see if he could intercept any revvie communications. The net didn't seem able to take the command, and he came up with nothing. With a gauntleted hand, he flipped up the lever on the shaft door and swung inside, setting his feet on the rung just below floor level and reaching back to close the door behind him.

Whhummmp!

The electronic scream of the net crashing ran through Trystin like a knife down his spine, and his fingers opened, half-deadened from the neural impact. Even with the implant cutouts dropping him off-line, Trystin stiffened and half slid down the three meters to the floor of the shaft, his hands barely breaking his fall with half-grasps of the metal rungs. He twisted off the ladder at the bottom, and his hip smashed into a side brace. Stars flashed across his eyes, and stabbing lines of pain lashed him.

Finally, he levered himself upright, feeling almost blind with all outside inputs to his implant cut off and the system down. He eased open the lower door a crack and looked into the maintenance room behind the vehicle garage—no revs in sight. The door to the garage was closed, as was the one to the lower-level main corridor. The station was dim, almost dark, with the power system off-line.

Slowly, he moved toward the corridor, his rifle ready. Underfoot he could feel vibrations, but couldn't sense their source. Again, he cracked the next door and looked down the corridor, using his internal controls to step up his night vision.

Two more of the barely discernible ghost-suited figures crouched with their backs to him, as if looking around the corner and up the stairwell.

Three quick shots were enough, and Trystin hurried toward the bodies, even harder to see when the revs were not moving. He still hugged the wall, not trusting that they were indeed dead.

Ping! Ping! Ping! More shots came from the end of the corridor ahead.

Trystin skidded down behind the half-visible bodies and tried to scan the section of the hall that led to the lock to the garage and the vehicle door where the armor shield had jammed.

Ping! Ping!

Shells spanged and pinged off the inside of the outer station wall behind and to the left of Trystin. His own breathing sounded like an overloaded ventilator, and he forced himself to breathe more deliberately as he fired three shots down the dim corridor.

Ping! Spang!

Plastcrete fragments from the revs' shots showered Trystin as he squeezed off two more rounds. He felt that there were only two revs crouched at the end of the corridor, but they had pushed in a turner blade for a shield—far more effective than the dead rev bodies he crouched behind.

Stifling a sigh, Trystin cranked up his reflexes to high and leaped sideways, then charged the revs. From a standing position, he had enough height to fire over the low turner blade—and sprayed the area in an effort to neutralize the revs he could see only as intermittent distortions.

Ping!

Only one shot came his way—one that creased his helmet.

He lowered his reflexes back to one notch above normal and crouched on his side of the turner blade, almost hyperventilating in an effort to relieve his oxygen debt, feeling both his overloaded suit and body straining.

"Shit . . ." he muttered. No system defenses, and who knew how many revs left. He could barely see the revs, and only if they moved. He was running through a stan's worth of oxygen in half that time by upping his metabolism to stay alive.

He remained concealed, but could hear nothing through the suit's limited "ears."

He'd killed at least four revs, maybe six—but what had happened to the rest?

Slowly he eased around the turner blade and headed for the lock to the garage. As he expected, the big door had been blown open. One rev body lay sprawled by the door, visible only where a slash across the suit had turned back the armored and insulated fabric—probably caused by door shrapnel.

Peering from behind the heavy plastcrete pylon at the flat ground around the station, he saw nothing moving. Outside, the badlands looked the same, and so did the one side of the single reclamation tower in his vision field. What was different were the dozen bodies and the fragments of composite armor strewn beneath the station walls.

Trystin stood, chest heaving. He wasn't thinking clearly, not at all, a sign of fatigue, and who knew what else. Fatigue? Idiot! He mentally tripped his reflexes and metabolism down to normal, and stood shaking. Step-up meant burning more energy, and he'd been in enhanced-reflex status for all too long. He almost slumped into a heap as fatigue washed over him.

He swallowed nearly all the Sustain in the suit's helmet nipple, ignoring the chills and cold jolt he felt as it hit his guts.

How long he waited, he wasn't sure, not until he checked his implant. With no movement for nearly a half stan, he doubted there were any revs left.

Then, picking up one heavy foot after another, he turned and headed back through the useless lock door to the tech section, and the emergency transmitter.

At the end of the corridor were two more bodies. One was a rev with the shoulder of his suit burned away; the other was Ryla.

"Shit . . ." Trystin swallowed; he was supposed to protect the tech.

He stepped slowly inside the tech section. The system console looked almost normal—the gray plastic dull as ever—except for the dead lights and the corner with the hole large enough for him to insert a gauntleted hand.

He levered open the shielded cover to the emergency transmitter, and the light winked green. With his implant working for short distances, he linked with the simple circuits.

"Perimeter Control, this is East Red Three, from Lieutenant Desoll. Station East Red Three is down. System is red. No station integrity. Rev attack neutralized—"

"Desoll, Major Alessandro here. How many revs? What's your status?"

"I'm in armor using the emergency transmitter. There were two to three squads with backpacked heavy weapons. They've got new shielding, and you can only see them on the fringe scanner frequencies and only at about a third of a kay. The vehicle-door shield jammed, and some blew their way in. Ryla—the tech—killed one, but they got him. I got six or so after I got in armor."

"Is the station secure?"

"It looks that way, but they blew a hole in the system

controller. So I don't know for sure. And their suits make them almost impossible to see."

"Do you want to hole up?"

"That's negative. You can't tell what's happening in the bolthole."

"Can you try to use a scooter to get to East Red Two?"

"That's affirmative."

"If the scooter isn't operational, let us know."

"Stet. East Red Three out." He off-linked and looked back around the tech office. Trystin had no real choices. Hanging on at the station for a tech cleanup team that could be days wasn't a choice, not really, not with all the damaged stations on both perimeters. He'd head for East Red Two, slightly closer than East Red Four.

He shook his head and looked at the slug thrower, then walked down the corridor and up the stairs to the cabinet. He extracted all the spare clips, putting a full one in the rifle and carrying the others, before heading back down. Standing around a dead station doing nothing wasn't exactly brilliant.

Then again, riding an unarmored scooter north for sixty kays wasn't exactly brilliant either—assuming he had a working scooter.

Both scooters were untouched, and the fuel cells and motors on both checked out. Trystin took number two because it had full tanks, and stuffed two additional oxygen tanks inside with the spare clips. He took both ration kits from the scooter he was leaving. Although eating in armor was a pain, what was even less desirable was handling other metabolic processes.

After loading and checking the scooter, he hurried back to the emergency transmitter, still carrying the rifle. He looked down at Ryla's body, and the open eyes. Finally, he went back into the workroom and found some plastic sheeting and slowly wrapped the tech's figure into the plastic, then laid him out on the long workbench. What else he could do, he didn't know, since the scooter would be cramped.

After that, he turned to the emergency transmitter.

"East Red Two, this is East Red Three."

"Trystin, interrogative you headed our way?"

"That's affirm. Me and my little scooter."

"We'll be watching."

"Stet. East Red Three out."

He closed off the transmitter and walked back to the loaded scooter, settling himself in the driver's seat and plugging his armor into the scooter's oxygen tank. He leaned the rifle where he could reach it almost instantly— at an angle across the narrow passenger seat. With a last look around the garage, he eased the vehicle through the ruined door. Once clear of the station, he followed the depressed and flattened ground of the shuttle track westward.

As he drove west, past where the turners had processed the soil, a darker earth had been mixed through the reddish surface cover and reset by the turners. Even so, Trystin could see the faint trace of the creepers beginning to grow over the combined mosaic of red and brown.

With each kay he headed westward, the low blue-green mottled creepers that looked like a cross between lichen and kudzu grew thicker, with less ground between the creepers and darker soil around them. As the bioengineered creepers grew, they slowly released the oxygen once bound into the soil eons ago. Already the free oxygen in the air was approaching five percent, but the total pressure was still half T-norm. Sometimes, looking westward across the creepered plains, he could almost see the gas rising. On a bright day around Klyseen, the gas from the most active creeper clusters cast wavering shadows.

The four-wheeled scooter bounced and jolted, without the air cushion of a shuttle or transport, and Trystin jolted and bounced with it. Scooters were not designed for long-distance travel. He also had to keep the scooter on the hard-packed soil of the track. If he bounced into the fine and gritty soil where the creepers grew, the scooter could easily dig in wheel-deep. More than a few turners had literally buried themselves in patches of ultrafine soil and sand.

By the time Trystin reached the north-south shuttle track and turned north toward East Red Two, the creepers grew almost calf-high in places.

As he drove, he continued to scan the terrain, now mostly mottled blue and green. The constant movement reminded him how much harder it was to check everything visually. His neck would be sore by the time he reached East Red Two. Even more sore, he corrected himself.

The scooter continued to bounce northward, and Trystin continued to scan the terrain, seeing only the endless kays of blue-green.

In time—after two uncomfortable stops, and four standard hours, he finally eased the scooter to a halt at the intersection of two shuttle tracks.

After looking at the track eastward and checking the small plot on the scooter console, Trystin turned the scooter toward Quentar's station and linked to the scooter comm. "East Red Two, this is East Red Three."

There was no response. Trystin shook his head. The scooter comms were supposed to be good for more than thirty kays on open terrain. He couldn't have been more than five from East Red Two. Had the tanks all been full on the scooter he took because the comm system wasn't that good?

As he headed eastward, the creepers became lower and more scattered.

After the scooter had covered another kay or so, and he could see most of the reclamation towers, Trystin tried the comm again. "East Red Two, this is East Red Three. I'm about three kays south."

Nothing.

He tried the helmet comm, with no results, and the scooter rolled on toward East Red Two.

"Approaching scooter . . . if that's you, Trystin . . . make a left turn, then a right, then a left back on your original heading. Then stop for a moment—the same number of times as your call number."

Trystin followed Quentar's directions, with three quick stops, trying not to mangle either creepers or the scooter, before resuming his course toward the station. He kept trying the comm intermittently.

Then he began trying the helmet link.

At about a kay, he got a response.

"You're coming in weak, Trystin."

"That's helmet comm. I can read you, but the scooter transmitter's shot."

"Revvie casualty?"

"Negative. Maintenance casualty, I think."

"Talk about it later. Natsugi is waiting for you."

"Stet."

Trystin guided the scooter toward the station. As he neared the garage entrance, both shields and door opened—in sequence. Trystin wondered if he or Ryla should have lowered the shields to East Red Three earlier. If he had, then maybe Ryla could have had time to repair the shield mechanism. Then again, maybe not. If the shield could have been repaired, they'd both paid for that oversight, Ryla far more than Trystin.

He swallowed again. It had still been his responsibility.

Natsugi waited at the vehicle door, a heavy rifle aimed at the scooter. He kept it aimed at Trystin until Trystin unhelmeted inside the station.

"Lieutenant Desoll, Natsugi."

"Pleased to meet you, ser." Natsugi didn't look convinced, but Trystin had encountered the problem before—he looked like too many revs.

"Maybe you could help, Natsugi." Trystin tried not to lean against the wall, but the armor was heavy, and he was exhausted. "The revs got Ryla. I couldn't bring his body, but I wrapped him in sheeting and laid him out on the tech table. If you could let someone know . . ."

"I'll see what I can do."

"Thank you. Quentar up in the center?"

"Yes, ser."

Trystin slowly walked up the stairs. Quentar waved as he saw the other lieutenant and motioned to the hard chair next to the command seat.

Trystin sat on the hard chair and took a deep breath.

East Red Two smelled like weedgrass and ammonia, but not so strongly as his station had.

"So what happened?" Quentar's eyes remained glazed, indicating that his attention was on his screens.

"A lot of revs, with heavy backpacked weapons, with really good visual and heat shields that kept them off scanner until they were within a couple hundred meters. The lower vehicle-door shield jammed. A bunch of them got past the gattlings and rockets and blew their way in. Ryla got one; I got six, I think, but they got him."

"You're lucky to be alive. According to PerCon, you had all six squads targeting you."

"I used a lot of rockets and almost all the gattlings. They still beat the armor to shreds."

"Our super high-tech composite boron plastic armor?"

"The same stuff."

"Did you think about the bolthole?" asked Quentar.

"Fine. I go down into that coffin and do what? Wait? Who'd ever come and get me? That's for when you're a basket case."

"Yeah. I feel that way, too." Quentar shook his head and pointed to the small console in the corner. "After you report to PerCon, you can use the off-watch cubicle and the shower. Let me know where they're sending you."

Trystin stood and trudged across to the console, linking into the system.

"Perimeter Control, Lieutenant Trystin Desoll, calling from East Red Two. Reporting status—"

"Desoll, this is Major Alessandro. Did you encounter any more revs?"

"No, ser."

"Can the station be brought on-line quickly?"

"I don't know. The upper right corner of the tech center got scorched with an HE round, but the rest seemed all right."

"How did they get in?"

"The vehicle-door shield jammed open after Ryla returned from a repair run, and we never got it fixed before the revs showed up."

"That's been a problem. Do you have any idea how many revs assaulted your station?"

"No, ser. The scanners wouldn't focus on their shielding right. I couldn't see anything either, not until I did a full-frequency scan, and that was only on the fringe, and they still seemed to flicker. . . ."

The questions seemed to go on and on. Trystin propped himself against the wall and kept answering.

Finally, Alessandro concluded, ". . . if we need any more information, I'll get back to you. There will be a tech team and a sweep team going in tomorrow, and they'll send a carrier for you—around zero seven hundred. Later on, we'll send out the rest of the station crew."

Trystin logged off and walked back toward Quentar, slumping back into the hard chair.

"And?" asked Quentar.

"They're sending a tech team out tomorrow, along with a sweep squad. They'll pick me up."

"Lucky you." Quentar paused. "No one else was there?"

Trystin shook his head. "The attack the other day . . . well, the revs bent a door and shield frame enough that the station stunk. So Voren and the techs bailed out. Gerfel had leave, and her replacement wasn't due until the late shuttle."

"Makes you wonder."

"Yeah," Trystin snapped. "How did they manage to locate the one under-force station on the entire perimeter—from orbit yet—and the only one with bad shields—and still get wiped out?"

"A lot of bodies?"

"What's a lot? I counted maybe a squad, but I didn't go looking. They're all still there."

"They're good for fertilizer, anyway. Except we've got to transport them." Quentar laughed. "You know the one thing I like about this job?"

"What?" asked Trystin tiredly.

"Killing revs. It'd be better if I could be a pilot. That way I could scorch a bunch, but the gattlings do a real good job. You know," Quentar said, his voice dropping to a more conversational level, "the revs aren't really human. They're part alien."

"I hadn't heard that."

"Oh . . . the policy types on Perdya hushed that up. They said it makes people too excitable. How else do you explain it? Would you run right at a gattling, Trystin? Would anyone human? How else can you explain it?"

"Their faith," suggested Trystin. "If they die in a holy war or whatever it is, they go to paradise."

"No real human could swallow that. No, they're aliens. They just look human." Quentar laughed again. "Wish I were a pilot. Then I could scorch a whole lot of them. Keep 'em from killing real people." His eyes half glazed at a message or some line input, and he added in a disinterested tone, his consciousness half elsewhere, "You need some rest."

"Yeah." Trystin nodded and walked down to the shower, concentrating on putting one foot in front of the other. A shower and sleep, those were what he really wanted—and not to think about alien-acting revs. Or Quentar's wanting to kill anything that moved. Just a shower and sleep.

6

 In the gray light before dawn, the troop carrier was even grayer than the morning, the thermoshield plastic that covered the composite armor blending into the western horizon. The beetle-shaped carrier bore twin forward-slanted antennae composed of Sasaki cannon. On each side of the bulge that held the fully automated guns was a single rapid-launch rocket tube. Under the guns were the cockpit portals—dark armaglass irises that looked like blind eyes.

Trystin watched as the carrier slowed outside the station,

putting its fans on bypass and settling down. He closed his helmet. The suit still smelled like a weight room, despite his quick efforts to clean it out that morning before redonning it. He stepped through the outer portal from East Red Two, walking quickly toward the armored carrier, aware that Natsugi had dropped the shields behind him as soon as he was clear. With each step, his boots sank ankle-deep in the powdery soil.

The carrier's armored side door swung down as he crossed the reddish ground that continued to vibrate under even the idling of the carrier's engines. As he put his foot on the textured plates that backed the door and served as a ramp, his implant linked with the carrier's order circuit.

"Lieutenant Desoll?"

"Stet."

"Major Juraki. Settle in for the ride, Lieutenant. I'd like to have you act as an observer once we're inbound to your station."

A trooper in a full-armor suit gestured toward a seat opposite the door.

"I'd be happy to." As Trystin answered the carrier commander, he took the vacant seat and strapped in, then slipped the seat's tube into his suit's oxygen plug. "Appreciate the ride."

"Our pleasure."

The armored door eased up into place; the fans hummed; and the carrier swept back westward along the shuttle trail, leaving a trail of fine red dust. The air-cushion shuttle didn't have any problems sinking into the soil, but it did leave a lot of dust. It could only carry about a third of its rated capacity, given the thinner Maran atmosphere, and the abrasion on the fans was murder.

Trystin glanced up at the monitor, which showed the shuttle track in front of the carrier, and then closed his eyes. He hadn't slept that well, not with dreams of exploding revs, and consoles and systems that didn't work. He'd even dreamed of revs turning into scaly aliens. He snorted. Quentar and his alien fixation—the revs didn't have to be aliens, not physical ones. Their blind faith made them alien enough. He pursed his lips. Quentar's cheerful admission of living to kill revs bothered him, but he couldn't say why he felt that Quentar was carrying it too far. After all, the revs had proved they were certainly out to kill him. He shook his head, recalling the fanaticism of the rev officer.

When he shifted his weight on the hard seat, his hip throbbed. It was still sore and promised to turn vivid shades of blue and yellow.

The carrier was far smoother than the scooter had been, and Trystin slipped into a doze, ignoring the faint hissing of the oxygen forced into his suit and the occasional clicks of the CO_2 cartridge system.

"Approaching East Red Three . . ."

Trystin sat up with a jolt and blinked. Had he slept that long? He wanted to rub his eyes, but the involuntary motion brought his gauntlet against his helmet. He yawned and straightened in the seat.

The sweep trooper beside Trystin thumped his companion on the shoulder and pointed at the single screen in the troop area, focused on East Red Three.

The pinkish light of early morning illuminated black holes in at least a dozen spots in the station's composite armor on the south side. The maintenance entry was a jagged dark cutout. Chunks of armor lay at the foot of the station walls and even meters away. Scattered between the fragments of armor were the dark figures of dead revs.

Trystin tried to count the bodies, but lost track at over a dozen.

"Desoll?" buzzed through his implant. "How does it look?"

"Looks the same as when I left. The shielding on the revvie suits seems to have worn off, though. I didn't recall that many bodies."

"Maybe we'll see how dead they are."

"Don't aim at a nearby body. Some are booby-trapped with organic HE."

"Organic HE? You got to be kidding."

"I wish I were. Take my word or check with RESCOM."

Trystin could feel the slightest jerk as the Sasakis let go.

A huge gout of flame erupted from a dead figure, and chunks of metal—weapons, respirator paks—clunked against the carrier's plates.

"See what you mean." Major Juraki's voice was dry through the implant. "We'll do a turn around the station—but all sensors indicate it's dead."

While the carrier slowed, it completed a full circle of the station before coming to a halt opposite the south side. Most of the damage had been there—where the entry portals were. The rest was on the east side, near the sensor conduits, at the level of the rocket launch and gattling portals, and around the armaglass port of the control center on the second level. The station's armor on the north and west sides was untouched. So were the reclamation towers. The shields still covered the power turbine fans.

Trystin frowned. The damage indicated that the revvie attack had been directed at all the defense installations. But that made a sort of sense, since once the defense systems were knocked out, nothing could stop the revs from destroying the rest of the station.

"Sweep team, stand by for reoccupation."

"Lieutenant Desoll"—that came through on the implant level—"stand back and let them sweep the place. We'll need you to identify what happened. After they're clear, come on up through the middle door."

The carrier eased to a halt and a full squad of the armored troops swept down the ramp and into the station. They moved quickly, if not on reflex boost.

When the armored door swung up again, Trystin unplugged from the oxygen line, going back to his suit supply, and stepped through the narrow hatch and climbed the three steps to the control deck.

The major, sitting in the left seat, motioned to the jump seat that folded down between his seat and the gunner's console. The gunner, wearing black armor, remained focused on his consoles. Trystin pulled down the jump seat and plugged into the auxiliary air jack.

"So far, so good." The major's voice was detached—

sounding through the implant, as if his attention were elsewhere. "Just dead revs."

"My tech is wrapped up in sheeting on the tech table," Trystin added. "It was all I could do."

"I'll pass that along."

Trystin waited, shifting his eyes between the screens and the armaglass portals. Both showed the same scene—flattened soil, fragments of composite armor, and the battered station walls. Beyond the station, he could glimpse the reclamation towers and the badlands. Two troopers were carting rev bodies to the carrier's rear cargo bay and stacking them. The revvie weapons went into the front bay.

"Station's clean, Lieutenant," announced the major. "Tech team's coming in, and they should have you back on-line before long."

"I hope so."

"Until the next attack. Damned revs. Wish we could just clean them out. Galaxy'd be a better place. But no . . . politicians in Cambria say that a big war would do us all in. This isn't? Every year, they send more troids, and every year the messes are worse." The major's hand pointed toward the station. "They're after real estate. What they all need is to buy the farm. You notice how they leave the reclamation stuff alone?"

"I'd noticed."

"They want us to do the hard work, and then, when the planet's set, they'll be ready to take it over. Hell . . . we've done enough here that without any more work, the air'll be breathable in another generation or so. Damned skimmers."

The implant circuit went dead, and Trystin waited.

"Tech shuttles are on your track. Only be a few minutes."

Again, the circuit went blank, and Trystin felt shut out as the major began to recall his team, and as the cargo-bay doors were closed and sealed, and the troopers reboarded the carrier.

Even before the carrier was reloaded, the three gray tech shuttles settled onto their braced fan skirts outside the station's vehicle door, and a handful of techs scurried into the dead station.

The last of the revs' weapons went into the carrier's forward bay, and the cargo-bay doors closed.

"Tech team confirms that the station will be up in a couple of stans. They'd like your input on priorities."

"I'd better be going." Trystin stood.

"We're off to the western perimeter. There's another crew of revs down, and reports that they brought some sort of EDI/radar-transparent carrier with them." The major shook his head. "Seems like there's always something new."

Trystin unplugged and headed down the three steps. "I appreciate the transport and help."

"That's what we're here for. You station guards are stretched pretty thin for all your fancy hardware." The helmet bobbed in a nod. "Luck, Lieutenant."

"Thanks." Trystin stepped back onto the red and brown soil outside East Red Three.

7

 "... there being a god, that god must be worshiped. Worship means raising the god above the individual, and liturgies often make the point that the individual is less than nothing compared to the deity. If this be done, then, when the god is invoked, the individual has so little worth that he or she may be sacrificed for the needs of the god. . . .

"And who speaks for the god? If all people do, then no one does, and there is no god. If the people accept a priesthood, or the equivalent, then those priests exercise whatever power that god's believers grant that god over them, and that elite may cause an individual to be worth less, to be exiled, or even to die or be killed. Yet such powers do not come from a deity.

"In modern history and science, never has there been a verified occasion of a god appearing or demonstrating the powers ascribed throughout history to deities. Always, there is a prophet who speaks for the god. Why cannot the god speak? If a god is omnipotent, then the god can speak. If he cannot, then that god is not omnipotent. Often, the prophets say that a god will only speak to the chosen, the worthy.

"Should a people accept a god who is either too powerless to speak, or too devious or too skeptical to appear? Or a god who will only accept those who swallow a faith laid out by a prophet who merely claims that deity exists—without proof? Yet people have done so, and have granted enormous powers to those who speak for god.

"More ironically, as technologies have advanced, men and women have gained powers once ascribed to deities, yet deistic faiths always claim greater powers for their deities and appear to seek equally great controls over their followers, over those followers' finances, and at times even over their sexual habits and private lives . . . and many people have accepted such controls, even with enthusiasm. . . ."

The Eco-Tech Dialogues
Prologue

8

 The perimeter station still smelled, not only of ammonia and weedgrass, but of oil, hot plastic, and burned insulation. Trystin coughed and wiped his nose. His eyes burned at the corners, and his hip remained sore from the bruise he'd gotten half falling down the emergency ladder.

He swallowed the last of the Sustain and cleared his throat. Then, for the second time, he called up the message that had been waiting for him when the station had come back on-line.

"Glad to hear you made it. Also glad it was you and not me. Ulteena."

Short and uncuddly, but nice to know that someone paid attention, even if he'd never met Lieutenant Ulteena Freyer. But a message wasn't enough. He needed to talk to someone, preferably someone female and sympathetic.

With a slow breath, he linked into the audio pubnet and tried Ezildya. She'd been out of her office earlier.

"Fernaldoi."

"Ezildya, this is Trystin. I'll be in Klyseen on sevenday afternoon. . . ."

"And the wandering Service officer wants a warm and willing companion? With so little notice?"

"The Service officer is the one who had six squads of revs tear down his station a few days ago. I've been some-what preoccupied with survival." He tried to keep his tone light.

"That was your station we had to cannibalize every-thing to put back together?"

"It wasn't that bad—just armor and more armor and about thirty percent of the main system console."

"Oh . . . you were number four. We didn't have that much left. . . ."

"Sorry I called."

"Trystin . . . it's been a long eightday."

"I know you had a long eightday. Me—I had a won-derful time. I really enjoyed going fifty kays in armor on a scooter with no comm, almost as much as I enjoyed hav-ing my tech killed and my station blown open."

There was a long silence.

"I am sorry, Trystin. Was it that bad?"

"If you're free on sevenday, I'll give you the details." As he talked, he flicked across the screens again, trying to ensure that he wasn't missing anything. There wasn't a flat prohibition on his using the pubnet, but it wasn't something he should drag out, either.

"I could take off a little early. Say seventeen hundred?"

"At your place?"

"That would be best."

"Thanks. I'll see you then. I've got to go."

"You on-line?"

"Of course."

"Trystin . . ." There was a sigh. "I'll see you sevenday."

Ezildya's sigh confirmed her displeasure at his calling on duty, but Trystin was tired of the unspoken restrictions of duty. He was more than a little tired of all the unspoken constraints that seemed to fill life—don't question this; don't ask about that—especially if you were a Service officer on a perimeter line.

After his own sigh, Trystin ran through everything again—screens, maintenance, power, and station-keeping. Nothing had changed, and even the trend-analysis screens didn't show anything, although the cloud buildups over the eastern badlands' hills registered heavier than usual. The perimeter lines were clear, and the turners, some kays south, continued to turn and process soil for creeper seeding. The turbine fans were generating forty percent of the load, and the organonutrient levels were down to twelve percent.

Trystin flicked off another reminder to supply, but all he got was the programmed acknowledgment.

"Lieutenant Desoll, ser?" The voice was that of Hisin, Ryla's replacement.

"Yes?" Trystin asked, half wondering if Hisin's rapid replacement of poor dead Ryla signified that Service personnel were as expendable as revvie missionaries. He pushed the thought away.

"I'm going to have to go off-line. The damned turners for the precrackers have jammed up. That means taking the scooter out."

Trystin zeroed in on the lower left screen, the satellite plot. There! "I make them about eight kays south and about a kay inside the line. Is that where you have them?"

"Yes, ser. Be a good stan 'fore I'm back, and that's without trouble."

"Check in if it's going to take longer, and take scooter one. The comm's shot on number two."

"The one they brought back from East Red Two, ser? It looks to be in better shape than number one, especially the tanks."

"That's the way it *looks,* Hisin. That's why I used it. That's also how I found out the comm was shot." Trystin shook his head. He'd totally forgotten to tell the tech about the faulty comm. "That's my fault. I didn't report it—I couldn't because the net was down, and I forgot to log it once we got things back together."

"Stet, ser. Once I get the turners working, if I can, I'll look into it. I appreciate the information. I'd hate to get out there with no comm."

"I didn't much care for it, either."

"You actually neutralized six squads of revs, ser?"

"I didn't count. Cleanup squad told me I got a few. A lot of it was luck. I couldn't sense much with their new insulated suits."

"Bastards."

"Yeah."

"Going off-line, ser."

"Stet."

Trystin checked the entire maintenance line, code by code and signal by signal. While all the major systems were functioning, a number of less critical areas were still awaiting maintenance action. The lower rear inside door to Block A was still jammed, and the replacement door to cell three in Block B still hadn't come in. Neither could be replaced without a new frame, and both doors and frames were back-ordered out of Klyseen central depot with no estimated delivery date. Surely a door frame, even a heavy-duty sector control station door frame, couldn't be that hard to fabricate? Could it?

He shook his head. While the tech team had been effective in restoring armor, station integrity, and weapons systems, internal items not necessary for the operation and defense of the station had a lower priority, and supplies were low after PerCon had been forced to rebuild nearly totally the three stations on the western perimeter.

His hip was still sore, and somehow itched. He started to massage it gently, then stopped. The massage just reminded him more of the soreness.

Hhhstttt . . . craccckkkk!!! The storm over the badlands discharged somewhere east of the tower, close enough that the first wave of the static knifed through the implant before the system's overload breakers cut in. Trystin's eyes watered even more, and he sneezed.

"Shit. Friggin' stormlash."

Was he getting more and more sensitized to stormlash, or was it just fatigue? Would the medical screening coming up the day before endday discover he was sensitized? What did medical screening have to do with the Farhkans? Who knew much about them, except that they were remarkably humanoid beings living in toward Galactic center who had been around a long time, and who had demonstrated, with rather convincing firepower, a few centuries earlier, that their desire to be left alone except through formal contacts was something that had to be respected.

The Eco-Tech Coalition had only lost one ship— officially. The revs had lost almost a hundred ships—and a major outlying Temple, along with a good portion of New Salem—before they had gotten the idea. The Farhkans had demonstrated close to total ability to annihilate the entire heavens of the Revenants of the Prophet before the revs had gotten the message.

Would the Eco-Tech Coalition have to do the same to stop the waves of revvie ships? He sighed. That wasn't his problem, and he doubted that the Coalition had either the ability or the will to wipe out entire systems. Still, he wished they'd do something, rather than just have perimeter officers like him sitting and waiting and reacting. Someday, he might not react quickly enough.

Once the Coalition and the revs had been allies against

the Immortals . . . but that had been a long time ago—before the Farhkans.

He frowned, realizing that he'd never really seen a Farhkan, not in person. According to the holos, they had pale gray skin and dark iron-gray hair that was short and bristly over their entire body, except around their mouth and single nostril. They had two red eyes and teeth that looked like greenish crystals which framed a double-hinged mouth.

With the rising wind, he reset the breakers and went back on-line to check the power screen, pleased to see that the fans were generating nearly sixty-five percent of the ambient load. So long as the winds held, the drain on organonutrient for the fuel cells would remain low.

Cling!

"All PerCon Stations. DefCom visual plot indicates two paragliders on entry envelopes. Paragliders are new beta class. Probable landfall coordinates follow. Full alert on perimeter stations. DefCon Two. DefCon Two . . ."

Trystin checked the coordinates. The probable landfall was beyond the western perimeter line, and the revs didn't miss by the width of the entire central plains—not by fifteen hundred kays. Not so far.

New beta-class paragliders! Now the revs were bringing down heavy equipment, and that equipment came off troids that had been launched from Orum or somewhere nearly twenty years earlier. What else had they developed that would be coming in the months and years ahead? He pursed his lips—better just to worry about the days ahead. Someone else could worry about the years.

Hhhsttt . . . craccckkkk! Crack!! Trystin only winced at the stormlash, and checked the metplot. The big storm was rolling westward and down toward East Red Three.

He tried to raise the scooter that sat, according to the satellite plot and the beacon, right beside the turners that Hisin was repairing.

"Hisin, this is Lieutenant Desoll."

"Barely read you, ser. . . ." The response was crackling, probably because of the approaching storm.

"We've got a big storm rolling our way. I'd estimate not more than a stan."

"I'm almost done. This time it wasn't that bad. Just had to clean out the toxics accumulator. The turners must have run through a bad patch here."

"Stet." Trystin checked the metplot again, but, if anything, the storm had slowed. That was good because Hisin would get back in time, and bad because a slower-moving storm tended to have more time over the station.

Supposedly, the storms would get worse as more oxygen and water vapor built up in the atmosphere, at least on the perimeter lines where old and new tended to mix. That had something to do with the slope of the hills at the edge of the high plains, not the perimeter lines themselves, although they had reached the badlands.

In another five years, the Service would have to begin to repeat the whole process on the western continent, and things would get even hairier.

Trystin stood and walked around the center, stretching his legs and glancing out the armaglass, where the eastern sky was continuing to darken.

The station still smelled of ammonia and weedgrass, and he rubbed his nose, so sensitive that the rubbing hurt, but his nostrils itched, and his eyes still watered. He blotted them on the back of his suit sleeve and headed back to the command seat.

After checking the four-screen once more, he watched as the scooter pulled away from the turners and curved back toward the station. Then he took another sip of the Sustain. Sometimes he felt as if he were living on the high-energy liquid nutrient. He coughed and cleared his throat. Sometimes he was.

"Back in-station, ser."

"Stet."

Crackk!!! CRACKK!!!! At the first knife through his skull from the clouds rolling out of the hills and across the station, Trystin winced, but the overrides cut him off-line again.

While he waited for the storm to pass so that he could

go back on-line, he called up the split screen on the console, visually scanning the displays, and feeling slowed and partly blinded by his loss of direct access to the network and station systems. His fingers were far slower than his mind.

Outside was dark, almost like twilight, as the heavy clouds passed over the station. The armor and walls couldn't block out the whining of the wind, or the gritty *tick, tick, tick* of sand against the armaglass window.

Crack! Another bolt of energy lashed from the storm.

Trystin shifted in the command seat, leaving his links to the system dead until the storm passed. There wasn't much sense in trying to go on-line and getting kicked out, especially since high-energy surges offered a chance of incremental neural degradation, small but definite.

The screen showing the area around the station continued to darken, as did the armaglass portal looking toward the eastern hills. At least the fans were generating enough to carry the entire load and actually load the backup accumulators.

The sand continued to *tick* against the window.

Crack! Crack! Two more lightning bolts flared down near the perimeter line, raising the illumination in the station and on the screen.

"Lieutenant, I'm shutting down the tech boards." The words came through the speaker, automatically turned on when the link system went off-line.

"Go ahead."

"Stet, ser."

Crack! CRACK!!!!

Trystin didn't need the red lights from the maintenance panel to know that the last discharges had mangled something, only to pinpoint where the damage was—main reclamation tower number one. Again, he should have been the one to suggest the cutoff earlier. He shook his head.

If it weren't the revs, it was the damned planet. He took a sip of Sustain and manually called the metplot onto the side screen before him. According to the scanners, the storm center had passed.

Crack!

That didn't mean the storm was finished with East Red Three, not as the station shook again.

Cling! This time, the tone came through the speaker, since his implant was off-line. Trystin fumbled with the console and shifted the message to the screen on the console. He hated being off-line. It was slow and clumsy.

"All PerCon Stations. DefCom has confirmed two beta-class paragliders with landfall near western perimeter. Both gliders are being neutralized. Landfall coordinates and estimated time of landfall follow. Full alert on western perimeter stations. DefCon One. DefCon One . . ."

Once more Trystin fumbled with the console controls and the keyboard before finally locating the landfall co-ordinates—directly across the plains to the west, and less than five kays into the western badlands.

He pursed his lips, not liking the phrase "are being neutralized." Was Maran Defense Control having trouble with the shielding on the gliders as well? More trouble than before?

Crack! The intensity of the lightning was lower.

Trystin continued to use his eyes to scan the screens on the console, begrudging the comparative slowness of his fingers in handling the displays. Still, the monitoring screens weren't that much work, and they were the only systems, besides basic station-keeping, that were on-line while the storm thundered westward over East Red Three.

As the storm faded, and the afternoon light rose, Trystin finally relinked to the system and began to reactivate the technical side, confirming as he did so that in addition to a number of minor circuits through the system, all systems of reclamation tower one were inoperative.

"Lieutenant, tower one is down. Down cold."

Trystin checked the metplot, but the storm was a good ten kays west of the station and beginning to break as it crossed the more heavily creepered areas. "Looks clear if you want to check it out."

"Stet. Scooter one is all right." A laugh followed. "I can always walk back." With the nearer tower one less than a kay away, Hisin would be close, not even out of helmet comm range.

Trystin checked the four-screen again, but could see no signs of more storms or revs—not that he had that much confidence in the scanners being able to detect anything the revs had until they were practically overrunning the station.

Then he used the net to scan the comm inslots, coming up with little more than routine messages.

Hisin hadn't been at the tower more than ten standard minutes before he called back. "Lieutenant, all the power links to the control boxes are fused. That last bolt from the storm overloaded the grounds, and . . ." Hisin's voice trailed off. ". . . haven't seen anything like this in a long time."

"There's a lot we haven't seen in a long time, and it's happening more frequently, I think. Do what you can."

"I'll have to come back to the station to see if we even have enough components."

"Stet." Trystin watched as Hisin reentered the scooter and rode back to the station. Just two more days before he could go to Klyseen. Medical exam or not, he was ready for a break.

Cling!

"Advisory for PerCon Stations. Revvie assault repulsed West Red Five. Full alert remains for western-perimeter stations. DefCon One. DefCon One . . ."

Trystin shook his head. Another long session for the western sector watch officers. Repulsion was not neutralization by a long shot, and that meant the revs had heavy weapons. And that meant trouble.

He shifted his weight to remove some of the pressure on the sore hip, then checked his own screens again, even remote-swiveling the outside scanners to the west for a quick sweep, but everything remained clear, not that he expected the revs to cross the high plains instantly.

Lifting the cup of Sustain, he looked at it, then set it down without drinking. He was already hyper, and being too hyper on the net was a recipe for headaches.

He'd had enough headaches in the last two weeks.

9

 "The time is zero four hundred ten." At 0410, the single sentence from the system was enough to jolt Trystin from sleep. He swung his bare feet onto the hard plastcrete flooring of the cubicle and sat on the edge of his bunk. He had a moment, but not much more, before he trudged to the shower and the chemically pure recycled water that had no zip. He rubbed his forehead, then struggled upright. Even so early in the morning, he could sense a faint static through the implant.

The shower helped—some, but even the hot water couldn't wash away the odor of ammonia and weedgrass. Trystin dried himself, wrapped himself in the towel, and trudged back to his cubicle. He dressed in informal greens, then made his way to the lock doors to wait for the shuttle.

At 0440, the ground shuttle stopped on the pad outside the center, and Trystin, respirator over his mouth, beret tucked in his belt, kit bag in hand, triggered the door to the pad, stepped out, and marched out and in through the shuttle's rear door. The passenger compartment was scarred green-gray plastic, with matching seats, and lit by a single glow-strip down the middle of the overhead.

A square-faced noncom looked at Trystin for a moment, scanned the uniform and pointed to a seat along one wall. Four of the twelve wall seats were taken, each by a junior officer, and each officer wore a respirator.

"Lieutenant Desoll?" came the faint indirect-link question.

"That's me," Trystin responded back through the static.

"Leave your respirator on, ser, but you can plug into the jack by your seat. We won't go to full oxygen till we finish the pickups."

As Trystin strapped in, the shuttle pulled away from the station. The faint hiss of the shuttle's air fed through the respirator, along with the odor of oil and metal . . . and ammonia and weedgrass. Trystin leaned back in the seat and closed his eyes, much the way the others had done, he suspected.

He didn't really sleep, or even doze, but sat there in a semiconscious daze, as the shuttle swayed through three more stops and starts before beginning its return to Klyseen.

"Full pressurization."

Groggily, Trystin opened his eyes and pulled off the respirator, unplugging and folding the mouthpiece into the pak. He rubbed his eyes gently, crusted as they were from the irritation of ammonia and weedgrass. Then he took a deep breath that was not quite a yawn.

"You're Trystin, aren't you?" The dark-haired officer next to him wore a star beside the double-linked collar bar, signifying her selection for major. Her nose was sharp, but fitted to her face, and the chin firm, squared, above the strong shoulders that were almost, but not quite, too broad. Her body seemed trim and muscular.

"Yes." Trystin looked again, realizing that the eyes were harder, the face older than he had first seen.

"I'm Ulteena Freyer."

"Congratulations." He nodded at the pin. "How long?"

"Next month. I'm one of the few with anniversary dates in Unodec." Her eyes fixed his.

"Could I ask how you knew who I was?" Then he grinned stupidly. They were all in uniform with the highlighted name badges below their shoulders.

"Actually, I picked you out before I could see the badge." She gave him a smile that was friendly, but not cuddly. "You're the only one who looks like a rev."

Trystin shrugged. "Can't do much about genetics."

"You from a long-term techie family?"

"Yes. One of the first on Perdya—believe it or not." He hated explaining that despite his rev looks, he was a techie through and through with family links that went back to the foundation of the Eco-Tech Coalition.

"I believe it. It also explains why you survived those booby traps the revs sent. You know Weslyn didn't? Neither did a couple of tech officers on the western perimeter."

"Why?" he asked politely.

"I'm sure you have to prove everything, and you and your family always have had to. Any failures in your family?"

Trystin understood the star beside her bars. Then he grinned. "You, too?"

The momentarily blank look was replaced by a grin. "Yes. Don't forget it, either, Trystin." Then the grin faded.

"I know. Next month, it will be 'major.' "

"It will. That's true. But your time will come. Ranks are temporary." She leaned back in the seat, closing her eyes.

What was that all about, he wondered? Except he knew. For whatever reason, Ulteena Freyer had as much to prove as Trystin did—maybe more. In a way, it was too bad. Despite the slightly sharp nose, he liked the way she looked, and her competence. It reminded him of Salya. He wondered how his sister was doing, then shook his head. Wondering wouldn't answer the question, and he settled back and closed his own eyes.

"Klyseen depot!" announced the noncom from the doorway.

Trystin jerked awake in time to see Ulteena step out through the shuttle's doorway into the shuttle depot. He stood and stretched, letting the others leave first. According to the implant, it was still only 0715, and he had more than enough time to get something to eat before his 0900 appointment at the Service medical center.

The tunnel from the depot was double-wide, nearly twenty meters across, with the side to Trystin's right—the eastern side—bearing a maroon stripe. The five meters next to the wall were reserved for electroscooters and open passenger carts. The carts each had three bench seats and were programmed to stop roughly every quarter kay.

Trystin ignored the carts, unlike most of the Service people, and walked away from the depot, situated under the center of Klyseen, southward toward the residential domes. On his days off, he had learned that the better cafes were there, with cross tunnels for pedestrians that led to the western Service dome—though the term "dome" was a misnomer, since the bulk of each structure was below ground.

Even with an interior and largely underground culture, most of the personnel on Mara had darker complexions than Trystin, not surprisingly, since the Eco-Tech heritage had been genetically mixed, to say the least. While he did not quite tower over the average Eco-Tech, at 195 centimeters he was taller than most, but he tried not to slouch.

He passed the first restaurant—the Tunnel Cubed—because it was crowded, with Service people at practically every table. Another half kay south along the tunnel, he stepped into the Marigold, where less than half the tables were taken.

After scanning the menu, he saw why. The prices were a good third higher than at the Tunnel Cubed. Hoping that the higher tariff meant better food, he tapped in his order at the service console—real eggs, toasted white algae bread, and browned potatoes. Potatoes could be grown almost anywhere. The console compared his thumb print and ID number and beeped its approval.

Trystin took the squarish slip with his number on it and walked over to the dispenser for some tea. The tea cost as much as the rest of the breakfast, but he needed something hot and real. He took a corner table beside the planter filled with live marigolds and rysya. The marigolds provided color and a bitter scent that Trystin found more acceptable than all the artificial fragrances that drifted past him. The rysya—planted everywhere in Klyseen—had only small white blossoms, but served as a supplemental oxygen regenerator. He could feel the directed heat from the laser-type sunsquirts in the ceiling.

Sitting at the green round plastic table in a green plastic chair, he sipped the tea and watched people walking, or riding, along the tunnel outside, separated from the cafe proper by the row of waist-high planters filled with the mixed flowers.

He still got curious glances from passersby, occasioned by his sandy hair, blue eyes, and broad shoulders, but once the eyes took in the Service uniform, especially the officers' bars, they tended to glaze over with the reassurance of the familiar.

Trystin took his time with the eggs, and enjoyed sipping the tea and studying the people who walked by—the Service officers and technicians in their pale green uniforms, the contract technicians in whatever they wished to wear, and a handful of dark-haired and dark-eyed children, usually in school tunics and trousers.

Children—he hadn't seen many since he'd left Cambria, not that most Eco-Tech families had more than two, if that.

He pursed his lips and finished the toast, then took another sip of the tea. Ulteena—somehow she fit his mental picture, and somehow she didn't. Certainly, she wasn't as openly warm as Ezildya, but her nose wasn't the beak he'd somehow visualized. And she was certainly competent.

He laughed. Ulteena was on the fast track, and before long, she'd be a major. She certainly had made that clear, but why had she mentioned that ranks were temporary? He took another sip of tea, sniffed the marigolds, and sat back to watch the pedestrians. He had time, more than enough time.

At 0820, he finally left the Marigold, walking quickly toward the pedestrian tunnel interconnecting Residence one to Service two.

At 0830, Trystin was entering Service two, the support dome of the Service. At 0840, he passed the exit for the botanical garden. He wished he'd left the Marigold earlier and had given himself enough time for the garden. Perhaps later. He missed the greenery. He kept walking.

At 0855, Trystin stepped through the front slider in the underground medical center, and walked to the console.

"Lieutenant Trystin Desoll—"

"Follow-up physicals are in corridor three B, Lieutenant. Follow the orange stripe to the blue. Make a right where the blue starts, and follow it to the next reception area." The dark-haired tech gave him a polite smile, then returned to his console.

Trystin shrugged and followed the orange stripe on the wall for nearly a hundred meters before turning right. Another hundred meters of turns led him to a waiting area. He stepped up to the tech at the console.

"Lieutenant Desoll . . ."

"Take a seat, Lieutenant. A med tech or Dr. Ihara will call you."

Trystin tried not to shake his head and turned. In the front row of the hard plastic chairs sat Ulteena Freyer. She smiled and motioned to the empty seat beside her.

"They don't care much for rank here," she observed.

"I noticed." Trystin settled into the seat. "How long have you been waiting?"

"About five minutes longer than you." She gave him a quick smile, and a sense of the warmth flashed over him and was gone. "I don't cut it quite as closely as you do. Women can't afford that kind of reputation, even today."

"I didn't plan on cutting it that closely. The med center is bigger than I'd realized."

"Your first time here?"

Trystin nodded. "My annual physical isn't due for another month. You think they'll combine it with this?"

"Not a chance. Regs say you have an annual Service physical, and you will." Ulteena brushed back a strand of hair scarcely longer than Trystin's.

"Desoll!" The med tech in greens by the console glanced around the room where the dozen young officers waited.

"Here." Trystin stood.

"Please follow me, ser." The "ser" was definitely a formality, without respect.

Trystin smiled at Ulteena. She offered a faint smile in return.

"See you later, at least on the net."

She nodded politely.

Trystin followed the med tech around the corner and to a line of curtained booths where the tech pointed at a booth with an open curtain. "Strip down to your underwear. Then stand in front of the console and let it wrap around you. Put your arms in the restrainers, and tap the stud under your little finger. There's one under either hand. Hold still. The console will take blood, skin, and a few other samples. When the tone sounds and the restraints lift, dress and walk up the corridor to delta four. Take a seat there, and wait for Dr. Ihara." The med tech looked at Trystin. "Is that clear, ser?"

"Clear."

The technician nodded and was gone.

Trystin closed the curtain and began to strip, beginning with his boots, setting them in the corner of the cubicle. With a deep breath, he stepped up and let the console embrace him, the plastic and metal cool against his bare skin. His hip twinged at the chill.

The implant flickered, indicating energy flows, in response to the brief sprays and energy probes that invaded him.

In less than five minutes, according to the implant, the process was complete, and the restraints lifted away. In spots, Trystin's skin tingled, and he wondered if he might have a few small bruises later.

He shook his head. Nothing to compare with the one he'd received from falling down the station's emergency ladder. He dressed quickly, opened the curtain, and walked up the corridor and around the corner. Another waiting area contained four chairs. Three were full, with a major and two senior lieutenants. One of the lieutenants was a woman with sandy-blond hair, not so fair as Trystin or his sister, but the first other blond Trystin had seen in the Service.

She looked up and grinned. He grinned back.

At that moment, a Service officer Trystin had never seen, also a lieutenant, stepped out of the room, shaking his head.

"Next. Lieutenant Berrie?" A heavyset doctor in dress greens stood in the open door.

The sandy blonde stood and followed the doctor. Trystin settled into the chair and closed his eyes, realizing how tired he really was.

"Next. Lieutenant Desoll?" A heavyset doctor in dress greens stood in the open door.

Trystin tried not to jerk awake, and rose as smoothly as he could.

"Don't worry about it. By the way, I'm Dr. Ihara. None of you perimeter types ever get enough rest."

Trystin followed him into the large office, where a halo of the western badlands filled the wall space on the right side of the room. The combination desk/console was bare, as was the credenza on the wall behind the console.

Trystin's eyes slipped past the panorama of fast-moving clouds to the third figure in the office—a not-quite human figure in what looked to be shimmering gray fatigues. The iron-gray hair and square face were the most human features of the Farhkan. Trystin tried to ignore the red eyes and wide single-nostril nose that seemed to flap with each breath. The crystalline teeth were not quite fangs or tusks, and seemed blunt.

Ihara shut the door behind Trystin. "This is Rhule Ghere, Lieutenant Desoll. He is roughly my equivalent with the Farhkan . . . hegemony."

Trystin nodded. The term "hegemony" was the closest description that matched any human term, although the Farhkans seemed to employ what really seemed to Trystin something like an ultrahigh-tech, self-policing, consensus-based, anarchistic democracy based on environmental understandings and an overall technology that the Eco-Tech Coalition could only drool over from a distance.

"Pleased to meet you, ser." Trystin offered a slight bow, feeling that some sign of respect was in order.

"It is interesting to meet you, Lieutenant." Ghere's voice

floated through Trystin's thoughts, almost as though unrolling on his mental screen, but more completely and more quickly.

"How?"

"I—we—have the ability to communicate, at short distances only, through your military communications implant. That makes communications easier—or possible."

"Dr. Ghere is here to interview those of you who volunteered to participate in the Farhkan project. I doubt you remember much, beyond the small annual bonus, about the project. . . ."

Trystin did remember, but not as much as he would have liked. Supposedly, in return for certain basic technology transfers, the Farhkans were following a small cohort of Service officers for a ten-year period—or longer—with periodic physical examinations, interviews, and some forms of mental tests. This was Trystin's second physical for the Farhkan project, but there had been no interview after the first.

"I recall the basic details, although I don't remember anything about interviews." He inhaled slowly, taking in an unfamiliar odor, a combination of an unfamiliar flower, a muskiness, and . . . cleanliness.

"You'll be getting an interview with each subsequent physical, unless, for some reason, the Farhkans find you unsuitable." Ihara offered a grimace. "We hope they don't. Please have a seat."

Trystin took the only seat in front of the console, opposite the Farhkan.

Rhule Ghere turned his red eyes on Ihara.

"The other aspect of the interview is that it is confidential," added Ihara.

Trystin repressed a snort. How confidential was an interview with a Service doctor present?

Ihara stepped to the second door and opened it. "Believe me. It's confidential. You'll see." He stepped out of the room and closed the door.

"We do have our ways," offered the silent voice of Ghere.

"If you wish to speak aloud or use your implant, it does not matter."

Idly, Trystin tried to access any net that might be in the structure, but found a blankness. He raised his eyebrows. "Won't they try to break it?"

"Of course. They have been trying for several years. That is one reason why they agreed to the bargain."

"Advanced technology?"

"They like the opportunity to steal technology. All humans do."

"So we're thieves?" As the words popped out, Trystin couldn't believe he'd said them.

"You do not like being a member of a species of thieves?"

"The thought doesn't please me much." Trystin shifted his weight in the chair.

"You find the idea of theft repulsive?"

Trystin paused. "I don't like being thought of as a thief."

"What about the theft of life?"

Again, Trystin paused. Was the alien a real alien, or was this just some fantastic screening device? But why would the Service go to such lengths? Would he know a real Farhkan from a phony one? "Do you have a spoken language? What does it sound like?"

"Yes."

A string of noise followed, except that the sounds twisted around each other almost poetically. Trystin felt a vague sense of longing and asked when Ghere had finished, "Is that poetry?"

"Of a type. It is the opening to what you would call my testament. But I could be lying. I could be a fraud."

"You could," Trystin admitted. "You act too human."

"Too human, or too intelligent?"

Trystin wanted to shake his head.

"You never answered my inquiry about the theft of life." The red eyes turned directly on him.

Trystin felt that the alien was looking beyond him, and that the alien was alien. Why, he couldn't say. He wet his lips. "War involves the theft of life. What are we supposed to do? Let the revs kill us off and take everything over in the name of their Prophet?"

"So you admit you are a thief?"

"You're twisting words."

"Am I?" A harsh sound issued from the Farhkan. "Am I?"

"If I'm a thief, so are you."

"I am a thief. I admit it. Are you?" asked Ghere.

Trystin didn't want to admit anything, even philosophically, especially since he wasn't sure what the Service might find out. He paused.

"Are you a thief?" asked Ghere again.

"Since any intelligent species must take from other living things, even if limited to food, in order to survive," Trystin temporized, "I would say that intelligence requires theft in the general sense."

"Is all taking a form of theft?"

Trystin shrugged. "I suppose taking implies possession, and, therefore, without ownership, taking would not be theft."

"But what is possession? Can any living form be said to possess something?"

"Temporarily, I suppose." Trystin felt warm, ready to burst into sweat.

"That is a careful answer, and it is true. Yet you will acknowledge that you eat. So why do you refuse to admit you are a thief?" Ghere shifted his weight in his chair, but so gracefully and silently that he made no sound.

Trystin sat silently for a few moments, suddenly conscious of the low-grade throbbing in his hip, and conscious of the absurdity of sweating through a moral argument with an alien—assuming Ghere was a real Farhkan.

The silence extended, so much that Trystin could hear the faint hiss of the ventilators.

"You have admitted that intelligent life must take from other life to survive. You know this is true. I have admitted I am a thief. You will not. Why not?"

"The word itself is unpleasant." Trystin felt the words being dragged out of him.

"Why?"

"Why? I don't know."

Ghere stood and pressed a stud on the console. "You need to think about that, Lieutenant Desoll. Thank you for your time." His mouth opened.

Trystin tried not to stare at the long, sharp, crystalline teeth.

Click. In the silence, the opening door sounded like a thunderbolt, and the Service doctor entered.

Trystin turned to Dr. Ihara.

"I will take a rest now, for a few moments," announced Ghere in the same mental "voice," even as he headed for the rear door, moving silently and closing it behind him—assuming Ghere was male, or the Farhkan equivalent.

Ihara looked at Trystin. "That was long—for him."

Trystin shrugged, wondering if he had failed some sort of test.

"Would you care to comment on the interview?" asked Ihara.

"Not really."

"No one ever does. No one." The Service doctor sighed. "All right, what about Ghere himself?"

"He seems real enough." Trystin shivered. "And alien."

"He's both," said Ihara wryly.

"Why do they want an interview?" Trystin asked.

"It's a game." Ihara glanced through the half-open door toward the empty waiting area. "The techs on the next level try to break his barriers, and he tries to get whatever he wants from you."

"He just asked general questions," Trystin said cautiously. "Nothing military at all."

"We've gathered that." Ihara pursed his lips. "They want something. They've got some sort of plan, but no one seems to know what."

"No one?"

Ihara lowered his voice. "The med higher-ups drug-probed one of the first interview subjects. Within days, we got a message telling us that all trade and information transfers would be canceled if it ever happened again." He laughed. "So no one can make you say a thing."

Trystin wasn't sure he believed Ihara, but he nodded.

"By the way, you're in good shape physically," the doctor added. "Upper ten percent. You work out regularly, don't you?"

"Pretty much."

"It shows. But there's some minor nasal irritation. Probably a little too much local atmosphere in your station."

"Is that all?" asked Trystin, looking at the closed door.

"That's all. But if you ever want to talk about it . . . or let us know . . ."

"I know where to find you."

As he walked from the med center, Trystin wondered exactly what it was that the Farhkans had provided that was so valuable that the Coalition would allow private interviews with promising young officers. It had to be valuable. No one, not even aliens, gave away technology for free.

Ghere, like everyone else, wanted something. But what? Certainly, probing the moral values of a junior Service officer didn't justify whatever technology the Coalition had received. Did it? Or was the whole thing a complicated charade? Trystin thought about Ihara. The doctor hadn't been lying. So what did the Farhkans want? Was it some type of information about a lot of officers? Or were they screening for something? What could it be? And why?

Trystin took a deep breath and kept walking.

10

 From the carved wooden bench, Trystin glanced across the five meters of grass separating him from the bushes and trees. A small red maple rose from the ivy. He didn't recognize the small brown bird with the red-shaded head, but watched as it cocked its head, then dropped from the branch and flew toward the south corner of the dome garden and a tree he didn't recognize.

Supposedly, the one-hundred-meter-square garden only contained flora and fauna that would fit the ecology of Mara when the planoforming was completed. And supposedly the purpose of the garden was to test the balance on a small scale. In reality, the garden was a reminder of what Mara could be, a reminder the Eco-Techs needed.

A green lizard wound its way up the trunk of a hybrid yuccalike plant with pale yellow flowers and spike-tipped leaves. The lizard's tongue flickered, but Trystin couldn't see the prey, or if there had been prey.

He shifted his weight on the bench, enjoying the smells of living things, the respite from the endless odor of plastic, ozone, and machine oil, and the silence from his implant. There were no net repeaters, at any frequency, within the garden dome where all his implant was good for was regulating his physical output—primarily sight, metabolic and muscular contractive speed, and reflexes—and for keeping time.

Tweeett . . .

The unseen bird's call blended with the rustle of the leaves moved by the hidden ventilator streams to simulate winds. The lizard crawled out of sight behind the yucca trunk, and Trystin looked to his left, toward the small grove of lime trees, if a group of four trees could be called a grove. He checked his implant—1643—almost time for him to leave for Ezildya's place.

Tweeet . . .

He stood and offered a salute to the hidden bird before heading out through the double locks toward Residential three. The odor of plastic and ozone struck him like a wall, along with the muttering of electronics picked up by the implant, and he almost stopped in mid-stride, but he kept walking.

He paused at the underground junction where the tunnels intersected, and where a handful of small shops burrowed farther back away from the tunnel. Finally, he stepped into one—"Niceties."

The plastic counters in the front held decorative boxes of dried fruits. Trystin picked up one and winced at the price. Still, it had to have come from off-planet, and translation costs were steep. But for fruit? When you could grow it anywhere if you knew what you were doing? He shook his head.

"Could I help you, ser?" A man in a motorchair glided toward Trystin.

"In a moment, I'm sure." Trystin offered a forced smile.

In the end, he bought a small, almost tiny, box of chocolates, paying more than he'd anticipated, but knowing that Ezildya had mentioned more than once that chocolate was what she missed most since she had left Carson.

Even after taking his time, at 1715 he tapped on Ezildya's door.

"Just a minute."

He waited . . . and waited.

Finally, the door opened. Ezildya looked up at him, golden-skinned face framed in fine black hair, green eyes somehow both tired—and sparkling. "I had to stay longer than I'd hoped."

Trystin handed her the small box of chocolates.

"Those are real Austran chocolates. You didn't have to do that." She closed the door behind him and carried the box to the low table beside the love seat where she set the chocolates, unopened.

"I know. You didn't have to take off early, either." He walked to the balcony and looked at the garden below, then across the domed courtyard at the sliding glasstic doors of the other quarters, all closed except for one where a man sat on the balcony with a child in his lap. The dark-haired child waved something in a chubby fist, and Trystin smiled. "It's quiet."

"Late sevenday's always quiet. Everyone's exhausted. So am I." Ezildya sat down on the small love seat covered with a handcrafted green and gray spread decorated with a series of stylized and interlinked evergreens. "A tenth of a gee doesn't seem like much, but . . . I'm tired."

Trystin looked up at the dome, seeing only a translucent

white, though beyond the dome the white light of Parvati shone through the red skies and slowly thickening atmosphere of Mara and upon the distant red hills.

"So am I." He walked back across the small room.

"You're from Perdya. That's high gee."

"Not really. It's just one point zero nine T-norm."

"You work out every day."

"Not every day," protested Trystin.

"Almost every day, and you're used to this. I can see all those muscles. Carson is point nine eight. By sevenday, I'm still wasted." Ezildya stretched her long legs out and put her slippered feet on the padded stool. "Could you just sit beside me?"

"Sure." Trystin sat down, letting his feet rest beside hers, and his cheek against hers, enjoying the faintest scent of fleurisle.

"I get so stiff." Ezildya leaned her head back and then dropped her chin on her chest, as if to stretch her neck. "The weeks are so long, sometimes. I wish they were only seven days, like back on old Earth."

"That was a long time ago, and all the months had different numbers of days, and you couldn't tell anything without a complicated calendar. Every year every day of the month fell on a different weekday. Here, the seventeenth is always oneday."

"I don't want to talk about history."

He shrugged, barely, and squeezed her shoulder with his left hand. "I'm glad you could get the time off."

"SysCon is pretty flexible." She grinned. "I will have to take Kentar's endday duty next week."

"That's an abort."

"Here? It doesn't matter unless you're into one of the club activities, and who cares for cycling in small circles? I've never liked my face in the water—must be because I was a synthwomb child. None of us are fond of swimming, even in these gees. I wonder why."

"Because you're a synthwomb child." Trystin squeezed her shoulder again, then took his right hand, caressed her cheek and tilted her face toward his.

Thhrrrrummmmm . . . The room shook with the vibrations.

Ezildya brushed Trystin's lips with hers. "That one was close. Must be headed for the south basin."

"The new south sea," Trystin corrected. "There's water now."

"Aren't the water comet transits hard on you?"

"Damned hard, especially if you're on-line and at full sensitivity. Even lightning out beyond the perimeter is bad." He squeezed her hand.

"Trystin . . ."

"Yes?"

"Just sit here. All right?" She squeezed his hand. "We can fix something later. I'm glad you're here, even if you call on such short notice."

Trystin bent over and kissed her neck. Her dark hair smelled fresh, clean, and he almost wanted to bury his face in it, to push away the memories of ammonia and weedgrass. Instead, he studied her profile, the almost pug nose and thin lips, the not-quite-flat cheekbones, and the faintly golden skin framed with fine dark hair.

Ezildya smiled. "That's one thing I like about you."

"What?"

"When you settle down, you're all here."

"I'm not sometimes?" Where was he? Thinking about Farhkans—or revs?

"You know what I mean. Sometimes people nod and agree and even carry on a conversation, and you have the feeling they're a thousand kays away, and they could care less what you say. You look at me, and you're here." She looked at Trystin. "Most of the time. But you're not now. Where are you?"

"I met a Farhkan today."

Ezildya shivered. "I met one a couple of years ago. They're creepy. They sort of look right through you. All gray, except for those red eyes and those greenish teeth."

"How did you meet one?" asked Trystin.

"They sent a technical team to Carson. To the shipyards there. My mother was an assistant to the translation engineer. She spent a lot of time with them, and brought one of them home for dinner. They're hydrocarbon-based, like we are, but they need a lot more arsenic than the traces we use." Ezildya shook her head.

"You didn't like him? Her?"

"Do they have sexes? I never found out. They're very private, and very polite—at least this Heren Jule was."

"So was the one I met," added Trystin, "but very insistent."

"Heren was, too. He, I guess he was a he, kept asking me about the reasons for having children. I was fourteen and I wasn't even thinking about children." Ezildya's laugh was short.

"Let's not talk about them." Trystin squeezed her shoulder again.

"You're still upset, aren't you?"

"Me?"

"Yes, you."

Trystin looked at the small hooked rug on the floor. "I guess so. I didn't realize it, though."

"We don't have to talk about aliens. Or revs. Or work." Ezildya leaned toward Trystin and kissed his cheek. "I've got some real Carson pasta. And I made real sauce—the tomatoes are working fine in the tanks." She stood. "Come talk to me."

Trystin followed her to the kitchen alcove, where he leaned on the wall and looked in, since there wasn't room enough for two people.

"This won't take long."

"Good."

"And don't leer. You won't get fed. And I won't offer you any of your chocolates, either."

Trystin leered.

"You're impossible."

"Not always."

Ezildya turned back to the small burners and the large water-filled pot too large for the miniature stove. Trystin waited.

11

"Wherefore shall it profit a man to gain all the lands under the heavens if the cost of those lands be that he take into his heart that which is an abomination unto the Lord?

"What be an abomination, ye ask? Ye are the people of the Lord, and I am His Prophet, and I say unto ye that an abomination is that which displeases the Lord and rejects His teachings.

"What displeases the Lord? A man who does not hold the Lord and His ways above all, or a woman who would place the ways of the world above her duty to bring forth souls and to nurture them in righteousness and in the ways of the Lord.

"Although there are indeed many mansions in your Father's heavens, any being, whether conceived in the depths of the most distant heavens or in the fires of the nearest stars, any being which does not accept the Lord and His commandments, such is displeasing to the Lord. For those who accept not the Lord have lost their souls to darkness and are to be counted as less than the dust under the soles of a man's boots, as less than the sand between a woman's toes.

"Even less are they who have known the Lord and rejected Him, for they have chosen nothingness over the substance of the Lord.

"This is the first and greatest commandment, that ye shall accept the way and the laws of the Lord, and ye shall have no other god before Him. And the second is like unto it, that no man and no woman shall turn away from the needs of another soul of the Lord.

"For the work of the Lord is the work of all faithful

souls, and woe be unto those who toil not in the fields of the Lord. Neither shall they know peace nor certitude, nor cool water upon parched lips, nor the succor of a loving Father. But they shall go unto nothingness troubled and despairing through all the days of their lives, which shall flicker out and be gone as quickly as those of the mayflies.

"The souls of the Lord shall live forever in the sight of the Lord, and He shall be glad to receive them, and they shall come to live in His mansions for so long as the heavens shall endure, and even beyond.

"As I have spoken, as the Prophet of the Lord, so shall it be, now and forever.

"For, as I raise my left hand to cause the lightning to flash, ye see and do not see. This flame I raise in the name of the Lord, and I have raised it with my lesser hand, and I am far less than the Lord. Would ye have me raise my greater hand? Or have the Lord bring His mightiness against ye?"

Book of Toren
Original Edition

12

 Ammonia and weedgrass still permeated the station, although the artificial cinnamon and rysya incense—Gerfel's latest attempts—muted the worst of the weedgrass odor. The tighter main door seals had eliminated any new infiltration of the fine grit, but there was more than enough remaining in the station to irritate Trystin's still-itching nose and to give him the beginnings of a sore throat.

He rubbed his nose gently and turned the command

chair to the left. Through the scratched armaglass of the window, he could see the clouds forming to the east. So far there was none of the static on the net that indicated electrical buildups, but that would come later. It always did.

With his right hand, Trystin massaged the back of his neck, trying to knead out tight muscles. Being away from the station had offered momentary relaxation, and so had Ezildya's presence and cooking, but the respite had been all too short.

Then he checked the reclamation systems. Tower one was still down, and one of the precrackers was operating at less than fifty percent. Hisin had requisitions in on both.

"Hisin, any idea when you'll get the stuff to fix the tower and that precracker?"

"No, ser. There's a lot of damage. That storm whacked a couple of mid-plains secondary systems, and you know what the revs did. It's hard for supply. We haven't been hit this hard all at once ever before."

"Any idea when we'll get the parts?"

"It'll be a couple of weeks, at least. I don't think the Klyseen techs were ready for these kinds of losses."

"A couple of weeks . . . well . . . we do what we can. Thanks." Trystin rechecked the fuel cells' organonutrient level. He still couldn't believe that supply had only refilled the tanks to sixty percent. Then he mentally spooled through the messages and even did a key-word search. None of the references to fuel cells or organonutrients showed anything except the delivery itself and the quantity. He shook his head, rechecking the four-screen display before accessing the tech console again.

"Hisin?"

"Ser?" The tech's voice sounded faintly irritated.

"There's nothing in the tanks. Do you have any idea why our fuel-cell resupply was only a half tank?"

"Half a tank, ser?"

"We were at around ten percent when I went to Klyseen. Now the tanks are at sixty percent. That's about a half tank."

"Oh, that. Lipirelli—he's the tanker tech—told me that

power loads were up and that they couldn't give us a full load because of the damage to all the stations. Just a temporary problem there."

"I hope it doesn't result in our being temporarily out of power when the revs show up."

"Ser?"

"Nothing. Thank you, Hisin." Trystin went back to the galley where he mixed another cup of Sustain. After one sip, he added more of the powder. That made the jolt harder when it hit his stomach, but he hated the watery taste that he got when he mixed the Sustain according to the directions.

He paced along the narrow space between the console and the wall, from the secondary console in the corner to the window and back. His guts were still tight, and he didn't know quite why. Was he worried about the Farhkan physical, or the interview?

Why had the Farhkan—Ghere, was it?—why had he/she/it been so hung up on getting Trystin to admit he was a thief—even in the general sense? Why had Ghere insisted that Trystin think about it? What did the damned interview have to do with the technical help the Coalition was supposedly getting? What kind of help was it? Ezildya had mentioned that her mother was a translation engineer. Were the Farhkans helping improve the translation engines of Coalition spacecraft? Why? How did he fit in?

He shook his head. Maybe his mother would know more about the Farhkans, not that he could ask her until he got home leave, and that wouldn't happen anytime soon. He took another sip of Sustain, pausing to look out the window at the slowly growing storm to the east.

Why was Mara suddenly receiving so much attention from the revs? Was it because it was nearing semihabitability and they were running out of room—again? Why were the revs always trying to take, take, take?

Cling! Trystin swallowed his sip of Sustain as he called up the message through the implant and headed back to the command seat.

"All PerCon Stations. DefCom visual plot indicates four

paragliders on entry envelopes—split pattern. Probable landfall coordinates follow. Full alert on perimeter stations. DefCon Two. DefCon Two . . ."

After plugging the coordinates into the system, Trystin cross-checked. Two of the revvie gliders were aimed into the midsection of the eastern badlands—making East Red Three a prime target.

Trystin hoped that the revvie pilots changed directions for evasive purposes, but he knew it wouldn't happen. He took a deep breath as he sensed another red light flare on the maintenance screen.

Hisin's voice fed through the implant. "Lieutenant, ser, that precracker's frozen, except for the mobility module. I knew it was going to happen, but, no, they can't spare the boards. I should disable it."

"You can't do it by remote?"

"There's no circuitry left to accept the signals. It's just going to waddle along doing nothing."

"How far is it out?" Even as he asked, Trystin used his satellite plot screen. "Ten kays, isn't it?"

"Nearer eleven, ser."

"Let it go for now," Trystin decided. "The techs made their decision. We've got revs coming down, and the last thing we need is for you to be out there if they start a firefight."

"Tech HQ won't be happy. Running nonfunctional wastes fuel."

"Let them be unhappy. Better than your being dead. Blame it on me."

"Appreciate it, ser. I can't say that I was looking forward to it."

"Don't worry. You'll have to do something once we deal with the revs, but you won't have to worry about them at the same time." Trystin clicked off-line and returned to his scans.

Nothing.

He continued to run through the scans and the satellite plots, but everything continued to register as before. Then he went through the maintenance levels. Besides tower number one, the malfunctioning and still-mobile pre-cracker, more than a few small problems remained, including the still-bulging cell door in Block B.

After reviewing the maintenance status, he scrolled back through all the recent messages, but most were just routine reports, except for Gerfel's report on an evening revvie attack he hadn't even known had occurred. From what he could tell, she'd neutralized them quickly. He studied the note about the use of rockets as flares. The new revvie suit fabric fluoresced some at night—or the light patterns looked that way. He'd try to keep that in mind, although he wasn't due for night-shift duty again for another month.

Cling! Trystin licked his dry lips and accessed the message.

"All PerCon Stations. DefCon One. DefCon One. Ambient atmospheric conditions preclude detection and neutralization of paragliders. Ambient atmospheric conditions preclude detection and neutralization of paragliders. Estimated landfall approximately 1256. Landfall estimated at 1256. DefCon One. DefCon One . . ."

Ambient atmospheric conditions? He checked the met-plot. The skies were more than half clear, nothing out of the ordinary. More like inability to penetrate improved revvie shielding. Why couldn't DefCom admit it? In any case, the revs were down without a rocket or a laser being laid on them, probably with more heavy equipment. Trystin called up all station shields, except those for the power fans, then accessed the tech console.

"Hisin, DefCom missed the revs, and they're on the ground, but no one knows where. We're shielding now—except for the power fans. With all the new revvie toys, they could be on top of us before the scanners register."

"Keeping the shields up is fine by me, ser."

"I'll let you know. That's if they don't announce their arrival otherwise."

"Maybe they'll pick on someone else."

"I think they've decided not to play favorites. We're all the targets."

"You are cheerful, ser."

"I try, Hisin." Trystin broke the link to the tech console and immediately checked the satellite plot, the scanners, even the EDI system—which usually wasn't much good for anything short of a spacecraft's energy discharges. He got nothing, except a growing tightness in his guts, probably compounded by drinking too much Sustain.

He felt better about his decision not to have Hisin shut down the defective precracker. If the revs attacked, and Trystin couldn't stop them, then the precracker didn't matter. If the revs attacked someone else and made a mess, no one would care about it, either. Not with four shielded paragliders that no one could track. He tried to concentrate on the screens.

As the minutes passed, Trystin kept focusing on the one screen, the full optical view, which only showed the few native cacti bending in the rising wind, and a few centimeters of grit scudding along the hillsides. Every so often, he tried the full energy scan screens. Nothing changed.

The storms built to the east, and then subsided. The wind rose and fell, and the odor of ammonia and weedgrass irritated his nose. Every so often, he sneezed, and his nose hurt more.

"Lieutenant, ser? Have you heard anything?"

"Not yet."

"The precracker's stalled out, ser."

"Well . . . it's not going anywhere, and you didn't have to disable it."

"The mobility module's probably shot, too."

"Blame it on me." Trystin shrugged. That's the way it would come out. Officers were there for people to blame so that the techs didn't have to worry about it. He went back to four-screen, but still found no signs of the revs.

Hssstttt . . . A thin wave of static singed the net. Trystin studied the metplot, but, by all indications, the afternoon storm was fading early.

Cling! Trystin let the message scroll through his mind.

"All PerCon Stations. DefCon One remains. DefCon One remains. Anticipate perimeter station attacks at any time. Anticipate attacks at any time. DefCon One. DefCon One . . ."

Wonderful. PerCon anticipated attacks. Where along the two-thousand-kay perimeter did PerCon anticipate the attacks?

He took a small sip of Sustain and stood, stretching. Under DefCon One, he had to remain in "close physical proximity" to the command console, but he needed to stretch tight muscles, especially if the revs were indeed coming.

After stretching, he walked behind the console and looked into the locker. His armor was there, and so was the slug thrower. He unsealed one clip and set it by the weapon that wasn't supposed to be loaded inside the station unless station integrity were broken. PerCon did not like careless officers punching holes in the station. The revs and Mara itself presented enough problems.

Trystin slowly walked back to the command seat and settled back down.

At 14:59.03, he spotted the puffs of dust barely rising above the hilltop to the northeast. He immediately dropped the scanners to the lowest band frequencies to find the distorted images of the rev missionary troopers.

This time, though, there were no images near the perimeter lines—only hints near the top of the hills beyond the perimeter line, and nothing clear, just intermittent puffs of dust that couldn't be natural. But the scanners didn't show what caused the dust puffs.

Trystin licked his lips, and checked all the defense systems, trying to compute a rocket trajectory for the backside of the hill.

Crumpt! The impact of the first heavy shell reverberated through the station, and at 15:01.12 alert-red spilled through the net. Trystin snorted. "A lot of warning from all this hardware." Then he hit the alarm for Hisin. "Revs! They've set up behind the hills, and it looks like we're in for a few shells. I can't see any signs of a troop assault."

"Friggers!"

Crumpt! Crumpt!

Despite the additional impacts, since they were barely above the soil line, Trystin held off lifting the shields for the power fans—for the moment—and fired off a quick attack report.

"PerCon, this is East Red Three. Desoll. East Red Three receiving fire. East Red Three taking fire. There are no revs in view or registering on any system. . . ."

Crumpt! Another shell exploded, this time in the soil less than three meters from the station's lower wall.

Trystin released a three-rocket spread.

Two more shells plowed into the station's composite armor, well away from the fans or the defense systems.

Trystin frowned. Why were the revs targeting that section? He called up the station schematic, noting that the fuel cells were beneath and behind the heavy lower walls there.

A gout of dust rose, barely clearing the hilltop, and Trystin froze the schematic, and released a pair of rockets.

Crumpt! The station shivered ever so slightly from the impact of the incoming shell.

Trystin split screens, but nothing showed—nothing but incoming rounds illustrated in screaming pink on screen three—the representative screen. Not even a single flickering image appeared on any band width. The revs were definitely not mounting their typical suicide-style approach, and that bothered Trystin.

Another alert-red flashed through the system, and Trystin's mouth opened as he watched all four screens. Three wide plumes of dust appeared on the one-screen, and before each what appeared to be a miniature hovertank with a comparatively oversized gun, made visible only by dust flowing around it. Absently, Trystin noted that the tanks had no turrets, probably to reduce weight, and used the hover fans to turn the whole tank.

"Hisin! Get into armor and get into the bolthole on the north side away from the fuel cells. Understand?"

"But—"

"Do you understand? There are three damned tanks

out there, heavy guns, and I don't know what else."

"Bolthole?"

"The armored caisson!"

"Stet."

Crumpt! Crumpt! Crumpt! The entire station shook.

Trystin, even as he was hurrying to the locker and pulling on his armor, was redirecting the gattlings, so that all the firepower was concentrated on the center tank.

He could sense the tank wobbling some, and as an experiment, targeted a pair of rockets into the low slope in front of the tank. The tank swerved, and both rockets exploded harmlessly across the composite armor.

"Shit!" Half into the armor, Trystin disabled the autoseek on the rockets and cut the gattlings. He didn't want to hit the tanks. The rockets wouldn't do a thing to that armor, not before the station was so much junk.

Crumpt! Crumpt!

The station shivered again, and amber telltales began to flash across the maintenance board.

Trystin directed three more rockets into the dirt in front of the center tank. With his armor in place, he grabbed the helmet and dropped back into the command seat as more shells shivered the station.

"PerCon, this is East Red Three. Under attack by light armor—all hovertanks—class unknown. Repeat, under attack by light armor." He added a few frozen screen images to the message and pulsed it off.

Crumpt! The station shivered once more under the impact of the little tanks' heavy shells. How had the revs gotten them planetside? He aimed another pair of rockets in front of the middle tank.

Crumpt! Crumpt! A single telltale flashed amber on the maintenance panel, but Trystin didn't check it. There wasn't a lot he could do.

Trystin's rockets exploded in the soil before the lead tank, and gouts of fine soil shrouded the hovertank. It nosed down into the small crater created by the rockets.

Trystin aimed the gattlings at the soil around the front of the tank, and dust billowed up and around the vehicle.

Trystin grinned as the unknown tanker overrevved his fans, and more dust swelled into a swirling plume.

Crumpt! Crumpt!

The grin vanished as the station shook again, and several more amber telltales flashed red. The remaining two tanks were less than four hundred meters away, their guns aimed point-blank at the wall above the fuel cells.

Trystin grounded more rockets in front of the left tank, and dirt and dust flew, but the tank swerved and kept coming, throwing more shells at the station's rapidly degrading composite armor.

Another brace of rockets went into the ground—and another . . .

"East Red Three! East Red Three, this is PerCon. Interrogative status. Interrogative status."

"PerCon, trying to repulse hovertanks. Will report later. Out."

Idiots! Automated direct-feed or not, he could only split his attention so many ways.

Another telltale went red with the next set of shells that rocked the station, and the upper bank of fuel cells began to lose power. Probably cracked cells, reflected Trystin. Perimeter stations hadn't been designed to undergo continuous heavy shelling.

Crumpt! Crumpt!

The station lights blinked, and flashed, momentarily, as the power load shifted to the accumulators. Trystin realized that the fans were still unshielded, and he left them open. He was going to need all the power he could get. As he shut down all the nondefense systems, he released another set of rockets, and followed with a pointed burst from the gattlings. The background hissing of ventilators died away.

Dust and plastic fragments filtered down around him from the ceiling and probably everywhere else, mixing with ammonia and weedgrass.

Kkkheewcchew! He sneezed, and an errant rocket flared into the hillside as Trystin rubbed his nose.

The left tank pitched nose down into a rocket crater, and

fans whined. Dust rose, higher and higher, and the tanker tried to rock himself out. Trystin permitted himself a tight grin as smoke curled out from the ghostly looking tank. The grit of Mara and the revvie tanker's impatience just might have cooked that tank's systems.

Crumpt!

Trystin checked his status—and wished he hadn't. He had less than a dozen rockets left and perhaps twenty percent of his gattling rounds. Surely, he couldn't have gone through an inventory that fast!

But he had to stop the damned tank, or he wouldn't have a station left. Another pair of rockets exploded into the ground in front of the last tank. Before long, it would be too close for his rockets.

Crumpt!

With one tank left, the odor of ammonia was stronger, and the number of amber and red warning telltales had gotten too numerous to count. Another system check indicated that the gattlings were down to ten percent, and that he had nine rockets.

Where were the rev troops? There had to be some—somewhere.

Another shell from the single functioning tank rocked the station. Above him the armaglass window cracked—probably from the flexing of the upper station walls under the pounding of the tanks' guns. Minitanks, at that.

Trystin studied the remaining mobile tank, which had suddenly turned and swept back toward the badlands. Then he nodded. His slim stock of remaining weapons had to be reserved for the troops that would follow.

The station shook, and Trystin licked his lips. The remaining tank stood back beyond the hill crest and lobbed shells into the lower walls. The fuel cells were plastic and twisted metal and spilled organonutrient—if that.

Crumpt! Crumpt!

AIR SYSTEM INTEGRITY LOST!!

With the holes in the lower levels, any vestige of breathable air was rapidly dissipating. Trystin jabbed the suit's external tube into the seat pak. He didn't want to use suit supplies any sooner than necessary, and he didn't want to leave the control center yet. He wanted a shot at the rev troopers, and the station's armor would hold out for a few more direct hits from the tank's shells.

Then he pushed the console jack into the suit's wrist slot, since, when he closed the helmet, he'd lose much of the implant's speed and range without the amplifier.

As more ammonia rolled into the room he closed the helmet. Somehow, the screen images felt metallic. That was the only way he could describe the sensation. Now, he could sense the flickering images of suited revs slipping from cover beyond the perimeter. They seemed to know that the command center was collapsing under the continued attack from the single damned tank.

Crumpt! Crumpt!

How many shells did the damned little tank carry?

Trystin licked his lips again and waited, checking the immobilized tanks. Both remained nearly gun-deep in fine red soil.

The revs, whose flickering images looked to be nearly eight squads, poured down the hillside toward the apparently dead station as more shells smashed into the collapsing armor. Trystin forced himself to wait, even as he noted the fire in the fuel cells, hoping he could hold on for just a while longer.

With a last shell, the hovertank swung wide and toward the south side of the station. Trystin understood that. The tank would use its shells to blast through the armor over the vehicle door.

He waited, calculating where the tank would station itself, and pretargeted the rockets.

The revs slipped closer and closer to the station.

The hovertank seemed to turn and center itself on the door. After refocusing the one-screen on the tank, Trystin felt as though he were looking right down the muzzle of the tank's gun.

The shells crashed against the armor shields of the big door.

Had the maintenance board been on-line, it would have

been bright red, Trystin knew, but he watched and calculated, watched and calculated, as the shells hammered their way through the vehicle-door armor, pounding an opening through composite and metal.

Then he triggered the last blasts of the gattlings, mowing through who knew how many revs, sensing vaguely, rather than really seeing, bodies falling across the shell-churned red powder that had been soil. As an afterthought, he also triggered the antisuit bomblets. They might get a few revs—maybe.

All nine rockets went off, one after the other, right in front of the tank. Trystin had counted on the tanker moving forward, in rage or reaction, and he had guessed right, as the tank dove into the pit.

Without waiting to see the results—with little power and no rockets or ammunition left, there was nothing more Trystin could do from the command center—Trystin unplugged the system jack and ran for the locker where he grabbed the slug thrower and the clip bag. He jacked his reflexes up one notch and bounded down the stairs.

Dust and soot and heat swirled through the lower layers of the station, hot enough that Trystin could feel it through the heavy armor. He made it to the lock doors to the vehicle bay, where the heat died away with the distance from the burning fuel cells.

Slowly, he cracked the door into the vehicle bay.

Spang!

The bullet ricocheted off the fragments of the outer door, where shredded metal framed a rough oblong in the metal. Fragments of composite armor formed a low barrier in the middle of the opening.

Trystin skidded and dived behind the largest pile, hoping that he didn't rip something vital in the armor. It was supposed to be tough, but so were perimeter stations and shell-shredded composite fragments.

He squinted through the helmet and through a narrow opening between two fragments of composite armor at the indistinct images. One rev was crouched behind the eastern corner of the station. Several appeared to be firing from where the last grounded tank lay silent.

Spang!

Trystin waited, the slug thrower ready. And waited. And waited. Finally, the rev behind the corner peered out. Trystin still waited. The rev lifted his head slightly, just enough, and Trystin fired.

The one shell ripped the juncture between neck and chest, and the rev pitched forward.

"Lousy, lucky shot," mumbled Trystin to himself, resigning himself to waiting, and checking his suit supply as he did.

Who would run out of air first? The rev suits used a concentrator and a supplement system, but he had no idea when they'd last been resupplied.

Spang! Spang! Bullets ricocheted through the garage.

There had to be at least a dozen of them outside. He checked the clips. More than enough ammunition for the moment. He squeezed off two rounds toward the figures around the last grounded tank.

They scrambled or sprawled deeper into the grit.

Another rev figure shambled, almost drunkenly, around the corner of the station—respirator problems or lack of oxygen, Trystin thought. Or a brush with a suit bomblet. Tough. Trystin brought him down with a single shot.

Then he waited, watching as another figure scuttled through the dust. The revs were low on air, and they intended to sneak around, trying to attack from both sides, and maybe from the tank all at once. It was a lousy plan, but they didn't have a lot of choice if they were short on air. Trystin frowned. Did they have grenades, or something like that?

That might make things less desperate.

He waited, still watching, as Parvati crept closer to the horizon, the sun's image getting redder and redder. He didn't like his minimal cover, so close to the door, but if he drew back into the bay, he couldn't see, and they could corner him inside.

So he stayed flat, rifle ready.

Then three revs exploded from holes, from somewhere,

toward the door Trystin guarded. One of the running revs hurled something, and Trystin fired once, bringing him down, but the cylindrical object flew over Trystin's head and deeper into the vehicle bay.

Thwump!

They had grenades.

He fired half a dozen times, maybe more, until no one was standing, then quickly replaced the clip. He had five clips left.

Parvati sank farther down, almost touching the western horizon.

As dozens of flickering figures appeared in the twilight, running toward Trystin, he kicked his reflexes into high as a shower of bullets *spang*'ed above and around him.

Trystin tried to concentrate, to make each shot deliberate, but there seemed to be far too many revs, and he switched to semiautomatic, running through the clip, and slipping the next into place, and then another. Figures fell, but more seemed to replace them.

The second grenade bounced off the door and exploded somewhere behind Trystin, spraying his leg with needles of shrapnel and pain.

He ignored it, and ran through another half clip before he looked at what seemed like rows of bodies strewn before the vehicle-bay door.

Lying on his side, he put the last clip in the slug thrower, and waited.

A flickering appeared to his right, then vanished. He watched. Another flicker, just momentary. Trystin nodded. The rev was trying a slow approach in the dim light so that Trystin wouldn't be able to see him.

After the next flicker, Trystin squeezed off two rounds.

The rev, less than ten meters away, launched himself toward the doorway, collapsing less than three meters from Trystin.

Trystin took a deep breath, realizing he didn't have much air left himself. There were aux tanks in the back of the bay, and the scooter tanks, but did he dare move? If he didn't, like the revs, he was going to be dead because he couldn't breathe.

Slowly, slowly, he inched himself back and to his right, trying to move so quietly that no rev could see. His progress was slow, since pain stabbed through his right leg, and the leg didn't respond well.

Once he was clear of the opening and behind the shredded edges of the door, he staggered up, rifle ready, as he backed toward scooter number one.

He could sit in the scooter seat and cover the door. It wasn't ideal, but it allowed him to breathe, which was better than the alternative, far better.

Another flicker caught his eye, and he fired. The image dropped from his sight. Trystin wanted to kick himself. He wasn't thinking well. He dropped his reflexes a notch and called up his night vision—except the effort brought stars to his eyes.

Edging backward, his intermittent vision on the opening blasted in the big door, he almost fell into the scooter. Awkwardly he tubed into the air supply. His vision cleared a bit, and his thoughts somewhat as well. Enough that he remembered to use the Sustain in the helmet nipple.

Then he waited, his night vision stabilizing.

The three grenades exploded where Trystin had been lying earlier, rearranging fragments of composite armor and metal and raising dust.

Trystin managed to struggle down to a position half sitting on the plastcrete floor while remaining connected to the scooter's air supply. His eyes were fixed on the opening in the door.

Thwump! Thwump!

The second set of grenades exploded farther back, raising dust and splinters of plastic, but none of the fragments went the nearly fifteen meters back to the scooter where Trystin waited, rifle ready.

Two revs burst through the door.

Trystin got the first one in midair.

The second turned in the wrong direction, looking toward the station lock doors, and spraying them with a short burst.

It took Trystin three shots in the near-darkness, and he yanked out his oxygen plug with the third.

Slowly, he levered himself back next to the scooter before replugging into the tank.

Then he waited. And waited. And waited. At some point, he remembered to drop his reflexes to normal—far later than he should have, but his thoughts weren't as clear as they should have been.

And his leg burned, and burned. And burned.

Trying to keep his mind off his leg, for a time, he tried to figure out the revvie tank design, and how the revs had managed to get them on radar-transparent paragliders. And where had all the shells come from? Shells had to have metal casings—or the equivalent—and casings were heavy. For all his speculations, he didn't really know any more when Parvati finally rose, bringing rosy light to the destruction around him. He did know that his leg was a mass of pain, and useless. Scooter one's oxygen supply was nearly gone as well. Still, he dragged himself to the corner, and pounded on the hatch before spotting the emergency comm jack. It took him a while to plug in.

"Hisin. This is Lieutenant Desoll. I think I need some help."

"Lieutenant. You been out there all night?"

"Call it guard duty." Trystin tried not to wince. "How's your oxygen?"

"It's about gone. I'd have to come out soon and get some more."

The hatch opened slowly, and Hisin's suited figure clambered out.

"Ser?" Hisin's voice rattled in Trystin's helmet.

"I'm here. Feel like shit, and can't move worth a damn." Hisin's eyes went down to Trystin's leg.

"Yeah." He swallowed, but his throat was dry and his tongue felt swollen. "I haven't seen a rev since early last night. So, could you see if you could raise us some help?"

Hisin looked toward the shredded vehicle bay door.

"They had tanks."

"Tanks?"

"Little ones, but they had big enough guns. Now . . . about that call for assistance . . ."

"Ah . . . yes, ser."

"First, help me over there where I can plug into scooter two's tanks." Trystin tried to straighten his leg, but couldn't, as he dragged himself into the second scooter's seat. His eyes blurred as he watched the tech edge across the bay and into the station.

Later, how much later Trystin couldn't say, not with the effort of trying to stay alert, Hisin clumped out from the tech room, his movements in the suit awkward. "Tech team is on the way, ser." The words were scratchy through the helmet phones.

"How soon?"

"I don't know. They didn't say. It couldn't be more than a few hours."

"Great." Trystin squeezed his lips together and looked down at the mangled mass of armor and leg. Then he looked at the line from the auxiliary oxygen tank. So far, the positive pressure was keeping his breathing supply clean. But Mara's slightly corrosive atmosphere was feeling more than slightly corrosive on the exposed parts of his leg.

"You all right, ser?"

"So far, Hisin. So far." He looked out at the shredded door to the vehicle bay, and at the bodies, and the one grounded tank. "I hope we've got plenty of oxygen. It's going to be a lot longer than a couple of hours."

"Ser?"

Trystin took a deep breath. They had no fuel cells, no place that was atmosphere-tight, except the bolthole, and there wasn't really any way he could climb down the ladder. There were probably revs and revvie armor everywhere. Somehow, he couldn't imagine PerCon exactly hurrying out to pick them up until the dust settled. He took another deep breath. It was likely to be a long wait. He hoped it wouldn't be too long.

13

The med center room smelled of rysya overlaid with an orange citrus odor too sharp to be real.

Trystin lay propped against the pale green pillows, his eyes flickering occasionally to the tubes and wires running to the fluid-filled harness around his right leg. The bedside table was empty except for the cup of medicated Sustain that tasted even worse than regular Sustain.

For about the third time in as many minutes he used his implant to flash through the med center's net library. Nothing looked interesting, and his leg kept burning. The med techs and doctors assured him that the burning was a good sign, that the nerves were regenerating as anticipated. That was fine. Their legs weren't burning. They weren't the one restricted to bed with tubes stuck everywhere to carry off the results of their normal bodily processes.

He tried the pubnet again, this time accessing a news update, one showing the brown-clad bodies around a perimeter station.

"... in a devastating demonstration of blind faith, revvie forces ..."

Trystin flicked off the pubnet. Blind faith? Some of the revs seemed blind, but the officer he'd questioned had made a deliberate choice to believe. Could anyone choose, intelligently, to follow such a faith?

Trystin looked up from the med center bed. A black-haired woman in Service uniform, wearing a subcommander's gold triangle on her collar, stood by the doorway, a green folder in her right hand.

"Might I come in, Lieutenant?"

Trystin gestured. "Please. I apologize for not being able to—"

"Don't worry." The subcommander slipped into the high stool beside the bed, her eyes level with Trystin's. "I'm Subcommander Mitsui, Midori Mitsui, integrative intelligence. My job is to follow up on the perimeter attacks." She raised the folder. "I also brought over some official papers you can look at later. No . . . don't worry." She set the folder on the table, then pulled a small recorder from the clip in her belt. She put the recorder on top of the folder and gently cleared her throat.

"This is official?" Trystin's eyes flicked to the recorder.

"Don't worry."

Whenever senior officers said not to worry, Trystin did.

"I know. Whenever a senior officer tells you not to worry, it's not a good sign." The commander smiled. "We've got a lot of problems, but right now, your biggest problem is to get your leg healed. Some rest won't hurt your neural system, either. What I want is background information on the attack on East Red Three—your impressions, your opinions, your conclusions. The scanners and data banks don't pick up those sorts of things that well."

"The scanners didn't pick up the revs too well, either."

"We're working on that. But how did you find them? According to the records, you reacted before the scanners did—almost two minutes earlier."

"I didn't trust the scanners after the past attacks. When we got DefCon One, I didn't want to be surprised again. I was looking for dust, changes in the light patterns, anything. I saw the dust first. Then we got the shells, and then the tanks. The rev troops didn't come until a lot later."

"What about the tanks? Did you notice anything unusual about them?"

"You've got most of that on the net, I'm sure. They were small and used hovering to turn the gun—no independent turret. That meant weight was a problem—either they wanted numbers, or they didn't have enough fuel for heavier tanks. It seemed like they were designed to cross the plains."

"Why did you think that?"

"I didn't—not then—but it makes sense now." Trystin ran his hand through his hair. It was getting too long. "Some of the badlands are rough. They'd have to be careful where they moved the tanks. Too rough, and they'd lose their air cushion—and the tank. That's not a problem on the plains. Of course, the hover assembly is lighter than treads. At least it should be, according to standard design." He shook his head. "I don't know. I didn't get close enough, and the scanners weren't worth an immortal's damn."

"Plains travel was one of the thoughts we had," she confirmed. "ResCom examined the immobilized tanks. They would have been very fast on the high plains, and, for hover vessels, they're extremely fuel-efficient. I wouldn't be surprised if we end up adopting some of the design features."

Trystin nodded.

"Was there anything else about the tanks?"

He pulled at his chin, then laughed self-consciously. "I remember thinking that they carried awfully big guns for such little suckers."

The commander nodded. "Very high projectile to gross ration."

"Big guns for little suckers," Trystin repeated with a grin.

Mitsui watched him, then asked, "How did you manage to immobilize them?"

"You know . . ."

"We know that you managed to ground them, but I'd like your impressions."

"Well . . . I tried the gattlings, and one of them wavered, but it didn't stop it. My first rockets just sort of splattered across the armor. So I figured that if those didn't even slow it, I'd better try something else. Some of the soil is really fine. . . ." Trystin licked his dry lips. "So I tried to blow holes in the ground just enough in front of them that they couldn't avoid nosing down. I sort of figured . . . It's really just a feel, I mean, you don't calculate that sort of thing when the revs are throwing heavy shells at you and the station's coming apart around you. Anyway, I felt that they didn't know how fine some of the subsoil was, and they were throwing dust when they moved. I had the feeling that they might dig in. And once they stopped, they'd settle, and rocking would just make it worse. Plus, I hoped that the grit—it's really fine—would help gum up their systems."

"All that happened. Two of the tanks at your station burned out their engines. How did you know that would work?"

"I didn't. I just knew nothing else was working, and I didn't have much time."

"That was another thing. Why didn't you use all the gattling rounds on the tanks?"

Trystin shrugged, then pursed his lips as the motion carried down to the immobilized leg and the tubes and wires around it, and a flash of fire ran back up toward his back. "It didn't seem like a good idea. That is, the revs just attacking with tanks. You can't take a station without troops. If I used all the rounds on the tanks, then what could I do when all those revs swarmed out of the hills?"

"So you let them batter the station when you still had weapons left that could have beaten them back for a time?"

Trystin opened his mouth, then shut it, before finally answering, "Not exactly. The rockets and gattlings weren't stopping the tanks. They did stop troopers."

"According to your tech and the pickup team, rather than use the bolthole, you stayed in armor almost twenty-four hours."

"Yes."

"Why? You were wounded."

"Because we'd have been dead if I hadn't done what I did."

"How do you know that?"

"Commander." Trystin tried not to sigh. Getting irritated at superior officers, even dumb ones, was not a good idea. "I've interrogated several revs. Most of them either wanted to kill me or tried to, or both. They regard us as golems, some sort of machines. They also don't have facilities for taking prisoners. That meant holding them off or getting killed. You can't hold someone off from a hole in the ground."

Even when Trystin thought there couldn't be any more questions, the commander kept asking them. Trystin tried to keep the irritated tone out of his voice, but knew he was failing.

Finally, when the commander had apparently exhausted her stock of what had seemed endless questions, he asked, "Could you answer a few of my questions, Commander?"

"I don't know. Ask."

"How did the other stations do? East Red Two—and Four?"

"East Red Four—Major Farli, I think—"

"Freyer, Ulteena."

"Major Freyer managed to immobilize all four tanks sent against the station and neutralize all revs. East Red Two was a total loss."

Trystin frowned. Quentar? "Personnel in East Red Two?"

"A total loss."

"East Red Four—how did Ulteena—Major Freyer—do that?"

"She used a turner to dig a line of trenches before the revs got there. She filled the trenches with ultrafine grit."

Trust Ulteena to figure it out ahead of time. Trystin took a deep breath. "Can you tell me how things turned out overall?"

"We managed to beat them back. We lost almost two thirds of the stations. They didn't have enough tanks to target every station. We had to bring in atmospheric space scouts and some very heavy weapons."

For a long moment, Trystin just sat there.

"That information is restricted, but you deserve to know. I will deny telling you, and you'll face serious disciplinary actions if you repeat it. But you and Major . . . Freyer were the only ones to survive assaults of more than a pair of tanks."

"How is she?"

"She's fine. She's on the way to her next assignment."

Trystin nodded, then licked his lips. "I've had some time to think. . . ." He forced a laugh. "I know that's always dangerous for junior officers. But I don't understand. When I first started as a station watch officer, we'd get a few rev attacks. Pretty scattered, never more than a squad, and we captured some, and killed some. Now, all of a sudden, we've been getting hammered. Lots of heavy weapons, at least heavy for respirator-suited troops to haul across the badlands, and enough firepower to crack stations they couldn't touch just a few months ago. So what's happening?"

"The revs were smarter than we thought." The commander's black eyes met his. "The attacks from the early glider drops were just to cover that they were bringing in those minitanks and guns. They've been caching equipment in the badlands for nearly three years—maybe longer. All underground with a couple of permanent depots."

"And no one could discover this until they wiped out half the perimeter stations?" Trystin found his voice rising. He tried to lower it as he spoke. Senior officers got upset when junior officers implied they were incompetent. In the back of his mind, he wondered if junior revvie officers had the same problems. They couldn't; they didn't think, did they, just followed their Prophet?

"Lieutenant. A planet is a damned big place. We're spread pretty thin. If we start building up defenses, then we have to divert from planoforming, and we'll never get the place habitable. Plus . . . the revs haven't been that sneaky ever before, and there weren't any signs we could pick up from the satellite scans."

"Exactly. If the satellite plots had better resolution, it wouldn't have happened."

"Maybe not," the subcommander admitted, "but better scanners cost more, and with as many stations as the Coalition has, what else do we do without?"

"So they'll keep doing it because we can't see them?"

She shook her head. "No. Now that we know what to

look for—and how to do it with the existing equipment—we've found and neutralized their caches/depots, whatever you want to call them. We've pushed them back to square one." Mitsui stood. "That information was sent to the perimeter stations this morning—those we have left."

"So I won't have to worry about a full-sized Sasaki-class tank—or whatever the revs call theirs—rolling over my station new month?"

"No, Lieutenant, you won't. You may wish it were that simple." She flashed a smile, a cool knowing smile. "I hope you're up and around before long." With a last nod, she walked out.

Trystin sat silent for a moment. Quentar, and who knew who else—dead because better scanners cost too much? How did that make the Coalition different from the revs? He pursed his lips. It was different. At least, the Eco-Techs didn't turn soldiers into living bombs.

He shook his head, then reached for the packet. After setting it in his lap, he opened it and riffled through the stack of papers. Then he set them flat and picked up the first one, a single sheet announcing that all Service tours would be extended by six standard months unless the needs of the Service required an earlier change of assignment.

Translated loosely, reflected Trystin, all short-term Service contracts were being extended. If you wanted to request or accept something more dangerous, the Service would be happy to oblige, all too happy to oblige you.

The second sheet was more interesting. Trystin scanned the page.

". . . Desoll, Trystin, Lieutenant, Service of the Ecological-Technocracy Coalition . . . results of your voluntary physical and the Farhkan follow-up study positive . . . retained in the follow-up cohort . . . annual pay bonus increased to five percent . . . reevaluation after next physical scheduled tentatively for Unodec 790 . . ."

Whatever he'd said to the Farhkan hadn't been enough to get him thrown out of that study. But what did they want? Would he ever find out?

Still . . . the extra pay was nice, even though he wasn't spending half of what he was making anyway. How could you spend credits when there wasn't anywhere to spend them? Even the best restaurants in Klyseen weren't that expensive, and they were about the only luxury the settlement boasted.

He smiled. Even the thought of that food started him drooling. The med center provided better food than a perimeter station, but not much better.

The next sheet he studied for a long time. There were five sheets, all identical copies—hard-copy orders. Voluntary, but orders. Propped up in the med center bed, with tubes and wires running to what was left of his right leg, Trystin kept looking at the hard-copy orders in his hands. Hard-copy orders, yet. He shook his head as he read the words in the second section.

". . . by accepting this assignment, you, Trystin Desoll, accept indefinite assignment in the Service, subject to the needs of the Service and the peoples of the Ecological-Technocracy Coalition. . . . Upon recovery and assuming full medical approval and clearance for duty, report to Chevel Beta for commencement of training no later than—"

Chevel Beta—that was the Service installation for training military pilots for deep-space combat and translation. Originally, he'd requested pilot training, but his request had been "deferred."

What had changed? Was it the revvie attack? He frowned. How could it have been? Service Headquarters on Perdya must have issued the orders as soon as they found out, because they knew he'd been wounded.

Did he still want to be a deep-space pilot? That meant he was basically being asked to volunteer for almost permanent isolation from his parents—and Salya—at least after the first few years. While translation slip/error wasn't that great for any interstellar jump, the cumulative effect was considerable. He'd still be young when his sister was frail and gray.

Tap . . .

He looked toward the door. There Ezildya stood, a tentative smile in place. He slipped the orders into the folder and put the folder in the single drawer of the table beside the bed. "Come on in. I don't bite." He looked at the harness around the leg. "I can't even move that much."

Ezildya edged up beside the bed, then bent over and kissed his cheek. The faint scent of fleurisle drifted to him, but dark circles ringed her eyes. "How is the leg?"

"It hurts. The med techs say it will be fine, maybe even a little stronger than the original, but probably won't be quite as sensitive in places."

"What happened?" She hoisted herself into the high-backed stool.

"What happens when people shoot things at each other. I got hit in the leg. Twice, I think."

"And they have to rebuild and partly reclone your leg?"

"Two days in shredded armor were more of a problem than the original wound. There was no way to get to us for a while." Trystin tried to shift his weight in the bed and was rewarded with a twinge of fire that ran from his lower leg all the way up into his back.

"It hurts, doesn't it?"

"When I try to move. The med techs say that's a good sign. That's easy for them to say. It's not their leg." He paused. "I'm glad you came."

"I didn't know for a while. I thought you were dead." She pinched her lips together. "A lot of the perimeter stations were destroyed."

"I heard that earlier today. I guess I was lucky."

Ezildya glanced toward the harness and raised her eyebrows.

"The alternatives were a lot worse." He frowned. "How did you find out I was here?"

"There was a public briefing sheet—not public, I guess, but for all of us in tech support. You and some major were mentioned as blunting the rev attack. It said you were wounded. After that"—she shrugged—"it was just a matter of finding out where you were."

"I'm sorry. I should have sent a message, but"—he

glanced around the small bare cubicle and then at his leg—
"I'm not exactly mobile."

"I can see that." Ezildya gave him a brief smile.

"How are things going for you? You look tired."

"I am. We've all been on extra shifts. I think everyone
in Klyseen is working every moment that they're not sleeping."

Trystin reached out and fluffed the black hair. "I'm glad
you came."

"So am I." She shook her head.

"What's the matter?"

"I guess I'm tired. You seem . . . different." She shook
her head again. "I must be tired. You are you . . ."

"I hope so." He looked to his right leg. "At least, most
of me is me."

"Is it true . . . you spent two days in armor with a
wounded leg? There's not enough oxygen . . ."

"I tubed into the scooter and aux supplies after the revs
stopped coming. Then Hisin helped me." Trystin saw the
confusion. "Hisin was the tech. I put him in the bolthole.
Techs don't have heavy armor. We're there to protect them,
and they run the reclamation side of the stations. You
know that. Anyway, once things were clear, he helped me,
and we waited."

"And you were rescued, and you're a hero."

"I was rescued. I'm not a hero."

Ezildya shook her head again. "I'm sorry. I'm supposed
to be cheering you up, and I'm really too tired to do a good
job."

Trystin touched her cheek. "Maybe you'd better go
home and get some sleep. I'm glad you came, but I don't
want to be the cause of your—" He forced a laugh. "I guess
I'm not thinking too well, either."

"Good-bye, Trystin. Take care." Ezildya slipped from
the stool and bent forward to kiss his cheek.

"You, too."

He watched as she walked to the door, turned, and gave
him a small wave.

After she left, he released a deep breath. Something was bothering her, but what? He shook his head, then looked toward the table that contained the orders for pilot training. Pilot training—if he still wanted it.

14

 "Examination of the genetic codes of all intelligent beings thus far discovered indicates a genetic predisposition to procreation at a precoded span in each organism's life. Although that procreation range occurs comparatively later in the life span of an organism with greater cognitive capacity, in all organisms studied to date that range coincides with the range of greatest physical health. . . .

"Thus, achieving individual organic physical nondegradation ('physical immortality'), defined as removal of all genetic tendencies for organic self-destruction on the cellular level, will by definition increase the reproductive rate beyond a neutral populace growth rate.

"Over a sufficient period of time, any organism with a positive level of populace growth—no matter how small that growth rate—unless checked by outside forces, will come to require virtually all the resources within its ability to acquire. . . .

"Any habitat can support a small number of virtual immortals or a much larger number of mortals. . . . Technology depends on a certain critical mass, however, often smaller than the number of immortals that can be supported by a given habitat. . . .

"The dilemma faced by any species with the capability to achieve individual physical immortality is whether to reject such physical immortality, to adapt genetic codes to lower populace growth, to develop cultural norms for stable populace growth, or to use technology to accommodate increasing habitat needs. . . .

"The use of technology to increase usable habitat will, in sufficient time, result in conflict with other species, and, in historical practice, the elimination of either the attacking or defending species as a threat to the other. . . .

"Can a species which refuses to adapt, either through genetic, biological, or cultural means, its reproductive expansion to its habitats be termed intelligent? Can mere survival of a species which employs diverse technology be termed a proof of intelligence? If one subculture of a species in conflict with another subculture demonstrates the ability and the will to limit its expansion, should we regard the favorably behaving and the unfavorably behaving subcultures as differing species? How can a species, even ours, ethically justify the use of force against another species on the grounds that the other species will in time use force to eliminate our species? Should we . . .

"These are the questions this colloquy has attempted to bring forth for discussion. . . ."

Findings of the Colloquy
[Translated from the Farhkan]
1227 E.N.P.

15

 As he waited for Ezildya, Trystin stared out through the closed glasstic door at the courtyard below and the small gardens where pebbled paths separated the differing shades of green into quiltlike patterns. A mother and her daughter picked beans from a plot in the far corner and placed them in a large brown sack.

The light of the setting sun turned the courtyard dome into a translucent pink, the last light of Parvati reflecting through the red skies of Mara.

The whispering of slippers on the hard floor alerted Trystin, and he turned. "Even through the dome, it's red."

"Yes. Like blood. That's fitting, these days, I suppose." In loose exercise clothes, Ezildya stood with her hands on the quilted spread that lay folded across the back of the cushioned plastic love seat. "How long have you been out of the med center?"

"A couple of hours."

"You came to see me. That was nice." Ezildya remained behind the chair, her faint golden skin somehow pale, her dark eyes fixed on Trystin.

"You came to see me when I was laid up."

"Yes, I did. What will you do now? Go back to your station? Or are they sending you somewhere else as a reward?"

"I've been offered orders to Chevel Beta. The orders were cut right after this . . . latest mess."

"Did they give you a reason?" Ezildya lifted her hands from the spread.

Trystin looked back at her, seeing both bleakness and relief in her eyes. "Just the standard wording. You know, the phrase that says, for the needs of the Service, and for further training before your next assignment?"

"Your next assignment?"

"Pilot training."

She winced. "You're willing to give up everyone, aren't you?"

"It isn't that way anymore. Translation error is down, generally only a couple of days, sometimes a few hours on the short jumps."

"Tell that to the people on the *Linnaeus*. Twelve years, was it, just between Perdya and Kajarta?"

"That was sabotage of the translation system."

"What about Lieutenant Akihito?"

Trystin flinched. Akihito had been the second test pilot

on the translation systems. He'd turned up all right, after everyone thought he'd died when the system had failed, and he had reappeared healthy and still young and enthusiastic—just seventy years out of time and place.

"It does happen, Trystin. My mother lost a year on a routine maintenance test, and she thought she knew what she was doing." Ezildya's voice was soft. "And the translation errors build so much . . . what will your family think?"

"I don't know. I'm going to Perdya. My father's always been behind me." Trystin laughed. "Even when he was convinced I was wrong."

"What about your mother?"

"She and my father generally agree. She used to be a ship systems engineer. Then she took up music, said it was the closest thing to the music of the spheres. She teaches now."

Ezildya nodded to herself. "Isn't this early for another assignment? You've only been on the perimeter for ten stamos, not even a full year."

"Eleven stamos when I leave. A year to fifteen stamos is the normal rotation. It's just a little early, maybe because schedules don't match. Besides, there's no station to go back to, not yet. Saboli—he was here when I got here—he left in less than a year. He said that was because the translation gates are dangerous in Duodec." Trystin laughed. "I think he was just trying to find a logical reason for an arbitrary decision."

"Where did he go?" Ezildya's tone was bland.

"Helconya orbit station. I told him to say hello to Salya. I guess he got there. I got a message from Salya suggesting that he wasn't her type."

"What does your sister think about your orders?" Ezildya shook her head. "That's stupid of me. She wouldn't know. She couldn't. What do you think she would say?"

Trystin chuckled. "I don't know. But she's the one who always wanted to be in on the Helconya project. She talked about it when she first studied biology." He shrugged. "I'd have to say that she'd say something like do what you really think you should."

"I see. You're all so . . . messianic. Does that come with the rev heritage, too?"

Trystin took a deep breath, feeling as though he'd been gut-punched. Finally, he asked, "What is that supposed to mean?"

"You really don't believe in people, Trystin. You're just like the poor revs you killed, except you're better at it. We've made you better. You're an Eco-Tech with blind faith, supreme confidence, and great hard-wired abilities. Just like the revs, nothing shakes your faith. Not rows of bodies, not almost losing your leg, not the real probability of your own death." She put her lips together tightly and blinked.

Trystin watched, then, as her cheeks dampened, limped forward, his leg stiff. The hint of fleurisle drifted toward him, a scent somehow misplaced in the oil- and plastic-tinged air of the Maran domes.

"No." She put out a hand. "I can't take any more hope. Do you know what it's like to lose someone twice? Of course you don't. You won't ever lose anyone, because you've never let anyone close to your heart."

"That's not fair."

"It's more than fair. You believe in your ideals more than in people. What comfort will your ideals give you when you're finally broken by time and age, or by the revs—not that that will ever happen. You'll break yourself. No one else could."

"Ezildya . . ."

"The grand and great Coalition may need you, and your type, but I don't." Ezildya looked at Trystin.

"What is that supposed to mean?"

"Just go . . . please, Trystin. If you don't know, then all my explaining won't mean a thing. And if you do, then"—she took a deep breath—"I really don't need to explain." She paused. "I'm sorry. I didn't mean to be so emotional. Just go. Go report to your training. Go save the rest of us. You can't save me, or yourself, but go save the Coalition."

Trystin stood there, a coldness seeping through him. He wasn't like the revs, not at all. Couldn't she see?

"Just go. You will anyway. Sooner or later. Just go."

Finally, he turned and walked slowly to the door. Nothing he could say would change her mind. That he knew.

16

The port tube-shuttle whispered to a stop at the EastBreak station. Trystin lifted his kit and shoulder bag and stepped out onto the green and gray tiles of the well-lit underground station. The glow-tubes overhead shed a soft light almost like that of the tunnels in Klyseen, but the air carried the faintest scents of the greenery that lay above and outside the station.

A mother and a small boy walked toward him across the clean and polished tiles of the station floor.

"He's a lieutenant," whispered the dark-haired boy, who dropped his mother's hand to point. "Like Daddy."

Trystin touched the edge of his beret briefly, then smiled at both the boy and his dark-haired mother. He walked quickly along the lighted tunnel to the steps up to the surtrans station, pausing to swipe his card through the reader to pay for the tube-shuttle—the same two creds it had always been.

As he started up the stairs, he tried not to limp. His leg didn't hurt, but it was still stiff, despite all the stretching exercises he'd done in rehab and even on the *Adams* on the way back to Perdya.

At the top, on each side of the wide staircase, framed in blue-stone, were miniature gardens, complete with the bonsai cedars that supposedly dated to the founding of Cambria. Behind them were the carved green marble slabs that bore representations of the evergreens of old Earth—

old Earth before the Great Die-off, before the forests had been turned to instant charcoal.

Trystin looked to the faded blue sky and the clouds scudding eastward to the Palien Sea. He took a deep breath of air filled with the scent of rain, of flowers he could not see.

The electrotrain, sliding silently above buried guides, did not arrive at the surtrans station for nearly fifteen minutes, but Trystin stood silently, drinking in the gardens, the green-winged heliobirds sipping from the tulip-tree blossoms, and the feel of moist air on his face.

He had the automated train to himself until the first stop, when two older schoolgirls got on, both slender and dark-haired. The thinner-faced girl, wearing a silver medallion over a pale blue shirt, looked at Trystin. Her eyes fixed on his uniform; then she looked away. The other girl put her arm around her friend, and both hurried from the train at the next stop. Trystin looked back as both girls dropped onto the bench by the surtrans garden. The girl who had looked away sobbed almost uncontrollably.

Trystin took a deep breath. Had she lost a brother, a boyfriend, someone dear? How many girls like that, or boys, was the war affecting? Except that it wasn't really even a war. The revs sent their military missions, and the system control ships and the planetary perimeter officers did their best to destroy them, no one said very much, not in public anyway.

He hoped it had been the uniform and not his fair skin and sandy hair.

At the next stop, an older woman, white-haired and trim, climbed aboard briskly. "Greetings, Lieutenant. Going to enjoy your leave? I assume it's leave."

"It is, and I hope so. Thank you."

"Don't thank me. Glad you're out there. Someone has to be. Did my turn back in 'thirty. That was when Safrya was really wild. Didn't have to worry that much about the revs then. Don't mind me, young fellow. Takes me back, though. Where have you been stationed, if I could ask?"

"Mara."

"That'll take some time. Then someday, you'll be telling some young officer about when Mara was really wild, and you'll wonder where the time went." She grinned. "As I said, don't mind me."

"You're probably right." Trystin offered her a smile, relieved at the diversion her sprightliness offered.

"Oh, I'm right, and someday you'll be right, too."

They sat in silence until the next stop where, after running his card through the reader, Trystin slipped off the surtrans with a wave to the white-haired woman.

The house was nearly half a kay from the surtrans stop, but Trystin walked up the lane slowly, flexing and stretching his leg when he thought about it, looking at the greenery, even the few native bluestalk trees that had thrived under the integrated ecology. The ornate and heavy wrought-iron gates at the bottom of the garden were open, as always, and he walked up the curving stone path laid by his great-great-grandfather.

He rapped on the front door, but no one answered. That wasn't a surprise, not if his father were working and his mother still at the university. He eased open the door and called, "Hello!"

No answer. So he set the kit and shoulder bag on the polished agate of the hall floor and closed the door behind him. His forehead was damp, and he wiped it on his sleeve, then tucked the beret into his belt. The kitchen was empty, except for the smell of some sort of dish from the ancient convection oven, and he stepped down the hallway to his father's office.

Trystin rapped gently on the side of the open doorway, then waited a moment, watching the screens before his father.

From what he could tell, the screens displayed diagrams or schematics, but diagrams or schematics with which Trystin was unfamiliar, although he gathered a general impression that one screen dealt with waste disposal of some sort. Even before he could really read the data, the screens all blanked into restful views of the eastern coast beyond Cambria.

The older man, the reddish-blond hair shot with silver and cut short, touched the keyboard and removed the headset. "Trystin! I'm glad you could get home." He stood slowly, then deliberatively moved toward his son to give Trystin a firm hug.

Trystin hugged him back.

"More muscle yet, I think." Elsin Desoll released his son. "Are you working out a lot?"

"Some."

"Good thing to keep up. You're still young enough it doesn't matter. Me, I've got to be faithful about it, or I'd turn to flab."

Trystin couldn't imagine his father turning to flab, not with the carefully managed diet, the gardening, and the daily workouts, both physical and martial arts.

"There are times when I think it would be easier to work with implants, rather than the headset, and see the screens in my mind, but that technology's for the Service, and this array is as far as I can strain my tired old brain."

"Your tired old brain? Is this the same tired old brain that designs obscure system keys for fun? Or theoretical encryption systems?"

"Those are just puzzles. The older I get . . . the more I cherish the obscure." Elsin's brow crinkled for a moment. "Have a seat. I whipped up a casserole, but it's still simmering, and Nynca won't be home for a bit."

"Is she still teaching at the university?"

"Still? Your mother will never give it up, and she's even managed to persuade the provost that since music enhances mathematical conceptualization, basic musical theory should be one of the required perspectives."

"She was working on that years ago." Trystin took one of the wooden captain's chairs by the chess table, leaving the one with the frayed purple cushion for his father.

"You'll recall that your mother isn't exactly one to quit on something she believes in. Of course, both of our offspring are so pliable and amenable to whatever their parents have suggested."

Trystin opened his mouth and then shut it. His father

still could prod him into reacting without thinking.

"Better." Elsin nodded. "Snap-juice or tea?" He paused. "Something wrong with the leg?"

"It's stiff. It got torn up in an assault, and they had to rebuild it. I don't have the flexibility back, but the doctors say it's fine, just a matter of time. I keep exercising, and it's getting better every day."

"You can tell us about it at dinner. No need to bother now. Your mother will ask for all the details. Tea or snap-juice? You didn't say."

"Tea, with lime, if you have it."

"Limes I have. More like liters of limes, now that I've got the balance in the upper garden right." The older man headed through the doorway and back toward the kitchen and wide eating area that overlooked the side garden, and the eastern side of Cambria.

Trystin turned in the chair to look at the garden, pleased to see sky without looking through a portal or a screen, or filtered through sensors and scanners. His eyes dropped back to the inlaid chess table beside him and the stone figures on it. The tabletop dated back eight centuries, and had supposedly been crafted by an ancestor on old Earth. Trystin smiled. It was old, but that old? The transit costs would have been prohibitive. If it were that old, it would be literally priceless, but only an immortal or DNA dating could verify the date, and neither of those was really feasible. The stone chess figures had been the contribution of his grandfather in his last years.

"Here." Elsin extended the heavy mug to his son, then sat and set his own mug on his knee.

"Thank you." Trystin let the steam waft around his face for a moment, savoring the scent and warmth of the tea and the fresh lime—far better than the translation-faded tea that had been so exorbitant on Mara.

Elsin sank onto the cushion with a sigh. "Let's see. How much translation distortion this time?"

"It wasn't bad. A little over one week. Transports have more distortion, they say." Trystin took a sip of tea, which tasted as good as it had smelled. "I miss things like this."

"I did. I'm not surprised that you do, too. No matter what people say, we do have an affinity for the land and its products."

Trystin nodded, thinking about the limes, the tea, and the garden—and the more than five generations the house and gardens had passed through, if greatly changed by each.

"You look a little thoughtful . . . even disturbed."

"Well . . . a woman I know said I was an idealist who didn't care much for people. She said I was just like the revs. She was really upset, too."

"It bothered you."

"I guess so." Trystin shrugged. "In some ways . . . well . . . you just wonder."

"Do you know why she upset you?"

"The people bit: I mean, I rode the surtrans from the tube station, and two girls rode one station with me, and one of them looked at my uniform, and she got off the train and broke down. I wondered who she'd lost. That was what I was thinking. And I think about Quentar. He was concerned when I had to make a run to his station because mine had been totaled. At the same time, he was talking about how he wished he could kill more revs, as if they weren't people. He's dead now. Instead of him killing them, they killed him. I don't know. I've always assumed that the revs were people, but that they weren't in a way. Quentar was honest about it. To him they weren't. I was. But I had to interrogate some revs, and most acted like machines, but one didn't. He said something like, while he believed, nothing I could say would shake him, as if faith were a choice." Trystin shrugged.

"You think that faith is something blindly imposed on people?" asked Elsin.

"I just hadn't thought about it. And I guess I was reminded of it because Ezildya accused me of blind faith, in a way. She said that if I put any sort of duty above human feelings I wasn't any better than the revs. In fact, she blamed my nonexistent rev heritage. If I look like one, I must be one. Does it mean I'm not human if I don't wear my heart on my tunic? Does it mean I'm a machine because ideals are important?"

Elsin laughed. "No. It means you're young and human. The young are cruel, and allowing others to see what you feel makes you vulnerable, and the young hate to be vulnerable. That's a luxury of age."

"Thanks . . . I think."

"I won't dwell on it. First, if I did, you wouldn't believe me, yet. And second, you'll see. Beware of women who want you to parade your emotions, and be equally careful with those who shy away from your feelings."

"That sounds like I should avoid them all." Trystin took another sip of tea. "I'll try to remember your sage advice."

"You won't. I didn't listen to my parents until I was older. No . . . that's not quite right. I listened to their words, and I could recognize their wisdom, but that wisdom didn't seem really applicable to me. I suspect that's true with every generation, but none of us live long enough to confirm that—not beyond our children's children, anyway."

Trystin nodded. There didn't seem to be much to add to his father's words, even as they seemed to slip away, for all their trite truth.

"Your message said that you'd been offered orders and training as a pilot officer, and that you'd decided to take it." Elsin took a sip from his own mug. "If you do much deep spacing, maybe you will live long enough to see the patterns in life."

"The translation effect is getting less." Trystin pursed his lips and shifted his weight in the chair, for some reason thinking about Ezildya's mother's work with the Farhkans. "I got the impression that the Farhkans were giving some help to our translation engineers."

"Occasionally, that has happened. You might ask your mother. I don't know much about it."

"What do you know about the Farhkans?"

"They're dangerous."

"Why?"

"Trystin, you're in the Service. So was I. You know everything I did, plus a lot more. Why don't you tell me? Besides, why do you want to know? Do you think I know something you don't?"

"You usually do," pointed out Trystin.

"All right." Elsin sighed. "They manage translation with virtually no time lag. Second, no one or thing invades their systems. We don't say anything, and the revs don't say anything, and the Farhkans don't say anything, but while the official line is that we lost one ship, we lost more than that. The difference is that we stopped trying. The revs didn't, not for a long, long time, and I'm not convinced that they ever have."

"What else?"

"The Farhkans are probably a lot better at integrating biotech and hardtech than we are." Elsin grinned and looked at his son. "You have that look on your face that says you know something, but I won't ask."

"Thank you." Trystin tried not to squirm in his seat. How had his father caught his thoughts about the Farhkans' ability to tap into his military implant? Had the Farhkan mental images been technology or an unknown physical ability?

"They have an agenda, and I'm not convinced that any alien agenda is necessarily for our benefit." Elsin rose.

"Who could say? It probably isn't."

"Since they're alien, I'd have to agree." Elsin cleared his throat. "This pilot business brings up something else."

"I know . . . the separation . . ."

"There's that. I know you must have thought about it, and I'm not one to try and bring up anything to make you feel guilty. That's not what I meant. I am an integrator, and I want you to consider how to protect yourself from the downsides. I mean in cold, hard financial terms."

"What?" Trystin shook his head.

"You're young, and you're healthy, but what happens if your translation engine cooks its mainboard, and throws you forty years into the future? The Service will, of course, pension you off with the standard retirement, or let you stay on for another few objective years and do the same thing. You need to be prepared for that."

"Oh . . ."

"It may not happen, but the chances are about one in ten that you'll have at least one translation error of more than two standard years if you stay for a career. If it doesn't . . . good. But . . . if it does . . ."

"I hadn't thought about that."

"The Service will gladly hold your back pay, and provide it in a lump sum, which, after taxes and inflation, will make it worth little enough."

Trystin spread his hands. "What do I do?"

"We set up a 'translation trust,' except we make it more general than that. Your pay goes directly into an institution where the funds are split into several accounts—an immediate credit account against which you can draw just like your regular credit account—but you specify a cap on it. Any funds received in excess of that level go into a diversified program. That way, if you're on extended duty, or not around, you can set up the program to pay any obligations and have the principal grow. It's more complicated than that, but fairly simple."

"How did you know this?"

"I didn't." Elsin shrugged. "When I got your message and thought about it, I started doing research."

Trystin took another sip of tea. He hadn't even considered what his father had seen nearly instantly.

"Hold on a minute. I need to check that casserole." Elsin slipped from the room.

Trystin looked back out the half-open window, letting the spring breeze flutter through his regulation-short hair. A few clouds were piled up to the east, above the Palien Sea, but not enough for a storm, not anytime soon.

A moment later, his father returned. "Things should be ready about the time Nynca gets here."

"She is regular," laughed Trystin.

"Someone around here has to be."

"You know, Dad. I've had some time to think. I still don't know what you do. You're a free-lance systems integrator. I understand every one of the words, and then I come home, and you pull something else up, like this translation trust, or I look at those screens, and they still look like Greek, or revvie gibberish."

"Sometimes they do to me, too." Elsin nodded. "I was working on waste-nutrient integration—"

"For Safrya?" Trystin's eyes strayed to the window, caught by the green flash of a passing heliobird.

"Slowships, no! It's a system for a place called Verintka, out your way, on Mara."

"That's on the south continent—but it will be another century before the atmosphere's really breathable."

Elsin grinned. "Maybe not. We're trying to do some tinkering. Newsin has a new bug that they think can use hydrocarbons and CO_2 and fix oxygen in the process."

Trystin nodded.

"It creates a gummy awful green sludge, plus a lot of water and oxygen. I'm trying to find a way to use the green sludge. I just might have it—but that's going to take more work."

Trystin heard a faint footstep and stood. "I think Mother's home. Someone just came in."

"Even without all that biohardware, you still had ears like a hawk. Now nothing can move without your hearing it."

"A hawk?"

"Predator of ancient earth. Supposedly could hear small rodents from kays away."

The woman who slipped into the office was stocky, but not heavy, with short hair half blond, half silver. Her green eyes smiled as she took in Trystin. "You look good."

Trystin stood quickly, stepping toward her, but his leg dragged ever so slightly. "It's good to be home," he admitted, hugging her tightly.

After a time, she stepped back. "Careful. I'm a fragile woman."

"Ha!" snorted Elsin. "Not very."

"Compared to your son, I am."

"My son? He's yours too, last time I heard."

"Poor man, he's starving. Can't you see that?" Nynca winked at her son. Then her expression turned serious. "What's wrong with your leg?"

"Projectile injury. The doctors say it's fine, just stiff. I need to keep exercising it."

"You didn't mention that in the message."

"I didn't want to worry you."

"So I have to worry now?" Nynca shook her head. "You and your father." She turned to Elsin. "He still needs to be fed. He's too thin."

"Dinner has been waiting for you, honored professor."

"Were you still working on that sewage project?" asked Nynca, stepping over to her husband and kissing him on the cheek.

"Of course."

She shook her head. "Can you afford to?"

"Not for money, but for Trystin and Salya."

"Always the idealist."

"How about dinner?" asked Trystin.

"I'll get dinner. You wash up," suggested his father.

By the time Trystin, still carrying his cup, entered the dining area that overlooked the middle garden, Elsin was setting the casserole on the ceramic and wood holder in the middle of the circular table. Greens and sliced fruits, topped with seasoned and crushed groundnuts, filled the big wooden bowl before Trystin's plate. Across the table, by the empty fourth place, was a basket filled with steaming dark bread.

Nynca opened the wood-framed sliding glass door, lifting the door frame slightly to ease it over a rough spot. "I can see I need to do some repair work here."

"Always the engineer." Elsin seated himself and turned to Trystin. "Help yourself. It's simple. Bread, salad, and casserole."

"It smells wonderful." Trystin waited for his mother to seat herself before settling into his chair.

"Isn't it always?" she asked. "I've gotten spoiled over the years."

Trystin waited until she had served herself, then heaped several serving spoons full of the churkey and rice casserole on the wide brown stoneware plate, followed by an equally generous helping of the greenery.

Elsin poured Nynca's tea and then helped himself to the food.

"Now . . . first things first. So I can get my worrying done. How did you get hurt?" asked Nynca. "Start from the beginning."

"That's what she always says." Elsin laughed.

Trystin finished the last of the tea in his cup. "The revs have been stockpiling equipment in the Maran badlands for almost three years, covering the stockpiles with continual off-and-on attacks on perimeter stations. . . ."

As Trystin outlined the background and the attack, Elsin refilled Trystin's cup.

". . . in the end, I really didn't have much choice besides staying in the armor. Then, while I was in the med center, I was offered the orders for pilot training and decided to take them. Part of it was the business about extending everyone."

"But not all of it. I'm not surprised." Nynca nodded. "Much as you love the house, it wouldn't be enough for you. Not now."

Elsin cleared his throat.

"Besides . . . we've talked about this. . . ." Nynca looked at Elsin.

"Talked about what?" Then Trystin nodded. "You mean that Salya will come back someday, and she really does love it enough to be happy here?"

His father nodded. "You, for years anyway, will be out there pushing the limits. You didn't want to hide away even when you were wounded, did you?"

"No," Trystin admitted with a short laugh. "I guess not."

"You've always liked being in control."

"And you haven't?" asked Nynca, looking at her husband. "Trystin will want to settle down sometime. You did."

"He might be ready in another half century." Elsin grinned. "It's a good thing we've got young people like you." He took a mouthful of the churkey and chewed. "Turned out good this time."

"It always does," Nynca said with a smile.

Trystin frowned. "What did you mean about having people like me? So that not everyone stays home and . . ." Since he couldn't figure out how to finish the sentence, he didn't.

"The situation with the Revenants." His father took another mouthful of casserole.

"What does that have to do with me? Or the house? Or Salya?"

"Haven't you figured it out yet, Trystin? We're losing."

"How do you figure that?"

"Because I'm an integrator, and I don't say much because there's no point in it. Everyone's doing everything they can. You don't help matters by screaming in a smoldering building. You just try to find more water." He shook his head. "I know. It's a bad analogy.

"On the surface, we've reached a stalemate. Our borders with the revs are stable, and we don't attack their fully habitable planets, and they don't attack ours—although we both could. Their population is growing—"

"Fast enough for them to re-create the Die-off within a few centuries on Orum."

"Try a millennium," suggested Elsin. "I've run the numbers. Planets are big. But your basic point is valid. We've opted to populate based on an integrated, sustained, ecologically and technologically sound basis—and a lot smaller population." He paused and looked at Trystin. "When will Mara be ready for initial air-breathing colonization?"

"Somewhere in sixty to eighty years, or, if the Newsin bugs or your treatments work," grinned Trystin, "a whole lot sooner."

"When will we really need it?"

Trystin shrugged.

"How about never?" injected Nynca with a laugh. "I've heard the sermon."

"When could the revs use it?" Elsin pursued.

"Probably now. That has to be why they're stepping up their attacks."

"Exactly. We're using everything we have." Elsin held up his hand and took a swallow of tea. "At some point, Trystin, advanced technology becomes meaningless. Does it really matter for most people in system-to-system transit if we've reduced translation lag from eight weeks to four days? In military terms, yes, we need that edge. But do the revs? What impact does that have on a troid ship loaded with enthusiastic young missionaries armed to fight for the Prophet? They don't have anyone to go back to, and if they survive, they'll become patriarchs and want for nothing."

"But . . . ?" Trystin tried to get a word in.

"You're designed as the ultimate military and killing machine possible. I don't even want to know how many revs you've destroyed. Has it stopped them? We have perhaps ten thousand young people like you, and maybe a quarter of those have the physiological strength to take full modifications. With our population, and the resources sunk in you, unless each of you kills thousands of revs, we lose every time a single Service member dies." Elsin broke off a chunk of warm bread, as though he wanted to tear someone's arm off.

"You think we should black-glass Orum and every other rev planet?"

"No. That's the problem. What kind of people do we become if we do that? We become our enemies. That's something that goes through the entire *Eco-Tech Dialogues,* and yet each generation wants to forget it."

"I don't see that." Trystin bristled inside at the gentle rebuke. He'd read every page of the *Dialogues.* "They haven't nuked us, and we're not considering that kind of barbarism."

"They won't. They need the real estate. But what about a nice four cubic kays of rock spiraling through Perdya's atmosphere? Then how civilized will we be?"

"Eventually, if I accept your argument, that would make sense."

Elsin laughed. "You shouldn't accept my argument. Find a better one. Or a way to refute it. Except that's why more time in the Service will be good for you."

"Can we talk about a few things besides the end of civilization?" asked Nynca. "We did see Salya last month, when she came in from Helconya."

"That's worse than old Venus, but they say it can be as green as Earth once was." Elsin sipped from the goblet. "Of course, it'll take a good millennium and the output of half a system. Intellectual lemmings, that's us."

"How is she?" asked Trystin.

"She's found someone—he's a major, I think, or a commander."

"He found her," suggested Nynca. "She wasn't looking."

"That's always the way it is. I found you, dear. You weren't looking, either." Elsin beamed.

"I'm still not, even when you bury yourself in the garden. You do have your undeniable charms, more so than ever."

"He seems to have mellowed," conceded Trystin.

"Mellowed? He's positively melted." Nynca laughed. "Do you remember the time that you and Salya undermined the little rock bridge and he went right down into the carp pond?"

"I didn't know he knew so many obscenities." Trystin grinned at his father. "What about the time that Salya put the fluorescent carp in the lower pond and told him that it had a carp-specific ichthyologic virus that had contaminated the old carp from Grandfather? Or the time that . . . ."

17

⯐ Trystin took a last sip of the green tea from the heavy earthenware cup, the solid green one his grandfather had made and given him on his tenth birthday. "Ahhhh . . . you miss these things. . . ."

"I think you've said that before." Elsin set his own smaller and more delicate cup beside the plate that had been filled with fruit slices.

"I probably have. I may have even said it more than once."

Elsin chuckled. "Do you want any more? You certainly huffed and puffed through that workout—"

"No. Not until later. You're working on the sewage thing this morning?"

"I could put it off. You mentioned that you wanted to go out to the Cliffs. We could do that."

"They're better in the afternoon. I just might take a walk this morning. I still want to stretch out the leg some more."

His father nodded. "If that's what you want. I'll finish this up then, and we can take the scooter out after lunch."

"That sounds good." Trystin stood and walked over to the sink, where he rinsed the cup. "When will Mother be finished? I think she was gone before I even woke up."

"She mentioned some sort of auditions. She won't be terribly late, but she didn't think she'd get away early, either. She's not the biggest fan of the Cliffs. So I think today would be a good day for that."

Trystin grinned. His father's observation about his mother's reaction to the Cliffs was an understatement, although how a former ships' systems engineer had such an aversion to heights was another question. Then, again, there were more than a few contradictions in his mother. "I won't be too long, but I did want to wander around some while it's nice out."

"Whatever suits you. We can leave whenever you get back." Elsin pushed back the heavy wooden chair, stood, and carried his cup and plate to the old-fashioned sink. After rinsing his own dishes, he reached for Trystin's plate.

"You don't have to do mine."

"It's no problem," Elsin said. "Go take your walk, or whatever, and I'll play with sewage, and then we'll go visit the Cliffs. We could stop at Hyrin's for lunch."

"That would be good. Do they still have that sautéed mushroom platter?"

"Last time I was there they did." Elsin racked the dishes, carefully moving the green cup to where it would not bang into anything.

"It's good. You can't get food like that on Mara." Trystin stood and looked toward the window and the clear greenish skies. "It's nice out . . . I won't be long."

"Just come and get me when you get back." Elsin gave his son a smile, but did not head for his office.

Trystin walked over and gave his father a quick hug. "I won't be long, but I really want to stretch my legs before we take a ride anywhere."

Elsin nodded and watched as Trystin headed for the front door.

Trystin closed the front door behind him, and paused there on the small porch, looking beyond the steps and down the winding walk, surveying the gardens, pausing to study the bonsai cedar in the circular planter where the stone walk split around it. The cedar didn't look measurably different from the way it had when he had left for duty on Mara—or from the first time he had noticed it as a child. It couldn't be quite the same, because bonsai required careful pruning and much more, but the differences were more subtle.

A light breeze brushed across his face, bringing the combined scent of the low pines from the sides of the garden and the mixed fragrances of the early season flowers. Seasons—he had missed the changes in the temperature, in the foliage. While the botanical dome in Klyseen had helped, dome gardens weren't the same.

Sometimes he wondered. When he enjoyed plants and trees so much, why was he accepting pilot training? What did he really want from the Service? Or was he there because it was expected and because he hadn't found what he wanted in life?

He walked down the steps and stopped in front of the small cedar, letting his eyes run along the lines of the shaped limbs. His fingers touched the moss around the base of the tree—a shade dry. The clear skies promised little rain, but that could change within hours.

The mid-morning sun warm on his face, Trystin walked down the walk from the house and then, his steps slow, down the lane to Sundance Boulevard, where he turned onto the narrower stone-paved walk that bordered Horodyski Lane as it curved back around the hill. Helio-birds flitted from the regularly spaced branches of the ancient Norfolk pines anchored in the middle stretches of the hill and that blocked his view of the hillside house. Below the trees, ten meters of turf stretched between the trees and the stone flower beds that separated the sidewalk from the grass.

A young heliobird, identifiable as juvenile by the pale green feathers, perched on a branch tip. It hopped and fluttered awkwardly to clear its wing of the heavy spider-ant web stretched between the branches of a Norfolk pine. After a moment and another flurry, the juvenile freed its wing and streaked uphill and out of sight among the trees.

Trystin smiled and resumed walking.

The trifels overflowed the stone-walled flower bed beside the walk, their long green tendrils dropping almost to the grass as the tiny purple flowers offered their honey-lavender perfume to the morning. A small electroscooter hummed down the lane carrying a dark-haired couple. The man offered a nod to Trystin; the woman stared.

Trystin wanted to stare back, but only nodded. Was it his imagination or were the stares more frequent?

He followed Horodyski Lane almost a half kay before he reached the vehicle gate and the edge of the Academy grounds. Outside the two stone pillars that framed the driveway up to the school, Trystin looked at the carved sign that proclaimed Cambrian Academy.

"Knowledge . . . faith . . . power . . . and understanding." He read the words on the four-pointed star logo under the name, recalling the words of the years-ago required readings from the original *Eco-Tech Dialogues,* not the more popular abridged versions.

"Without power, knowledge is useless. Without knowledge, faith is tyranny. Without understanding, humanity is blind, and without all four, it is doomed."

Of course, he reflected, no one had wanted to use such a negative statement publicly. So the Academy had come up with the four words and the four-pointed star—knowledge, faith, power, and understanding.

The polished blond wood of the sign looked the same as when Trystin had left the Academy almost a decade earlier, and probably no different from when his father had graduated. His mother had gone to the Science Academy.

The low, square-trimmed hedges served as a barrier, channeling visitors toward the drive or the stone archway that covered the main pedestrian entrance.

Trystin walked along the lane toward the main entrance, the spot where the surtrans still stopped, although, unlike many students, he had lived close enough to walk to school, even on the rainiest of days.

The main gate was open, but Trystin did not go in. He sat on a stone bench under the pagoda-type roof where so many students had clustered to avoid the rain while they had waited for the surtrans.

The athletic fields to the right of the classroom buildings were empty, and the whole complex seemed silent. Only a faint humming from open classroom windows gave any indication that the Academy was in session.

As he watched, a student in the green blazer of a top former walked briskly from the physical science building toward the older brown-bricked main building. Then the

student entered the building, and the illusion of stillness returned.

Trystin stood and began to walk back toward the house, passing the sign and the four-pointed star again. Understanding—that was the hardest for him, and for most people, he thought. He looked uphill and continued walking, hoping that he saw no other electroscooters.

18

 Carrying his kit and shoulder bag, Trystin stepped through the Perdya orbit station's lock doors and onto the quarterdeck of the *Roosveldt* and into the faint smell of ozone and heated plastic. "Lieutenant Desoll, reporting for transport. Permission to come aboard?"

"Granted, ser," said the rating with the stunner in her watch belt. "Your orders?"

Trystin handed across his orders and the Service ID card and placed his hand on the scanner.

The green light flashed.

"You'll be sharing stateroom four with Lieutenant Yuraki." The rating nodded and handed back the orders and the card. "He's the supply officer. Two and four are on the left as you head aft. One is the captain's. Five is the officers' mess. We'll be separating in less than an hour."

"Thank you." Trystin eased down the narrow corridor, sensing the humming of the ship's net through his implant. He turned sideways as he passed an officer with a major's triple bars holoed on the breast of her shipsuit. Above the bars and the name "Laurentian," she wore the antique wings.

"Sorry, ser," he said.

"No problem, Lieutenant. You're our passenger, the one who's going to see if he can be a pilot?"

"Yes, ser."

Major Laurentian nodded. "This is a short hop—a non-duster. After you get settled, come on forward. You can watch and see if you know what you're getting into."

"Thank you."

"You can thank me later." She was gone, heading forward.

Though bigger than most translation ships, the *Roosveldt* was still a small ship, tiny compared to the revvie troid ships, but then most translation ships were, given the limitations that Trystin didn't fully understand, but suspected he would come to learn. The entire corridor extended no more than thirty meters, the last twenty comprising the section aft of the entry lock and minuscule quarterdeck.

Why it was called a quarterdeck, Trystin didn't know, except that the name dated into antiquity. Stateroom four was just forward of the open third-aft safety hatch. Out of courtesy, he tapped on the stateroom door, but there was no response. He tapped again, waited, and then slid the thin sheet-plastic door open. Because of weight considerations, and practicality, the *Roosveldt*—and every other noncombatant translation ship—was constructed in airtight sections, but without significant airtight barriers within the subsections. So internal walls and doors were thin.

Trystin stepped into the stateroom and stopped. The tiny workspace built against the airtight third-aft bulkhead was an array of data file cases stuffed with two-centimeter data disks surrounding a compact console. At the console sat a bulky man with light brown hair and a creamy brown skin. Trystin could almost feel the hardwired signals running from the console, but he always had been more sensitive to the nets than most—and that sensitivity had been one of the reasons why the Maran storm feedback had been harder on him than on most. He carried his bags inside and set them down on the plastic-textured deck, sliding the door shut behind him.

After several moments, the officer on the console finished tapping the keys and stood. He wore the single gold bar of a junior lieutenant, but the fine lines running from the corners of his eyes indicated he was considerably older than Trystin. "Sorry. You must be Lieutenant Desoll."

"Trystin."

"I'm Elgin Yuraki—the one who's in charge of stowing, balancing, and retrieving cargo, not to mention food supplies, air regeneration, and all the other nonpropulsion and navigational details of the mighty *Roosveldt*. Welcome to our humble craft, cramped as it may be."

"Thank you. I didn't mean—"

"That's all right. We should apologize to you. We're carrying two very senior commanders. They got the two good transport cabins, ecobalance and protocol forbid that they should share with anyone."

"I'm sorry. It sounds like you've got a full load. How many on board?" Trystin asked.

"Not really that many. The crew's just six. The captain and Lieutenant Hithers, me, and three techs. But we've also got you and the commanders, and five more techs in transit. We're configured more for cargo than passengers. A barge like the *Udahl* could handle thirty supercargo easily, sixty in a pinch." Yuraki paused and gestured toward the console. "Sorry . . . but . . ."

"You must have a lot to do right now. Just tell me where to put things, and I'll get out of your way." Trystin offered a smile.

"The lower lockers are empty, and the bottom bunk's yours."

"Fine. Can I sit in the mess to get out of your way?"

"That's where I'd be if I didn't have all this . . ." Yuraki grimaced. "But you should have it to yourself."

Trystin slipped his two bags into the lower locker, where they barely fit. By the time he had straightened, Yuraki was back at the console.

The mess was just abaft the aft-third bulkhead on the right—and empty. Six light gray plastic chairs clustered around a long narrow table, and three more were stacked in the corner. The combined odors of strong tea and the false citrus of Sustain permeated the room. After looking around, Trystin found a spare cup and thumbed the spigot on the samovar.

The steam carried the smell of relatively fresh hot tea, and Trystin burned his mouth with an incautiously quick first sip. He slumped into a corner chair. While connected to the orbit station—and the station's power supplies—the *Roosveldt* remained at full Perdyan gravity.

A face peered into the mess. "Lieutenant?"

Trystin turned around and then stood as he recognized not only the commander's uniform but the green shoulder braid that signified something on the Service Command Staff. "Yes, ser."

"Could you rustle up a cup of tea for me? I'd appreciate it." The woman in the uniform had traces of actual gray in her short-cropped black hair. "I'm in number six."

"I'll see what I can do, ser." Before Trystin had finished responding, the commander had vanished.

With a slow, deep breath, he went to the wall cupboard and took another plastic cup from the rack inside, then filled it. He turned right outside the mess and walked to number six, where he rapped on the door. "Your tea, Commander."

"Come on in."

Trystin opened the door and stepped into the stateroom, no bigger than the one he would share with Yuraki. The commander's eyes were faintly glazed as she concentrated on the largest portable console Trystin had ever seen. The display seemed to contain a three-dimensional star map, and he couldn't resist mentally trying to adjust his implant to pick up the signals.

"I wouldn't. The standard implant isn't equipped for that kind of data flow." She took the tea. "Thank you." Her eyes glazed over as she turned in the chair back to the console that sat on the built-in desk shelf.

Trystin stood there for a moment, then realized he had been dismissed. He closed the door and returned to the mess, where he sat and took a deep swallow from his own cup.

He really hadn't even been there for the commander, except as a piece of equipment. He got up and poured another cup of tea from the samovar.

As slowly as he sipped and waited, no one else entered the mess. No one even passed the open door.

"Stand by for seal-off." Major Laurentian's voice echoed from the speakers. "Stand by for seal-off."

With the announcement, Trystin rinsed off the empty cup, reracked it, and slowly walked forward past the now-empty quarterdeck and the sealed hatch through which he had entered the *Roosveldt*.

As he neared the open hatch to the cockpit, the major's voice again echoed from the speakers. "Stand by for power changeover."

Trystin reached out and braced himself between the narrow bulkheads.

The noncom at the screens in the alcove to his left grinned.

Then the lights flickered; for a moment the hum of the ventilators stopped; and the gravity dropped to point five, ship standard.

As always, Trystin's guts twisted slightly at the transition. He licked his lips, leaned forward and peered into the cockpit. The consoles in front of the captain and the first officer blazed with lights.

Trystin eased up the receptivity of his implant—and staggered slightly as even a fraction of the complete data load seemed to drown him before his cutoffs blocked the flow. His eyes watered, and his head throbbed. After a moment, he licked his lips again. Did all pilots have to carry and monitor that much data—or was he accessing the wrong channels?

He shrugged. It could be either, and he wasn't about to ask.

". . . Pelican two . . . cleared for low-thrust separation . . ."

". . . Pelican two separating this time . . ."

The representational screen, easiest for Trystin to recognize, showed the separation of the *Roosveldt* from the orbit station.

Trystin watched as the signals apparently cascaded across the boards, and as the screens flashed the latest data. Neither the major nor the pilot officer in the second seat used their hands, but those hands rested lightly on the manual controls, and Trystin could see that both officers clearly cross-checked the purely visual screens, almost as if they did not fully trust their implants and the direct links to the *Roosveldt*.

"Lieutenant?" The first officer looked at Trystin.

"Yes, ser." Although Hithers couldn't have outranked Trystin much, Hithers was the first officer in the line of command, and Trystin responded.

"We won't be translating for almost three hours relative, and it's likely to be rather boring. Go get some tea or something."

"Could I get you anything?"

"No, thank you. It might be boring for you, but we'll be occupied."

Trystin took the hint and headed back to the mess, where Elgin Yuraki was pouring himself a cup of tea.

"You all right?" Trystin asked.

"Fine. Last-minute stuff." Yuraki glanced toward the door and lowered his voice. "Commander Milsini—she's the one in six—she dumped something like five tonnes of shielded equipment on us. That's a bitch to handle at the last minute—shielding, weight and balance, and recomputing all the mass for translation." The supply officer cleared his throat. "I was afraid we'd be over the translation limit, but we've got a good two tonnes to spare."

Trystin nodded politely. Two tonnes on a large ship didn't sound like that much of a safety margin.

"See . . . the total mass isn't as much of a problem as the accuracy of the mass calculation. The closer the calculated mass is to the translation power approximation, the less the translation error—all other things being equal, which they're not. Anyway, you'll learn all that better than I know it. All I know is that the captain gives me hell if the mass calculation isn't as good as I can make it." Yuraki took a deep swallow of the boiling tea without even wincing. "And when some commander dumps stuff whose mass is mostly unknown on me . . . how do you tell a commander it's a problem? All they say is that I should solve it."

"That's right."

Both junior officers glanced up.

The second commander—a stocky dark man with the holoed wings over the name "Chiang"—stood by the samovar. "When you're a junior officer, you have to solve problems. When you get to be a commander, you get to create them. When you get to the senior staff level, you have to tell the commanders which problems to create." He snorted. "Enjoy problem-solving while you can. It's easier." With that, Commander Chiang carried his cup from the mess.

"Who are they?" Trystin asked. "Do you know?"

"Commander Milsini works for the planning branch of the general staff. Commander Chiang—I don't know. Except all the pilots sort of whispered when they heard he was coming. He only brought three cases of stuff, and the mass computations were taped to each case."

"Thoughtful of him," observed Trystin.

"He was, or is, a pilot. If all pilots are like the captain, they never forget the importance of mass computations." Yuraki stood and poured another cup of tea, then added a heap of Sustain powder to the steaming liquid.

Trystin winced. "How can you drink that?"

"You get used to it." Yuraki took a deep breath. "Besides, I've got more to do. See you later." He carried the cup out of the mess.

Trystin helped himself to a half cup of tea, without Sustain, and slowly sipped it. He must have dozed, because he sat up with a start, checking his implant for the time— over two hours since he had left the cockpit. He must have been more tired than he thought.

Another cup of tea, with some Sustain, helped wake him, and he finally walked forward to the cockpit, past the tech in his shipsuit, still monitoring the ship's maintenance systems through the six-screen panel.

"Not bad timing," said Hithers from the right-hand seat. "Be another fifteen or so." His eyes glazed over.

Major Laurentian never glanced toward Trystin.

The cascade of lights across the board seemed to slow, more and more lights winking out with each passing minute. Were systems being powered down prior to translation? Trystin didn't know. This was the first time he'd watched a translation from the cockpit, and the time slipped past.

"Prepare for translation. Prepare for translation." Hithers's words spilled from the ship's speakers. "Thirty seconds to translation."

The whole ship went totally silent. The ventilators stopped. The screens blanked. The gravity went, and Trystin thrust out his legs and awkwardly braced himself, inwardly damning himself for his forgetfulness.

At the moment of translation, the entire ship seemed to turn inside out, and black turned to white, and dark to light, for an instant that seemed momentarily endless—yet was totally subjective. No clock ever designed had been able to measure any duration for a translation.

Then, with a stomach-wrenching twist, the ship was back in norm-space. The screens in front of the pilots began to flash, slowly, and then more quickly, as the tell-tales reported system information.

The hissing of the ventilators resumed, and ship's gravity dragged Trystin perhaps ten centimeters to the hard deck.

But neither pilot moved, although Trystin could almost sense the stepped-up flow of information through the cockpit.

The representational screen twisted, and reformed, showing the *Roosveldt* heading in-system, toward Chevel Beta, and the first officer reached out and tapped a stud beside the console.

"Translation complete. We are heading in-system. We are heading in-system."

Somewhere on the inbound leg to Chevel Beta, the *Roosveldt* would use its receivers to pick up the simultaneous dual and continuous signals beamed from asteroids on opposite sides of the system in synchronous orbits. The signals contained coded algorithms that, when deciphered and with the computed parallax, allowed incoming Coalition ships to determine real time and thus their translation error.

"That's it, Lieutenant. We'll see you later." Hithers offered a brief smile to Trystin.

Trystin understood the dismissal. "Thank you, ser." He slipped back into the narrow corridor behind the crowded cockpit.

From the tech alcove beside the hatch, the noncom in the shipsuit glanced up. "Good luck, Lieutenant."

From what he'd seen, Trystin wondered if he'd need a lot more than luck, a lot more.

19

 The only instructions Trystin had received when he had checked in at the Chevel Beta training command and received his room assignment were to report to room B7 at 0900 a week later with everything on his checklist taken care of. Room B7 meant second level, relatively high for an asteroid station. Report to B7 and wait, not that he'd been doing much besides waiting. Taking another physical, updating his personnel files, being issued shipsuits and fitted for deep-space pressure armor hadn't taken all that long. The most complicated thing had been arranging all the paperwork for his translation trust. Neither payroll nor the admin section had been terribly pleased, but his father had provided a step-by-step procedure and all the Service and legal cites. That hadn't exactly pleased Major Turakini, and her reaction had given Trystin the distinct impression that should anything happen to one Trystin Desoll, the Service really wanted to hang on to his pay and everything else for as long as possible.

The other time-consuming, necessary, and boring item had been a screen-based intro class to the basics of spatial coordinate systems. He'd spent a lot of time in the station library, using his implant to àccess all the general information on piloting, and on translation engines, and more than a few hours in the high-gee exercise room. With the station gravity kept at point five, probably because the energy consumption to maintain standard gee would have taken a pair of large fusactors alone, high gee was classified at one point one, or a trace over Maran norm.

Trystin tried not to bound or bounce as he walked toward the up-level ramps. His quarters—a cube four meters on a side carved out of solid rock and sealed with plastic—were on J level.

The ramp corridors, zigzagging back and forth toward the surface of Chevel Beta, were plastic-coated rock, bare except for the air-collection vents set midway between each level.

Between E and D level, a noncom brushed by Trystin, her eyes flickering to his name patch as she muttered a low, "Excuse me, ser."

As he nodded and moved aside, wondering at her glance at his rank and the totally perfunctory nature of the request, Trystin cranked up his hearing and caught the words, ". . . 'nother frigging greenie . . ."

Would the whole training program be like that, with perfunctory respect covering scorn for junior officers by the deep-space noncoms? Trystin took a deep breath and kept going up the ramps.

Room B7 smelled faintly of sweat and ozone, but looked like an old-style classroom, with a dozen flat consoles and scratched gray plastic chairs. Trystin glanced around. Three lieutenants and a major returned his glance.

The major, a dark-haired and fresh-faced woman who looked little older than Trystin, despite her triple bars, nodded. "Make yourself at home, Lieutenant. I'm Ciri Tekanawe."

"Trystin Desoll."

"Jonnie Schicchi." The stocky and dark-skinned lieutenant who looked older than anyone was the first to respond.

"Constanzia Aloysia." Lieutenant Aloysia was thin-faced, with short light brown hair that frizzed around her face.

"Suzuki Yamidori." The lieutenant's thin lips barely opened, and her syllables were clipped.

Trystin slipped into a chair behind a console equidistant between Major Tekanawe and Lieutenant Schicchi, his implant indicating that it was 0855 standard space time.

At 0859, a squat, dark man with the subcommander's gold triangle on his chest beside the name insignia that read Torowe stepped into the room and glanced across the group of five officers. Above his name and rank insignia was the implanted holo of an antique-looking pair of wings. Finally, he asked, "Any of you sing?"

Trystin frowned.

"Never mind. It was a bad joke—obscure anyway. Most pilots—those who survive—end up with dated and obscure senses of humor. You'll get used to it, and about the time you do, everyone except the older pilots will give you blank looks because what you thought was funny they haven't got the referents for." Torowe shook his head. "Just file it away. You'll understand someday."

Trystin moistened his lips. He hoped that all the instruction would not be nearly so obscure.

"All of you have survived perimeter-station duty. That's not a great recommendation, but it's a good indication that you are either extraordinarily lucky or marginally competent, and it saves us the trouble of doing gross screening. We like that here, because real stupidity costs us ships and, occasionally, instructors. As an instructor, I have certain biases, especially against stupidity." Torowe paused again.

"Lieutenant Desoll, in the next day or so, we could up your implant and direct-link you to the vette or the troop barge you're going to be the owner, master, and flunky for, and you'd probably be able to handle just about anything. So why don't we?"

"Because just about probably isn't good enough."

"There's no question about it," said Commander Torowe. "As far back as decent military training goes, the records indicate that a disproportionate amount of time has been spent training officers in control of vehicles on how to handle situations that happen one percent of the time—or less. Some non-Service efficiency experts still occasionally suggest that such devotion to rarity is the height of cost-inefficiency—unless an emergency occurs on the ship they're taking." He smiled. "The problem with emergencies is that most of the time you lose all or part of your normal operating systems, and that's one reason why we just don't turn you into part of the machinery—the revvie insults notwithstanding.

"And, by the way, you'll also be required to use hardcopy manuals for systems, in addition to on-line tutorials. Do you have any idea why, Lieutenant Schicchi?"

"No, ser."

"Think about it, Lieutenant. How can you figure out how to repair the power system if the information you need can only be accessed through a system powered by the ship and you don't have power, which was the problem to begin with?"

"Oh. . . ."

"Think! You all need to think more." Torowe shook his head sadly. "After this indoctrination, you won't see me for a long time. You'd better hope you don't." He offered a slow smile. "Now . . ." He looked at the five again. "We're going to disable your implants—just temporarily—and send you back to school. You will learn everything you need to learn to pilot without any on-line assistance. You won't become pilot officers unless you can. Major Tekanawe, can you tell me why?"

"Implants or linkages fail under some conditions, and unboosted ability may be necessary to complete a flight or mission," Ciri Tekanawe answered.

"That's the correct long answer. The short answer is that it might save your ass. You're going to have a class in estimation. Why? With calculators and implants, you can get precise answers. Fine. What's the square of sixteen? Can you tell me without your implant? How about the square of that?" Torowe's finger pointed at Lieutenant Aloysia.

"Sixty-five thousand five hundred thirty-six, but I doubt I could do it in my head."

"No, but you'd better be able to estimate the general magnitude in less than a second, because that may be all you'll have." The commander turned back to Trystin. "Lieutenant Desoll, try to imagine this. You have the kind of static in your head that's worse than direct-feed from a badlands storm—yes, I've been on the Maran perimeter line—and your implant is down. You have a spread of torps flaring at you, and you have no plots and no input except the visuals on a flat screen. And you have less than a minute to decide. Now what?"

Trystin winced.

"I think you might have the vaguest idea of what faces you. Maybe." He paused. "Then again, maybe not. I said you had a minute to decide, but I didn't tell you that if you guess—or calculate—wrong, you'll watch disaster coming for a good stan, and you may not die until your emergency life support blows, and that could be a long time."

The commander straightened. "Your first stop is medical for your implant deactivation. That's right. No reflex boosts, and no cheating by overhearing what you should have gotten the first time. Medical's in C fifty. After deactivation, report back here, and your packets will be waiting with your schedules for classes and simulators. I won't be." He turned and walked out of the room.

Trystin nodded. No repetitions of directions or instructions. No redundancy. You either got it, or you didn't. He stood and followed Major Tekanawe out the doorway and back toward the ramps to the lower levels.

The medical door was marked with the antique red cross.

"Ah . . . the latest crop of lost ones . . ." Trystin picked up the whisper from the tech standing behind the console.

"Major, you're first. Lieutenant, take a seat, and you'll be next."

Trystin sat in the battered black seat, and watched as the major walked through an archway and out of sight around a corner. The three other lieutenants slipped into the room and sat, following the age-old dictum of letting the senior and the brave face unfriendly fire first.

Shortly, a somber-faced Major Tekanawe walked back through the archway.

"Lieutenant?"

Trystin stood and followed the woman tech down the short corridor and into a room with little more than what looked to be a dental chair in it.

"Lieutenant, sit down right here." The tech gestured to the chair.

As he slipped into the chair, Trystin looked up at the assembly of electronics that vaguely resembled a folded-back helmet.

"Don't worry, ser. It only looks like a torture device. It doesn't take long, and it doesn't hurt at all."

The tech lowered the device and slipped the sections down and around Trystin's head, fitting the smooth plastic along Trystin's jawline and around his ears until only his lower forehead, eyes, nose, and mouth remained uncovered. The plastic of the long chair felt clammy against his back.

The tech touched several keys on the console but said nothing aloud.

"Can you hear this through your implant?" The words/sounds rolled through Trystin's implant so loudly that he winced.

"Yes."

"You're one of the sensitive ones—or you got some high-class work there."

The tech touched another key, but Trystin heard or felt nothing.

"That's good. No harmonics there."

"Let's try this. . . ."

Trystin almost bolted through the apparatus when the white noise knifed through him.

"Sorry, Lieutenant. You're definitely a sensitive. Pluses and minuses there. This should do it."

Trystin shivered as his implant went dead—leaving him completely alone for the first time in years. Even the background static he'd learned to tune out was gone. His skull was indeed silent, and he would be unable to communicate except by impossibly slow words or by physically manipulating console dials, switches, studs, and whatever.

"That's it." The tech began to peel back the equipment.

He stood slowly and walked out of the medical section, feeling somehow off balance, and somehow as if everything were designed for exactly that purpose.

20

 "What is this crap?" asked Jonnie Schicchi as the four officers walked toward the lecture room.

Trystin shrugged. "You know as much as I do. We're scheduled for four of these 'Cultural Ethics and Values' seminars."

"They're mandatory," added Lieutenant Aloysia, bobbing her head.

"Isn't everything?" Suzuki Yamidori bestowed a smile on Constanzia Aloysia, who ignored it.

The four were almost the first ones there, and Trystin took the opportunity to sit as far back as he could. The three others took the three chairs in the second row next to him. The room smelled dusty, and Trystin rubbed his nose. He didn't really want to sneeze.

Kkhccheww! Suzuki did sneeze. "Sorry."

"My nose itches, too," admitted Schicchi.

Trystin just watched as other student pilot officers straggled in.

At 1028, a dark-haired man, slender and wearing dress greens and a commander's insignia on one side of his collar and a cross and a crossed olive branch as the other collar insignia, stepped into the room and nodded. He set a stack of papers on the table and said quietly, "Handouts for later."

"Frigging ethicist . . ." mumbled Schicchi.

"A chaplain by any other name," answered Yamidori in a low voice.

The chaplain turned to the dozen-odd officers. "Good morning. I'm Commander Matsugi, and I'm the first lecturer in your series of seminars on Cultural Ethics and Values." His dark eyes traversed the room. "This seminar has been called boring. Dull, even. There's another term for it. Call it necessary. No, you won't be tested, not here anyway."

Several sets of lungs exhaled.

"I won't attempt to insist that this will save your life or your career." A grim smile played across Matsugi's face. "And I don't have the marshal's power or charisma. So you will have to bear with me."

He cleared his throat.

"The Revenants of the Prophet are the declared enemy of the Coalition, but what raised that enmity? That enmity arises from fundamental cultural differences, and those differences arise from religion, from belief systems dating to antiquity . . . even from basic economic precepts . . . and from the Coalition's emphasis on rationality. Rationality is the enemy of any closed faith. What do I mean by a closed faith? One that relies on a dogma that cannot be questioned without the threat of death or exile. The Revenants are closed to what you might call outside truths, and their culture is so stable internally that change from within is highly unlikely. I'll put it in terms that are simple. Minds, like ancient parachutes, function better when open, but, like fists, they strike harder when closed . . . call that a cultural parallel . . ."

Trystin stifled a yawn, trying to keep his eyes open. Still, he kept missing words, even though what the chaplain said seemed to make sense. But he was so damned tired, and Matsugi's voice seemed to drone on and on.

Crack!

Trystin jerked awake with the sound of the impact, gazing at the front row where one lieutenant struggled into his seat, red-faced, apparently so asleep that he had toppled right onto the floor.

". . . trouble for Herrintin . . ."

". . . wait til Folsom finds out . . ."

Trystin swallowed another yawn.

"I am glad to see you were not hurt, Lieutenant," the chaplain added. "I would hate to obtain the reputation for injurious seminars."

Faint laughter ran through the officers.

"Now . . . as I was discussing . . . the fundamental differences in beliefs between the Revenants of the Prophet and most beliefs within the Coalition lie in two areas. First, the Revenants believe, deeply, in a single set of revealed truths, as expounded by Toren, the Prophet of God, while few belief systems within the Coalition are so rigid as to exclude all possibility of entertaining other truths. Exclusivity is one factor . . . the second is the participation of a revealed God in the workings of life and the universe . . . this dates back to Judaism—that's the forerunner of the old Christian religions that were the forerunners of both Mahmetism and Deseretism, which in turn were the forerunners of neo-Mahmetism and the Prophet—for those of you into history . . ."

The commander wiped his forehead. "The participation of God. Even Christianity, which arose from Judaism, believed in a god who cared, who gave his son up to save those who believed. . . ."

Trystin stifled a yawn and forced himself to concentrate. Maybe he should read some of the handouts.

". . . Jesus of Nazareth walked into the Temple of the old Jews, which had taken forty-six years to build, and said that, if the Jews razed it, he would rebuild it in three days

. . . according to old scriptures, he really referred to the temple of his body, which, in the Christian tradition, God resurrected in three days . . . and on three occasions after that he showed himself to his disciples.

"Here too God descended to the level of daily living, involving himself. This long tradition of deistic involvement did not start with the fusion of the neo-Mahmets—the so-called white Muslims—and the followers of the Prophet into the Revenant culture. Rather the Revenants affirm and believe that tradition. A daily living God is totally real to them . . . it permeates their entire culture and value system. . . ."

Idly, Trystin wondered how the Revenants would react if some modern-day prophet actually appeared and created miracles. Beside Trystin, Jonnie Schicchi shifted his weight and yawned. Constanzia Aloysia took a long and slow deep breath.

Commander Matsugi droned on, and Trystin tried to concentrate.

21

 The warning light on the fusactor systems remained amber, signifying that power output was less than seventy percent. Running at less than ten percent, with all the telltales red, the accumulators were close to burning out.

The smell of ozone and worn equipment seemed to press in on Trystin, but he checked his closure against the ambient space-dust density, breathing a sigh of relief to learn that he could initiate translation, even as his fingers toggled the sequence.

"Translation power-up beginning. Four minutes to translation."

The representational screen flashed red momentarily, and Trystin glanced from the translation plot to the EDI where the tracks from the revvie system patroller were wider, indicating more power output and a higher closing speed. An amber circle dropped over the center point in the screen—representing the damaged corvette Trystin was trying to get out of the revvie system—and a single *ping* issued from the screen speaker.

"Shit . . ." he mumbled. The rev had a lock-on. Trystin lost a few instants trying to coax an answer from his dead implant before his fingers flickered across the console. Everything seemed to take so long manually.

Three minutes and ten seconds until the translation systems were on-line and synchronized. System power output was at sixty-five percent and dropping. Full shields would drop the available power level below the fifty-five percent required for translation. The revvie patroller was less than fifty thousand kays away—only a fraction of a light-second—and closing, and semitranslation torps ran just below light speed.

In the half-gravity of the cockpit, Trystin's stomach was rising into his throat. He pulsed the shields, then toggled them off as the available power dropped to twenty percent. As he watched, the available power level began to climb back . . . twenty-five percent . . . thirty-five percent . . . forty-five percent . . . forty-eight percent. . . .

"Present free power flow insufficient for translation," the main console scripted. "Interrogative delay of translation initiation?"

He ignored the question and wiped his forehead, conscious that the small cockpit smelled of stressed human as well as stressed equipment. Not only was his forehead damp, but his whole body was damp. What could he do?

He cut the power to the artificial gravity, and felt his body both rise against the straps and be pressed ever so slightly against the pilot's couch from the continuing acceleration of the in-system thrusters. His guts rose farther up into his throat in the near null-gee.

"Two minutes to translation." The mechanical words

scripted across the console in front of Trystin.

The representational screen flashed red, and a series of dotted pink lines flared toward the screen center—toward Trystin.

Bzzzz! Bzzzz! The power warning light flashed. "Power below fifty-five percent," scripted across the console.

Trystin's eyes flicked between the screens and the power meter in the corner of the console, and to the digital clock readings, as he tried to calculate his options. Finally, he toggled off the environmental systems, then watched until the power output inched over fifty-five percent. Then he flicked the guard off the emergency translation stud and slammed it down.

The cockpit flared white, then black, before the entire board powered down with a dull whining sound. The cockpit turned into inert plastic, metal, and electronics, lit only by the faint red emergency lights.

"Systems Inoperative!" The red words flashed across the top of the screens perhaps three times before they too died in the darkness, burned out by the back-power surge created by translation without accumulators.

Trystin wiped his forehead, trying not to shake his head. What else could he have done? Dying a slow death in the cold without power or getting incinerated instantly—what a choice. He sighed.

The door at the back of the cockpit opened.

"You couldn't do a damned thing, Lieutenant. Not at the end. Once you got to the point where the torps had you bracketed with no accumulators and less than enough power for both shields and a translation, you were dead one way or the other. A blind early jump was the best option you had, but you'd still probably end up freezing somewhere in an outer orbit off some system without even enough juice to call for help and not enough heat to survive even if you were heard." Subcommander Folsom shrugged. "Unstrap. We'll go to briefing room B." The slender officer disappeared, leaving the hatch open and Trystin alone in the simulator.

Trystin unbelted and slipped out of the worn pilot's

couch. Then he eased his gear bag from the locker beside the empty noncom's couch. After ducking through the hatch and stepping across the gap from the simulator to the fixed platform, he slowly climbed down the ladder to the gray rock floor of the simulator bay.

By the console stood now-Major Freyer and her instructor, a subcommander Trystin did not recognize who was talking to the simulator tech.

"How did it go, Lieutenant?" asked Ulteena Freyer.

Trystin wiped his forehead. "I froze to death in deep space . . . slowly."

"Endgaming." She nodded.

Trystin frowned and paused.

"It's a old chess term—the game, you know. Look it up. If one player can think a move farther ahead than the other, then he can force the less perceptive player into making apparently logical moves that lead to a trap." She glanced toward the commander.

"Head on up, Major."

She smiled briefly at Trystin and lifted her gear bag. "Hold tight, Trystin."

Trystin nodded back at her and then walked slowly out of the bay and into the corridor off which were the seemingly endless small debriefing rooms. Kind as she was, why did Ulteena always act so superior? He snorted. Probably because she was. Back on Mara, she had figured out how to defeat tanks before they arrived. He hadn't even figured that the revs might have tanks.

He took another deep breath and stepped into briefing room B.

"Sit down, Lieutenant." Subcommander Folsom smiled.

Trystin sat.

"Do you have any idea why you ended up where you would have frozen into a cold cometary lump in some forsaken outer orbit?"

"Was the situation designed to sucker me in?" Trystin wiped his forehead. "Or designed to let me sucker myself in?"

Surprisingly, Folsom leaned back in the plastic chair and nodded. "Now why would we want to do that to you? And why do we use what appear to be antique physical simulators, rather than modern neuronic simulators?"

Trystin had pondered that question himself—certainly more than once, but the rigorous schedule had left him limited time for questions. The entire Service left little time for questions, and only when he was too exhausted to ponder them. "I had wondered that. My first thought was that they're expensive, and that they probably take a lot of maintenance."

Folsom half nodded, then pulled at his chin. "That's partly right. The underlying reason is because we're still full-body creatures. A lot of feedback to your brain is nonconscious, but you're still aware of it. The more we can duplicate the entire environment, not just your mental processing of that environment, the more real it seems. Sure, I suppose we could hook each of you up in suits that fed inputs into every nerve in your body, but every damned one of those suits would have to be custom-designed. The physical simulators are much more cost-effective. Also, we don't have to worry nearly so much about monitoring your system. The physical simulators also have physical limits." He paused. "Although we have lost a few idiots who screwed things up so bad that the overrides couldn't compensate quickly enough."

Trystin swallowed.

"That doesn't happen very often. But back to the original question. Why did I set up this trap for you?"

"So we recognize that kind of situation before it gets out of hand?"

"It's worse than that." Folsom squared himself in the seat. "There's an ancient saying about forgetting that your objective was to drain the swamp when you're ass-deep in allodiles. Now, what that means is obvious enough . . . and it's not. When you're out there alone in that vette, or when you're the one in charge of piloting a cruiser or a transport with other people's lives in your hands, and when everything starts to go wrong—and it does, more than we like to make public—there's a terrible temptation to let the patterns you've learned take over. After all, reflexes, especially implant-boosted reflexes, are far faster than stopping to think, especially when you feel like you only have minutes or seconds to respond. Boosted reflexes make that even worse, because you can respond with trained patterns far more quickly than you can analyze a situation. That's why you have to anticipate."

Trystin waited.

"Anticipation—that's the key to being able to think and react, simultaneously. We try to help you at first by deactivating your implants to slow down your training patterns. Later, you'll have to handle these things at full speed or even at full reflex boost—and it may not be fast enough. Remember, a lot of the time you're going to be on the wrong side of the time-dilation envelope, and that means you'll have to react instantly and correctly, while the rev has all the time in the world—comparatively."

Trystin moistened his lips.

The brown-haired subcommander took out a series of sheets and laid them on the small table. "First . . . your handling of the fusactor dump was quick and effective. Nicely done. I probably would have cross-checked the accumulators earlier, but that's something you learn with time, and it's not in the tutorials."

Trystin wiped his still-damp forehead.

"Why would the accumulators have blown, Lieutenant?"

Trystin frowned.

"I know. They blew because I told them to . . . but what sort of problem could have caused that to happen?"

"Well, ser . . ."

"Don't stall."

"Poor maintenance or too many rapid temperature changes. Either that or physical damage—a close-in laser or shrapnel—but that wouldn't seem likely, since—"

"Since anything close enough to inflict physical damage would probably be enough to take you out. You're right." Folsom cleared his throat. "The two biggest causes of equipment failure are the same as they always were, even back when people tried to slash and bash each other with broadswords—operator error and maintenance or construction error. Take it from there."

"Operator error," began Trystin, trying to get his brain to operate more quickly. "Would a pattern of dumping too many quick load shifts on the system eventually wear out the accumulators?"

"That's right. Sure, that's what they're designed for, but save that ability for when you really need it. I know, station controllers want you off the lock *now.* And tactical coordinators want you to react even more quickly, but an extra minute to allow a gentle buildup of thrust and a smooth power transfer won't change anything, and it might mean those accumulators won't blow when you really need them."

Trystin winced, thinking about his abrupt power shifts.

"You all do it to begin with. It's part of the process. What about maintenance?"

"Does that mean better preflight of equipment?"

"That helps. How would you tell a stressed accumulator from one that wasn't?"

"I don't know," Trystin confessed.

"There are ways. Some are in the tech library. Some are in the minds of the better techs. I won't tell you. I'm not being cruel. I've told student pilots before, and most never remembered. So I don't. The ones who want to live go find out."

Trystin repressed a groan. Another item to dig out of obscure files, manually no less, since his implant linkages didn't work for anything.

"Back to your flight. Once the accumulators went, why didn't you just bat-ass above the ecliptic for a dust-free zone and translate?"

"I was still running at eighty-five percent—"

"Until you ran into the dust and had to beef up the shields."

Trystin was beginning to see the pattern. The power he had shifted to the shields was meant to be temporary, but with his out-system velocity and the extended dust belt, the power load had strained the capacity of the fusactor, and its efficiency and output had dropped, and then the rev patroller had shown up.

"So why didn't you tilt for the ecliptic after you cleared the dust?"

"I shut down all EDI emissions and thought I would be able to coast clear of the first rev."

"You did that all right, but by then you were in the detection envelope of the second without enough power to outrun a solar-sail ore carrier or a water asteroid on a slow spiral."

Trystin nodded.

"Do you see, Lieutenant? Each decision you made seemed perfectly logical. Except for one. That toggling of your defense shields was unnecessary, probably the only really overtly stupid thing you did, not that it would have changed the outcome much. Anyway, there are times when you'd just better cut your losses and run for home."

Folsom stared at Trystin. "Now . . . I understand young pilots. None of you want to admit that there's something you can't handle. There's a saying that dates back to the first years of atmospheric flight. It's still true. 'There are old pilots, and there are bold pilots, but there are no old bold pilots.'

"The other thing that you had to be considering in not choosing a high ecliptic exit was the compounded translation error. Is saving a month—or a year—in elapsed time worth the rest of your life? Some pilots have thought so. I hope you're not one of them. After all, we do have several million credits already invested in you, one way or another."

Trystin nodded once more, trying not to reveal that the commander had caught him out again.

Folsom picked up the papers from the table and stood. "Not too bad, all in all. Especially if you learn something from it."

Trystin stood. "Yes, ser."

The slender commander walked out, his steps slow and deliberate.

After packing up his notes, Trystin flicked off the debriefing room lights and walked down the corridor toward the ramps. He'd have to hurry if he wanted to get a shower before his translation-engineering class, and the way he smelled, he needed a shower.

The simulators were on nearly the bottom levels—that was because it was easier to cancel the grav fields generated by the equipment nearer the center of the small moon—or big asteroid—that was Chevel Beta.

He had almost reached J level when he heard someone come out of a corridor below and start to follow him up the ramps.

"Trystin?"

He stopped and turned.

Jonnie Schicchi trudged up the ramp behind him. "I saw you had Commander Folsom as your setup instructor. Constanzia says he's a mean old bastard."

"He's tough," Trystin conceded.

"Everything here is tough." Schicchi looked down at the ramp. "You figure out the power-translation problems?"

"Most of them, except the second one. As far as I could figure out, you can't make a translation." Trystin wiped his still-damp forehead. "But the worksheet asks for power requirements, maximum distance, and a coordinate envelope. I don't know."

"So what did you do?"

Trystin shrugged. "Put down the calculations indicating it couldn't be done. I probably overlooked something, and Commander Eschbech will make me feel like an idiot." Trystin looked up the ramp. "I've got to get moving. I need a shower before class."

"So do I, but I'm too tired to rush."

"See you later." Trystin hurried up the ramps toward J level and his cubicle. Luckily, all the classes were on D level—as were the few administrative offices.

"Right. Maybe Yamidori can help me with the engineering stuff."

Trystin didn't rise to the bait, although he felt vaguely sorry for Schicchi. Supposedly, Jonnie had great instincts, at least in the simulator, but equally great difficulties with more abstract exercises.

Trystin began to unfasten the shipsuit even before he was fully inside his cubicle.

22

 "Before we approach the tactical aspects of translation, such as the virtual impossibility of synchroneity, that is, the synchronization of translations and emergence from translation by separate spacecraft, we need to discuss translation error. We talk about 'translation error,' but is it really an error? Of course not." Commander Kurbiachi nodded at his own answer to his question. "We call it an error because we cannot determine in advance exactly how much apparent elapsed time passes in our space-time universe while a ship is in the process of translating between the congruencies created by a translation engine. Two identical ships with precisely, or as precise as we can make it, the same cargo and personnel can routinely emerge at the same point in space with differences in translation time as great as two months. The problem is that each ship, each point of translation, each time of translation is unique. Thus, even attempting to determine the impact of literally hundreds of subtly different variables upon a translation through what can be roughly called chaos, though it is not, becomes a mathematical problem beyond the capabilities of any equipment yet developed. Oh, our estimations have gotten relatively precise, but they are only estimations, and they are really only even halfway precise for a single ship . . . most references do not account for the impact of the so-called translation error upon multiple ship movements . . ."

Sitting in the second row of the dozen-plus would-be pilots, comprised of officers at three slightly different practical training levels, Trystin stifled a yawn.

"As established by the noted academician Ryota more than a century ago, because so-called translation error is a function of the unique properties linked to each translation, the result approximates a random distribution within a range limited by the gross variables of the situation." The commander paused as a major in the third row raised her hand. "Yes, Major?"

"I might be getting ahead, but theoretically," asked Ulteena Freyer, "theoretically, if you had a large enough group of ships, and you attempted simultaneous translations, effectively wouldn't you end up with groups of ships emerging at roughly coincident times?"

"That is certainly theoretically possible, and it was one of Ryota's theorems that such would be the case—the Distribution Theorem. However . . ."—Kurbiachi paused before continuing—"the number of variables involved would have required, according to Ryota's calculations, based on the translation engines of that time, a fleet in the neighborhood of ten thousand ships. Today, my modest adaptations of the Distribution Theorem suggest that to achieve a barely acceptable distribution, that is, twenty groups of ten ships emerging from translation chaos with the ships in each group translating into real space within a day of each other, would still require almost a thousand ships." Kurbiachi bowed slightly, his short jet-black hair unmoving.

"Thank you, Commander."

"Your question illustrates the problem of achieving synchroneity, which is obviously the basis of tactics on any level above that of the individual ship. Theoretically and practically, synchronizing multiple ship movements through interstellar distances remains impossible, even using advanced chaos-perturbation modifications."

"What about the Harmony raid?" asked someone behind Trystin.

"Ah, yes. That is a good question." Kurbiachi smiled.

With the smile, Trystin saw why he didn't want Kurbiachi as a check pilot.

"A good question, indeed. You are familiar with the Harmony raid?" Kurbiachi paused. "For those of you who are unfamiliar with the details, I will elaborate slightly. In Septem of 720, the Coalition effectively attacked the Harmony system with a fleet of nearly one hundred translation ships and destroyed all the feasible military targets within the system, then the main staging base for the Prophet's missionaries. That success has never been repeated, nor is it likely to be. The Coalition began to translate ships into the sub-Oort region of the Harmony system nearly four months before the attack. To obtain one hundred and eight ships—the precise number that began the attack—required attempted translations of over two hundred ships. Eighty ships missed the attack window through wide variations in translation and returned unharmed, although the last did not return to Chevel Beta until nearly three years after the attack. Twelve ships attempted the translation and did not return. The assumption is that those twelve missed the sub-Oort free dust zone and translated into nontranslatable zones. . . ."

"Boom . . ." came a muted whisper from the front row.

"Exactly," agreed Kurbiachi. "Then, of the one hundred eight ships that commenced the attack, twenty-seven survived and returned." He bowed to the lieutenant who had asked the question. "After the Harmony attack, the Revenant military authorities widened their patrols to include the outer fringes of their systems. That tactic, while somewhat costly, precluded any Coalition attempt to evade the synchroneity limits through a phased buildup of forces within a system. . . ."

Trystin pursed his lips and took a deep breath through his nose, trying to avoid a yawn. History and more history! The conclusion was simple enough: No one had yet figured out how to have two ships translate at the same time and emerge close to each other, either in time or space, although time seemed to be the bigger problem.

"... As a result of the synchroneity limitations, pitched interstellar battles between fleets are highly unlikely, and the system defense provides, with the development of EDI technology, certain advantages to the defender. ..."

Trystin stifled another yawn. While Kurbiachi was a brilliant tactician in his own way, his lectures were boring. Out of the old parashinto mold, he was polite and refused to adopt more interesting classroom techniques because they might cause his students to lose face publicly.

Rumor said he was far more taxing in private. Trystin hoped never to find out.

"... likewise the Tompkins' Limit restricts the capacity of translation engines to masses of less than roughly two thousand metric tonnes ... and translations involving masses exceeding one thousand tonnes have certain ... difficulties ..."

In the engineering class, Trystin reflected, Subcommander Eschbech had begun on the mathematics of the Tompkins' Limit, and Eschbech was far more interesting.

"... in combating both the synchroneity restrictions and the Tompkins' Limit, the Revenants of the Prophet have returned to what might appear to be an anachronistic approach—the use of fusactor mass conversion-boosted asteroid ships, with modified translation-effect acceleration and deceleration, based on ..."

Trystin doodled out what looked like a chunk of iron asteroid, then added his conceptualization of the so-called deceleration module. Sooner or later, Kurbiachi had to get into tactics, rather than why there weren't tactics. At least, Trystin hoped so.

23

 "That's all, ser. Your implant will feel strange for a while with the wider band receptivity, but everything checks, and your neural system's in better shape than when you checked in." The tech folded the equipment away from Trystin's face. "We'll give you another check before you leave on your assignment, but everything should be all right. If anything hurts or burns, get back here immediately. That shouldn't happen, but it does sometimes." She coughed. "You ought to feel better, at least until you give it a workout."

"First rest it's had in a while." Trystin stood and stretched. In fact, it had been eight standard months since he had used his implant.

"Glad it's you and not me."

"Why?" asked Trystin.

"You ever see someone with a burned neural system? Those who don't die? They shake and shiver all over, and every time they move, their faces twist, like each movement sends needles through their brains. No thanks, Lieutenant. You can have it." The tech shook her head.

The first sensation he was aware of was that the silence in his skull was gone. The trickling signals even from the medical equipment registered, like a background hum, and he could sense the main Chevel Beta net, though he didn't have the protocol to tap into the signals.

"Thank you." He turned to the tech before leaving.

"You're welcome, ser."

Did he hear a note of sadness in her voice? Resignation?

He checked the time through the implant—1320, more than enough time before his simulator session for him to stop by the library and work out the references he needed to complete the problems that Commander Eschbech had dumped on the engineering class.

Why weren't there hookups in their rooms? All it took was cabling and inexpensive, or relatively inexpensive, hardware. Trystin rubbed his forehead. In a way, it didn't make sense. Yet, so far, everything that the Service did had a reason, not always a reason Trystin accepted, but a reason. Was it too expensive? Or old habit? He pursed his lips. That question would wait for later. He still had to figure out a series of problems on superconductivity lines and translation engines.

The workstations at the south end of the library were all vacant except for two—one in each corner. Trystin did not recognize either officer in the room. He took the console in the middle, easing his gear bag as far under the shelf that held the console as it would go, and toggling the screen controls before realizing that he could again use his implant.

The implant link-connect was soft, almost flat, but faster than he recalled as he called up the engineering index and began to race through the superconductivity entries.

As usual, none were exactly what he needed, and he wondered if Commander Eschbech designed his assignments just that way so that they always required four different references, interpolations, calculations, and sometimes just plain guesswork.

How was he supposed to come up with the specifications of a ceramic-carbon-helix design for a supercon line designed to handle a translation engine with a thousand-light-year limit on optimality? And why? Trystin took a deep breath.

After completing three of the problems, Trystin rubbed his forehead. The noise of the implant still bothered him, enough that he had a slight headache.

"Good luck this afternoon," said a soft voice.

Trystin looked up at the round face of Constanzia Aloysia, who had cut her hair so short that the frizziness almost did not show.

"Thank you." He looked at her again. "Why?"

"I saw the assignments board."

"Not Commander Mitchelson?"

"Not that bad." She smiled. "Commander Kurbiachi."

"Thanks."

"You're welcome." She looked at the few notes he had scrawled on his pad and at the screen that showed his engineering work to date. "You do those problems? He said that they were optional."

"If I don't do it all, I get in trouble."

Lieutenant Aloysia shook her head, then brushed something off the sleeve of her shipsuit. "I thought you wouldn't want to be surprised."

"Thank you." Trystin tried to put more warmth into his voice.

"That's all right. I'll see you in Engineering."

As Constanzia left the study area, Trystin checked the time. Although he hadn't finished the last problem and couldn't figure out how to set it up, he was out of time. He gathered his gear and downlinked from the library system. He hurried out, but no one looked up.

After bounding down the ramps at a speed less than dignified, Trystin stepped up to the assignments board in the square foyer off the south end of the simulator bay. A name in glowing letters appeared next to his—that of Commander Kurbiachi. He moistened his lips. So far he had been lucky enough to avoid the commander, although the rumor was that he was fine in class, all right in the simulator, and murder in actual corvette trainers. Trystin headed down the corridor toward briefing room three B, the heels of his boots whispering across the textured plastic floor sealant.

Although his steps had always been heavy—Salya had claimed the Academy knew when Trystin left the house—the half-gee field in the station kept even Trystin from sounding like a reclamation tractor.

In the briefing room, Commander Kurbiachi was waiting, his informal greens crisp, his face smooth and unlined.

"Lieutenant Desoll, ser."

"Sit down, Lieutenant." The commander handed Trystin the worn briefing packet, but did not sit as Trystin eased into the scratched gray plastic chair. "You have just had your implant reactivated—is that not correct?"

"Yes, ser."

Kurbiachi nodded. "In this session, you will be doing a standard recon run, through the Jerush system, looking for a rev drone or scout. The parameters are as accurate and as up-to-date as we can make them. In fact, this session is modeled after such a run. Yes, we do infiltrate rev systems, and they occasionally infiltrate ours. Space is quite large, remember."

In turn, Trystin nodded, trying to look alert, despite the distractions provided by the increased noise of his "improved" implant.

"This session is a review, Lieutenant, for very good reasons. First, you are going to have difficulty in adjusting to the greater data flow from your implant. You will be confused and trying to use both manual and implant input to control the corvette, and you may have difficulty learning how to tone back on your increased sensitivity. You can do that, you know, but it takes work and practice, and we haven't given you enough of that yet. Finally, the readouts and data flows will all be speeded up so that you experience the full impact of operating under dilation effect."

The commander half turned and took several steps toward the door, hands behind his back, before turning and walking back toward Trystin. "This simulator session is usually the most difficult for all pilots, Lieutenant," said Commander Kurbiachi. "That will not be because there is anything new, however."

"Yes, ser." Trystin nodded.

"As I said, most pilots have great difficulty handling the volume of the data flows through the implant. I must remind you that for the next several sessions, you will only be receiving the tactical and basic-maintenance data. The actual mission is merely a flight from the Jerush Oort area on a recon runby. You will probably encounter rev patrollers, since they do investigate any EDI tracks within their system, as do we.

"Unlike most simulator sessions, on this one you may take as long as you wish on your setup. I would recommend that you do so." Kurbiachi nodded and bowed ever so slightly.

"Thank you, ser." Trystin bent and picked up his gear bag and followed Kurbiachi out into the simulator bay and the smell of plastic, ozone . . . and tension.

Kurbiachi merely nodded at simulator six, and Trystin climbed the ladder easily. When he opened the simulator hatch, Trystin staggered, feeling the same overpowering flow of data that he had sensed in entering the cockpit of the *Roosveldt*. The signal intensity was lower, no doubt on purpose, and the amount of data flowing through the implant was less, but Trystin still felt as though the entire Maran Defense Net were attempting to take up residence in his skull—and what he experienced wasn't even the full scope of what was supposed to be routine for a pilot officer. He glanced at the empty noncom couch. He didn't even have to deal with the technical data that would normally be going through the tech boards.

He wiped his forehead. Kurbiachi had said he could take as much time as he needed.

First, he checked the hatch and the air system before sealing the cockpit and stowing his gear in the locker. Then he strapped in and began the checklist, fumbling because he was used to the manual toggles and studs, and not his implant.

"Precheck," he instructed the system through the implant.

"Full or abbreviated?" came the system query.

"Full."

Trystin was deliberate, his directions through the implant considered and precisely triggered as he tried to get a more complete feel, although every rush of data seemed to bring another sweat to his body. His entire shipsuit felt soaked long before he signaled for switchover from "station" power to "ship" power. Just as in the *Roosveldt,* the moment of weightlessness twisted his guts before the half-grav of pseudoship-norm reasserted itself in the simulator cockpit.

"Coldrock one, station control. You are cleared for low-thrust separation. . . ."

"Beginning separation." Trystin demagnetized the holdtights, and, as Kurbiachi had predicted, found both his hands and implant toggling the repeller field. The screens twisted, indicating somehow Trystin had managed to separate at an angle and with a tumbling motion. With ship gravity centered in the hull, he didn't feel the tumbling, but the screen inputs and the data net confirmed his clumsiness.

Slowly he pulsed the field until he had the "corvette" on course line and stable. Theoretically, he could have tumbled for a long time without too much damage, before the oscillations created by the conflict between the minute but real solar and planetary fields began to build. But the inputs from the net would have given him a headache, and Kurbiachi definitely would have fried him for overstressing the simulator.

Don't think like it's a simulator, he told himself as he confirmed the thrust and course line. Think like it's a corvette. It is a corvette.

"Dust density is point zero six and rising," scripted the message from the exterior monitors.

Trystin inched up the shield power, noting the increased heat in the accumulators, then recalculated his path, trying for an arc above the dust line that generally centered in the ecliptic.

"Outside system parameters."

He tried again.

"Will require one hundred ten percent of system power."

While he could get the power from an accumulator dump, that wasn't a good idea, and he recomputed with lower thrust, knowing that the lower thrust would drag out the elapsed time.

"Dust density point zero five and dropping."

As he recomputed again, Trystin smiled grimly, through the headache that was steadily worsening. It was going to be a long session/mission.

24

 After adjusting the arm units to near-maximum resistance, Trystin stepped up on the inclined treadmill and began to jog, pumping his arms rhythmically against the resistance units.

Each minute ticked by slowly, ever so slowly, in the one point one gee section of the workout facility that he usually seemed to have to himself. After less than twenty minutes, his legs felt like lead, but he kept jogging. At forty minutes, his arms felt like they were ready to cramp into inert lead.

He slowed the machine to a quick walk an hour after he had started, and to a slower walk after another ten minutes. His exercise shirt and shorts were drenched, but there was no point in taking a shower—not yet, not until he cooled down more.

After walking slowly for another five minutes, he stepped off the equipment and into the reading-room section of the workout facility where there were four consoles, all of which seemed almost new. He pulled the sturdy chair over to the end console, the one closest to the overhead ventilator. If student pilots couldn't get enough time to exercise, the guidelines recommended as much time as possible in the higher-gee environment. Trystin tried to do both as much as possible. Unlike some student pilots, he had no trouble sleeping. Waking up, yes, but not sleeping.

He flipped the power switch, absently using the small towel to blot his forehead as he used the implant to interface with the station library. He began his daily search through the maintenance manuals to see what else he could find to follow up on the hints he had picked up from various instructors. All of them seemed so straightforward, but none of them were. Commander Folsom's suggestions about detecting accumulator problems had led him through reference after reference, and more than a few talks with senior noncoms, most of whom had just said something like, "I really can't say as there's any specific thing, ser. It's a feeling you get with experience."

Trystin didn't have the experience, and by the time he got it, it might be too late, and that had led to his ongoing search of engineering and maintenance manuals. Between Commander Folsom and Commander Eschbech, it seemed as though he'd read every engineering reference in the system, and he still couldn't answer half the questions they asked.

He wiped his forehead and took another deep breath.

As he began to cool down, he wiped his forehead again before going back to the material on the screen. Then he glanced up and, through the glass, saw a trim but muscular figure in an exercise suit begin a warm-up routine in the next room. The woman's back was to him, but she looked somehow familiar. After a minute or so, since her face was away from Trystin and he couldn't figure out who it might be, he went back to the net and the library.

The engineering manual indicated that minute power surges often foreshadowed accumulator failure, but unless he installed a recording monitoring system on every ship how would that knowledge help? He needed a clue that was visual. What did power fluctuations affect? He couldn't find anything on that, but that led him down the line of tracking power flows—

"Exercising in the sitting position, Lieutenant?" asked Ulteena Freyer, sweat pouring down her forehead as she walked into the reading room.

"I already spent an hour on the treadmill and weights," Trystin snapped.

"Touchy, aren't you?"

"Major, I apologize for any offense I may have caused. Certainly, none was intended. I may have been somewhat preoccupied with my work."

"You are touchy."

Trystin repressed a sigh and offered a smile. "Only when I'm tired."

"I'm sorry, Trystin. I spoke out of turn. The other day I came in here and found every console taken, but not a one of them had even raised a sweat."

"That's all right."

"What are you working on?" Ulteena took the console closest to the door.

"Engineering . . . sort of. Stuff on accumulators."

"Hmmmm . . . is that new? I don't recall much on them." She wiped her forehead with the small towel taken from the waistband of her exercise shorts. Like Trystin had been, she was soaked in sweat.

"Something that an instructor suggested I check out . . ." Trystin admitted. "I've been sandwiching it in."

"Then it's either Kurbiachi or Folsom." She wiped her forehead with the back of her forearm.

"Folsom."

"That figures. He's a translation engineer. Kurbiachi gets you with sensors and nav equipment."

"I seem to have had them both."

"You're fortunate." She laughed, and the sound was actually musical. "That's assuming you survive."

"Right."

"You will, and you'll probably appreciate them later."

"I keep trying to hold that in mind. It doesn't always help, since they're always coming up with something else."

Ulteena laughed softly. "That's the problem with all of us. We've never time to think about the past, and we're always planning for the future. And since the future's always the future, we never live in the present."

Trystin paused. He'd never thought of Ulteena as philosophical. "I hadn't thought of it quite that way."

"Try it. You still have to prepare for what will happen, but it might help." Ulteena wiped her forehead. "If you'll pardon me, I do have to do some of that preparation myself."

"Of course." Trystin nodded as she turned to the console. He looked at her back for a moment, then wondered why he bothered. While she was friendly enough, sometimes surprisingly warm, they were headed for different ships, perhaps totally different parts of the Coalition.

Never live in the present . . . don't have time to remember the past . . . planning for the future . . . her words swirled in his mind. Then he wanted to laugh as he looked down. He didn't really have time to consider what she'd said—not if he wanted to avoid having Folsom and Kurbiachi or Commander Eschbech all over him.

Did the Service design it so no one had time to think, really think? He still hadn't found time to finish reading the handouts on Revenant theology, perhaps because he kept getting hung up on the whole question of why anyone would believe a prophet without any real physical evidence of a god.

He shrugged and flicked his console from accumulators to translation subsystems.

25

 Trystin checked his armor and the seals on the helmet again, holding on to the railing inside the access tube. The short figure in armor arrowed down the tube toward him in the streaking bound that those experienced in min-gee affected. He caught the subcommander's insignia—not that any of the instructors were less than subcommanders with at least two complete ship tours—and the dark hair before he saw the woman's name—duValya.

"You're Lieutenant Desoll?" She braked easily and

stared at him, dark eyes matching dark hair, a face regular enough to be attractive, except for the penetrating intensity of the eyes. Why did all the attractive women have such perceptive eyes? Or was he only attracted to perceptive women?

"Yes, ser."

"We've got number ten, Lieutenant. Armor ready?"

"Yes, ser."

"We'll do the preflight first, and then I'll brief you after you've had a chance to familiarize yourself with the feel of the systems."

"Yes, ser."

"Some pilots feel that you don't need to preflight the outside of a corvette, especially if you're the only one piloting it, every flight. That's probably true. On the average, what can happen in space? Then again, it's your life, and a half hour of time. Do you want to gamble your life against half a standard hour, especially when your translation error can run days?"

The subcommander's logic was sound, but all those half hours added up, and pretty soon they amounted to days, and he wouldn't always have days.

"Now, I know that all the little safety edges can add up, and there will be times that you feel you just don't have the time . . ."

Trystin repressed a groan. Did all of them read minds?

". . . so the best policy, I have found, is to do everything whenever it is at all possible. Then, when the mission comes when you really don't have time, you've laid the odds in your favor." Subcommander duValya bobbed her head, but her short thick hair didn't move.

Trystin nodded.

"I know you know the preflight sequence, and you've practiced it on the exterior dummies in the simulator bay for at least the last six months, but it's different when you're weightless and floating around." Commander duValya cleared her throat. "You start with the lock seals, even before you head out. Then, once you're suited and sealed, you cycle the exterior side lock. I know it's part of the station and not the vette, but . . . it could be embarrassing, or worse, if the lock were to jam with you on the outside. Cycling generally prevents that. There's some loss of atmosphere, but given that you represent close to a billion creds, a little air is cheap insurance. . . ."

Trystin listened as duValya repeated, so close to word for word that she might have written them, the preflight manual's instructions. Maybe she had. All the instructors seemed to be experts on something—and everything.

". . . is that clear?"

"Yes, ser."

"Fine. It's all yours. I'll watch. You can ask questions without penalty, this time, but if you forget something or have to ask a question later, I won't let you forget it. Now . . . you go out first."

Trystin sealed his suit, triggering his implant. "Comm check, Commander?"

"Check, Lieutenant."

The training corvettes essentially floated in heavy reinforced composite docks off the spiderweb of access tubes and locks. Since Chevel Beta was a largish chunk of rock with minimal gravity, providing artificial gravity outside the station proper would have been a waste of power.

Remembering all the briefings, after he exited through the narrow lock, Trystin immediately clipped the retractable tether line to the recessed ring by the corvette's hatch.

Seemingly slumping in the ship cradle, the BCT-10 looked more like a partly deflated oval bladder made of metal than a ship.

"Good. Don't ever forget that tether clip. You can make a real mess of yourself if you have to use attitude jets. Here they have enough power for escape velocity." The commander's voice rang hollowly in the armor's speakers.

Slowly Trystin pulled himself across the corvette's hull, noting replacement plates, and the many signs of repairs, such as the scratches around the sensor bulges and the heavy layers of heatshield. As he had been instructed, he only did a visual inspection of the orientation jets and the mass thruster nozzles. He avoided even floating/bouncing behind the nozzles.

"Is there anytime you actually physically inspect the exterior of the thrusters?" he asked.

"Not unless you're an engineer and you've locked the ship and frozen the internal comm nets so that no one can play with the power. Even then, I wouldn't do it. The ECR of even stray boosted ions is enough to scatter you and your armor across a very large system. Besides, what would it tell you?"

Trystin nodded inside the helmet. Dumb question, but sometimes he did ask dumb questions, no matter how hard he tried.

After the preflight, they used the lock back into the access tube and then the ship's lock, still in full armor. Trystin released the mechanical holdtights, leaving the ship only held in place by the magnetic holdtights.

Once he confirmed that the ship's pressure was sound, he flicked on the heater switch and cracked his helmet. His breath steamed in the cold air, and he could hear the whine of the ventilators as they forced slowly warming air through the ship.

He unsuited and racked the armor. The commander racked hers in the second rack, the one used by the tech noncom in a standard corvette.

Trystin began the interior preflight by walking to the rear of the corvette and sliding open the lower-deck access panel.

"What happens if the panel jams?" asked the commander.

Trystin looked blank. He hadn't read or heard anything about jammed access panels. Then he looked at the half-open panel. There were four heavy recessed hex sockets around the door. He peered underneath. "I don't know, ser. It looks as though you could lift the whole assembly if the hex nuts were removed."

DuValya smiled. "You get one for quick thinking, but that's about it. This isn't something that's on exams, but it happened to me once. Very embarrassing. I did just what you suggested. I even carry a hex socket." She pulled the socket wrench from her thigh pouch. "I suggest you get one. Not for this, though. If you have any gravity, the assembly will fall straight down on the converter. If you don't, it masses too much to move quickly and has a tendency to slide aft under pressure, where it will crimp or slice the supercon cables."

Trystin winced.

"The best thing to do is call for overhaul, because any ship where the hatches are jamming is a mess. Of course, you can't do that in real life. So, what do you do?"

Trystin waited.

"You leave it alone and use your handy hex socket to undo the vent-duct access cover here. It comes out right between the translation engine and the converter for the accumulators." She pointed to a plate on the deck forward of the access hatch. "Then you slice through the duct tubing—it's just plastic—and remove the access cover from the back on the other side. An old tech showed me that." She paused. "Go ahead, Lieutenant."

Trystin slid the access plate back and down into the grooves, then pulled himself down into the space below. The BCT-10 felt tired, even more tired than the worn simulators. Tired, and bigger, more real. The odor of heated and cooled plastic, of ozone cooked into walls and equipment, and the faintest odor of once-hot machinery and oil seeped into his nostrils. Although the main systems had virtually no moving parts, lots of the subsidiary systems did, like heating and ventilation, or the loaders for the single torp tube.

Trystin glanced around the power center, then began by inspecting the supercon lines, especially noting the line from the accumulator was dust-free.

The commander said nothing, just watched as he methodically went through all the steps of the internal preflight beginning with the aft power section and heading forward until they reached the cockpit.

"Go ahead. Strap in." Commander duValya stood beside the noncom's couch, rigged in the training corvettes to combine both override controls and technical boards.

Trystin didn't see how the instructors managed the instructing, the overseeing, and the tech inputs. He'd been having enough trouble just piloting a simulator, and now he had to do it for real.

As Trystin strapped into the pilot's seat, the commander pulled out a data cube. "This is a typical mission cube, with all the information you'll need. It's the same information that you found in the simulator system, and the displays are the same, but, obviously, corvettes can't be hardwired into the simulator training bay.

"Now the one thing we don't do until your last training flight is to have you do a real translation. There's nothing special about translation, except the setup, and if we did many translations in training, we'd never get you trained, not without taking three times as long in elapsed Chevel time.

"In the real world, you may get a mission cube days in advance and have time to study it, or you may get it just before you strap in. We assume the worst—that you'll never get time." She handed him the cube. "You have fifteen minutes before separation."

Trystin slipped the cube into the reader, fumbling a bit in the nearly null-gee of the corvette and wishing his guts were a little more settled.

Then he went through the power-up sequence, step by step, relaxing when the half-gee of ship norm hit and his stomach settled.

After that, he studied the cube . . . and managed not to groan. In order to save fuel and extend the fusactor's range, for the entire mission, ship gee was to be at point two gees. He had to take the corvette to the inner Oort belt and find an abandoned rev hulk. The hulk was real, probably placed there for training purposes.

As he studied and began setting up the board and the computations, the commander strapped into the noncom seat. Unlike the ancient aircraft or ships or modern flitters, it made no difference where the commander sat, not since all navigation and observation data were relayed from the sensors and through the ship net.

"Ready, Lieutenant?"

"Ready, ser."

"Then let's get out of here."

"Beta Control, this is Hard Way ten. Requesting clearance for separation." Trystin called up the docking module into his mental screen, waiting for clearance to demagnetize the last holdtights.

"Hard Way ten, cleared for separation upon submission of mission profile."

Trystin grimaced. At least control was giving him a polite reminder. He scrambled through the profile assembly and zapped the profile through the net. "Control, this is Hard Way ten. Mission profile is filed with commnet, key Beta Charlie one zero three one four."

"Hard Way ten, cleared for separation this time."

Trystin felt like wiping his forehead, but didn't, instead demagnetizing the holdtights, and pulsing the orientation jets to separate the corvette from the docking cradle.

The nav signals poured into the representational screen before him and into the one in his head, creating a doubled image, before he scanned the power flow and the accumulators. Recalling Commander Folsom's advice, he let the fusactor output build rather than pumping power from the accumulators.

Through the direct-feeds, he could feel the BCT-10 lifting/floating/separating from Chevel Beta. He could also feel the dampness of his shipsuit, and he had barely begun.

26

 "Why do we have to do another one of these?" As they walked toward the large lecture room, Jonnie Schicchi turned toward Trystin. "You're on top of things. Do you know?"

"They've scheduled four of these 'Cultural Ethics and Values' seminars. We've only had two so far," Trystin said, hoping that there weren't too many more handouts. He barely finished reading the last set, struggling through the selected excerpts from the *Book of Toren*.

"Both were boring," added Suzuki Yamidori, brushing short heavy hair back off her forehead, "mandatory or not."

Ahead of them Major Tekanawe stepped through the lecture-room doorway.

"Even the major has been at every one," added Schicchi. "It must be even more boring for her."

"She never lets it show," observed Suzuki.

"She doesn't let much show," Trystin said.

The three took the remaining chairs in the second row and waited. Trystin rubbed his nose, trying not to sneeze. His nose kept itching, reacting to something in the air, or the fine dust that even the most effective filters couldn't remove from a closed recycling system. The dust was worse in the lecture rooms, or maybe it just felt worse there.

At exactly 1030, a white-haired man, stocky but apparently solid, walked into the room and stopped in the open space before the dozen chairs. He wore a black tunic and trousers, without rank insignia or decorations. "Good morning. I'm Peter Warlock." He glanced around the lecture room at the dozen or so officers with an amused smile that quickly faded. "Although the seminar is on Cultural Ethics and Values, and even though you have already had two sessions, I'd like to start with my reasons why these seminars are necessary. There are two great commandments in warfare. The first and greatest commandment is to know thyself, and the second is like unto it. Know thine enemy." Warlock laughed easily. "I apologize for the antique rhetoric. Attribute it to my own antiquity. In these few seminars we have been trying to deal with the second great commandment—knowing the enemy. In the past, all too often people have fought wars through ignorance, through creating simplified stereotypes of their enemies, or even, in some twentieth- and twenty-first century—

old-style calendar—conflicts, becoming so involved with trying to understand the enemy that they lost the motivation to fight."

Trystin tried to stifle a yawn. Like the others, this seminar promised to be long, and interesting as some of the material was, he was so tired that if he sat in a classroom too long he wanted to sleep.

"Too little understanding or too much ill-founded sympathy—it doesn't matter which—lead to the same problem, and that is reduced motivation and mechanical performance of arduous duties. One sure result of mechanical performance is death." Warlock paused.

"Now, as an ancient and now-obscure author said, 'It is far easier to mourn the dead than to protect the living.' What Levinson meant by this goes beyond the significance of the mere words . . ."

Suzuki looked at Schicchi and rolled her eyes.

". . . it's a lot easier to say I'm sorry that a comrade died or a ship got totaled than to roll up your sleeves and work at understanding what makes the revs tick."

"Who's he to say?" whispered Schicchi.

The amused smile returned even as Warlock continued to speak.

". . . why do the revs let themselves be sent on their so-called military missions? To be crowded into asteroid ships in cold storage for decades? Why did they pick the Coalition as the target for their so-called missions? In our terms, it doesn't make sense. But what about their terms? Why do they have virtually no crime on their home planets? And few police officers? A value system exists because it works. How does the Revenant system work? How does it control behavior? Whether you approve or not, you need to understand." Warlock's cold black eyes raked across the junior officers, and Trystin felt like shivering, without knowing exactly why. Did he really want to understand? Maybe it was better to adopt Quentar's philosophy that the only safe rev was a dead rev. Then . . . Quentar was dead. Trystin bit the inside of his cheek to try to remain alert.

Beside him, Schicchi shifted his weight and yawned.

27

 "All right. I want you to put the ship behind that rock—the nickel-iron one. Set it up so that you're shielded from EDI detection from two six zero to zero eight zero off the outbound solar prime." Subcommander Folsom coughed, then added, "Then cut all thrust and attitude adjustments and shut down. The ship should stay in the envelope."

That left only a ten-degree latitude on each side of the too-small asteroid, and Trystin had to put the corvette behind the asteroid so it stayed, without constant course or attitude adjustments. After nearly six months of practice runs through the Chevel system, that sort of accuracy was supposed to be the norm, but on a full check-ride it was usually harder.

Trystin studied the asteroid—not much bigger than the BCT-15. Of course, that was the idea—to see how precise his piloting really was. Then he calculated the angles off the sides of the irregular rock.

For the training corvette to be shielded, according to the commander's specs, he'd have to bring it within four meters, sideways. And he'd have to do it gently, because too much thrust from attitude jets would either push the small asteroid away from the ship or result in a collision.

Trystin frowned, then nodded to himself, slowly feeding power to the thrusters and edging the ship around so that it lay barely "behind" the asteroid's orbit, not that anything but the most sensitive detectors would have shown such motion so far from the sun. Then he edged the corvette forward.

The detectors showed an eight-meter separation as the nose crept past the metallic mass. Trystin gave the outboard jets a puff, the tiniest of pulses, forcing himself to wait for a moment, then followed that with a quick decel pulse, so tiny that the instruments barely showed it.

Seven meters of separation . . . six . . . five . . .

Another millisecond pulse.

Five . . . four and a half . . .

Trystin waited, checking his fore and aft clearances, but the ship seemed stationary behind the asteroid.

. . . four and a third . . .

Trystin decided against any further attempts, although he continued to check the separation, holding at a shade over four meters. The perspiration oozed across his forehead.

"We're shielded, ser."

"We are?"

"Yes, ser."

Trystin could sense the commander's presence on the net, but he just sat and waited . . . and waited . . . and sweated . . . and waited . . .

. . . and waited.

"All right, Lieutenant. We could sit here for days, and we wouldn't move, it looks like. But I don't like that much nickel-iron that close. So pull us off to a more comfortable distance."

Again, checking the separation, Trystin eased the corvette to a position a good two hundred meters from the asteroid and checked the sensors. Nothing else registered.

Trystin wiped his forehead and waited.

Beep!

He pulled up the warning, tracking it to the EDI and then the representational screen. A series of dashed lines appeared on the representational screen, confirmed by the EDI, but the dashes were spaced far differently from anything he'd seen and bore a reddish overlay.

"Incoming ship, ser. I can't identify the type."

A moment passed.

"That's a Farhkan, one of their fast couriers, I'd guess," the subcommander explained. "You haven't seen that track before?"

"No, ser."

"We see them now and again. They all look something like that." Folsom paused. "Don't mess with them. Rumor has it that they once just lifted a whole ship of Revenant high-muckety-mucks, examined them within a gram of their lives and let them go—after fusing all their torps."

"Why?"

"I don't know, Lieutenant, and I'd recommend that you never get in a position to find out." The commander cleared his throat. "Now, an Ursinian track, since we're on the subject of alien EDI patterns—that looks more like a series of ovals, and they're very slow compared to the Farhkans."

"The Farhkan track has almost a red overlay," Trystin commented. "What about the Ursinians?" Trystin knew next to nothing about Ursinians except that they came from a sector even farther from Galactic Center than old Earth and that they resembled a cross between intelligent cats and small bears.

"You're a sensitive? That's interesting . . . well, I can't see it, but I've been told that an Ursinian EDI track holds a shade of maroon. Have you seen a real revvie track?"

"No, ser. Just through perimeter sensors."

"Supposedly, the revvie tracks shade to the blue, if you can see it. The Hyndji tracks are green, but fainter than ours, and Argenti tracks shade to the silver. The shades are a result of the harmonics in the drive tuning scales we use. It's a maintenance thing." Folsom cleared his throat. "Now, we're going to do a short recon run." He stretched his hand toward Trystin. "Here's another cube."

Trystin popped out the previous cube, the one that had the data for the outbound flight, stored it in the recessed rack, and slipped the new cube into the reader. The data poured through the net, and he had to frown because the recon run wasn't through the Chevel system, with a simulated translation, but through the Kaisar system. Kaisar wasn't inhabited, not by any life-form detected by man, not without water planets and nothing but hunks of molten rock or gas giants.

That meant a real translation.

He continued to scan the profile. "Do you want me to send a revised profile to Chevel Control?"

"It might be nice, just in case we run into trouble."

Trystin flushed, but compiled the profile, and zapped it out on ED standing wave.

Then he checked the ambient dust density—a shade over point four—before adding thrust outbound. If the attenuation remained standard, they would be clear of the fringe within ten minutes.

As they moved outward, he checked the screens for other debris—water comets, dark asteroids, but the screens remained blank. He studied the Kaisar profile, but it seemed straightforward enough—a high-speed pass by the outer gas giant with a full-scan sweep, and then a return and translation home. As Trystin began the translation power-up, he wondered what else the commander had in mind.

As the power built, he ran through the mission profile.

"Are you set up for translation, Lieutenant?"

"Yes, ser."

"Then translate. This is for real. Translate us to the outer Oort range of Kaisar."

Trystin punched the translation stud and pulsed the initiation key through the net. Translation was about the only maneuver that took both physical action and neural command. In an emergency, the stud would work alone, but only if the internal net were off-line.

Darkness became light; noise became silence; and order flipped to chaos as the ship turned itself inside out. So did the ship's systems, and all the data streamed through Trystin inside out, meaningless gibberish, yet with the hint of something . . . something beyond chaos.

Thud!

The sensors showed no overt change. The temperature outside the corvette was still only a handful of degrees above absolute zero. No stellar bodies registered within light-hours. But the EDI screen was blank, and the representational screen showed a new solar system.

Trystin accessed the temporal comparators, then the representational comparison system, but the comparators registered first. "System matches Kaisar profile."

He adjusted the thrusters and eased the corvette on the course line toward Wilhelm, the outer gas giant, letting the acceleration build, bleeding off the artificial gravity and feeding the saved power into the acceleration.

Shortly, the temporal compensators clicked in.

"Translation error was five hours and twenty-four minutes."

"Not too bad."

Trystin continued to scan the screens as the corvette swept in-system, noting that the temporal comparators began to jump as actual velocity entered the time-distortion curve.

He looked back to the tech seat, where Subcommander Folsom sat, eyes closed, apparently dozing. Trystin shook his head, then almost laughed. Why not? There wasn't much the commander could do, and he probably had his implant connected to the out-sensors and a dozen other warning inputs.

Trystin just wished he dared to take things that easily. He did take a long swallow from the Sustain bottle in the holder by his knee.

In time, he began to program the data sweeps of the big gas giant—Wilhelm. Why would anyone name a gas giant Wilhelm?

He took another swallow of Sustain and rubbed his forehead. Still a good standard hour on the corvette before they began the sweep. He didn't even try to figure the out-of-envelope elapsed time.

Eventually, Wilhelm appeared large in not only the representational screens but in every other way.

The full-scan information poured through the sensors, leaving Trystin inundated with data on everything—just beginning with temperatures, natural EDI, magnetic fields. . . . And all the data were not just energy bits inscribed and recorded in the ship's data banks, but sensation and more sensation, to the point that Trystin's head ached. Beyond the standard, there was . . . something. . . .

With another gulp of Sustain and a deep breath, he forced his mind through the data. Feeling like he was mentally wading through a mass of numbers that sliced at him, he forced his concentration back toward the anomaly, the peaked and pulsed energy source. He frowned.

"Commander, there's what seems to be a locator beacon there."

"Where?"

"Best I can make out, north latitude about thirty degrees, about eighty apparent on scan four."

"Put it on my screen three."

Trystin obliged.

"It is a locator beacon, and it's what you were supposed to find. Take us home." Folsom closed his eyes and leaned back in the tech/instructor couch again.

Trystin adjusted the course toward the nearest low-dust, low-ecliptic translation point. Nothing great, nothing spectacular—just find a locator beacon without being told. What if he hadn't? Would he have found himself back on the Maran perimeter line? Or driving transports or in-system solar sails?

From the rear seat came the soft sound of snoring.

Trystin watched the temporal envelopes curve up, wondering how much time they were jumping, but feeling too tired to really care. Seldom did the short missions around Chevel Beta involve time distortion beyond an hour or so.

Less than a subjective hour later, Trystin punched the translation stud for the second time and pulsed the initiation key through the net. Darkness again became light; noise became silence, and order flipped to chaos as the ship turned itself inside out. So did the ship's systems, and all the data streamed through Trystin once more, still with the hint of something beyond chaos.

Thud!

The sensors showed no change. The temperature outside the corvette continued to register a handful of degrees above absolute zero, and no stellar bodies registered within light-hours. The EDI screen was alive, mainly with the emissions of training corvettes.

Trystin again accessed the temporal comparators and the representational comparison system, and the system comparison registered first. "System matches Chevel profile."

"Good. Nice to know we got where we were supposed to."

Shortly, the temporal comparators clicked in.

"Translation error was three hours and fifty minutes. Total error of nine hours and fourteen minutes. Time-envelope dilation in the Kaisar system was eleven hours."

"So . . . this one flight jumped us forward in time, so to speak, a little more than a standard day. And the error was minimal. That's why we use Kaisar. Do you see why we don't do translations as a matter of course in training?"

"Yes, ser."

"What's the power flow on the fusactor? Fuel reserves?"

"Running eighty percent. Reserves are down to ten hours objective."

"Poor bucket's ready for overhaul." Folsom sighed. "Aren't we all, sooner or later. Don't answer that. It's not a question."

Trystin moistened his lips and kept watching the screens, cross-checking them with the implant data-feed. Was this really his last training flight? Had he made it? Or was he so bad that he was done—headed back to perimeter duty somewhere?

He hadn't done anything wrong, not that he knew. Finally, he toggled the comm band. "Beta Control, this is Hard Way one five. Request cradle assignment."

"Hard Way one five, interrogative status."

"Control, one five, status is green."

"Tell them green beta," suggested the subcommander.

"Control, this is one five. Status is green beta. Green beta."

"Understand green beta."

"That's affirmative."

"Your cradle assignment is delta four."

"Understand delta four."

"Stet, one five."

"Green beta," added Folsom conversationally, "means all right for short hops around the base. Fusactor output dropped off almost fifteen percent with the last translation, and you had it set up right, with optimal dust density on both ends. But I wouldn't want to take her out on another translation."

"Does that kind of drop-off happen often, or just before trouble?" asked Trystin.

"Nine times out of ten, it's before trouble, but not always. That's like everything else in this line of work. Nothing's absolute, and you have to go with the odds. The only thing that's absolute is death, and not even that, if you believe the revs." Folsom stretched again. "It's all yours until we're cradled. Try not to crash into anything." He grinned, then leaned back and closed his eyes.

Of course, Trystin realized, he scarcely needed his eyes with his implant, not for monitoring the ship. Trystin kept on the net and the screens, occasionally wiping his forehead, making tiny corrections and easing the corvette toward Chevel Beta.

"Beta Control, this is Hard Way one five. Approaching cradles this time."

"Stet, one five. We have you. Cleared to delta four this time."

"Stet, Control."

Trystin dropped the closure rate to meters per second, then meters per minute, finally easing the corvette into the apparently frail docking cradle. By the time he shut down the thrusters and attitude jets, his forehead and shipsuit were damp, for the first time in almost a dozen flights.

"Beta Control, Hard Way one five is cradled. Shutting down this time."

"Stet, one five. Congratulations."

Congratulations? Trystin wiped his forehead, and magnetized the holdfasts, then began the shutdown procedures.

"We're cradled, Commander."

"Soft cradle. Nice touch."

"Thank you." Trystin continued methodically through the shutdown, ignoring the twisting in his guts when he flicked off the artificial gravity.

"By the way, what did you think of Marshal Warlock's talks on ethics?" Commander Folsom asked as he stood.

Trystin gathered up the mission data cubes and handed them back to the commander, trying not to swallow too hard. The stocky man had been Marshal Warlock, the hero of the Safryan Standoff?

"He doesn't like to announce himself, but he insists on giving some of the ethics lectures. What did you think?"

"Well . . . I understood the theory behind what he was saying, and I've read all the handouts." Trystin shook his head. "I keep having trouble understanding how intelligent people can swallow such crap about self-declared prophets. I mean, I know they do, but I can't make the connection between that kind of self-delusion and how understanding it makes us better pilots. Or whether it matters when you've got to stop a troid ship or even a tank assault on the Maran perimeter line."

"In short, you thought it was useless fertilizer?" Commander Folsom smiled.

"I didn't say that," Trystin said quietly, holding back a surge of anger. After all, he was one of the few who had actually read and studied the materials. "I just don't know how to apply it."

"Well, young fellow, if you're a top pilot, you've got a long career ahead of you. You might end up on the Planning Staff. Or as a perimeter commander. Or in Intelligence. You might even end up being an agent—don't look at me like that. You look like a lot of revs, and it's a lot easier to take someone with the right genes than to rebuild people who don't have them. And most Intelligence agents are former pilots, you know."

That was something Trystin didn't know, and he swallowed.

"If that happens, what Marshal Warlock said might come in handy," continued the commander. "Then it might not. You might die young." Folsom paused. "You ever find out a way to detect a stressed accumulator?"

"Ser?" Trystin wondered what stressed accumulators had to do with ethics.

"A stressed accumulator? I think we discussed this, didn't we?"

"Oh, yes, ser." Trystin cleared his throat. "I couldn't find any one foolproof way, but there are a couple of things I did find out. One was a check of the average system dust densities encountered. I didn't know this, but the maintenance system holds the records of all ambient conditions over the last ten missions. Ships with more than five missions out of ten with a dust density over point four five show a thirty-percent greater rate of accumulator problems."

Folsom nodded. "Go on."

"Also, accumulator problems occur more often on ships with frequent short-jump translations. The only physical thing I could track down is that some of the techs say that if you start getting dust on the supercon line, you'll have problems." Trystin shrugged.

"Not bad," admitted Folsom. "You spent a lot of time tracking down information on one subsystem of your ship. You're going to be spending a career chasing and being chased by revs. Maybe a little more work on understanding the information you've picked up on the revs would be helpful in keeping your posterior intact." Folsom unstrapped from the rear seat. "You know, Marshal Warlock was one of the few survivors of the first wave at Safrya. He's one of the few to make a dozen successful recon runs through the Jerush and Orum systems. He's also one of the few experts on rev ethics and culture." Folsom paused. "Anyway, Lieutenant, it was a good run, and you should be pleased. You're basically a good pilot, and you might get to be really good someday."

Folsom cracked the hatch to the station lock. "Take what's left of whatever day today is off, and tomorrow go collect your orders—and your wings—in personnel. I do have to finish the record-keeping and data entries." Then he grinned. "The techs were right about the dust on the line, even if the engineers deny it."

Trystin began to unstrap. Then he gathered his gear and armor, not shaking his head until the commander was out of the lock and out of sight.

He was a pilot officer . . . after nearly two years. Why didn't he feel like one?

28

 As he waited for the shuttle to the orbit station at Chevel Alpha, Trystin glanced at the orders, the top hard copy already smudged from his continual scanning, and then down at the antique wings on his tunic above his name. He still couldn't quite believe they were there. One thing that had helped was the clear increase in his pay, although the notation that went with the itemization was somewhat sobering—"extra hazard pay." Of course, it would swell his Pilot's Trust translation account. He shook his head and looked back at the hard copy of his orders.

"... on or about 15 quint 791 ... report to Medical Center, Cambria, for Farhkan f/up study. ... Upon completion of home leave, no later than 30 quint, report Perdya orbit station and wait for arrival of *U.C.S. Willis* and assignment as pilot officer. ... Report Service commander orbit station for temporary duties as necessary. ..."

In short, first he had to have another physical, right after his flight-training detachment physical, and he hadn't even gotten a corvette, but second officer on a light cruiser. It could have been worse. He could have been assigned as second officer on a troop carrier or a cargo bus. And while he was waiting for his ship to arrive, he'd be assigned every grunge duty the orbit-station commander had

He folded the orders and slipped them into the thin case next to the message from his father, asking Trystin, when his training was complete, to let them know if he would be getting home leave and when. Elsin had added a cryptic phrase about not needing to worry, and that made Trystin worry. Why did people always say not to worry? Still, he had sent the message, wondering if it would get there before or after he did. With translation errors, one never could be sure, although his actual detachment had taken more than a week of hurrying and waiting, including his detachment physical and implant calibration.

At his feet were three bags, the two he'd brought and the third with his armor and associated pilot gear. He glanced at the status board, but there was no status information on the shuttle yet.

While he'd heard of many Coalition ships, the *Willis* hadn't been one of them. So he'd looked up the name. Kimberly Willis had been a corvette force leader in the Harmony raid and almost single-handedly responsible for destruction of the troid battlecruiser *Mahmet*. According to some battle analysts, the destruction of the *Mahmet* had ensured the success of the Coalition forces—if success meant less than twenty-five percent of the Coalition ships returned and that none of the revvie ships had survived.

Trystin wasn't sure he would have been able to translate himself into an enemy troid—not at all.

"Where are you headed?" Ulteena Freyer walked across the shuttle bay toward him.

Trystin still admired her carriage and mind, even as he steeled himself without knowing why. "Perdya. How about you?"

"Arkadya, but I meant your assignment."

"Oh, the *Willis*. Light cruiser. What about you?"

"Chief everything on the *Yamamoto*—corvette—not that I'd get anything else." She glanced up at the status board, where glowing letters finally indicated that the shuttle for Chevel Alpha—more accurately, the main orbit station off the planet itself—would be arriving in ten standard minutes.

"They didn't have any choice?"

"It's simple enough. I'm a major, a very junior major, but a major. You're a lieutenant. Even if you're a moderately senior first lieutenant, they can put you anywhere, and almost any pilot will outrank you. No problem."

Trystin understood. "This way, if you survive, you get a bigger ship as CO on the next tour."

"You've got it."

Trystin frowned.

"Why the frown?"

"I was thinking about Major Tekanawe."

"She'll make a wonderful transport pilot—good and stolid."

"If she survives corvettes."

Ulteena's laugh was short and harsh. "I'll bet she got perimeter patrols in the Helconya system."

"That seems . . ." He frowned again. "I think she did. How did you know?"

"I didn't. She's very solid, without much imagination, and those types of pilots are hard to find. People with quick thought, quick reflexes, and the willingness to leave everything behind usually hack the system rather than follow the program to the last line of code—but transport pilots need to follow their orders to the last byte. To follow a schedule." Ulteena laughed easily. "How would you do at that?"

Trystin laughed, too.

"You see what I mean? Do you really want to be a transport pilot? Or on border patrols off Helconya?"

"No."

"I didn't think so." Ulteena glanced over her shoulder. "Here comes Ardyth. I'll see you later. Do take care of yourself, Trystin." She smiled warmly and turned.

Trystin looked at Ardyth, a large and stolid lieutenant, also with pilot's wings above her name. The two pilots walked toward another officer—male—at the end of the waiting area, but Ulteena turned and gave him a last warm smile.

Trystin returned the smile, trying to keep a puzzled look

off his face. He was finding too many unanswered questions, including the one called Ulteena Freyer. He pursed his lips. One minute she was warm, the next formal. Yet she was the type that never did anything without a reason.

Finally, answerless, he hoisted his bags.

29

Trystin paused at the first turn in the walk, where the stone-walled bed still held the purple-flowered sage—sage his father insisted had a pure genetic line to old Earth. He set down the three bags. Bending over, he inhaled, trying to pick up the fresh scent. Smelling the sage was so easy when he crushed the dried leaves, but more difficult with the growing plant.

Springtime had almost left, and the late-afternoon heat that heralded summer oozed in over the garden walls, not that summer was all that hot in Cambria. Why did he always seem to come home in the spring? Coincidence?

He straightened and looked at the stones of the bedding wall that held the sage. He remembered building the wall—chipping and fitting the stones so they would hold without mortar and with no more than the width of a heavy knife blade between any edge. All that as punishment for swinging at Salya because she'd teased him about—who had it been—Patrice?

What had ever happened to Patrice? The last he'd heard, she'd married another Service officer, and they'd been shipped to Arkadya. Arkadya—that was where Ulteena Freyer was headed. Ulteena must have been from a tech family, because Arkadya wasn't open for colonization—at least it hadn't been the last time he'd checked.

Trystin bent down again. The blue-shot gray stones of the wall seemed unchanged, still rough in places, despite the fifteen years that had passed since he'd built it. Then, fifteen years wasn't anything to a stone. Or a translation pilot, his mind added. He pushed away the thought and concentrated on the wall. In some places the gaps had been a bit wider than the back of the replica knife his father had used as a gauge, but not much, and Elsin had just smiled and said, "They're close enough. You'll remember, and that's additional punishment enough."

At the time, Trystin had just been relieved. Now . . . he looked at the gaps in the stones, not quite narrow enough, and laughed. But he understood what his father had meant, especially as he stood and wanted to reset the stones. He laughed again before picking up the three heavy kit bags and heading up through the boxwood maze toward the low stone and wood house set amid the gardens. That the house had greater depths and vistas was never apparent, except from within.

Trystin wondered if that reflected all of the Desolls, or if such an image were merely vanity. And what lay in his depths?

He paused again when he came to the bonsai cedar—the same and yet not the same. He could come home, and the cedar was always the same and not the same. Another image? Shaking his head, he walked up the stone-paved path quickly, enjoying the scent of the pines and the heavy but distant odor of the early roses. Was he stalling in the garden, enjoying the plants, because he feared the message beneath the message his father had sent?

After a quick glance back across the gardens, Trystin rapped on the door and waited. He rapped again.

The oak door opened, and a blond woman, wearing the Service uniform, smiled at him.

"Salya! You're the reason Dad sent that message—and I was so worried."

"Silly!" Salya hugged him even before he got inside, and his bags scattered across the stones as he hugged his sister back. Then she stood back and looked at the dress green Service uniform. "You really made it—Pilot Officer Desoll."

"I always said he would," observed Elsin from the foyer.

Trystin mock-glared. "You had me worried with that message."

"You had us all worried with pilot training," pointed out Salya.

"Let the man get inside," suggested Nynca. "You've scattered everything he owns all over the front porch."

Trystin gathered up his shoulder bag and flight bag, and Salya hoisted the third bag and followed him down to the lower bedroom, the one off the office.

"I can't believe you're here," he said to her, setting the bags by the closet door.

"I can't believe you're here." Her dark blue eyes studied him for a moment. "My brother. Not even my little brother anymore."

"I'll still be your kid brother."

"Thanks."

They looked at each other for a long moment.

"I think Mother's got some goodies waiting. They've been waiting for a couple of days." Salya started out the door and up the half-flight of stairs.

Trystin's eyes lingered on the room, the single bed, the slightly dusty wooden model of the antique corvette hanging above the desk where his school console had been. Finally, he shook his head and followed his sister.

By the time they reached the great room, Nynca had a tray of miniature cakes on the table, with steaming pots of both green tea and greyer tea on the old carved wooden trivets.

"It looks good," Trystin observed.

"It had better. Your mother spent most of her endday baking and filling and dicing and slicing."

"I did help a bit," added Salya.

"You ate as much as you fixed." Nynca's eyes twinkled.

"I imagine she was as deprived as I was," Trystin said, lifting the pot of greyer tea and filling the heavy green mug. "I can't imagine that food on Helconya station compares to what comes from your kitchen." He turned to Salya. "Green or greyer?"

"Green."

As he filled his sister's mug, he looked to his father. "Do you want any?"

"The greyer."

After filling his father's and sister's mugs, Trystin just poured the green tea for his mother. She'd never liked greyer tea, calling it perfumed water. "There."

"He still pours his tea first, but now he's learned to pour everyone else's before he gulps his down." Salya grinned.

"I love you, too."

As the four settled into the captain's chairs around the light wood of the game table, Elsin looked toward Trystin. "How does it feel to be a certified pilot?"

Trystin finished munching the chocolate nut cake and sipped his tea, holding up a hand.

"Let him have something to eat, dear. It's not as though he'll be disappearing tomorrow."

"With the Service, you never know." Salya glanced toward the half-open slider to the middle garden, her eyes taking in the fast-moving clouds beyond the trees.

"In some ways, it's not much different at all, except that you look back and realize you're doing things you couldn't have imagined before."

"Such as?"

"Nestling two hundred tonnes of plastic, metal, and composite up beside a nickel-iron asteroid and floating there in darkness a few degrees above absolute zero." Trystin took another sip of the tea and held the cup under his nose, letting the steam circle his face, closing his eyes for a moment.

Salya lifted a lemon cream cake. "These are good."

"Don't eat too many," said Elsin. "I do have a special dinner."

"We'll eat late. We always do."

Elsin rose quietly and picked up both the dark gray teapot and the green one, carrying them back into the kitchen. "I can see we'll need more tea."

"How are your projects going?" Trystin sipped of the greyer tea.

"We're getting there." Salya paused and sipped her tea. "The airspores are beginning to impact the upper troposphere, except you really can't call it that, and we're getting some cooling from water comets, although right now what's left after transit just vaporizes. Still, that overloads the absorptive capability of the surface, and the high-temperature bugs we seeded down on the rocks are beginning to release free oxygen and reduce the CO levels. . . ."

"When will we be able to live there?"

"This one's long-term, really long-term. Say eight hundred years, if we're lucky."

Nynca shook her head.

"It's not so bad," Salya said. "For one thing Helconya's effectively a sterile planet. That means whatever we do doesn't get tied up in unforeseen ecological knots. And then there are the ethical concerns. . . ."

Trystin nodded. "You mean the old arguments about whether a planoformed place would have developed intelligent life in time?"

"Right." Salya reached for another lemon cake, then put her hand back in her lap and lifted her mug with the other.

"There." The mostly silver-haired man set both teapots back on their trivets. "I turned down dinner a bit." He settled back into his chair. "You mean I won't be called upon to develop integrated biosystems there?"

"Not in this lifetime, Father. Not unless you're an immortal and have been keeping it from us."

Elsin ran a hand over his thin hair. "Does this look like an immortal's hair?"

Both Salya and Trystin chuckled.

"Where are you going?" Nynca looked at Trystin.

"I don't know." Trystin's hands flailed for a moment. "I've been assigned to a light cruiser—the *Willis*—and I'm supposed to report to Perdya orbit station after leave—no later than the thirtieth of the month."

"You've got three weeks," observed Elsin.

"I also have a physical at the main medical center on the fifteenth, but that should only take a half-day."

"Don't they give you detachment physicals?" Salya frowned.

"I volunteered for a follow-up study on young officers." Trystin offered a grin. "There was a pay bonus involved."

"Trust Trystin to follow the easy credits." Salya shook her head.

"It's not that bad. Just an additional physical every two years or so with a follow-up interview. Besides, Dad said I'd need all those credits if I were to become a pilot officer."

"The psychology people." Salya snorted. "I told them, 'No, thank you.' I didn't want any of their notes in my files, not even for their money. Just be careful what you tell them."

Trystin thought about his struggles with the ethical issues of theft. "I've tried to be careful." He picked up another cake.

"They're sneaky." Salya looked at the tray, then finally took another lemon square. "This is the last one for me."

"Who's counting?" Trystin grinned at his sister. "Feeling guilty? Or worried that someone might see a bulge in the midsection?" He watched Salya blush. She'd always blushed easily.

"She doesn't need to worry," said Nynca.

"What about this major?" asked Trystin. "Mom and Dad had mentioned—"

"Oh, you mean Shinji? He's just a friend. He'd like it to be more."

"Shinji?" asked Nynca. "As in the legend of Shinji Takayama?"

"How did you know his last name?"

"Just a guess."

Trystin could sense the sadness his mother masked with a quick smile, although he had no idea why a mere name would cause it. "What about him?"

"He's tall, but not so tall as you. Dark hair, of course, parashinto heritage, but he does have blue eyes."

"They must be very blue," opined Nynca.

Salya blushed again.

"And he's just a friend," said Trystin with a grin.

"Trystin . . ." Salya cleared her throat and looked down at the table, then up, brushing back the short blond hair away from her face. "He's the head of the atmospheric transport section—they do the upper-atmosphere sampling, run the drones, and occasionally they provide shuttle pilots. They're not deep-space pilots, though."

"Where's he from?"

"Perdya, but he's from Kaneohe, and he went to the Service Academy." Salya turned to Trystin. "What about your romantic life?"

"It's nonexistent. Has been since I left Mara."

"I can't believe you haven't found someone—or they haven't found you."

"The only one who's found me is a major who gives me advice and grief in equal doses, with an occasional smile."

"You're intrigued, aren't you?"

Trystin frowned. "I think so. But she's also scary. Anticipates everything . . . way in advance."

"And like a typical man," laughed Salya, "you're worried about losing control."

"I doubt I'd ever have it," Trystin admitted.

"For men, that's even worse." Salya shook her head. "She probably even makes you think the deep thoughts, the ones you've always avoided. Like why you're even in the Service."

"That's unfair," Trystin protested.

"Probably, younger brother." Salya grinned. "Unfair . . . but true."

"Salya . . . I could start on how you devour men. . . ."

"I'd rather you didn't. Let's talk about your major and why you refuse to be intrigued by her."

Elsin rose. "I think dinner's ready. Bring your tea with you." He picked up both pots and carried them toward the long black table in the dining area. Nynca stood and followed him.

Trystin took a last sip from his mug and looked at Salya, who had raised her eyebrows. "It's simple enough. She'll be running a corvette somewhere, and I don't even know where the *Willis* operates. With my luck, I won't see her again until I'm old and gray."

"I have my doubts about that. I can't imagine you being old and gray. And life is never simple."

"Pilots often don't—"

"I'm sorry. I shouldn't have even hinted at it. You don't have to say it. We all know." Salya touched his arm, and he could see the dampness in the corner of her eyes. "Let's go eat."

Trystin swallowed and followed his sister.

30

 Trystin recovered his card from the surtrans reader, readjusted his beret, and stepped from the surtrans.

After crossing the covered stones of the platform, he walked up the wide stone steps to the main Service medical center on Perdya, just off radial three on the east side of Cambria. Beside the steps were stone flower boxes filled with rysya and trefils, each species about to bloom.

Once inside, he headed for the information console.

"Lieutenant Desoll, reporting for a follow-up physical."

The civilian technician at the front console nodded politely. "What kind of physical, Major?"

"The Farhkan study." He laughed politely. "And while I wish to be a major, I'm still a lieutenant."

"I see. You're one of those. Let me check. What was your name?"

"Desoll. D-E-S-O-L-L."

"Here we are. Go to the second floor, all the way to the rear on the south wing to Dr. Kynkara's office. Someone there will tell you where to go from there."

"Thank you."

"You're welcome, Major."

Trystin repressed the urge to correct her again and turned toward the wide ramp. On the way up, he passed two lieutenants, one walking stiffly with the measured gait of someone rehabbed from spine damage. Another casualty from Mara? Or somewhere else? Before Trystin got to the far end of the south wing, he reached another technician at another console.

"Ser?" The dark-haired woman looked up at him, waiting, her slightly slanted eyes skeptical.

"Lieutenant Desoll. I'm here for the Farhkan follow-up study."

"Follow me, ser." Without another word, she took off down a side corridor and around two corners until they reached four cubicles. Three had open doors. Inside each was a diagnostic console. "I'm sure you're familiar with these." She looked at him. "Your ID, ser?"

Trystin handed it over.

She swiped it through the scanner, and the console ready light winked green. Then she handed it back.

"Just disrobe to your underwear, and let the console take its measurements and samples. When the restraints loosen, you can get dressed. Go to gamma three—that's at the end of the corridor—and take a seat outside Dr. Kynkara's office. They'll find you there."

"Thank you." Trystin nodded, but the technician was gone. He disrobed, winced as the cold console enfolded him, and waited as the equipment measured and probed. When he could, he dressed and walked to the end of the corridor, where four plastic chairs lined the wall outside a closed door with the name Kynkara on it.

Somehow, the directions he'd received in the lobby didn't match where the doctor's office was, but he'd managed. He sat in the gray plastic chair and waited . . . and waited . . . and stood and walked around . . . and waited.

According to his implant, he waited nearly an hour before the doctor, a gray-haired woman, arrived with a Farhkan in tow. This Farhkan—as had the first one he had met—wore shimmering gray fatigues. Red eyes were set in the iron-gray hair of the square face, with longer and darker hair covering the top of the skull. Was this one the same, or did they all look alike?

"Lieutenant Desoll? We apologize, but Dr. Ghere was delayed. Oh, I'm Isabel Kynkara."

"I understand." Trystin nodded, inhaling slowly and taking in the vaguely familiar odor, the mixed scents of an unfamiliar flower, a muskiness, and cleanliness. "I believe I have met Dr. Ghere once before."

"That is correct."

Again, Trystin was surprised by the feeling of the words scrolling through his mental screen.

Isabel Kynkara fiddled with the entry plate on her door, then stood back. "I'm just here to facilitate things. I'll be in the next office, the one that says 'Staff,' waiting for Major Gresham and Lieutenant Ohiri."

"Thank you." Trystin wondered why he was thanking her, but gestured for the Farhkan to enter the office.

Ghere entered without speaking, and Trystin flicked on the interior lights, although the window—overlooking the med center gardens—really supplied enough light.

As Trystin closed the door, he had the feeling of the same silence as the last time he had met with the Farhkan, but with his enhanced implant he could sense more clearly the total block on communications that settled upon the room. How did the Farhkans manage it? And why did it matter, if they only wished to talk philosophy?

Ghere settled into the chair behind the desk; Trystin took the plastic seat before it.

"You thanked the doctor because you would like to make her comfortable, even if it was a form of a lie."

"Don't you engage in such niceties?"

"Not if the niceties involve untruths. I admit to being a thief, but not a liar." A hint of amusement followed the words.

Trystin nodded, not exactly surprised that the conversation had gone back to theft. The Farhkan appeared persistent, and that bothered Trystin.

"Have you thought about theft recently, Lieutenant?"

"Not until I realized I would be speaking to you. At

least, not recently. I did think about it after our last conversation."

"What did you conclude?"

Trystin pursed his lips. "I suspect theft, in the broadest sense, must occur in all intelligent species, at least if the species is to survive."

"An interesting speculation. Perhaps . . . I would have to consider that at greater length. What about you? Are you a thief?"

Trystin did not answer. Ghere bothered him. In some ways, the doctor felt alien, in others, all too human.

"I have upset you. Why is this so?"

"You're both alien and too familiar."

"That is true. You do not like to lie, do you?"

"No," Trystin admitted.

"Do you know why you dislike lying?"

"Not really, except it feels wrong."

"So . . . you live in a society that requires theft, and you refuse to admit you are a thief. You live in a society that encourages lying and avoid it. Is not living in a society where theft is necessary but refusing to admit it not a lie? Are you not a liar?"

"I try not to be."

"Are you a thief?"

"I thought we had agreed that intelligence, by nature, requires a form of theft."

"I do not recall agreeing exactly to that concept. Are you a thief?"

"In your terms, I'm not sure what you mean by theft," Trystin said slowly.

"Let us lay that aside for a moment. There is an old saying. Force creates good."

"I don't recall that." Trystin paused, licked his lips. "Might makes right?"

"Is there a difference between good and right?"

"I'm not convinced that what people think is good is always right."

"Would you explain?"

"Many people feel that what they believe in is good. A

poor man would say that all people should be rich, but the Great Die-off showed that any world has a limit. It is right not to destroy a world's ecology—" Trystin stopped, realizing that he was uncomfortable talking about destroying ecologies when, in effect, planoforming was destroying one ecology to replace it with another—and even in his terms, that was theft.

"You are upset again."

Trystin said nothing. Anything he said would get him in deeper.

"I think that is enough, Lieutenant. I would request you think some more about theft. And about whether any good is absolute." Ghere stood.

"Of course it's not."

"Then why do you humans persist in trying to impose such absolutes on others, even using force to do so? And why do you persist in refusing to identify yourself in terms of absolutes while trying to persuade others to accept those absolutes?"

"We're human."

"Is that good?" Ghere stood.

Trystin could feel the comm screen—or whatever it was—vanish.

Ghere nodded.

Finally, Trystin turned to open the door and to get Dr. Kynkara, wanting to leave, but knowing that the questions the Farhkan raised wouldn't vanish, not for a time, if ever, and that bothered him, too.

Later, as he walked out of the medical center, he tried not to shake his head. He still didn't understand what the Farhkans wanted. Maybe he never would. They might be roughly human-looking, but that didn't mean that they thought like human beings.

They clearly wanted something. The question was what, and Trystin didn't even know where to begin to seek the answer—or whether he should, or would have the time. He had the feeling that before long surviving was going to become difficult again.

Ulteena had said something about living in the present,

and perhaps he should, at least while Salya and his parents and he were all together.

He kept walking toward the surtrans station, his thoughts swirling together.

31

 Trystin stood at the chest-high barrier, leaning forward, his arms resting on the golden logs polished smooth by craft, time, weather, and other arms. The wind whipped through his regulation-short hair, swooping up off the water and past the lookout on the edge of the Cliffs. Behind Trystin the Cliffs rose even higher, to nearly three thousand meters, but the jagged tops were lost in the clouds created by the moist air coming off the dark green waters of the Palien Sea.

Five hundred meters below the sheer drop-off, the waves crashed against the basalt walls, sending fine spray halfway up the Cliffs. In regular lines, the waves marched in and shattered themselves against the jagged rocks.

While cultivation and home-building and gardens had softened much of the land over more than eight centuries, nearly a thousand years of young and rough waters had not blunted the sharp edges of the Cliffs, although trees did poke from odd crevasses above the reach of the slightly salty sea.

"I never get tired of watching the sea." Trystin's words barely carried over the rushing of the wind and the crashing of the waves below. "It's always relaxing."

"It must be something in the blood." Salya brushed her hair, not that much longer than Trystin's, off her forehead.

"Not from Mother."

They both laughed.

"Does Shinji like the ocean?" Trystin paused. "He must, if he's from Kaneohe."

"He does talk about the time when there will be oceans on Helconya."

"That's going to be a long time."

"You have to have dreams."

Trystin nodded. "I suppose so. You're lucky to have the same ones."

"They're not quite the same," she said wryly.

"Oh. That's why he's still mostly a friend?"

"Something like that." Salya straightened. "If you want to have time before dinner to stop by the market and see if they have carnot nuts, we'd better get back to the car."

"All right." Trystin watched one more line of waves crest, white running along the tips, then break over the jagged needles at the base of the Cliffs. He straightened and turned, almost running into a Park officer, who stood in the middle of the stone walkway that led back up to the parking area. The dark-eyed officer's right hand rested on the butt of the holstered shocker.

"I see you were enjoying the view. It is rather spectacular, not something that someone sees on just any planet." The Park officer paused before continuing. "Might I ask where you are from?"

"Cambria," Trystin answered.

Salya's face blanked.

"Cambria is a rather large place these days. Almost anyone could claim to have come from there."

"Cedar Gardens, Cedar Lane, on Sundance Boulevard off Horodyski Lane. I grew up there, and my parents still live there."

"Cedar Gardens does not sound like a real address, although that would only be my humble perception."

"I'm sorry, Officer. That is the address." Trystin slowly took out his wallet and offered both his Service identification and his vehicle license to the Park officer.

"Hmmm . . . I would be most curious as to where you got these." The words of the black-haired and dark-skinned officer remained even and polite.

Trystin stared at the man, then nodded politely. "I received my first vehicle license at the constabulary on Hyroki Avenue eight years ago. The service identification was just issued on Chevel Beta last month when I got my pilot's wings. I'm on home leave."

"Your . . . friend . . . is also rather tall."

"My sister? Yes, she is. Siblings do tend to resemble each other."

The Park officer handed Trystin's license and Service ID back to him, turning to Salya. "If I might trouble you . . ."

Salya, still blank-faced, dug her Service ID from the pocket of her shorts and handed it to the officer.

"Desoll—even the same name. Well, I suppose you would have the same name if you were brother and sister." After studying the ID for a time, and comparing the holo to Salya, he handed it back. "Thank you."

"You're so welcome, Officer," Trystin said politely.

The Park officer stared at him. Trystin met the gaze, refusing to waver. Finally, the officer looked away and stepped back.

Trystin nodded again, even as he stepped up his system into high-reflex, unarmed-combat mode, his ears intent on any sound as he and Salya walked up the steps and along the walk to the parking area. There, Trystin turned back, but the Park officer stood at the top of the steps, still looking toward them.

"Your sarcasm probably wasn't such a good idea." Salya opened the door on her side of the electrocar.

"Probably not, but his whole attitude bothered me. His job is to protect the ecology, not to run around harassing people."

"You looked about ready to kill him."

"I should have gone into combat mode."

"It wouldn't have done any good," Salya pointed out. "He's the type who's convinced that anyone who is tall, blond, and blue-eyed must be a rev. Besides, then he would have tried to use the shocker, and you would have hurt him or made him lose face. Where would that have gotten you?"

"In restraints, no doubt, and out of the Service." Trystin shook his head. "But it bothers me." He shifted his weight in the small car, and checked the safety harness before pulling out of the lot.

"It bothers me too, but what can you do with people like that? You can't kill them, and nothing less will change their minds."

How was the Park service officer any different from the rev officer he'd questioned years before? Trystin was half-surprised that the thought crossed his mind. They both had fixed perceptions independent of contrary reality. His eyes checked the mirror. "They're following us, two of them in an official car," Trystin observed. "I think we'd better head straight home."

"This is really absurd. Why are they after us? You can't counterfeit a Service ID."

"It's because we look like revs, but the Service ID should have stopped that. You can't be an officer and be a rev. The screens are too deep."

"Prejudice isn't always rational."

"Great."

Trystin continued to watch the Park officers all the way into Cambria. He drove the electrocar straight into the garage, triggering the door while he was still on Cedar Lane.

After they left the garage, he stepped up to the wrought-iron railing atop the stone wall and executed a stiff para-shinto bow—twice—in the direction of the dark green official car, before turning toward the house.

"That was childish," said Salya.

"I feel childish. I've spent the last three years doing the bidding of the Service. I've been attacked, shot, wounded, and damned near lost my leg, and some silly little Park officer is convinced that I'm a rev spy—as if the revs would ever be stupid enough to send a spy who looked like I do."

"There's a lot of hatred growing."

They walked silently along the path and up toward the house.

Elsin opened the door before they reached it. "We didn't expect you back so soon."

"We were sort of chased back. Some throwback pseudosamurai decided we had to be revs. He wasn't impressed with my vehicle license or my Service ID. So they followed us home."

Elsin frowned. "That does seem odd." He stepped back, and the two walked into the foyer.

"It didn't happen when I was with Shinji the other day, and he's almost as tall as you are." Salya pursed her lips.

"I suspect Shinji is somewhat darker than I am," Trystin said wryly.

"You think it's coming to that? I hope not." Salya looked across the gardens toward Cedar Lane, but the green electrocar had disappeared.

"So do I," answered Elsin, but he frowned.

<h1 style="text-align:center">32</h1>

A juvenile heliobird whirred across the darkening garden, his wings a blur as he swooped for the nest in the corner pine. The faint whirring of insects almost drowned out the underlying static of Trystin's implant. Although he had damped down the receptivity to nil, somehow he was still aware of the background noise, even away from the Service and its systems and nets.

"Do you really understand what being a pilot means?" asked Salya.

"Probably not," Trystin answered.

"Why did you accept the offer?"

"I've always wanted to be one."

"I know." Salya's voice was low, and she leaned back on the bench. "You made models. You read books. You even bought the pilot simulator for your console and installed it in a secret drive."

"How did you know that?" Trystin looked at his sister in surprise.

"Who helped you with basic console programming? Besides, I was testing some ideas Father taught me about cracking systems."

Trystin spread his hands. "Between the two of you no system would be safe."

"Not from Father, except he's so ethical he'd never look."

"As opposed to nosy older sisters?"

Salya offered a faint grin before asking, "Is being a pilot what you thought it would be?"

"Better. I feel like I'm doing something. When I was on the line on Mara, we just waited and took what the revs handed us. I was lucky, and I made it through. A lot of perimeter officers didn't. The official line is that things are improving—some commander told me that. But things still keep getting worse. No one seems to want to act. I asked about that, and the commander who was debriefing me nearly took off my head." He paused. "It wasn't that bad, but I felt like it was. She said that a planet was a damned big place, and that we didn't have the resources."

"We don't."

"If we don't have the resources . . . we lost almost all the plains stations. Only two of us survived their minitanks."

Salya moistened her lips. "You didn't tell us about that."

"So I got a commendation. I survived, and most didn't."

"There's nothing on the news about those kinds of losses."

"I'm not surprised. Before that, when the revs wiped out five stations on the western line, I was called down for using a data pulse to find out."

Salya sighed.

Trystin turned on the bench to face her. "That doesn't surprise you, does it? Not much, anyway."

"It doesn't surprise me, Trystin. It doesn't surprise me much at all after that incident at the Cliffs. But it bothers me. What sort of people are we becoming?"

"We've always been thieves. Now, we're becoming liars as well?"

"You've done some thinking, haven't you?"

Trystin offered a short laugh. "I've had my thinking prodded."

"You still want to be a pilot?"

Trystin shrugged. "You still want to be a xenobiologist?"

"Fair enough." Salya stretched, then added, "You know . . . anytime you translate could be the last time you see Mother and Father."

"I know. That's true every time you travel between here and Helconya, and it would be true even if I stayed a perimeter officer."

"But the probability goes up with each translation, and pilots make a lot more translations."

"I've thought about it. That part wasn't easy. Father and I talked about it. He even helped me set up a trust."

"He would."

"Yeah."

"Dad was right. You do have a restless spirit."

"I still like to come home," Trystin reminded her. "And I miss the gardens."

"Not enough. Someday, you'll come home, still young, and we'll all be gone." After a moment, she added, "We'll make sure it's here for you. We all would want that."

Trystin swallowed.

"I'll miss you." Her hand touched his gently.

"I'll miss you."

They sat side by side in the growing twilight, the insects twittering, the evening coming down like a purple shade, while the heliobirds settled into the pines for the night. The heavy scent of roses dropped into the twilit garden and almost made Trystin forget the faint static of the implant—almost.

33

Trystin waited in the bay for the *Willis*, his bags stacked neatly beside him. He was glad to escape the drudgery of junior operations duty officer for Perdya station—much more than glad.

"Who are you waiting for, Lieutenant?" asked the tech standing by the lock control panel.

"The *Willis*."

"This is the place." The noncom glanced at Trystin and his bags. "She's a cruiser, not a transport."

"I know."

The tech's eyes flicked to the wings on Trystin's uniform. "New pilot officer?"

Trystin nodded, then asked, "You know anything about her?"

"CO's Major Sasaki. He's pretty senior. They say he's related to the armaments people."

"He could be. Anything's possible, but Sasaki's a pretty common name."

"You haven't met the major." The tech shook his head.

A dull thud, followed by a second thud, echoed through the station frame. Shortly, the green light flickered above the lock tube.

"Little rough," announced the tech, "like always, but she's here." His fingers danced across the lock console.

Trystin could sense the locking-system data flows through his implant, and with more time, could probably have tapped them, but there was no point in it. Instead, he waited for the clunking of the mechanical holdtights.

A row of green lights flashed across the console.

"All set. Ready, Lieutenant?"

Trystin hoisted his bags and followed the tech down the

lock tube, heavy frost on its permaplast sides. His breath steamed.

The noncom checked the seals and exterior holdtights again before pulsing the entry clearance. With a hiss, the cruiser's door slid open.

"Ah, it's you, Liendrelli." Standing in the lock was a woman with dark mahogany hair in the uniform of a senior tech, a belted stunner in place.

"Who else would it be? Everyone else goes to the other side of the station when you people dock."

The ship's tech glanced beyond Liendrelli to Trystin. "Lieutenant Desoll. Major Doniger will be pleased to see you, ser. I'm Keiko Muralto, ship's senior tech."

"Pleased to meet you, Tech Muralto."

"Keiko, please, ser." She finished checking the lock seals, and ensuring that the emergency closure lanes were free. "You can set your gear in the locker here for a while. Welcome aboard." Then she turned to Liendrelli. "We're low on organonutrient—we take the alpha class—and just about everything else."

"You cruiser types . . ."

"Don't complain, Liendrelli. The captain wants us out as soon as possible after Major Doniger's replacement shows, and since he's here . . ."

"All right, Muralto. We'll get on it."

Keiko Muralto smiled sweetly at Liendrelli.

Trystin decided he wanted the tech on his side. "You're certain putting my gear here won't be a problem?"

"Not at all. Just set it in the alcove there." She stepped back and pressed a stud. "Captain, Lieutenant Desoll is here."

"Send him forward, Keiko."

Trystin carefully stacked his gear in the space, keeping only the thin case with his orders, data cubes, and records.

"Yes, ser."

The tech gestured toward the passageway heading forward. "I'm sure you can find your way, ser. I need to pound on Liendrelli some more."

"Give me a break, Muralto," protested the station tech.

Trystin smiled and stepped through the area that functioned as a quarterdeck, half nodding at the familiar scents of plastic, ozone, Sustain, and human beings.

The forward passage was empty, and he found himself stepping through the hatch to the cruiser's cockpit, where a small officer stood, waiting.

"Lieutenant Desoll, Major." Taking into account the name and the apparent parashinto background of Major Sasaki, Trystin offered a slight bow to the Captain of the *Willis.*

"So you're the new second? You look more like a rev than most revs I've seen." Major Sasaki brushed the black hair that was on the long side of the Service-recommended length back off his forehead and offered a boyish grin that emphasized his sparkling white teeth.

"My family helped found Cambria, ser."

"I'm sure. Don't worry about it. It's what you do that counts, not how you look." Major Sasaki glanced around the cockpit. "I wanted you to meet Andrya before she left, but when she heard you were already here, she went back to get her stuff."

"I left my gear with your senior tech."

"Don't worry. Just put your stuff in the mess until Andrya clears out. She won't be that long." Major Sasaki gestured toward the *Willis*'s aft section.

"Your senior tech mentioned that the second was a major?"

"She was just promoted, and the Service doesn't like wasting two majors on the same ship these days."

Trystin noted the faintest edge to the words, but said nothing as he heard steps heading toward the cockpit.

"Here she is. Trystin, this is Andrya."

The stocky major with short and frizzy brown hair extended a hand, took Trystin's with a firm grip and shook it. "I'm Andrya Doniger." She glanced toward the commanding officer. "Don't let James here get the better of you. He's bright; he's a good tactician; he understands Service politics; and he's a second-rate pilot with first-rate connections. And yes, he's from those Sasakis." She smiled at Major Sasaki.

Trystin felt as though the ship had been dropped right out from underneath him. "It's nice to meet you. Where are you headed?"

"Me? I'm getting one of the new cruisers—the *Tozini*. Smaller than the *Willis,* but faster, more torps. Very deadly." She looked at the three bulging kit bags. "I need to be going. They're holding the *Adams* for me. I managed to pull a few strings. No sense in waiting another week for the *Morgenthal*. The station CO would have too good an idea of what to load on me. Good luck to you, Lieutenant."

With a quick nod she hoisted the bags. "It's been interesting, James. If you want to make commander, though, let him do the delicate piloting."

"If he's as good as you think . . . why not?"

Trystin swallowed a smile. What a pair! The Doniger family had been in the ecological hierarchy of the Coalition as far back as the history texts ran, and the Sasakis had evolved from using metalworking to bury nuclear wastes on old Earth into becoming the premier arms producers of the Coalition.

And now he had to take orders from Major James Sasaki.

"Let's go have something to eat." Sasaki smiled his broad and boyish smile. "They don't tell you about it, but there's a small restaurant on the lower level that has some real seafood—if you know enough to ask."

Sasaki's eyes glazed over momentarily, and Trystin could feel the net link. "Liam? The new second and I have to go stationside for a couple of hours. You've got it. Keiko's on the deck."

The major's eyes unglazed. "Liam's weapons and comm. He's a former senior tech, and he can be duty when we're docked. Otherwise, it's you when I'm not around or have to sleep. Contrary to rumor, CO's do sleep." He smiled again. "Let's go. I'm ready for some decent food."

Trystin followed the major out to the quarterdeck.

"Keiko, Trystin and I have some things to do station-side. Liam's got the duty until we get back."

"While you're gone, I'll have the lieutenant's gear put in his stateroom." Keiko smiled pleasantly. "Have a good meal, Captain."

"I'm sure we will."

"I can do that when I get back," Trystin protested.

"Don't worry about it, ser."

Trystin tried not to shake his head as he walked beside Major Sasaki back out the lock tube he had entered what seemed only moments before.

The major led him through a maze of corridors Trystin had never seen in his two weeks on the station.

The restaurant lay behind a bronze-colored plastic door panel bearing the name Le Tank. Trystin frowned, but followed Sasaki inside, to find eight small tables with real linen cloths upon them. A single table was occupied, by a woman wearing a single marshal's four-pointed star.

"Major!" A rotund woman in white bounced across the floor.

"Vivienne." Sasaki bowed. "This is my new pilot officer, Trystin Desoll. Trystin, Vivienne LeClerc. This is her domain."

"Welcome back, James." The dry voice came from the marshal at the corner table.

"Thank you, Marshal Toboru." James Sasaki bowed.

"Don't mind me. By the way, your father is looking well. I saw him last month . . . and your brother." The marshal returned her attention to the soup in the gold-trimmed white porcelain bowl before her.

Vivienne led them to the table in the corner farthest from the marshal.

"I'd like anything that's fresh from the tank," requested Major Sasaki. "And then whatever your special is."

Vivienne nodded and looked at Trystin.

"What are my choices?"

"For appetizers, the raw fresh seafood is either clams casino or octosquid today. We also have slizirki mushrooms, sautéed, and fresh greens."

"The mushrooms, please."

"The specials are soft-shelled spotted crabs or broiled young silver trout amandine."

"I'll have the crabs." The major added, "Don't worry, Trystin. This is my treat. You'll earn it later."

"Thank you," said Trystin. "I'll have the crabs also."

With a nod, Vivienne stepped back, only to return with two crystal goblets and a bottle. "The Villa Tozza is the only white right now."

Sasaki shrugged.

Trystin just watched as the woman poured half-glasses for each of them and left the bottle in the holder.

"Not bad, although I still think the Mondiabli would have been better."

Trystin sipped the wine, enjoying the slightly nutty, slightly fruity scent as much as the taste.

"You like wine, don't you?" asked Sasaki.

"When I don't have to be on duty."

"How do you know you won't be?" The major laughed and offered the boyish grin again.

"I don't, but you aren't likely to just hand the ship to me."

Vivienne set one of the gold-rimmed porcelain plates, filled with sliced white circular objects, in front of the captain, and a second, filled with steaming browned and buttery mushrooms, in front of Trystin.

"Where are you from, Trystin?" Sasaki used the silver seafood fork to pick up one of the white slices and began to chew.

"Cambria, Academy district." Trystin took a second sip of the Villa Tozza. Even the background hiss of his implant seemed muted.

"Are your family academics? That's an expensive place to live." Another swallow of the white food followed.

"Actually, my great-great-grandfather built the house and donated the land to the Academy."

"It must have been difficult, especially in the early years."

Trystin repressed the urge to strangle his superior officer. "My father worries that there's more prejudice now than there ever has been."

"How is the octosquid, Major?" asked Vivienne.

"Good. Very good. My congratulations."

"Thank you. It did take some doing. I appreciate your help."

"It wasn't much." Sasaki frowned. "The slizirkis look good. Could I have just a few?"

"Certainly. Most certainly."

While the two talked, Trystin had several bites of the slizirki mushrooms, which carried a crispness, a warmth, a tanginess, and an unidentifiable flavor.

"I take it they are good?"

"Very," answered Trystin. "How did you find this place?"

"I didn't. I helped Vivienne get started. It's good to have someplace decent to eat that's not planetside." Sasaki refilled his glass then looked back at Trystin. "I take it you come from a large family."

"No. I have one sister. She's Service, too. A senior lieutenant in charge of a biological modification section on the Helconya project."

"What about your parents?" Sasaki chewed more of the raw octosquid. "Not bad for a tank animal. Almost like the real thing."

"My mother was a ships' systems engineer. After she retired a few years ago, she got a second doctorate in music. She teaches at the university. My father's an independent integrator."

"Job-shop stuff?"

"Actually," Trystin said, "he's been designing integrated regional sewage and disposal systems for stage three planoforming projects."

"One of the big boys, then. Interesting. Quiet, longtime anglo family. Well-off, cultured, and very highly educated. Probably not many of you left."

Vivienne slipped a small plate of the slizirki mushrooms onto the table.

"Thank you." Sasaki chewed one slowly. "Very good."

Vivienne smiled, nodded, and backed away.

Trystin ate several bites more before taking another sip of wine.

"Why did you choose to go Service?"

"I always wanted to be a pilot. I spent a tour on Mara—perimeter officer—before I went to Chevel Beta."

"These days, most pilots do. It's a good idea. You test your warriors first, sort of like the old Shintos . . ." Sasaki let his words trail off as Marshal Toboru paused by the table.

"Don't try to corrupt him too fast, James." She offered a smile and a pat on the shoulder before she slipped out of the restaurant.

The major took a long swallow from his glass and refilled it.

Vivienne removed the empty plates.

"So many of our problems with the revs date back to antiquity, even before the Great Die-off. If the old Shintos had won the second global war, or whatever they called it, then the anglo forerunners of the revs couldn't have built their power base and amassed the fortunes that they took to Orum. And that would have meant that the white neo-Mahmets. . . ."

Trystin held in a sigh. It was likely to be a long tour.

"Do you want any more wine?"

"Not yet, thank you."

"It's good. Not great, but good . . . anyway, as I was saying, all of those problems relate to the economic relationship between the Shintos and the anglos . . ."

Trystin nodded, hoping the main course would come soon, even as he pushed out of his mind the thought that the meal might be costing the equivalent of a week's pay—or more. Instead, he took another, very small, sip of the Villa Tozza. It was good, but he had the feeling that everything associated with James Sasaki had a high price.

34

 Trystin put the last of his uniforms into place in the locker beside his bunk, then refolded the two bags into small oblongs that he tucked into the back corner before he closed the locker door.

He'd had to wash and wipe out the locker first, getting rid of a residue of powder. He'd also wiped the dust off the console screen. Clearly, Major Doniger hadn't been the neatest of people. She had left what appeared to be a complete and updated set of hard-copy manuals on the *Willis,* though, with paper slips inserted throughout. Trystin walked over to the console and picked up the top manual, opening it to one of the slips.

"... peak power limitations of the F4-A(R) fusactor ..."

A single paragraph was highlighted. Trystin read it, and was surprised to learn that each of the twin fusactors could actually deliver one hundred ten percent of load for five minutes without damage—or one hundred twenty percent for two minutes. Would he ever need to use that knowledge? He frowned, deciding that it might not be a bad idea to study the manuals, and to start with the noted sections.

Major Doniger might have been personally messy, but she had essentially told him that the captain was a lousy shiphandler, and the manuals laid out on the narrow space next to the console conveyed another message—that the captain might not be any great expert on systems, either.

Trystin took a deep breath, feeling the ship's net around him. For the moment, he was the duty officer, and he hoped nothing happened. While he supposed he should have been up front, with the net it didn't matter where he was, and he wanted to get settled as quickly as possible.

There was a rap on the door.

"Come in."

Keiko Muralto stood in the doorway.

"Yes, Tech—Keiko?" he corrected himself.

The tech carried two flat volumes in her hands. "Before she left, Major Doniger asked me to get duplicate copies of these for you."

Trystin looked at the two thin volumes. "What are they?"

"This is the manual for the translation system, and this one is the programming layout for the ship's infonet."

Trystin shook his head and pointed to the manuals beside the console. "She left me quite a stack already." He took the two. "Looks like I've got a lot of studying to do."

"Yes, ser." Keiko's face was almost blank.

On impulse, Trystin kicked up his reflexes and hearing, before asking, "Do you think it's very important for me to learn all this as fast as I can?"

"Yes," came the subvocalized response. "You would know best, ser."

"There's a lot I don't know, Keiko. I'm still a rather junior pilot. Which one of these"—he gestured—"would be the best place to start?"

"Infonet." Keiko paused. "You could start anywhere, ser."

"I'll have to learn it all, anyway."

". . . soon . . ." The tech waited, then answered clearly, "I suspect that it's something all pilots are expected to learn."

Trystin caught the glint in the tech's eye. "You've worked with a lot of junior officers off the perimeter lines, haven't you?"

"Yes, ser."

"Well," Trystin said casually, "I appreciate having all of the manuals, and I'll work through them as quickly as I can. Sometimes, you almost have to read between the lines to figure out what's important."

"I would imagine so, ser."

"I appreciate it." Trystin didn't have to fake the warmth.

"Thank you, ser." Keiko paused once more, then added,

"The captain will be introducing Lieutenant Akibono to you once they get back."

"Akibono? Oh, is he the weapons/nav officer? Liam?"

". . . *watch it* . . ." "Yes, ser."

"It'll be good to get the names and faces straight." Trystin nodded. "Do we have time for you to introduce me to the rest of the techs?"

"Yes, ser." Keiko Muralto smiled for the first time.

Trystin tried not to swallow, wondering exactly what kind of mess he'd stepped into. "Let's do it."

He followed the senior tech out of his stateroom, number two, predictably, and aft. The first technician he met was a young, broad-shouldered and brown-haired man.

"Lieutenant Desoll, this is Tech Albertini. Albertini, this is our new pilot officer, Lieutenant Desoll."

"Pleased to meet you, ser."

"I'm pleased to meet you, Albertini."

After that, he was introduced to two other technicians—Muriami and Reilli. Trystin and Keiko then headed forward.

"Albertini is new on board. He's barely been here a month. He handles low-level maintenance. Muriami—she's a wonder on individual components, but has trouble with systems. Reilli is pretty much the weapons tech."

"And you do everything," suggested Trystin.

"I try."

As they reached the quarterdeck, Trystin heard feet in the lock tube, and he dropped his reflexes back to normal, trying to slow his breathing.

"Must be the captain. He was up in station operations," suggested Keiko.

Major James Sasaki stepped through the open lock and tucked his beret into his belt. A squarish officer followed him, dark-skinned and black-eyed, with the muscles of a power lifter.

"Ah, I was going to look for you, Trystin." He paused. "This is Liam Akibono. He's the best weapons/navigation officer in the fleet. He's also a damned good supply officer."

Liam offered a bow.

Trystin returned the bow, but with a shade less inclination. A ghost of a frown flicked across James Sasaki's face. Had Trystin revealed too much of the early martial arts training he had received with and from his father?

"We're headed back to your old stomping grounds, Trystin—back to Parvati system," announced the captain. "The revs are really pushing there, and the Planning Staff has decided to beef up the patrols off the outer orbit control platform. We'll hit Mara first, though. We've got some dispatches."

"When do we leave?" asked Trystin.

"About ten hours. That's enough time for you to get some sleep, and to spend some time in the cockpit familiarizing yourself with the feel of the ship. Andrya reminded me that early familiarization was important. The systems aren't that different, but there are a few things you should know." He shook his head. "Quite a person, that woman. Quite a person."

Liam only raised his eyebrows.

"Do you have your gear stowed?" James refocused on Trystin.

"Yes, ser. I had Tech Muralto introduce me to the rest of the crew, and I was starting to go over some of the system manuals."

"Good. Do whatever you need for the next hour or so. Then come to my stateroom, and we'll go over the ops plan, and after that we'll go through a fam routine in the cockpit."

"Yes, ser."

Major Sasaki turned to Liam. "As soon as we're loaded, let me have the mass plan. See if we could squeeze a few more torps on board."

"Yes, ser." Liam turned and headed aft.

James Sasaki's eyes flicked to Keiko Muralto. "Did you find the problem with sensor three?"

"There's a flaw in the command module, and that's a solid matrix. Tech support is trying to find us one."

"Who's in charge of tech support?"

"That's Commander Bulari, ser."

"Who's his boss?"

"Marshal Toboru, I think."

"You'll get your matrix, Keiko." James Sasaki smiled and turned toward the cockpit.

Keiko raised her eyebrows, and Trystin felt a chill go down his back. He followed the captain as far as his own stateroom, where he stepped inside and closed the door behind him.

He picked up the infonet manual and began to read, noting that, once again, a few paragraphs were highlighted. He stopped reading in sequence—he wouldn't have time to get through all the manuals before he was supposed to meet with the captain—and scanned through the highlighted sections.

He swallowed and read through them again.

He should have known, and in some ways it was predictable. A complete ship's net worked both ways. Anything that could monitor all the occurrences within the ship could and did record everything. Everything. So why had Keiko Muralto subvocally insisted that he know that from the beginning?

He nodded slowly. James Sasaki was political—very political.

Trystin recalled the smile on James's face when he had promised Keiko the replacement module for the scanner. Anything that Trystin said—had he said too much at dinner?—would be recorded, recalled, and used, if possible.

Andrya had managed, but she came from power and position. Trystin only had faster reflexes and better shiphandling ability—and the knowledge. Still, a junior Major Doniger had certainly been open about assessing Major Sasaki's piloting abilities—or lack of abilities. So that wasn't any secret, and part of Trystin's unspoken duties was to ensure the *Willis* didn't get into any embarrassing shiphandling situations.

Clearly, another part of the game was not to let on that he knew about James Sasaki's political maneuverings, even within the ship—to appear even younger and more naïve than he was. But why had Keiko warned him about the in-fonet's capabilities?

He nodded again. Because if James had trouble getting a handle on Trystin, he might be kept in check? Or was there something more?

Trystin took a deep breath and kept reading, feeling as though he had far too much to learn in far too little time, and far too many questions.

His eyes crossed the other small pile of paper, the hand-outs on the Revenants that Commander Folsom had suggested he study. When would he have time for that? He sighed. It didn't help that he knew Folsom had been right, not when plodding through revvie theology was as attractive as digging his way out of a Maran dust pit.

35

 Thud!

Following translation, as the *Willis* settled into the sub-Oort, dust-free zone, James Sasaki leaned back in the command couch. "You've got it, Lieutenant. Take us to Mara."

Trystin understood. The run into Mara should be easy, and he needed greater familiarity with the ship and its systems.

He scanned all the screens, from the representational to the maintenance boards, then went back to the representational screen. At the system fringe was the faintest trace of an incoming ship—too far to locate accurately. It had to be a troid, because no Coalition ship would be in real space that far beyond Kali—the outer planet of the Parvati system. For future reference, he noted the sector—orange—and added the observation to the transit report to be filed with Mara operations when the *Willis* locked there.

"Keiko—send someone up with a couple of teas." James shifted his weight and closed his eyes again.

Trystin let his consciousness drop into the power system, trying to trace the odd pulsation he'd noted from the beginning, almost as though the accumulators were hiccuping power.

For a moment, he split power from the fusactor, running one thruster off the fusactor and the other off the accumulator. Little peaks appeared in the thrust output from the accumulator-powered thruster, then the thrust dropped off as the accumulator load bled down. Trystin restored normal operations. He wanted to check the accumulators more, but not millions of kays from anywhere.

"How much envelope distortion, ser?"

"As much as you please. There's no difference to Mara control, and we don't get as tired."

Trystin cranked up the thrusters—slowly, in order not to put additional strain on the accumulators.

"Your teas, Captain, Lieutenant." Albertini stood in the hatchway, a cup in each hand.

James took his cup silently.

"Thank you." Trystin sipped the tea slowly. The heat seemed to help a throat that seemed slightly raw, but for a moment his senses scrambled, and the scent of tea, the feeling of its heat, and the flow of data from the net twisted together. He shook his head, and concentrated on the screens, especially the representative screen.

He had to be more tired than he thought. That was when sensory scrambling occurred. Then he checked the comparators.

"Translation error was one standard day, seven hours and thirty-one minutes, Captain. Estimate another three-hour loss from envelope effect."

"Not too bad." James sipped his tea, his eyes slightly glazed.

Trystin rechecked their progress. "Estimate seven hours to Mara orbit control."

The captain nodded.

For the next four hours, Trystin guided the *Willis*, spending as much time investigating infonet readouts and maintenance records as he did navigating, noting that the captain apparently did not care that the distortion envelope reached fifty percent. Maybe that was why he looked so young.

Two hours out from Mara, Trystin began deceleration. James said nothing, seemingly lost in his own thoughts.

When the *Willis* dropped out of the time-distortion envelope, Trystin pulsed the orbit station.

"Mara Orbit Control, this is Iron Mace two, approaching zone this time."

"Iron Mace two, squawk four."

"Squawking."

"Mace two, we have you. Proceed to gamma three for docking. I say again gamma three. Cleared for low-thrust approach to gamma three."

"Control, cutting to low thrust this time."

The station appeared on both the representational screen and the unadjusted optical presentation. Trystin checked his closure and flicked in another set of deceleration pulses.

"Control, Iron Mace two approaching gamma three this time."

The captain opened his eyes and stretched, watching as Trystin eased the *Willis* toward the docking portal.

Once the cruiser was within a half kay, James nodded. "I'll take the con."

"You have the con, ser."

Trystin kept his face impassive as James corrected and overcorrected and finally bumped—gently—the ship into place.

"Whew!" The captain wiped his damp forehead.

Trystin magnetized the holdtights, and signaled Keiko to extend the mechanical holdtights for the station crew.

"Stand by for power changeover. Stand by for power changeover."

Trystin welcomed the full grav, tired as he was.

Once the standby checklist was complete, he looked at James. "Now what?"

Liam Akibono appeared in the hatchway as Trystin finished speaking.

"We'll be here for just a few days, until we can get resupplied. Then we'll be spending the next year, maybe longer, chasing revs from Parvati outer orbit station."

"That's a long way from anywhere," pointed out Liam.

"It's where things are happening."

"Yes, ser."

"As Hantariki wrote, 'the sky is brighter for the storm.' Remember that."

"About the dispatches . . ." began Liam.

"I'll take the dispatches," James announced. "I need to stop by and see Commander Maldonado anyway, and Liam's going to try to get us some of the newer high-drive torps."

"So I've got the ship?" Trystin asked.

"You'll do fine." James flashed his boyish grin and picked up the dispatch cases. "I'll be a while."

"Ser?"

"Yes?"

"Is there a good restaurant here?"

Liam raised his eyebrows, but James laughed. "Not yet. Not yet."

After the captain and the weapons officer left, Trystin accessed the maintenance records through his implant. From what he could tell, the accumulators had not been replaced or had major maintenance at any time in the last three years, although they had been inspected in detail at the five-year (ship objective) overhaul.

He wanted to discuss them with Keiko first.

Trystin stood and walked back to the quarterdeck where Tech Muriami stood, wearing the watch stunner. Mara orbit control smelled the same—even to the faint odor of plastic and weedgrass, though Trystin couldn't imagine how weedgrass ended up in an orbit station.

"How you doing, ser?" The woman continued to watch the lock tube.

"Fine, Muriami. How about you?" Trystin inspected the tracks for the emergency seals.

"They're clear. I always check them first thing."

Trystin sniffed. It hadn't been his imagination. The station atmosphere still smelled like weedgrass.

"Smells funny, doesn't it?"

"It's weedgrass. Used to get into everything. Always made my nose run."

"You were a perimeter officer, weren't you?"

Trystin nodded.

"Ever kill any revs?"

He nodded again.

"How many?"

"Enough."

"Ever get a commendation?"

Trystin nodded reluctantly.

"My brother's a perimeter tech. He says not many officers get commendations. That true?"

"I don't know." He added absently, "I only know of one other officer who did."

"Who was he?"

"She. Major Ulteena Freyer. She's the CO of the *Yamamoto*—corvette somewhere."

"Must be a tough woman."

"She is. Doesn't look that way, though."

"Like you."

"Me? I'm not tough."

Muriami laughed. "Service wouldn't send spring flowers here. The captain'd eat them alive."

"The captain?" Trystin grinned.

So did Muriami.

"Do you know where Tech Muralto is?"

"Up in station maintenance."

"When she gets back, would you tell her that I need to talk with her?"

"Yes, ser."

With a nod, Trystin turned and headed for his stateroom, his implant still tuned to the ship's net and status board. After a second thought, he paused by the mess for a cup of the strong green tea, which he carried into his room. Setting the tea by the console, he sat down in the plastic chair and opened the fusactor manual. He had to start somewhere.

When he got too bored, he'd go down to the tiny exercise room behind the mess—or go back to studying Revenant culture. While he understood why the economics worked, he still couldn't figure why people bought into it. Maybe he never would. Maybe Quentar was right—but Quentar was dead.

He began to read the fusactor manual.

36

 "Tradition. It's important." The captain set his empty cup on the narrow mess table.

"Yes." Trystin tried not to yawn as he stretched and got up to pour another cup of tea from the samovar.

"Pour me some, would you?"

Trystin picked up James's cup and refilled it, setting it in front of the captain. In the corner, Albertini, the junior tech, sipped instant cafe. Trystin wrinkled his nose at the raw odor. He'd never liked cafe. After refilling his own mug with the strong green tea, he sat down across from the captain.

The *Willis* was cinched up to the ready lock, on standby in case any revvie scouts or ships should appear. For the last two weeks, after leaving Mara, the *Willis* had been rotated through standby duty on Parvati station, but the system had been quiet. Standby meant the crew could be anywhere aboard, so long as the captain and the second were on the link.

"Tradition," repeated the major. "Even words have a tradition." He paused. "Have you ever heard Moritaki?"

"No." Trystin took a long sip of the plain green tea, not

nearly so good as what his father brewed, but better than Sustain or cafe.

Cling!

Trystin jolted alert in his seat. So did James.

Albertini, not direct-linked, saw the reaction and mumbled, "Oh, frig . . . trouble . . ."

"Iron Mace two, badboy at your zero two zero, elevation amber, eighty light-mins. Incoming at plus four." The direct-feed comm shivered through both pilots.

"Control, Iron Mace two. Powering up this time," announced James.

Trystin emptied his cup and racked it, then scurried forward and mentally called up the checklist.

"Prepare for separation. Prepare for separation." James's voice blared through the speakers.

They both strapped into their couches, and Trystin continued running through the short checklist while James linked the data from control into the ship's data banks.

"We're ready for changeover," Trystin reported.

"Stand by for power changeover."

"Standing by," Trystin affirmed.

"Ready for changeover," acknowledged Keiko from the duty tech station behind Trystin.

The lights flickered; the ventilators' hum stopped, then resumed; and the gravity dropped to point five, ship standard. Trystin's stomach twisted, and he proceeded through the rest of the checklist, using the mental screens, occasionally cross-checking the manual screens before him.

He could still remember the first time he had sensed the full pilot data load, and how it had threatened to drown him. His lips curled momentarily.

"Ready to separate, ser," he reported.

James nodded, his eyes half-glazed with his concentration on the data and nav plots.

"Outer Control, demagnetizing this time." After the acknowledgment from James, Trystin sent the report.

"Iron Mace two, understand demagnetizing. Cleared for separation this time. Maintain low thrust for three."

"Stet, Control. Will maintain low thrust for three."

Trystin relayed the instructions to James, trying to ignore the sweat beading up on the major's forehead.

"Iron Mace two, separating this time . . ."

On the representational screen the amber point that was the *Willis* began to move away from the red square that represented the outer orbit station.

"You have the con, Lieutenant."

"I have it, ser." Trystin smoothed out the power flows, trying to rest the accumulators and slowly boosting the flow from the fusactor.

"Steady on zero two zero, green—until we're clear of the dust."

Trystin kept boosting power to the thrusters, noting that the rev's image on the representational screen was as much blue as white. On the full-system and representational screens, the *Willis* seemed to creep away from Parvati outer orbit control, but quickly on the visual screen as orbit control vanished into the darkness. Parvati herself was no more than an extraordinarily bright star.

The revvie ship was inbound toward outer orbit control, angled from the innermost point of the Oort cloud, as if the pilot had been trying to use debris and cometary masses of the cloud as a screen.

"To oppose something is to maintain it," James intoned.

"Is that traditional, ser?"

"No. LeGuin, anglo preimmortal writer who understood culture."

Trystin tried not to frown. Was the captain being deliberately obscure? Finally, he asked, "What's being maintained by what opposition?"

"Outer orbit control. We created it as a staging point to hit the troid ships before they get too far in-system. They build up forces to take it out, and that means we have to add more forces to keep it."

That made sense—in an odd way. Trystin refocused his scan on the orange sector of the representational screen, increasing the scale exaggeration. As he kept watching, the rev's previously constant bearing began to shift.

"Badboy's edging toward the red. Looks like he's going to line into Krishna."

"Could he use a slingshot mag-warp to get head-to-head?"

Trystin hadn't even thought of that, and he recomputed. After a moment, he answered. "Probability is above point eight."

Trystin should have thought of it. On a high-speed head-to-head, the rev had an improved chance because his cross section was smaller and open for a shorter period of time. The added speed of the maneuver might cancel the shield-strength advantage possessed by the *Willis*.

The two dots on the screen crept closer and closer to each other and Kubera—the outer gas giant—and its scattered moons and dust envelope. The rev dropped lower.

"Recommend going into the plus, ser."

"Go ahead, Lieutenant. You have the con."

Trystin began to ease the *Willis* above the absolute plane of the ecliptic, trading away closure for position, but still maintaining the cruiser between orbit control and the rev. If the rev did slingshot, his low position was going to haunt him afterward.

Trystin hesitated, then triggered the restraints warning.

"All personnel take restraints. All personnel take restraints."

The time-dilation envelope had a nasty side effect—partly countered by reflex step-up—which affected two ships with high, but differing absolute speeds. Although nontranslation speeds were limited to around point nine lights for any ship, experienced elapsed time shrank more quickly on the ship farther into the time-dilation envelope, effectively giving the pilot less time to react.

James looked at Trystin and nodded, but said nothing.

The lieutenant continued to track the incoming rev as the *Willis* steadily narrowed the distance, approaching both Krishna and Sithra, the gas giant's big fourth moon, nearly a third the size of Mara.

"Lot of power for a rev," observed James.

"We're seeing what they did twenty years ago, and I'm

not sure I want to know what's twenty years ahead."

James arched an eyebrow, but said nothing.

Once the rev grazed Krishna, all Trystin could get were confused signals from all the screens. Then two quick-dotted lines—torps—appeared on the representational screen, streaking toward the *Willis.*

CLING! CLING!

Trystin bled off all power from the gravs and nonessential systems, feeding it into the thrusters as he twisted the cruiser into an impossibly tight turn to angle in front of the fourth moon of Krishna.

The turn ran to nearly three gees, a lot for a deep-space ship, with James and Trystin pressed into their couches.

"Shields going up!" snapped Trystin, the words following his actions.

All the input from the sensors blanked, and, of the screens relaying exterior information, only the representational screen continued to function, but its "data" was based only on estimated updates.

The smallest of shivers rocked the cruiser.

Trystin waited for another two minutes before lowering the shields.

The rev had used the slingshot effect—to accelerate translation torps even faster than normal and to change his course back toward sector green without killing his speed.

Somehow Trystin had slipped the *Willis* through a tighter turn, while not losing too much speed, and the cruiser was actually nearer the rev than before.

"Good reactions," said James.

"He's running for Kali."

Trystin and the captain watched as two blips on the screen seemed to converge on the small ice planet.

"We've got him." Trystin watched the lock-in click, even as the rev slid toward Kali, his path as close as he could make it without generating a blister field. Even outer planets had some atmosphere.

Another series of torps, two and then another two, flared from the rev, but not toward the *Willis.* The four torps ran toward Yama—the small ice-and-rock moon of the outer planet.

Trystin frowned. The revvie corvette would barely be shielded by the planet before the torps impacted.

James froze, but Trystin could feel the captain's presence on the nav side of the net, demanding a series of calculations.

"Lieutenant!" snapped James. "Full three-gee turn red, two seven zero."

Crazy! The captain had lost it, but Trystin triggered the alarms and restraints again, and slammed the ship into the turn without a protest. As he did, he continued to track the rev, watching as the corvette swung low and angled in-system. Pressed back into his seat, he calculated another vector, and nodded.

Rather than speak, he threw the request through the net at the captain.

"Again?" came the response.

Trystin broke down the request, showing how the *Willis* could use the free-dust area above the ecliptic to gain the angle on the rev, especially once the corvette hit the Trojan points off Shiva, since the rev's maneuver had forced him above the ecliptic as well.

"You're cleared."

Absently, Trystin scanned Yama. Most of the small ice-and-rock moon wasn't there. Even under the gee load, his stomach lurched. The rev had basically used his torps to throw a screen of ice and rock across the *Willis*'s approach. At the acceleration Trystin had piled on, either the screens would have shredded or the accumulators blown, or both.

No . . . the captain hadn't lost it, and the rev had been clever, but not clever enough.

The *Willis* continued to gain on the rev, and Trystin grinned. He had the angle, and no matter which way the rev went, any course change worked to the advantage of the *Willis*. If the rev stayed above the ecliptic with the *Willis*, it would be only a matter of minutes before the *Willis* got EDI lock-on. If the rev dropped toward the center of the system plane, the dust would slow him faster than the *Willis*.

The EDI track faded into a point.

"He shut down all his systems."

Trystin increased his sensitivity and strained the ship's systems, mumbling. He could barely sense the rev, but he doubted that the torps' energy sensors could. That meant firing the torps literally to a point and hoping the absolute heat sensors could find the revvie corvette.

"Fire one." He pulsed out the first torp.

After adjusting the signal again, he initiated the second. "Fire two."

All in all, it took Trystin five torps to neutralize the rev. By the fifth he was sweating, and his shipsuit was soaked, and a rapidly cooling mist of metal, vapor, and synthetics was dissipating and leaving the screen clear.

"Captain?" came Keiko's voice. "Are we clear to lift restraints?"

Trystin blushed. "Clear to lift restraints. Rev neutralized."

"Did you need five torps, ser?" That came over the net from Akibono.

James looked at Trystin.

"This rev was rather good," Trystin said.

"Very good," added James, "but not good enough."

Trystin wiped his forehead. He tried not to imagine being in a silent, shut-down ship hoping someone would miss.

"I'll take the con, Lieutenant."

"You have the con, ser."

"Could we have some tea up here?"

"It will be a few minutes, ser. The samovar wasn't as restrained as we were."

The boyish grin crossed James's face. "That's fine. Water or anything will be fine."

"I think we'll be able to do tea, once we mop up."

"Casualties of war," observed the captain.

Trystin wiped his forehead again, before leaning back.

In less than ten minutes, Albertini arrived with two cups of tea.

"Wild ride, ser." He looked at Trystin.

"I'll try to make it smoother in the future."

"That was fun, ser."

Trystin took his tea after the captain did, sipping it quickly, and burning his tongue. How had they gotten it that hot that quickly? Fun?

He took a deep breath and sat back, trying to relax.

"It's different, isn't it?" asked James, after perhaps a half hour had passed silently as the *Willis* headed back to Parvati outer orbit control.

"Yes."

The captain pointed to the EDI screen. "There. It looks so quiet, and unless something like that last bit happens, it is. Most of the time, it's a matter of angles, a matter of power, and a few torps, and one ship or the other's neutralized. That's it."

Trystin looked at the visual EDI, not the mental screen. The EDI still showed the blue-tinged blips of the incoming asteroid ship, well beyond the patrol fringe, well beyond accurate detector position. Every time the *Willis* crossed the orange sector, the EDI showed the incoming ship, and reported the data to SysCon. Nothing changed.

"Why don't we refuel and go get it?" asked Trystin.

"Get what?"

"The troid."

James raised his bushy black eyebrows. "How? We don't even have a decent vector. It's still a tenth of a light out there, and the potential translation error is enough that we could end up chasing it all over the sky."

Trystin frowned. There had to be a way.

James laughed. "You youngsters are all the same. If you can see it, you can hunt it down." The boyish grin faded. "Look . . . I know I'm not the greatest shiphandler, but shiphandling isn't all there is to being a pilot—or a marshal. How big is that troid—if it's the standard revvie operation?"

"Probably . . . what? . . . no more than two kays across?"

"Why can we detect it?"

"Because it's using a ramscoop-powered fusactor with thrusters. They register on the EDI."

"At between a tenth and a fifth of a light, what's the probable margin for error—not translation error, but jump error?"

"It could be a couple of light-days, maybe more." Trystin was beginning to see where James was heading.

"How far would we have to go into the distortion envelope after we translated?"

"Pretty far . . . and that takes a lot of fuel, plus system strain . . . and the translation error could be a week, maybe two, each way."

"Exactly—and while we're blundering around out there, what's likely to be happening back here?"

Trystin sighed.

"And," continued James inexorably, "what are the chances of one cruiser against a troid ship?"

"About one in four."

"That's why we wait until they come to us."

James wasn't stupid—just clumsy with shiphandling.

"Outer Control, this is Iron Mace two, confirming badboy neutralization. Badboy neutralization."

"Mace two, Control. We confirm neutralization. . . . Gave you a run there. Yama won't ever be the same."

"What's a little ice here or there?" quipped James.

"Better you than us, two. Cleared to epsilon three."

"Mace two, commencing approach to epsilon three." James nodded and turned to Trystin. "They'll probably pull up the *Sebastopol*. You take the con for a while."

Trystin rechecked the accumulators. The power hiccuping on the outbound side was still faint, but stronger.

"Ser . . . the hiccuping off the accumulators is stronger, not a lot, but stronger."

"Record it. Have Keiko run it by the station logistics engineer, through the maintenance system, and you put a note in the ops report."

"The log engineer will just say it's normal, but it's not."

"I know that." James smiled. "It takes time."

Trystin nodded.

"Patience is like tradition. They're important," announced James.

"Yes." Trystin struggled to listen, while still computing the course line to bring the *Willis* to rest in berth epsilon three of the outer belt defense station. Parvati was so far away that the screen bore the legend "SCALE DISTORTED."

"Have you ever heard Moritaki?"

"No. I can't say I have." Trystin had never even heard of Moritaki, except when the captain had brought up the name before they had scrambled.

"Very old. He wrote in old Shinto—eight centuries before the Die-off. Very beautiful."

"What did he write?" Trystin pulsed the thrusters again, dropping the closure rate to meters per minute.

"I had to memorize some of his verse as a boy."

Trystin waited. Sooner or later, James would get there, but never in direct fashion.

The captain spoke the words softly.

> "A falling petal
> drops upward, back to the branch.
> It's a butterfly."

"I've seen some butterflies like that." Trystin adjusted the approach again.

"How about this?"

> "The morning glory—
> another thing
> that will never be my friend."

James paused before adding, "That was Basho."

"You know him?" Trystin asked.

James laughed. "He died fifteen hundred years ago. Tradition. It's important."

"What's a morning glory?" Trystin wanted to keep James talking. Things seemed to go better when the major was the center of attention.

"A flower. A blue flower. It opened at dawn, and it folded up in the full light of day. None of them survived the Die-off." James looked bleakly at the screens.

Trystin swallowed, wondering at the captain's sudden change of mood.

"Iron Mace two, closure is green."

Trystin nodded and pulsed back, "Stet, Control. Holding green."

"Do you want the con, ser?" Trystin asked.

"You're doing fine. Take her in."

"Yes, ser." Trystin shifted his weight in his couch.

"Mace two, cleared to dock. Maintain low thrust."

"Control, this is two, beginning final approach." Trystin moistened his lips and pulsed the thrusters again.

The *Willis* crept in toward the wall of metal and composite—slowly, slowly, until, with a faint *chunk,* she slipped into place.

Trystin magnetized the holdtights. "We have lock-on. Apply mechanical holdtights and prepare for power changeover." He began the shutdown list, and the items and replies went back and forth over the net, silently, between him and the captain.

"Accumulators . . ."

". . . discharged."

"Fusactor . . ."

". . . stand by."

"Compensators . . ."

". . . open."

Trystin nodded.

"Senior Tech . . . power changeover."

"Changeover, ser."

As the full grav of orbit control pressed Trystin into his couch, he realized just how tired he was. "Whew . . ."

"You're not done yet, Lieutenant. We have to go up to ops and debrief."

"Yes, ser." Trystin dragged himself out of the couch.

"After that, you get to go and talk to the maintenance people about the accumulators, not logistics—Keiko will handle that—but Commander Frenkel's assistant, Lieutenant what's-his-name."

"Isuki. But he won't do anything."

"I know. But make sure you talk to him, and talk to his tech assistants. That's so everyone knows that you've been there, and give him a hard copy of the note from the ops report."

"I don't have—"

"Make one. I'll wait."

Trystin sent the command over the net and wiped his face, then pulled his beret from his belt and walked back to the tech room where the printer waited for him.

Behind him, James smiled.

37

The *Sebastopol,* the *Willis,* and the *Mishima* formed a rough arc—as shown by the representational screen. At the center of the arc was the blue pulsing sphere that was the revvie troid.

In front of the Coalition cruisers were nearly a dozen fast corvettes, matched by nearly as many Revenant scouts that led and protected the troid.

"I told you we'd get a chance at that troid," pointed out James. "Are you still interested in taking it on alone?"

Trystin studied the EDI tracks on the screen, noting the bearing from the *Willis* and the closure rate—nearly half a light. He'd never seen anything that big move so fast—not as close as the troid was. The revvie scouts and the corvettes moved closer—only centimeters apart on the physical screen in front of Trystin—but those centimeters still represented nearly ten light-minutes.

"What the mother is that?" asked Albertini as he handed

the cup of tea to the captain, his eyes on the pulsing blue ball in the visual screen.

"Is that your first troid up close?" James took the mug of green tea.

"Yes, ser." Albertini extended the second cup to Trystin, but the tech's eyes were still on the screen.

Trystin took the cup, and a quick sip before setting it in the holder by his right hand.

". . . the friggin' revs . . . how long those corpsies been chilled?" the tech whispered.

"Now, now, they're just on a mission for the Prophet." James set his tea down.

"Twenty years, give or take a few," answered Trystin.

"You'd better get back and strapped in," suggested James.

"Yes, ser."

On the screen the green-shaded points of light—the Coalition ships—moved toward the blue-shaded points of light.

The Coalition corvettes were higher-powered, with heavier shields, and somewhat less maneuverable. The revs accelerated faster and formed into a wedge, close enough that they merged on the screen, possibly close enough that their shields overlapped.

The wedge arrowed toward the forward arc of the Coalition corvettes.

Nothing happened as the ships drew closer. Then a series of green-dashed lines flickered from the Coalition formation toward the lead revvie scout.

The torpedoes intersected the arrowhead, and two points of light flashed, but the remaining revvie scouts reconfigured into two smaller wedges and split apart, sending their own torps out.

A Coalition corvette went up.

Concentration of firepower—that was the game.

Another Coalition corvette vanished—just vanished—from the screen.

So did a revvie scout.

A blue-dashed torp course line flared from the right

revvie arrow toward the trailing corvette on the left flank of the Coalition formation.

Trystin watched, and it appeared that the corvette never saw the torp. The ship just flashed into red, then disappeared from the screen. How could a pilot not sense a potential lock-on?

The Coalition corvettes let loose another barrage of coordinated torps, then peeled away from the oncoming revs in a circular sweep that seemed designed to bring all the corvettes back onto the left revvie wedge a few light-minutes in-system.

The right arrow of revvie scouts swept toward the cruisers. The left arrow of revvie scouts swept across where the vanished corvette had been.

Abruptly, a blue point of light appeared—behind the revvie wedge—released three torps in rapid succession, and then accelerated into a sweeping left turn.

Two more torps flew, and blue and green lights merged, before another pinlight of sun flashed across the screen.

Two revvie scouts went up in light to the torps of the destroyed but previously "vanished" corvette, and the Coalition corvettes converged on the weakened left wedge, with torp lines crisscrossing on the screen.

A single revvie scout remained, apparently left alone, as the remaining six corvettes accelerated on a stern chase after the four revvie scouts that closed on the cruisers.

"Full shields," ordered James.

Feeling the captain's control of the torps, Trystin waited as the *Willis* and the revs closed on each other.

Another series of torps flared from the Coalition corvettes, and more revvie scouts vanished, leaving two revvie scouts headed toward the cruisers.

"Fire one!"

Trystin felt the command through the system, rather than heard the words.

"Two! Three! Four!"

Four torps that quickly?

Trystin watched as the torps impacted one right after the

other on the shields on the lead rev—and the scout flared into dust.

Absently, Trystin realized that the remaining rev scout from the other wedge had surprised another corvette with what seemed like a suicide dash. Both scout and corvette flashed into nearly pure energy.

The remaining scout pounded toward the *Sebastopol*, somehow avoiding the first torp from the cruiser, and the second, and launching its own torp.

The *Sebastopol*'s shields flared amber, and stayed amber, but the rev went up in energy with two more torps from the remaining three corvettes.

Trystin wiped his forehead, then computed closure rates. The *Willis* remained three light-mins out from the rev—an enormous absolute distance, and a very short time to closure.

"Iron Mace two, this is Sledge Control. Coordinate dump follows. Coordinate dump follows."

"Sledge Control, Mace two, standing by for coordinate dump. Standing by this time." James nodded to Trystin.

The coordinate dump was just that—a blast of data—with detailed coordinates outlining the two target points on the troid. In too many places, even the heavy troid-killer torps would slam into the nickel-iron without much impact—or not enough to disrupt the course or mission of the troid.

Trystin reviewed the dump, then plugged the coordinates into the targeting parameters. "Target points established, ser."

"Stet, Lieutenant."

Ghostlike images flared from the troid, more than a dozen, and then another wave of revvie scouts rose from the hidden locks of the troid, only five in all, but only the three corvettes remained in front of the cruisers.

Trystin nodded to himself, knowing that the ghostlike paraglider wings were on their way to Mara, and, with their radar-transparent silhouettes, by the time the battle around the troid was over, system control would be lucky to find half of the paragliders, if that.

"Holding back scouts to keep us from going after the gliders," James said quietly, then asked, "Interrogative time to launch point."

Trystin ran the comps again, letting the figures spin through him and across the circuit to the captain.

"They'll be here before we're there." The captain paused, then added, "Weapons, stand by on torp changeover. Badboys incoming."

"Standing by, Captain." Liam's voice sounded tinny on the net, the result of converting vocal vibrations to neuroelectrical pulse.

"Lieutenant, you have the con. Get us to the launch point in one piece, and take as many of them as you can along the way. Standard torps will fire at twice normal rate."

Trystin noted that the captain neither closed his eyes nor relaxed.

"Yes, ser. I have the con. Torps will fire at twice normal rate." Immediately, Trystin began bleeding back the power flow to the thrusters slightly, cutting acceleration levels by five percent. He checked the accumulators again, but the hiccuping, while reduced, still occurred. Why could the *Willis* fire torps at twice the standard rate? That could wait for later.

Trystin triggered the restraints warning. "All personnel take restraints. All personnel take restraints."

"Shit . . ."

It might have been Albertini's voice, but Trystin ignored it, and dropped the shields to half-power while lifting the *Willis* above the past battle plane. He boosted the power flow to the accumulators, until they registered at a hundred percent, then slowly eased up acceleration.

Two of the revvie scouts veered from their centerline toward the *Willis*. Trystin kept the cruiser lifting for another minute, then dropped the nose back to a direct vector toward the troid, although it would take a while to overcome the rising vector—which was fine. He didn't have to worry about drag—not that much in space.

Trystin kept studying the revvie scouts, watching . . .

With the first flicker in their EDI envelope, he acted.

"Full restraints!"

"Shit . . ."

Even before Albertini had finished swearing, Trystin had poured all the stored accumulator power into the thrusters and dumped the nose even more, hoping his calculations were correct. Scouts didn't have beefed-up thrusters and accumulators. He also dumped the artificial grav and poured that power into acceleration.

The acceleration pushed him into the couch, and he let it, watching as the torps flared toward the *Willis.*

"Fire one!"

"Fire two!"

He paused, checking the incoming lines.

"Fire three!"

Out of time, he dropped off enough power to bounce up full shields, and the "gravity" in the cabin slumped to a shade over normal, but it was pure acceleration effect.

"Shields! Desensitize!" he announced after the fact, as the *Willis* powered toward the troid, and as Trystin calculated the wave fronts, then lifted desensitivity, ready to reimpose it.

There were no torps. There were also no revvie scouts near the *Willis,* although one scout seemed to be fleeing the *Mishima,* and the two others did not register on the screens.

"Approaching launch point in one minute ship time," Trystin announced.

"Stet. Time for the big ones." The captain pulsed back to Liam. "Put the regular torps on standby and drop in the reds."

"Loading red one and two at this time, Captain. Three and four standing by."

The red torps—the troid busters—required both the action of the weapons officer and the pilot in command, unlike ship-to-ship torps. The weapons officers also underwent rather intensive screening, Trystin understood. After the experiences following the Die-off, the Coalition had a fetish about nuclear and nucleonic antimatter weapons.

"Let me know when they're ready, Weapons."

"Stet, ser."

On the screen, the *Willis* moved closer to the large pulsing blip that was the revvie troid.

"Point five," Trystin announced.

"I have the con, Lieutenant."

"You have it, ser."

"Red one is ready." Liam's voice was tinny and calm.

"Ignite red one," ordered James.

"Red one is go," responded Liam.

"Red two!"

"Red two is go."

Trystin swallowed and waited for the reload, which took longer with the reds.

James appeared calm, then pulsed the command. "Red three!"

"Red three is go!"

"Red four!"

"Red four is go."

"Changeover to standard torps."

"Changing over this time."

"Shields!"

"Shield in place, Captain," Trystin responded.

"Desensitize."

"Desensitized."

Trystin could feel the pressure as James turned the *Willis* until she accelerated away from the troid, to eliminate the possibility of a collision with large objects resulting from the fragmentation of the troid, since the ship was traveling faster than the troid. Still, the path taken by the troid would have to be monitored, since flying through the planned troid course line would be dangerous for the next few days. After that, it wouldn't matter.

Trystin glanced around. With the screens dead, and all external contacts cut, the cockpit felt more like a coffin, except for the gentle hissing of the recycling system and the holo displays of the internal status of the *Willis*. He wiped his forehead, and his eyes flicked toward the blank red-tinged boxes where the rest of the visual screen displays should be, then triggered the implant simulation through the representational screen, which showed the dotted course line of the huge torpedoes as they closed on the revvie asteroid ship.

At the moment of projected impact, nothing happened, except the dotted line on the display vanished. Trystin waited for the *Willis* to shiver . . . for something . . . but nothing occurred.

"Calculate," he direct-fed, asking the mainframe for wave-front clearance.

"Wave front has passed, assuming all input parameters are accurate." The words scripted across his mental screen.

"Let's wait a moment," suggested the captain.

Trystin couldn't argue with that. Wave fronts didn't always follow the calculations, and who knew what else might have been in the troid?

Shortly, James nodded and ordered, "Remove desensitizing."

"Receiving input."

The representational screen showed almost the same view as before—the outer planets, orbit control station—but only a faint luminescent haze marked the spot where nine superaccelerated torps had met the five-kay-diameter asteroid and translated a great deal of mass into nearly pure energy.

Two blue-dashed trails appeared on the screen, heading toward the *Willis,* nearly head-to-head.

"Shit . . ." mumbled Trystin.

"You have the con, Lieutenant. You have eighteen torps left. Use what you need." James's voice was cool.

"I have the con." Trystin calculated—two minutes to their torp range. The hell with it.

He dropped the *Willis* into a marginal-gee acceleration, at a slight angle to the oncoming scouts.

"Shit . . . now what?"

Ignoring the comment from one of the techs, who probably felt as though his or her stomach were about to depart, he waited until the first flicker of the EDI, then slammed full power into the thrusters, turning the ship into the oncoming torps.

"Fire one! Fire two!"

He waited only until the tubes were reloaded.

"Fire three! Fire four!"

Then the shields went full up, and he waited, watching, without desensitizing for a moment.

"Control, Weapons. Loader on tube two is jammed. Tube one will fire at twice normal rate."

"Stet, Weapons." More sweat poured down Trystin's face, and he wiped the dampness away from his eyes.

After another moment, Trystin dropped the shields momentarily—firing through shields was usually fatal.

"Fire one!" He waited. "Fire two!"

He raised the shields . . . and waited, conscious that the hiccuping from the accumulators was becoming a stutter.

The accumulators began to grab for power, and Trystin dropped them off-line.

The acceleration dropped to point seven, all the fusactors could maintain.

Trystin held his breath, releasing it as two and then four torps flared past the *Willis*.

The right rev flared into energy.

Dropping shields, Trystin fired another torp, hoping another wouldn't be necessary. It wasn't.

After a moment, he wiped his forehead.

"Rather effective, Lieutenant."

Trystin wiped his forehead again. His shipsuit was soaked. "Thank you, ser."

"Clear to lift restraints," the captain announced.

Trystin flushed. That was something he always forgot.

Liam Akibono stood in the cockpit hatch. He had a bruise on his forehead.

"Sorry," Trystin apologized, with a quick look at the weapons officer. His senses went back to the screens, but the system seemed clear. From what he could tell, only two corvettes, the *Mishima,* and the *Willis* were left from the original Coalition strike force.

"Don't be. I'd rather be battered than dead." Liam

looked at the captain. "The number one new loader needs a lot of work. The second one might last another mission. Maybe."

"There's another set at the station. See if you can get them installed. The company's getting its field test." James grinned wryly. "We have a few other repairs to take care of. So we're not going anywhere soon."

The weapons officer glanced at the screens. "Those revs are crazy. Head-to-head?"

Crazy? Trystin thought not, but offered nothing, knowing James was watching.

"I don't think so, Liam," said James. "One could almost respect them for doing the honorable thing."

Trystin shivered. Honor was cold comfort, sometimes, and the captain's words bothered him. So did the red telltales. "Captain, accumulators are shot. So are the right rear sensors." He wondered how and when that had happened.

"Take us home, Lieutenant."

"Yes, ser."

"If we have a samovar left, Keiko, could you send someone up with some tea?"

"It might take a moment, ser, while we put it back together."

Running on fifty-percent power, with no accumulators, the *Willis* limped back toward Parvati outer orbit control.

James sipped green tea, hair unmussed, apparently unruffled.

Trystin also sipped tea, but his hair stood on end, and he smelled like he'd been working out on the high-gee treadmill for days. He tried not to shiver in the damp shipsuit, after he finally docked the *Willis* firmly in place at lock epsilon four.

He wiped his forehead again. He was still sweating more than an hour after the last torp had fired.

"Let's get to the debriefing, Lieutenant. After that, I'll be gone for a while," announced James. "You did file that last report on the accumulators, didn't you?"

"Yes, ser. I've filed one after every mission. Isuki doesn't ever want to see my face again."

"Good." James offered a smile, not the boyish one.

Trystin raised his eyebrows.

"After the ops debriefing, I'll be seeing Senior Marshal Kovalik. So I might be a while. You need to get back here and relieve Liam. He'll have to work fast to get the loaders replaced and to get us resupplied."

"Yes, ser." Trystin had an idea what Major James Sasaki was about to do with the commander of the outer orbit control station, and he was just as glad he wasn't going to be around. Commander Frenkel might not be around much longer, either.

The torp loaders were another question. Trystin wondered what else lay hidden on the *Willis*.

38

★ "... As cultures advance in knowledge and power, the conflict between reason and faith becomes apparently greater. Not only have people attained through technology the powers of old gods to cast thunderbolts or to heal or to destroy, but they have exercised those powers, and they know that divinity is not required. They can determine that sufficient power determines destiny.

"The problem with technology is that it rewards the able while also empowering those who are less able. A man who cannot fathom a computer or an infonet can destroy those who can, and who have been rewarded for their skills.

"Yet, if each individual obtains and wields the power within his or her scope, few individuals will survive. By placing power in a greater being, a deity, in some force greater than the individual, or even into a belief that the community is greater than the individual, an individual is expressing a faith in the need for an entity greater than mere personal ambition or appetite. That faith . . . allows the individual to refrain from exercising power, yet it also places such an individual at the mercy of those without such faith.

"While it can be and has been argued that all people are created equal, genetics and environmental analyses have verified that such equality ceases at birth, perhaps even earlier.

"With unequal power and unequal ability the lot of humanity, religion has sought to establish a common ground by subsuming all to a mightier god, yet reason and technology have conspired to communicate that no such god exists—or that such a god does not interfere—and that some form of might makes right. And no god has, in recent historical times, destroyed the side with the bigger battalions and mightier technology.

"So . . . how can a rational individual confront the problem of power? In the same way that all the faithful have throughout history—by sharing a set of ideals and a spirit of community more highly valued than individual application of power. . . .

"One of the cries of the true believer is that there are moral absolutes that can only be set forth by a deity. Yet if life is sacred, as many deities have proclaimed, how can a deity command people to kill in his name, as most deities have done? How can we even exist, since we must consume, in the natural state, some other organism, and that means killing? Likewise, if life is not sacred, then the injunction to be fruitful and multiply is a military command, not a deistic one. . . .

The Eco-Tech Dialogues
Prologue

39

✦ "Prepare for power changeover."
"Standing by for changeover."
Trystin tensed slightly as the lights flickered and the gravity dropped to point five, but over the years his guts had learned to flip around a lot less with the switch from station normal gravity to ship grav.

The humming hiss of the ventilators stopped, then picked up, and Trystin proceeded with the checklist, running down the mental screens called up through the implant, only occasionally cross-checking the manual screens before him to ensure that the manual controls still worked—or that his implant wasn't malfunctioning.

"Ready to separate, ser," Trystin added.

"Stet."

"Outer Control, demagnetizing this time." James flashed Trystin the boyish grin after reporting to station control.

"Iron Mace two, understand demagnetizing. Cleared for separation this time. Maintain low thrust for three."

"Iron Mace two, separating this time. Will maintain low thrust for three." Sweat still beaded up on the captain's forehead.

The representational screen depicted the separation as the amber point that was the *Willis* began to move away from the red square of the station.

"You have the con, Lieutenant."

"I have it, ser." Trystin monitored the power flows, trying to check the new accumulators while phasing in power from the fusactor. The sooner the accumulators were carrying a full load the happier he'd be.

"Steady on zero one five, red," ordered James.

"Stet."

Neither spoke as Trystin eased the *Willis* away from already distant Parvati and toward the pulsing blue globe on the representational screen.

"Weapons, loader status?"

"The new loaders and fixes seem to be holding, Captain."

Trystin nodded to himself. Once again, contacts helped. James had managed to get the new high-speed loaders installed on the *Willis*. That just might have been because they were Sasaki loaders. Now they had the first upgrades, since the initial version had had a tendency toward jamming—not exactly wonderful in combat.

"Let's hope so." James's voice was calm, as if testing new systems in combat were expected of him.

Trystin pursed his lips. For James, such tests were—part of the parashinto honor concept. Trystin was still discovering how complicated the man was.

"Sledge team, this is Sledge Control. Datadump follows."

After the net picked up the data burst and arrayed it, both Trystin and James sat silently, using their implants to scan and digest the information and the plans sent from the *Tokugawa* and Marshal Guteyama.

"Too complex," James finally announced.

Trystin nodded, and the *Willis* accelerated toward the orbit of Krishna.

"This is deadly . . . and boring," reflected James into the near silence of the cockpit.

"Boring?" How could anything that could kill you be boring?

"The revs send a troid and scouts. The scouts and troid want to destroy our defenses and take over the system so they can raise more little revs to take over other systems. We go out and kill them, and they kill some of us, and we destroy the troid. Then we build more ships and train more people, and they send another troid, and we do it again. For us, it's even more predictable. A few hours of stress and excitement and then more days or months of waiting. All very predictable. All very boring."

Trystin tried not to frown. Was James testing him again? "Is there some way we could get out of the pattern?"

"If you—or I—could find it, I'm sure Headquarters would like to know. We can't squander resources the way they can in trying to attack their systems, and they don't seem inclined to stop attacking ours. Somehow, you'd have to shake their faith to its foundations, and I don't see that happening." James laughed. "Or we'd have to change, and that's about as likely as the revs giving up their faith."

That wasn't likely, thought Trystin, not after what he'd seen of the revs on Mara. And what could the Eco-Tech Coalition change? It wasn't as though the Coalition wanted anything that belonged to the revs.

Still, he couldn't think of any other logical response to James's declaration that war was essentially boring. But he wasn't sure that he'd call anything where he could get killed boring. The weeks or months of waiting between troids *were* boring—except for the occasional long-range rev scouts. He shook his head and concentrated on integrating the data and the ops plan.

Nearly a standard hour passed before the representational screen showed the six cruisers forming a semicircle to face the oncoming troid. In the two center positions were the *Tokugawa* and the *Mishima*. The *Willis* was at the left end, the *Muir* at the right. At the right middle position was the *Izanagi*, while the *Morrigan* held down the left middle position. Twenty fast corvettes, split into five groups of four with overlapping shields, moved ahead of the cruisers and toward the troid. Fifteen revvie scouts comprised five triplets that sped toward the corvettes.

Abruptly, the revvie triplet groups split—each of the five accelerating into a curving course designed to arch over the oncoming corvettes.

As they accelerated, the ports on the troid opened, launching, and spewing forth in rapid succession, paraglider after paraglider.

"Shit . . ." mumbled Trystin. As usual, by the time the Coalition ships were free, the paragliders would be cold and inert, drifting at high speeds toward Mara, ready within days, or at the most, weeks, to emerge from their cocoons and assault the perimeter lines. Space was just too big to find all of the paragliders, and ships could cruise within kays of one of them and not even spot it because there were no energy emissions, no reflections, and almost no heat radiation.

Data bursts flared across the net, and Trystin responded, driving the *Willis* in toward the *Tokugawa.* He was too busy to shake his head, but that was his feeling, between the troid, the scouts, and the paragliders.

The central quad of corvettes intercepted the middle revvie triplet, and torps flared. The corvettes' overlapped shields held; those of the revs did not, and four converted to energy, leaving a single rev, screens pulsing amber, curving outward before vanishing from the screen.

Trystin noted the location of the vanished rev, but could detect no energy radiation as he eased the *Willis* closer to the *Morrigan,* until their screens flicked across each other.

Two groups of the revvie scouts joined in an attempt to wedge between two other corvette quads, doubling shields and arrowing toward the far side of the cruiser line, straight toward the *Muir,* which was joining shields with the *Izanagi.*

The remaining two revvie groups combined and drove toward the *Willis* and *Morrigan.* In turn, one of the Coalition corvette groups peeled down to intercept the revs headed toward the *Willis.*

The three corvettes remaining from the first attack and the other quad headed to intercept the triplets aimed at the *Muir* and *Izanagi.*

Trystin waited, since any torp he fired might well home on the energy emissions of one of the corvettes before it could seek out a scout. Space was so big that without energy-searching or a very precise location, no single torp would likely hit anything.

Three of the revvie scouts heading toward the *Willis* veered toward the intercepting corvettes; the other three toward the *Morrigan.*

Torps began to flash, and the representational screen

was filled with blue- and green-tinged energy dashes. Two scouts flared into energy, as did one corvette, and then another.

Another scout went up, and then there were two scouts between the corvettes and the *Morrigan*.

Trystin calculated, and pulsed his commands across the net. "Fire one! Two!"

Both torps were aimed at the revvie scout closest to the *Morrigan*. Two torps from the *Morrigan* followed.

Trystin turned the *Willis* into a head-on-head course, and, once the tubes were reloaded, fired two more torps, this time at the trailing rev, followed by two more salvos of two each.

Again, the *Morrigan* lagged in releasing torps.

Two revvie torps flared against the *Morrigan*'s shields, but, though they pulsed amber, the shields held.

Those of the revs did not, and the scouts vanished into dust and energy.

The troid ship lumbered on, and one of the corvettes, apparently trying to avoid something, veered toward the troid. A flash of energy jabbed outward from the mass of nickel-iron, and the corvette vanished.

Trystin got the readouts, even as he kept the *Willis* turning.

"Modified thruster—they've got enough power on the troid to handle that sort of deviltry," said James.

A thruster that could deliver enough punch to blow a corvette's screens at four hundred kays?

The two groups of cruisers edged forward as the troid inexorably bore down on them.

"Approaching launch point in one minute ship time," Trystin announced.

"Stet." James pulsed back to Liam. "Regular torps on standby; load and arm the reds."

"Loading red one, and two, at this time, Captain. Three and four standing by."

On the screen, while the *Willis* seemed to move toward the large pulsing blip that was the revvie troid, the actual data showed the asteroid ship was the one doing most of the moving.

"Point five," Trystin announced.

"I have the con."

"You have it, ser."

"Red one is ready." Liam's voice was tinny and calm.

"Ignite red one."

"Red one is go," responded Liam.

"Red two!"

"Red two is go."

Again, there was the pause for reloading.

"Red three!"

"Red three is go!"

"Red four!"

"Red four is go."

"Changeover to standard torps."

"Changing over this time."

"Shields!"

"Shield in place, Captain," Trystin responded.

"Desensitize."

"Desensitized."

Although the ship grav remained, Trystin could sense the stresses as the *Willis* turned and accelerated away from the troid. The cockpit remained a ventilated coffin, and Trystin focused on the implant's simulation of the troid-busters' course line toward the rev.

"Calculate," he direct-fed, asking the mainframe for wave-front clearance after the moment of impact had passed.

"Wave front has passed." The words flicked across his mental screen.

Trystin waited for a time before announcing, "Plus three after impact."

"Remove desensitizing. You have the con, Lieutenant."

"Receiving input. I have the con."

The screen showed ten corvettes boxing in the last two revvie scouts near the orbit of Kali—and a faint point of energy inside the screens of the *Tokugawa*.

Trystin triggered the implant—too late.

EEEEEEEeeeeee . . .

The eruption of white energy that had been the *Tokugawa* blasted across all wavelinks and shivered right through Trystin. For a moment his thoughts froze, and his nerves burned, even down to his fingertips.

The rev that had dropped off the screen had just stayed put, totally shut down, hoping for a shot from inside a ship's screens. And he'd gotten it.

The revvie scout went up in energy at the impact of three torps from the *Mishima* and the *Muir*.

"Guess we'll have a new marshal." James shook his head.

Trystin tried not to frown, instead scanning the screens. No revvie scouts remained, and only warm chunks of fragmented nickel-iron registered on the cruiser's screens.

"Sledge team, this is Sledge Control Alternate, return to base. Return to base."

Trystin eased the *Willis* into a thirty-degree turn and backed off the thrusters, automatically checking the accumulators. They were fine, no roughness or hiccuping or roughness in power transfers in either direction. He nodded to himself.

"That was better," announced James. "It helps to have a few more ships."

"This time."

"They've got a twenty-year lag," the captain added.

"I thought that when I was down on the perimeter, too."

"You think they'll keep escalating the amount of force they throw at us?"

"One way or another." Trystin rechecked the accumulators as he spoke. The power flows remained smooth. He eased the thrusters back even farther, since the *Willis* was the last cruiser in the formation, and there would be an approach bottleneck anyway.

"Iron Mace two, this is Sledge Control Alternate, interrogative status."

Trystin flicked across the maintenance boards. Outside of two marginal sensors, the *Willis* was in relatively good shape—except for having only eight torps left. Logistics was not letting Liam overstock torps, one Major Sasaki or not, not after the rather hurried and unpleasant departure of Commander Frenkel. The *Willis* now got everything it rated—immediately—but not one thing extra.

Trystin pulsed the status information to James. "Green, ser, except for sensors and torps."

"Sledge Control, Mace two here. Status is green beta—armament."

"Stet, Mace two. Interrogative status upon resupply."

"Sledge Control, this is Iron Mace two. Anticipate status will be green upon resupply."

"Thank you, two."

Trystin looked at the captain.

"They're trying to figure out the standby duty rotations. Probably all that went up with the *Tokugawa.*"

Trystin wiped his forehead with the back of his sleeve. Why was it he sweated so much and James, except when piloting in and out of locking status, seemed so cool?

After waiting for the other cruisers to complete their approaches, the *Willis* crept in toward outer orbit control, slipping up beside the wall of metal and composite—slowly, slowly, until, with a faint *clunk,* she melded with the station.

"We have lock-on. Apply mechanical holdtights and prepare for power changeover." After magnetizing the holdtights, Trystin called up the shutdown list.

"Accumulators . . ."

". . . discharged."

"Fusactor . . ."

". . . stand by."

"Compensators . . ."

". . . open."

Trystin cleared his throat of the dust that never quite seemed to leave the ship, no matter how scrupulous the cleanup.

"Senior tech . . . power changeover."

"Changeover, ser."

As the full grav of orbit control pressed Trystin into his couch, he took a deep breath.

"Time to go up to ops and debrief. It should be short this time."

Trystin slowly pried himself and his damp shipsuit out of the couch.

40

 Trystin's boots whispered on the heavy plastic of the locking tube. He glanced back past the automatic locks that would close if the pressure dropped, but the lower corridor was almost empty, except for a young tech headed back to the *Mishima.*

Trystin wiped his forehead, still warm, even though he'd had a cool-down and a shower after his exercise in the outer orbit station's high-gee workout room. At times, he wasn't sure whether the downtime of two to six months between troids was better or the busy times when the revs were attacking. He didn't run the risk of getting killed in downtimes, just being bored. The outer orbit station's facilities were limited, and strained by the force buildup, and James had a tendency to philosophize too much about the old Shinto times.

Since Mara inner orbit control hadn't ever been built to support large numbers of Service craft, most ships had to dock at Parvati outer orbit control, although they were all rotated through Mara orbit station for relief.

Trystin sniffed. The corridor, like all station corridors, smelled faintly of plastic, metal, and ozone, with an underscent of oil. He paused at the lock as Muriami, wearing the duty stunner, stepped toward him.

"Lieutenant?" asked Tech Muriami. "The captain was asking for you earlier. He's in his stateroom."

The tech's careful tone alerted Trystin.

"Did he say what he wanted?"

"No, ser."

"Thank you, Muriami."

Trystin carried his exercise bag to his stateroom and dumped it next to the console. Pretty soon, he'd have to do more laundry, and that was a pain. He went back into the passageway, closing his door.

The captain leaned out of his stateroom. "Trystin . . . need to talk a moment." A lock of short black hair fell across his face, and he slowly pushed it back.

"Yes, ser."

James left the door open. He was sitting in the plastic chair with the purple cushion on it when Trystin closed the stateroom door.

"Sit down." The captain gestured at the chair on the other side of the small circular plastic table anchored to the deck. A half-empty glass bottle rested on the table, and James held a glass in which two fingers of an amber liquid remained.

Trystin sat. His eyes flicked to the half-empty bottle and the label.

"Scotch. Actual Cambrian Scotch. Not . . . so good as the old Earth kind, but that's gone . . . damned Immortals." James took another swallow from the glass, then poured another three fingers into the glass. "Yes . . . I'm drunk, soused, stoned, fried, shroomed—you name it. Wouldn't you be?" He looked owlishly at Trystin. "Only reason I'm alive is you. You know how that feels?"

"I wouldn't say that."

"I would. In fact . . . I did." James fingered the glass. "Damned fine pilot you are . . . ought to be a major. You'll make it . . . but you won't make subcommander. Know why?"

Trystin waited.

"Because you look like a friggin' rev, and nobody wants a commander who looks like a rev. . . . It's going to get worse," James emphasized, overannunciating, pausing between each word. "They have people in their belts smelting—belts . . . smelts, nice rhyme—mining, building. They got people everywhere. And they all produce. What do we have? We had technology and honor, but they got technology now, and honor is not enough." He paused and looked at Trystin. "You got honor, but it's not enough."

"I'd like to think so."

James snorted. "You don't drink, do you?"

"Wine, ser."

"Sit down."

"I am sitting." Trystin was glad the ship was in standdown. Then, being in stand-down was probably why James had the bottle. Where had he gotten Scotch at three hundred creds a bottle? Of course, three hundred creds probably meant nothing to a Sasaki.

"Do you drink?"

"Wine."

"You drink wine. So you're not a dyed-in-the-blood Revenant, and you drink tea, and they don't. How about cafe?"

"I don't like the taste."

"Good man. Tastes like boiled revvie boots, even if they don't drink it."

"Ever tried sake?"

"Once. I like wine better."

James took another quick swallow. Trystin waited.

"You believe in revealed truths, Trystin? Like the revs believe that every so often the Prophet will return? Jesus, then Brigger or Younger, whatever his name was, and then Toren?"

"They believe it," Trystin said slowly. "Personally, I have a hard time believing in a God that has to use prophets to deliver his word."

"So do I. Honor, that's what's important. You got honor, Trystin. Look like a friggin' rev, but you got honor. . . ." He picked up the bottle. "I'll be fine. We're on stand-down. Another two months before that next troid arrives. Plenty of time to get sober." He poured more into the glass. "Get out of here, and let me drink."

Trystin closed the door behind him, after a look back at the dark-haired major holding the two-thirds empty bottle. He paused in the narrow corridor.

Did the captain drink just because of the stresses? Or the isolation? Captains were isolated. And James, because he was a Sasaki, was more isolated than most. Who could a Sasaki trust as a pilot officer? A Doniger, with equal prestige and position? A Desoll, of old stiff-necked anglo heritage? If he were James, would he trust Trystin? How would he cope with the isolation, the looks, the implications that he only had the triple bars because of his name?

Trystin frowned. They were all isolated, when you got right down to it. In a strange way, the connection of the system nets and implants isolated Service officers more than their ancient predecessors. Allowing instant data access reduced the need for contact, and the politeness and formality of the whole Eco-Tech culture made personal contacts so superficially smooth that most people didn't even see the isolation. At least Trystin hadn't, not with his having to worry about survival on one level or another.

He shook his head. Had anything really changed since he'd left Mara? He was still waiting and trying to stop revs, except the stakes were higher. Still waiting and reacting—and knowing it wasn't enough, because too many of the damned paragliders still got through. No wonder James drank.

And as for the drinking . . . anyone but a Sasaki or a Doniger or a Mishima would be in trouble . . . but who was about to accuse the captain? And why?

Trystin walked past his stateroom and up to the near-dead cockpit, calling up the visual screen, so he could look out at the cold, cold stars, and out into the darkness beyond the unseen Kali where the seemingly endless line of Revenant troid ships continued to bear down on Parvati.

41

Trystin squared the ship on its troid-buster course. "I have the con, Lieutenant."

"You have it, ser."

"Red one is ready." Liam's voice—tinny as always—reported through the net and both pilots' implants.

"Ignite red one." The captain's voice was cold.

"Red one is go."

"Red two."

"Red two is go."

The wait for reloading was shorter, but still perceptible.

"Red three."

"Red three is go!"

"Red four."

"Red four is go."

"Changeover to standard torps."

"Changing over this time."

"Desensitize."

"Desensitized."

"Full shields. Get us clear, Lieutenant."

"Shield in place, Captain. I have it." Trystin rechecked, and dropped ship's grav to point two while throwing the extra power into the shields, and dropping the ship's nose almost straight down, while torquing up power from the fusactor and the accumulators, letting the fusactor rise to one-hundred-ten-percent output for almost a standard minute before dropping output to just shy of max.

Scattered telltales began to flash amber.

Trystin shut down the ventilation system and shifted the last of the power for gravs into the thrusters.

With what he'd done, the internal simulation of the ship's position was almost useless, and he ignored the simulated position on the representational screen, waiting until he felt the wave front had passed.

Trystin swallowed. With the screens essentially dead, the ship's ventilation off, and the grav system bypassed to throw power to the thrusters, the cockpit was again a stuffy coffin, except that the steady acceleration pinned the crew in place.

He moistened his dry lips, his eyes flickering toward the blank red-tinged visual screens. Finally, he said, "Removing desensitizing."

"Receiving input."

Three blue-tinged blips continued to close on the *Willis*, but all that was left of the troid was a debris cone shrouded in an energy haze.

This time, the damned troid had carried almost four dozen of the scouts, and they'd shredded most of the Coalition corvettes.

Trystin calculated, and recalculated. The *Willis*'s shields were strong enough for perhaps two simultaneous torps—once.

With the three scouts coming, and no one close enough to help—only the *Mishima,* the *Izanagi,* and the *Morrigan* had reached the launch point—Trystin was on his own.

"Fire one! Two!"

He didn't expect too much from the torps, except that the scouts would have to raise full shields, and that meant a slight loss of acceleration.

Then he cut the thrusters, and slewed the ship sideways—at a right angle to the course line—with the attitude jets.

Even before the cruiser was reoriented, he loosed two more torps, these at the flanking scouts, followed by two more. Then he pulsed the thrusters once at full power, and shut down all external radiation from the ship. Without shields, the *Willis* veered slowly away from her previous course line, but her primary vector remained along the high-accel route set by Trystin after the red torp launch.

Trystin watched the positions of the rev scouts, hoping their energy detectors had locked on the thruster pulse.

The blue-tinged blips drew nearer, nearer.

Trystin kept calculating, his breath coming faster, faster than he wanted, but there was no way the *Willis* could stand off three of the beefed-up revvie scouts at once, not just with screens and torps.

"Close . . ." James's words came through the net, as if he were whispering.

"Need them to be close . . . real close."

As the scouts probed, screaming toward the cruiser that had "vanished" off the energy-detection screens, Trystin released two torps, forced one hundred twenty percent of fusactor output and full accumulator loads through the thrusters for thirty seconds, then dropped the fusactor to normal, released two more torps, and jammed the shields to full with three-quarter max acceleration.

"Shit . . ."

A dull thud followed the exclamation.

Trystin ignored the possibly injured tech and checked the screens. Unless the revs were playing dead, and Trystin didn't care so long as they didn't combine to chase the *Willis,* the ploy had worked. The thrusters had sliced through one rev, and that was certain, because the detectors showed hot metal. It looked like a torp had gotten the second, and the third was making a wide turn, trying to escape the *Willis.*

Trystin sighed and lowered the shields to half-power, while cranking up the thrusters, and heading into a stern chase.

The rev began to slow, fractionally.

Trystin shook his head.

Instead of closing beyond max torp range, he began to fire torps, one after the other, in pulsed intervals.

The rev flared into energy after the seventh torp.

Trystin eased the ship into a long arc back toward outer orbit control. As usual, as the attack had progressed, the damned troid had spewed forth its cargo of radar-transparent paragliders and their shielded and deadly cargoes destined to create more havoc for the hard-pressed Maran perimeter troops.

There might not be any scouts or troid left, but there had been more than thirty, at Trystin's rough and quick count, of the ghostly gliders sent forth. He hoped the patrols off Mara could pick up most of them.

"Iron Mace two, this is Sledge Control. Interrogative status."

"Status is green beta—armaments and propulsion." The accumulators were hiccuping, and Trystin didn't blame them after all the different power demands he'd thrown on the equipment.

"Understand green beta."

"That's affirmative."

"Stet, Mace two."

"Accumulators?" asked the captain.

"Yes, ser."

"I'll take her in. You've been through it."

"You have it, ser."

Trystin wasn't damp, but soaking wet, and he pulsed the tech station. "Is there any tea or water or anything intact in the mess?"

"Not much, ser. We're working on it."

In the background, he heard Albertini muttering. ". . . after that, he wants tea?"

"After that, you're alive," snapped Keiko at the junior tech. "We'll send something forward, ser," she replied to Trystin.

Trystin took a deep breath. He didn't like what he was doing to the ship, or the crew, but it seemed as though every troid attack required more from him.

He leaned back in the couch. How much more could he give? How many more new angles could he try without turning the *Willis* into scrap metal or ionized gas?

Keiko handed him a cup of Sustain. "Sorry, ser."

"That's all right. Thank you."

She turned to James. "Captain?"

"I'm fine."

Trystin sipped the Sustain slowly, hoping it wouldn't hit his stomach with too much of a jolt.

"Iron Mace two, closure is green."

"Stet, Control. Holding green," answered James, brushing limp black hair off his forehead, almost as damp as Trystin's.

"Mace two, cleared to dock. Maintain low thrust."

"Control, this is two, beginning final approach."

The *Willis* crept in toward the wall of metal and composite—slowly, slowly.

Thud!

Trystin winced as the *Willis* clunked up against the outer orbit control station.

"Relax, Trystin. That's less than you just put the old lady through." James flashed a boyish grin. "With all the stuff the revs are throwing at us, I need some practice somewhere."

James magnetized the holdtights. "Lock-on. Apply mechanical holdtights and prepare for power changeover." He began the shutdown list, and the items and replies went back and forth over the net, silently, between the captain and Trystin.

"Accumulators . . ."

". . . discharged."

After the captain announced power changeover, and the full grav of orbit control pressed Trystin into his couch, he just sat there for a time while the techs ensured full docking.

He'd thought twenty-percent losses per battle had been bad enough, but this time . . . what? Three cruisers left of eight, and a handful of corvettes. So far, there had only been a troid ship every four standard months, or thereabouts—two since his near-disastrous first troid encounter, and now they were back to where he'd started, except that the Coalition was losing even more ships.

Finally, he stood, picked up the mug, and walked back to the mess where Albertini stared at a dented samovar. "Ser, what do you have against the samovar?"

"Nothing." Trystin grinned. "I like tea. But the revs don't, I guess."

"They're crazy, all of them." Standing in the corner,

Liam Akibono took a deep swallow of double-strength Sustain.

Trystin winced at the thought of what that much Sustain would do to his guts.

"You don't agree?"

"I don't see how your guts stay in place with that much Sustain."

"What about the revs? Better if we could use hellburners on all their planets. We don't want their real estate. Why can't they leave us alone? They're crazy, that's for sure."

"They can't be totally crazy. Otherwise they wouldn't have been so much of a threat for so long." Trystin blotted his forehead.

"You ever met any?" Liam took another pull of Sustain.

"I had to interrogate some of them when I was on the perimeter. Some were just like those in the corvettes, ready to throw anything away to kill me. Some were very thoughtful and analytical—those were the officers." Trystin set his cup in the rack and wiped his forehead. He'd need a shower after the debrief, and it was going to be long, that he knew.

"So . . . the revs have a lot of idealistically crazy cannon fodder led by analytical and thoughtful officers?" asked Keiko as she reracked a chair in the mess-cabin corner.

Trystin shrugged. "That's what I saw. I also saw a lot of new equipment and tactics."

"Someone has to be giving it to them. They're not that smart. No one who believes in all that crap their Prophet spouted can be that smart." Liam refilled his mug with more Sustain.

"Lieutenant Desoll, to the quarterdeck, please. Lieutenant Akibono, you have the ship."

Trystin got the message on the link a second or so before it hit the speakers. "Time to go. You have it." Trystin grabbed his beret.

"Yes, ser," answered Liam.

Trystin met James at the quarterdeck. The captain even looked slightly frazzled as they walked toward the station ops center.

"I couldn't help but hear Liam's comments about the revs," the captain said slowly. "Do you think we have traitors?"

Trystin took a deep breath. "I guess anything's possible, but . . . I remember talking with a senior commander after the first big revvie assault on Mara, and she pointed out that a lot of the technology in the new rev tanks was better than what we had. . . ."

"I wonder if it's being funneled to them first?" mused James.

"It wouldn't seem likely. Those tanks were designed before I was born. They sat on a troid ship for more than twenty years. How could anyone sit on technology that long without it leaking out?" Trystin forced a laugh. "Unless half the Coalition leadership were in on it?"

"Maybe they are. Maybe they are. Then again, maybe we just *think* that technology is that old."

Trystin pursed his lips. "I don't see how they could translate to a troid ship. It's hard enough to hit a whole stellar system. And the number of translations they'd have to make would show on the sensitive EDIs."

"Maybe." James shook his head. "Maybe. What about the damned Farhkans? They could be in on it?"

"They could," Trystin agreed. "But we've gotten better translation stuff from them, stuff the revs don't have."

"They've got to have an angle," mused James.

They probably did, Trystin reflected, but it wasn't technology, and that bothered him—because . . . what was more important than technology?

They pulled themselves up the grav tubes to beta deck and continued onward toward the debriefing room.

Two techs stood in the corridor. The one with the toolbox gestured, and Trystin absently cranked up his hearing sensitivity. "Those two . . . the devils . . . captain, he's a Sasaki. Commander Frenkel shorted him . . . sent Frenkel to run the rev camp on south island . the other . . . stand a ship on end . . . and laugh . . ."

Trystin lost the words as they turned into the debriefing room. Him. laughing about what he did to the *Willis?* As if he had any choice. He looked around and swallowed. Twelve pilots, six from the cruisers, and six corvette pilots—out of more than nearly forty that had been at the prestrike briefing.

They called him a devil? For doing what he had to in order to stay alive? He tried not to think about it . . . but couldn't there be a better way?

How? It was taking everything the Coalition had to hold the revs to what seemed to be a stalemate—at least that was what he saw from the *Willis*. The real situation might be worse than that, if people with connections like James were talking about traitors. Or Farhkan interference.

"How do you like being a devil?" asked James quietly as he eased into one of the briefing-room chairs.

"Oh . . ." Trystin paused. "Better a live devil than a dead angel, I guess . . . though I wonder sometimes."

"So do I."

They sat waiting for Commander Atsugi.

42

 A good third of the telltales in front of Trystin winked amber, and the net crackled under the system overloads. He calculated the vectors to the oncoming revs and triggered the torp releases.

"Fire one!"

"Fire two!"

"Both loaders jammed, ser!" That was the response from weapons.

The oncoming revvie corvettes, five blue blips, shields locked tight together, loomed nearer in the representational screen, closing to less than a fraction of a light-minute.

The single torp from the *Willis* flashed harmlessly against the joined screens.

His guts jumped up in his throat as Trystin dumped all the power maintaining the ship's grav into the shields. The accumulators began to hiccup, and power surges created static across the net, as more of the telltales flashed amber, then red.

The ventilators' hissing died away, and the odor of burning insulation seeped from the ducts.

None of the other Coalition ships were close enough to blunt the revvie attack, and Trystin yanked the ship's nose almost straight up, then jammed on max overload power from the fusactor and the accumulators. The fusactor lined out at one hundred twenty percent.

The rest of the telltales began to switch from amber to red, a movement that began to cascade across the board in front of Trystin.

Even with the ventilation system down and all the power shifted into the thrusters, the blue blips closed in on the *Willis.* The accumulators gave a last hiccuping surge, and crashed.

Abruptly, Trystin shut down all external radiation and applied full desensitization.

Crump! The ship actually shuddered with the torp explosion, not a direct hit, but close enough, and a faint hissing grew into a low roar, and what felt like a wind swept across the cockpit.

The telltales gleamed red, those that remained operational. Then the cockpit boards began to blank out. The emergency lights on the left side of the cockpit flashed, then went black.

Crump! With the near-impact of another torp, the *Willis* shuddered.

Trystin's ears popped as the atmosphere poured out of the *Willis.* He unstrapped and clawed his way, weightless, through the air toward the armor rack, feeling his eyes bulge as he did, trying to keep his mouth shut.

All the lights failed, and the entire cockpit went black. Trystin groped for the armor behind the pilot's couch, trying to hold on to the couch against the air loss that threatened to rip him out of the cockpit, feeling his skin bulge, his closed eyes close to popping from his face, the air seeping from his nose, and vacuum burning down his nasal passages—

He bolted upright in his bunk, gasping, sweat pouring down his face, his underwear as soaked as after an engagement.

He tried to laugh—the dream had been an engagement, a brutal one—but with the dryness in his throat, all that occurred was a rasping cough.

Slowly, slowly, he swung his bare feet onto the cold metal deck and lowered his head into his hands.

"Frig . . . frig . . ." he muttered to himself.

Like all violent nightmares, it had felt so real. His heart was still pounding, his mouth dry. Even his eyes felt like they had been vacuum-burned.

Why now? What did it mean? That his subconscious was telling him that he was running out of time and tricks?

How long could he keep pulling new tactics out of his ass? How long could he push the *Willis* to the edge of the envelope before systems failed in a catastrophic cascade? Just like the one he had experienced in the nightmare.

For a time, he just held his head.

At that moment, the whole damned war seemed so futile. Both sides just kept escalating, yet what could he do? There was no doubt that the revs wouldn't stop, even if the Coalition surrendered Mara and half—or all—of its planoformed real estate.

He took a long shuddering breath, and stood in the darkness, walking in a small circle in his cabin, letting the air from the ventilators dry him and his soaked underwear.

Tomorrow he'd be all right. He would be. Tomorrow.

He kept walking in tight circles, trying not to think about the dream. It had only been a dream. A dream. Just a dream.

43

As the *Willis* slipped up to Mara orbit station, Trystin scanned the representational screen again, still amazed at the numbers of EDI traces.

Nearly a dozen corvettes crisscrossed the orbit of Mara, trying to track down inbound paragliders. According to the official reports, the paraglider neutralization ratio was seventy percent.

Trystin snorted. Seventy percent of the *verified* troid launches, but he'd seen the official paraglider counts, and those counts were half what he'd seen—and he'd been there when the rev gliders had spewed forth from the troids.

Nearly a year and a half earlier, when he and the *Willis* had arrived from Perdya, the standard force had been three cruisers and a dozen corvettes at outer orbit control. Now, outer orbit control was twice its former size, and host to nearly three times the number of ships. And nearly three times as many corvettes patrolled Mara as part of the stepped-up effort to try to stop the assault gliders.

The greater numbers allowed use of interlinked shields and multiple formations, and the newer longer-range torps had helped even more, but not enough. Each troid ship had more and more scouts, and the revvie scouts were now nearly as big and as fast as the Coalition corvettes—and they carried more torps.

A red-tinged pulse clung to the screen representation of the orbit station itself—just a single red pulse.

"There's a Farhkan ship docked here, ser."

"They dock here every so often, the insidious aliens."

Trystin reflected. The Farhkan that had interviewed him in Klyseen would have had to use the orbit station, but he hadn't seemed insidious. Persistent, but not insidious.

"Iron Mace two, cleared into gamma three."

"Stet, Control, approaching gamma three this time."

Trystin pulsed the thrusters ever so slightly and then trimmed the ship with the attitude jets. The *clunk* was barely perceptible.

"Very neat . . . as usual." James stretched.

Trystin magnetized the holdtights, and they went through the shutdown checklist.

After the power changeover, Keiko's voice came through the speakers. "Lieutenant? There's a tech here with something official for you."

James looked at Trystin.

Trystin looked back and shrugged.

"Don't tell me they're detaching you. I know SysCon's short of pilots, but . . . it is a little early."

Trystin could understand James's concerns. The captain had the tactical and political savvy, but not the instinctive and reactive abilities. They made a good team. Without a second as good as Trystin, the *Willis* could have been another energy-conversion statistic. Without some of James's insight, Trystin would have gotten himself backed into situations from which extrication would have been difficult, if not impossible. But he still had nightmares . . . and they were getting more frequent.

Trystin unstrapped and walked aft to the quarterdeck.

"Lieutenant Desoll?" The harried-looking tech thrust a folder at Trystin. "This is for you, ser." Then the tech, with several other folders under his arm, was gone.

Keiko and Liam, who had appeared from nowhere, watched as he opened the envelope folder.

He read, and then he laughed, shaking his head. "I have to go get a special physical in the station's medical center. That's all." He knew why the Farhkan ship was docked there, probably making the annual or biennial trip, or whatever rounds the Farhkan doctors needed to make.

"We're still stuck with him," James said with a smile.

"What can I say?" He frowned. "This says 'soonest,' and I'd better hurry."

He headed back toward his stateroom.

"The Farhkan study?" asked James.

Trystin stopped. "Yes."

"That came after my time. How do you see them?"

Trystin paused. "Strange. Not what you expect. Somehow too alien and too human all at the same time."

"Insidious. They've got their own agenda, and we'd be better off without it, but we need their help."

"I'd like to know what they really want," Trystin admitted.

"So would half of Service HQ, but we need the technology, and they parcel it out in return for seemingly useless information. Insidious . . . worse than the revs." James shook his head, then added, "I may be out when you get back. Liam needs to check with logistics. He's still having problems with the loaders. So touch base with him. All right?"

"We'll work something out."

After a quick shower, Trystin pulled on his informal greens, rather than a shipsuit, and headed for the med center.

The station still reeked of plastic and weedgrass—oily weedgrass—and of too many people.

When Trystin walked into the med center, buried down on the fifth level, and checked in, a familiar face greeted him.

"Sit down, Trystin. It'll be a while." Major Ulteena Freyer smiled ironically at him.

Trystin sat down. "I didn't know you were here—in Parvati system, I mean."

"I haven't been here long. I'm the new CO of the *Mishima*."

"Congratulations."

"I'm not sure about that. You've been getting pounded pretty heavily."

"Where were you?"

"Safrya. They got a bunch of troids, but the lag time meant—"

"Lag time?"

"Safyra took less time to planoform than Mara has.

The early projections were just the opposite."

Trystin nodded, finally understanding. The Revenants usually targeted the planets where real estate was closest to habitable, but Mara had lagged, and Safyra had proved far easier, due to more frozen CO_2 and buried water than discovered in the initial survey. But the revvie troid ship attacks had been planned thirty to fifty years earlier, right after the Harmony mess.

"Of course, that doesn't always hold true. Look at the mess that just happened in the Helconya system."

"What mess?" Trystin's voice sharpened.

"You haven't heard? They sent a big troid through there. I guess we managed to hold them off, but some of their scouts actually attacked the planoforming orbit stations before they were destroyed. Someone from your group—Tekanawe—a major, I think, spearheaded the counterattack. She got the Star. Posthumously."

Trystin shook his head. That was all he could do. How could he find out about Salya?

"Are you all right?"

"Damned revs . . ." He pursed his lips. How could he find out? "Is there any way to find out more?"

Ulteena shook her head. "I don't think so. I had a cousin there, but no one would tell me anything. What's the matter?"

"My sister was in charge of one of the biological airspore projects."

"I'm sorry." Ulteena looked at him, her dark eyes showing concern. "She could be just fine. They told me the stations survived, and if they did—"

"Some of the people did." Trystin moistened his lips. "I hope so. I hope so."

"You're close to her."

Trystin nodded.

"I'm sorry. You might try the admin office. Sometimes, they know—transfers and the like."

"Thanks. It's a thought." Trystin licked his lips. Salya—how could he find out?

They looked up as a technician appeared.

"Lieutenant Matsumi?"

A stocky officer got up and followed the tech.

"Sometimes . . . sometimes, I'd just like to smash them all." Trystin forced his fists to unclench.

"Force works—to a degree. If the other side survives, though, it can make things worse," observed Ulteena.

"I could destroy Wystuh and everything on the continent, perhaps life on all of Orum."

Ulteena nodded.

"Don't humor me. It's simple enough. Take the largest translation ship available and accelerate it to the max with subtranslation drives—beefed-up versions of what we use for torps. Then aim it at Orum." Trystin wiped his forehead.

"What would stop them from doing the same thing?"

"Theoretically, nothing. Except the revs need living space more than we do. Right now, we're fighting on their terms, where every person we lose hurts us more than the thousands they lose."

"The planning staff won't buy that sort of destruction."

"What kind would they prefer?" asked Trystin.

"You're also proposing using a bigger hammer. They could decide to use an even bigger one—like running troid ships into planets, and where would that leave any of us?"

"About as dead as we're going to be if this war continues the way it is."

"It isn't that bad."

"No? How about this?" Trystin deepened his voice and quoted, " 'Ye shall consume all the people which the Lord thy God shall deliver unto thee; thine eyes shall have no pity upon them . . .' That's from their friggin' *Book of Toren*."

"You are cynical, Trystin. You've got that open, trusting face, but . . . a lot more goes on than most people see." Ulteena half laughed, half frowned. "Maybe that's why . . ."

"Why what?" he asked belatedly.

"Nothing." She smiled, an expression half wry, half warm. "It won't be long before you get the third bar. Promotions are stepping up."

"More casualties. It makes sense."

Ulteena lowered her voice, and Trystin had to kick in intensified hearing. "There are more and more battles where Coalition ships are unaccounted for."

"So?"

"There's a rumor. If you slew the ship and apply power just as you translate—it increases the translation error severalfold, maybe more."

"Pilots are doing that?"

"It's better than waiting for a torp spread you won't survive, isn't it?"

"But that means you'd have to climb—"

"If you get a chance, keep your eyes open, Trystin. You'll see what I mean." Ulteena shifted her weight in the plastic chair as a tech approached.

"Major Freyer?"

"Take care, Trystin." Her hand brushed his almost casually, except for the pressure of her fingers on his skin, and she was gone, following the med tech.

The warmth of her touch lingered, and he wanted to shake his head. What was she saying? In how many ways? One moment she was almost approachable, and in the next she was talking about pilots translating to escape being torched. Certainly, that made a sort of sense. Even Commander Folsom had pointed out that returning to fight was better than being fried. But stretching out translation effect to avoid returning to combat immediately—or at all?

Was Ulteena telling him that the whole war was useless, to escape with his skin if he could? He took a deep breath. Was it that bad? He tried to consider it—rationally, as his father would have said. Both sides were putting more effort and materiel into the war, and all that seemed to be happening was that more people were being killed and more materiel being lost. Could the Coalition do anything any differently? He snorted. How would he know? Those on the front lines knew little enough about the big picture and had too many concerns about staying alive.

All too soon, the tech was back.

"Lieutenant Desoll?"

He did not see Ulteena as he headed for the diagnostic console, nor as he later waited for his interview.

A squat dark-haired doctor reclaimed him from the narrow plastic chair outside two adjoining offices in the corner of the medical bay, where the odor of disinfectant warred with weedgrass, plastic, and ozone. Trystin's nose itched, but he did not rub it as he rose and followed the woman.

"Lieutenant Desoll, I'm Dr. Suruki." The Service physician nodded her head toward the Farhkan. "This is Dr. Naille Jhule."

"Greetings, Lieutenant." Again, Trystin could feel the words scripting through his implant.

"Greetings."

This Farhkan was different from Ghere, even if the green tusks and red eyes were the same.

"You know the drill, Lieutenant. I'll be in the next office." Suruki shut the door.

The comm block dropped around the room as Trystin settled into one chair and the Farhkan into the other.

The alien's tongue flickered, not quite touching the green crystalline teeth. "Are all human cultures composed of thieves, Lieutenant?"

Trystin took a deep breath. Why did all the Farhkans focus on theft and ethics? "As I told Dr. Ghere, I suspect that all intelligent cultures must practice theft in some basic degree in order to survive."

"Are you a thief?"

"As I also told Dr. Ghere, the way that question is phrased bothers me. Yes, I have taken others' lives so that I, or others, might live. I suppose that could be termed theft, but I don't know that that makes me a thief."

"Is it the word or the idea that bothers you the most?"

Trystin shrugged. "I've pretty much admitted that the term 'thief' bothers me."

"If you do not admit you are a thief, does that not make you a liar?"

Trystin swallowed. More ethics. "That assumes that I accept your definition . . . and the values behind that definition."

The Farhkan did not respond immediately.

Trystin waited.

"Should values change from species to species?"

"They do. Whether they should is another question."

"Should your species and mine have different interpretations of what values are the most important?"

"I suspect we do."

"But should we?"

Trystin frowned.

"Should you and the cultural group you call the Revenants have different interpretations of what values are the most important?"

"We do. Some of them are very different."

"Should you? Are there absolute universal values?"

"Some say so."

"I would ask that you reflect upon those questions." The Farhkan rose and waited for Trystin to stand.

"All right." Trystin bowed slightly and opened the door, stopping to knock at the adjoining door. "We're finished, Doctor."

"Thank you." Dr. Suruki opened the door and smiled. "Thank you, Lieutenant."

Trystin walked back out into the main med-center area, then into the corridor, wondering why the Farhkans were asking about value differences between the Eco-Techs and the Revenants. That implied they had studied both cultures—but for what purpose? James was right; something insidious was going on, but the Coalition was afraid to look too deeply, and that meant even more trouble. Even Ulteena had hinted at that.

"Trystin?"

He looked up. Ulteena Freyer, standing alone in Service greens as station and other ship personnel passed, gestured.

"Yes?" He walked toward her.

"I wanted to say good-bye. You look disturbed. I hope you're not taking the Farhkans too seriously."

"How can I not take them seriously?" He forced a laugh. "They keep asking these questions that pilots shouldn't consider."

Her forehead crinkled.

He could see the fine lines running from the corners of her eyes, and wanted to reach out, but his hand never left his side.

"They ask you questions?" she finally asked, as if each word were a struggle.

"Usually about ethics. What about you?"

"Mathematics. That was my doctorate. They ask about the applicability of certain . . . parameters."

Trystin found himself moistening his lips.

"I have to go. I'm already late to report." Her hand touched his shoulder for a moment, and dropped away as she smiled briefly. "Good luck. I mean it."

"Same to you."

He watched her brisk stride for a moment until she disappeared around the curve in the corridor. She had seemed almost human. He snorted—more than human—like a real live woman, or was he imagining that?

Finally, he turned and started up to admin. He needed to find out about Salya before he headed back to the *Willis* to relieve Liam. If they'd tell him anything . . . And Liam could wait. So could his questions about the Farhkans, at least until he was back on the ship.

<h1 style="text-align:center">44</h1>

 The *Willis* slewed as Trystin recomputed the red torp launch to compensate for a multiple-thrust vector created by his efforts to avoid the seemingly endless lines of revvie scouts.

"Take her in, Trystin," James ordered. "Weapons, the

lieutenant has the con. Follow his commands."

"Stet, ser."

"Commence torp changeover," Trystin ordered.

"Commencing changeover."

A single revvie torp flared against the *Willis*'s screens, and Trystin punched up the thrusters to one hundred ten percent for twenty seconds as soon as the rev's torp energy flared away.

"Red one is ready." Liam's tinny voice reported through the net and both pilots' implants.

Trystin juggled the multiple inputs of the three scouts converging on the *Willis*, recorrected the course line, and swallowed. At least there weren't five of them all at once—this time. His forehead was streaming sweat, and he automatically wiped the dampness away on the back of his shipsuit's sleeve.

"Red one go!" His voice was ragged.

"Red one is go."

"Red two."

"Red two is go."

Trystin kicked in more thrust for another quick pulse as the loaders set up the next two red torps.

"Red three."

"Red three is go!"

"Red four."

"Red four is go."

"Changeover to standard torps."

"Changing over this time."

Even before Liam acknowledged the changeover, Trystin was twisting the ship into a head-to-head with the lead scout, using his implant, and feeling the lines of figures flowing through him, like powered arrows. His stomach was in his throat, unsurprisingly, since the ship had been on minimum internal gee for most of the engagement.

Even with the possible sensor overload, he couldn't afford to desensitize, not with three revs nearly on top of them, not for more than a moment or two at least.

To get close enough to the troid had meant letting the

revvie scouts cover the escape positions, and there was no way the *Willis* would survive running through the debris caused by the troid's explosion.

"Changeover complete," Liam reported.

"Fire one! Two!" Trystin snapped the direct-feed commands into the system.

As the tubes reloaded, Trystin shifted full power to the left thruster momentarily, then recomputed on the nearly head-to-head course with the first revvie scout. He wished the *Willis* had greater simultaneous torp-fire capability, like the new cruisers.

Stop wishing! Idiot! He pursed his lips.

"Fire one! Two!"

Two more torps pounded out toward the rev that blocked the *Willis*.

Less than two seconds to red-torp impact!

"Desensitizing!" he snapped, ignoring the check-cross-check procedure, shutting down the sensors. Then he dropped the thrusters off-line and fed the excess fusactor output into the ship's shields, letting the *Willis* run toward the rev blindly.

Ten seconds after computed impact, he barked, "Removing desensitizing."

"Receiving input."

The beefed-up shields flared with another torp impact, and the amber telltales flared on the capacity board.

Trystin ignored the amber warnings, just as he ignored the nightmares and the might-have-beens and the what-ifs.

"Fire one! Two!"

The representational screen showed that the revvie troid ship had not fragmented totally, but split into two, no, three, large chunks.

Finally, after six torps, and two that seemed to impact, the one revvie scout flared.

Two more blue-dashed trails continued to converge on the *Willis*, and Trystin lowered the shields to normal and powered the cruiser into a three-gee turn. He could almost feel the plates creaking as the ship centered head-on-head on the next rev. While head-on-head was a hard torp shot, the position gave the *Willis* the greatest shield advantage and the smallest target exposure, and with the cruiser's multiple-torp firing capability, a greater opportunity for potting a scout.

Theoretically, the shields would brush aside a scout, but Trystin didn't ever want to try that. Besides, the shields wouldn't stop a pair of torps that impacted simultaneously at the same point, and that was exactly what a revvie pilot should try in those circumstances.

"Fire one! Two!"

Trystin rechecked and torqued up power from the fusactor and the accumulators, letting the fusactor rise to one hundred ten percent output for almost a standard minute before dropping output to just shy of max.

As more scattered telltales began to flash amber, Trystin shut down the ventilation system and, as soon as the tubes reloaded, loosed two more torps.

The system redlined him a message that he was down to four torps. He swallowed, breathing against the gee load and trying to ignore the sudden stuffiness of the cabin.

He moistened his dry lips.

In the screens, he could see two scouts hammering at the *Mishima,* with another pair working toward the *Izanagi.* The *Morrigan* was already dust and expanding energy. But the *Campbell* was free and sliding out to support the *Izanagi.*

"Fire one! Two!"

Although the rev raised full shields, they weren't enough, and Trystin permitted himself a tight smile, until he realized that the third scout was tailchasing, and that was the *Willis*'s weakest shield point.

He calculated, though the data took nanoseconds, then cut the thrusters, and used the attitude jets to flip the *Willis* end over end. Another full blast on the thrusters, and then he diverted the power to the shields. They flared amber as the rev's torp impacted. Flared amber, but held, as the rev flashed toward the *Willis.*

"Fire one! Two!"

Trystin flipped the ship again, ignoring his own nausea

and a retching sound from aft, and put full power on the thrusters.

The combination of the thrusters' energy flow and the torps was sufficient, and entropy was increased with the scattered fragments of another revvie scout.

Trystin scanned the screens, noting that heavy green-tinged dashes ran from the *Campbell*'s screen image toward the fragments of the troid. All three troid killers impacted, and this time the fragments were of suitably infinitesimal size.

Continuing to power the thrusters, Trystin pushed the *Willis* toward the *Mishima*.

One of the rev scouts flared away from the other cruiser. Trystin calculated and grinned.

"Fire one! Two!"

The dashes representing the last two torps streaked across the screen toward the broadside exposure of the fleeing revvie scout.

"No torps remaining. No torps remaining!" the system redlined at Trystin.

The revvie scout vanished from the screen with the twin torp impact.

"How . . . ?"

"Shield malfunction. That was probably why he broke off the attack." Trystin answered the captain's unfinished question as he continued to scan the system.

Two corvettes and the *Willis*, the *Mishima*, and the *Campbell*—those were all that remained.

Trystin nodded as his senses verified that the *Mishima*—and Ulteena—had made it. He hoped the next troid was a long time coming—a very long time—as he eased back on the thrusters.

"Sledge team, this is Sledge Control Alternate, return to base this time."

Trystin looked at James as the captain broadcast. He hadn't realized that James was the senior officer remaining. Trystin wasn't sure that James had known it either until he'd taken stock of the casualties.

Trystin wiped his forehead again. He'd need to do more

laundry once they returned to outer orbit control. This one had been almost as bad as his recurring nightmare.

The accumulators were hiccuping again, and the shields were still running in the amber, and most of the sensors were operating at reduced efficiencies. He couldn't mentally sum up the smaller amber warnings.

At least the most sensitive EDI screens showed no troids in range, and that meant a few months' respite—maybe more.

The crew and the ship all needed it.

So did Trystin.

Maybe he could find out about Salya . . . except no one knew, or would say. Maybe he could make more sense out of a war that got bigger and never changed. Maybe he could understand what the Farhkans wanted. Maybe . . . he shook his head.

Across the cockpit, James frowned.

45

 Trystin eased the *Willis* into the docking slot. The recon run had shown no troids and no revs—the marshal occasionally sent out the cruisers to take advantage of their longer-range EDI detection capabilities.

"Magnetize holdtights."

By the time he and the captain had finished the checklist, through the implant and the ship's net, Trystin could sense that Muriami had fastened the mechanical holdtights.

"Power changeover."

"Standing by for changeover."

Once full station gravity hit the cruiser, Trystin unstrapped and sat up.

"Captain?" came from the quarterdeck.

"Yes?" answered James.

"Dispatch case for Lieutenant Desoll," Albertini announced. "They had it waiting. One for you too, Captain."

Trystin forced himself to walk slowly back to the quarterdeck.

Albertini extended the case toward him.

Trystin wiped his forehead again with the back of his shipsuit's sleeve before he took the case and opened it. The first sheet of paper was simple.

Effective the first of sixta—eighteen days away—he was Major Trystin Desoll.

The second sheaf comprised hard-copy orders. He began to read.

"Congratulations, Trystin." James flashed his boyish grin. "I'd guess it's your promotion to major and orders to your own command."

"Maybe . . . I did get promoted."

"When, ser?" asked Muriami.

"One sixta." Trystin continued to read, focusing on the key words.

The captain slowly opened his case. Like Trystin, he frowned.

After a moment, Tech Muriami finally asked, "Captain, ser . . . if it wouldn't be too much trouble . . . could someone tell us what's happening?"

Trystin looked at the orders again.

". . . on or about 15 septem 796 . . . report to Medical Center, Cambria, for Farhkan f/up study. . . . Upon completion of home leave, no later than 32 septem, report SERCOM . . . FFA . . ."

Another Farhkan physical, not that he minded that much . . . and then some staff assignment at Service Command? Relatively junior majors didn't get staff assignments these days—those were for screenpushers or incompetents. Had he screwed up somewhere that he didn't know?

James Sasaki frowned, then smiled.

"What is it, ser? If I might ask?" Trystin added.

"There were four sets of orders. Yours—and congratulations again—your replacement's, mine, and my replacement's."

"What?"

"They're phased. You go first, and you're actually being replaced by my replacement for a month or so, and then your eventual replacement comes, and I go."

"That's a little odd, isn't it?"

"Not really. You're being groomed for something, Trystin, but for what I couldn't tell you." James frowned again, and Trystin wondered whether he were just trying to cheer Trystin up. "Someone wanted you to be familiar with larger ship operations first."

"Where are you going, ser?" Trystin wondered if the major had finally gotten his promotion, but didn't want to ask.

"Strat U." James grinned.

"Does that—?"

"Absolutely. I can put on the triangles immediately."

"That merits two sets of congratulations."

"Ser?" pleaded Muriami.

James flashed a boyish grin. "My promotion was effective fourteen days ago. So I can put on the triangles now. Lieutenant Desoll will put on the third bar in eighteen days. Sometime in the next month, Major Watachi will report, and he will take Major Desoll's place while he gets familiar with the ship. Then around the first of octem, a Lieutenant Valada will report, and I will leave. Is that clear?"

"Mostly," said Albertini. "We got to break in two new officers."

"Major Watachi was the second on another cruiser, and had a tour in corvettes."

"It sounds like there's some experience there," Trystin offered.

James nodded.

Trystin looked at his orders again. For further assignment? Was that good or bad? He didn't know. He didn't even know anyone who'd ever received orders like that.

"Often, indefinite orders like that mean something special that no one wants to put on the net." James looked at Trystin. "I told them that you were the best pilot I'd ever shipped with."

"They asked?"

"I got a questionnaire from the Service detailer a while back."

Trystin tried not to take too deep a breath. His orders might be very good, but he had his doubts. He forced a smile. "Time for a celebration."

"How, Lieutenant? We're on outer orbit station."

"I don't know. I'm sure the captain could find a way." James nodded slowly.

Trystin closed the dispatch case and put it under his arm. He had some thinking to do, but it could wait—a little while.

46

 Trystin looked at the kit bags on his cabin floor and at the flimsies in his hand. The wrinkled top one was simple enough, except that it wasn't.

Major Trystin Desoll:
   The commanding officer of the *Mishima* would request the honor of your presence prior to your departure for further assignment . . .

What did Ulteena want? Their schedules almost never coincided because the *Willis* and *Mishima* anchored the two opposing long-range recon sections. And how did one offer small talk to a cruiser's CO? Or even get to see her? He couldn't just march up to the lock and announce himself.

Even now, the only way that he'd been able to work out any time was between Major Watachi's arrival and the next shuttle to Mara. So he'd been like Major Doniger, packed and ready to depart when Eleni Watachi's boots touched the lock. James had been faintly surprised to find that Major E. Watachi was female.

Keiko Muralto hadn't even smiled when Trystin had asked her to confirm that the CO of the *Mishima* would be available. The senior tech had nodded and then brought back the second flimsy as he'd been sealing the last bag.

"Major Freyer will be available for Major Desoll"— that was all it said.

"Old friends," Trystin had said. "On the Maran perimeter."

Keiko had smiled then. "Major . . . no one on this entire station will question either one of you."

"It's not like that."

The senior tech had just grinned and left.

Trystin shook his head, then folded the flimsies and slipped them into the data case that held papers and orders. What did Ulteena want? And why? Still not knowing, he hefted his gear and stepped into the corridor toward the quarterdeck.

The corridors around the quarterdeck were crowded.

"Good luck, Trystin." James stepped forward.

Trystin had to put down the bags to shake James's hand. Eleni Watachi nodded politely.

"Ser?" Keiko Muralto handed him a short tube with a thin red ribbon around it. "It isn't much, but we wanted you to have it."

"You didn't have to—"

"It's just a thin-film holo of the ship, with inserts from the whole crew."

Trystin swallowed. Thin-film holos didn't come cheap, and he wondered how they'd even gotten one of the ship. "Thank you. Thank you." He carefully eased the tube into the second kit bag, then straightened. "I'll always keep it."

"You still don't know where you're headed, ser?" asked the senior tech.

"No. What about you?" Trystin asked.

"My orders just say the tech command on Fuji." Keiko smiled. "Any school there would be fine, but it'll probably be systems."

James stepped forward again. "If I can ever help, let me know, Trystin." He shook the younger man's hand again and grinned. "Even if you look like a rev, you've as much honor—or more—than anyone could ever ask for."

"Thank you, and I will." Trystin had the feeling James meant every word, that for once his words weren't calculated or political.

James flashed the boyish grin a last time, and Trystin smiled back.

"Good luck, Major," called Albertini as Trystin lifted the three kit bags and crossed the lock into the outer orbit station.

"Give 'em hell, Major!" added Muriami.

"All of you take care," Trystin said as he stepped out through the lock.

"You, too, ser."

Several officers nodded or waved as Trystin made his way to the delta locks, and to the *Mishima*.

"Yes, ser?" asked the slim tech guarding the access to delta four.

"Major Desoll to see Major Freyer. I think—"

"You're expected, ser. The captain's in her stateroom."

"Can I leave these here? I probably won't be long." Trystin extracted the data case from the pocket on the top bag.

"Yes, ser." The slim rating helped Trystin ease all three bags against the quarterdeck bulkhead, an area more spacious on the newer cruiser. "We're in stand-down, so it's not a problem."

"Thank you."

"First forward on the left."

"Got it."

The door was ajar when Trystin rapped.

"Yes? Oh, Trystin, I'd hoped you'd be able to come." Ulteena opened the stateroom door. She wore the standard shipsuit with the antique holoed wings and triple bars. Her eyes looked gray, and they met his.

He shrugged and offered a wry grin. "I'm here."

"I'm glad. Would you sit down?" Ulteena closed the door.

"For a bit. I've only got a few hours before I have to catch the shuttle." He sat with the data case in his lap.

Ulteena turned one of the two gray chairs and sat down facing Trystin. "The last time we talked was right after the mess on Helconya. I ran some inquiries," she said slowly, "but I couldn't find out anything about your sister, even through a few back channels. I'm sorry."

"You didn't have to—"

"You remember the last troid battle? You got one of the last scouts pinging on us."

"I was just the second pilot," Trystin said cautiously, still wondering where Ulteena was headed.

"Trystin," she said wryly, "the entire system knows that the reason the *Willis* is the oldest cruiser left and the only one in its class not in scattered leptons is that Commander Sasaki had the brains to let you pilot her. Since you're being difficult, I'll make it simple. Our screens were going amber, and you saved our ass. I'm grateful." She held up a hand. "That's not why I asked you to stop here."

Trystin wanted to shake his head, but didn't. He waited.

"When I first met you, even over the perimeter net, I thought you were some spoiled anglo rich kid. You know, I grew up on Arkadya, and my parents were tech-grunts. The Service was my way out, and I hated people like you that had everything."

"I didn't have everything. . . ." Trystin paused, then added, "Well, maybe I did, compared to you, or most people."

"That's what I like about you, Trystin. After that first initial defensive reaction, you stop and think, and you really listen. It's hard to find people who listen. And you care. You know why I asked everyone I could find about your sister? Because when you found out about the Helconya raid, there on Mara station, the look on your face told me and the whole universe that you loved your sister." Ulteena rose from the chair and walked toward the corner that held her bunk, then turned and walked back toward Trystin. "I wished I could give you good news. Or even bad news and console you." She shrugged, and another wry smile appeared briefly. "The universe doesn't care much what we wish."

"No, it doesn't." Trystin didn't know what else to say, or exactly what Ulteena was getting at, and he felt he should.

"Trystin . . . I wish this were another time, another place. But it's not. We're on outer orbit station, and you have a shuttle to catch, and in another hour or so the *Mishima* is back on the duty roster. I'm worried for one reason, and you're worried for others." She paused, and the gray eyes met his again, almost with a shock. "This is difficult."

She cared? The efficient Major Ulteena Freyer cared?

"I know," he said slowly, fidgeting in the chair. He stood and set down the data case on the seat.

"You're from all the schools and places I was determined to be better than. . . ." She stopped. "That sentence doesn't even make sense, and it doesn't matter, does it?"

Trystin shook his head.

"Trystin . . . I'm not one for love before the battle. I'm not one for making merry because tomorrow we may die." She swallowed. "This is hard. Very hard."

Trystin reached forward and put his arms around her, and hers came around him.

They just held each other silently . . . for a long time.

She stepped back a half-step, not quite letting go. "I don't know what will happen. I can't promise. I won't. But I couldn't just let you go off without . . . somehow . . . letting you know that . . . things weren't what they seemed. I couldn't do it again." She swallowed. "I can't promise anything, but I . . . Do you understand?"

Trystin forced a grin. "Probably not everything. You felt the way I felt."

"You felt?" Ulteena looked surprised.

"When I was lying in that med-center bed, and I'd heard

that you'd stopped all those tanks, and you'd even figured out that there would be revvie tanks and how to stop them, I lay there, thinking how brilliant you were, and how stupid and just plain lucky I was. And when you talked about endgaming on Beta, you probably saved my ass. It felt that way, anyway."

Ulteena gave a slight laugh. "I wanted to slug you, though, when you made that supercilious comment about already working out on the high-gee treadmill for an hour. You looked so . . . so . . . anglo . . . and composed."

"I was sweaty and tired, and you looked so neat and trim," Trystin protested.

"Neat?" She snorted.

"Neat."

"We could rehash it all, but . . ." Her arms went around him again, and she continued, "We already lived it."

He squeezed her to him for a moment.

After returning the full-bodied embrace, she stepped back. "It's stupid, and it's not, but I told you—"

"You're not one for love before the battle, so to speak."

She nodded, and her eyes fell. "It's stupid. I'm a major and the CO, but some things don't change."

"I wish I'd known before."

"You almost didn't know now. Except your tech asked Geilir for some help in making up a farewell gift for you, and I overheard that you were leaving, and no one knew where." She paused, and the gray eyes were brilliant with unshed tears. "I wish we'd had more time. I wish I'd made more time."

"Hindsight is a lousy gardener, as my father always said." He held her again, more gently, his hand stroking the short dark hair. "I didn't know how, and I'm glad you did, and it doesn't matter about love before the battle, because . . ." Trystin stopped and swallowed. "You know . . . I really think I'd screw it up."

"That's a terrible pun. . . ." She shook her head.

"What else have I got?"

"More than you know."

Again, for a long, long time, they just held tight to each other.

Later, after more words, never mentioning love, and more embraces, Ulteena straightened, and brushed her short hair back. "Duty, frigging duty, calls."

"As always." Trystin had heard the implant warning as well.

"Take care, Trystin."

"Me? You're still on the line. You take care."

A last quick hug, and both straightened their uniforms—singlesuit and undress greens. Ulteena walked beside Trystin to the quarterdeck.

"Your bags are here, Major Desoll," offered the duty tech as Trystin stopped at the quarterdeck. Her eyes were grave, thoughtful, then she added, "We'll miss you. Good luck."

"Thank you." He offered a smile, both to the tech and to Ulteena.

The smile he received from Ulteena was more than mere formality but still guarded, but he understood that . . . now.

As he hurried toward the shuttle lock and the trip to Mara station, Trystin glanced back at delta four—just another lock. Just another closed door. He shook his head as he carried the three bags toward the shuttle. Why hadn't he seen? Why hadn't she seen?

He shook his head. Would it have changed anything? The Service didn't post people for their convenience. At least . . . at least he knew she wasn't crisp and competent in everything. Next time . . .

He swallowed. Would there be a next time? Or would he find a dataclip announcing the disappearance of the Coalition ship *Mishima*?

He tried to push that thought away. There had to be a next time. Didn't there? But there hadn't been for Salya . . . or her major. He pressed his lips together and kept walking.

47

✺ With a quick look back at the underground shuttle port tube-station, Trystin swiped his new ID through the reader and stepped into the tube-shuttle along with a handful of others in uniform, glad to be heading home, even if the local hour did happen to be before dawn. There was only one fifteen-degree segment on one planet that coincided with Coalition standard space time. Add translation error, and just about every interstellar journey required readjusting to the local planetary time.

By the time he had reached the tube-shuttle from the port, it was past dawn, and even later when the shuttle whispered to a stop at the EastBreak station. There Trystin lifted his three bags and followed the half-dozen other Service personnel out into yellow light cast by the glow-tubes. Soft as the light was, it tended to wash out the color differences between the green and gray tiles of the underground station. Even in the underground station, the air smelled like the warm rain of summer. Trystin took a deep breath, glad to escape the odor of plastic, ozone, and recycled water and people—except for one major he felt he had found and lost simultaneously.

Two young men, wearing militarylike school uniforms Trystin did not recognize, looked at him, then quickly looked away as he passed. A white-haired man with an erect carriage nodded politely, and Trystin returned the gesture. At the reader, Trystin flicked his card through the scanner, and swallowed at the five-cred price. The price of the trip from the port to EastBreak had more than doubled since the last time. Then he shrugged. He couldn't spend that much of his pay anyway.

A light rain was falling when he reached the top of the stairs, and the eastern sky was fading from purple into the sullen gray of low nimbus clouds. He scrambled down the walk through the small gardens in order to catch the electrotrain. As he stepped aboard, two dark-haired youths, in more typical school uniforms, also looked away from Trystin as he slid into the second seat. One jabbed his furled umbrella against the floor.

Trystin didn't need to step up his hearing to catch the whisper.

"Rev in our uniform . . ."

"Not just your uniform, young ser. I was born here, and so was my great-great-grandfather, and every one of us has served."

Both boys stiffened, but neither spoke.

"The revs reject people who don't look and think like they do. I always thought we were better than that."

Neither youth turned or uttered a word.

"Of course, I'm sure you know better than I do. After all, I've only spent a tour fighting them on perimeter duty, and another one busting troids."

The surtrans whispered on to its next stop, where a pair of girls stepped aboard and carefully furled their umbrellas. They took the seat across the aisle from the schoolboys.

The brown-haired girl looked at Trystin for a moment and offered a tentative smile. Trystin nodded back as the surtrans moved away from the station. The girl with dark mahogany hair glanced sidelong at the youth who had jabbed the umbrella.

A flock of heliobirds, mostly juveniles, swooped by the surtrans as it slowed for the second stop. Two more schoolboys boarded, one a gangly youth with light brown hair who offered Trystin a shy grin.

"Another one . . ." whispered the boy in front of Trystin.

Trystin smiled at the gangly youth, who sat across the aisle from Trystin and behind the two girls, and then said quietly to no one in particular, "It really is amazing how some young people feel that short stature and small minds are a sign of superiority. I wonder what ever happened to decency and courtesy?"

Both youths in front of Trystin stiffened. The gangly youth grinned more broadly, and the brown-haired girl nodded ever so slightly.

The third stop was Trystin's, and he nodded politely to both students before he ran his card through the reader. Neither returned the head bow.

Like the tube-shuttle, the electrotrain fare had also more than doubled. He shook his head.

When he stepped away from the surtrans, he could hear one of the boys hiss, ". . . still a dirty rev . . ."

"Shut up, Goren," snapped the gangly youth. "Did you see the row of decorations?"

Trystin wanted to shake his head—decorations weren't the point, either. Instead, he shifted his grip on his bags.

"Ser?" A Domestic Service officer stepped through the increasing rain toward Trystin, then stopped. His eyes ran across the holo symbols on the greens below Trystin's name. "Those for real, Major? *Six* troid battles? As a pilot?"

Trystin nodded.

"I never saw anyone who survived six. I was a tech on the *Izanagi.*"

"You were rotated off? I was there when—"

"Where?"

"The *Willis.*"

"After my time, Major. That was five stans ago."

"I was running a perimeter station then." Trystin shook his head, then wiped the dampness off his face. The beret didn't help much, and he hadn't thought about a waterproof. There wasn't rain on ships and orbit stations. "The captain made it through nine troids."

"He must have been something."

"He still is. He's a subcommander now."

"Good to know . . . where you headed?"

Trystin shrugged and offered a smile.

"Sorry. I shouldn't have asked."

"That's all right."

The Domestic Service officer paused. "Be careful, ser.

Some of the young bloods are a little wild these days." He laughed. "I'm sure you'd have no trouble."

"I'd rather have none," Trystin admitted.

"You going home?"

Trystin nodded. "My folks live up at Cedar Gardens."

"You one of those Desolls?"

"I'm on home leave."

"Well . . . take care, Major." The Domestic Service officer nodded again as Trystin hiked up the gentle hill.

Trystin had never seen a Domestic Service officer near the house, especially one with a shocker, holstered or not. He continued to walk, shifting the bags around. After a time, they got heavy. The rain intensified, warm drops beginning to fall in sheets, battering their way through the summer leaves of the overhanging trees and through the symmetrical branches of the Norfolk pines.

The front gates to the house and gardens were locked, and a small speaker box had been installed in a matching extension to the stone posts. Beneath the speaker was a button. Trystin pushed it.

"Hello . . . this is Trystin." He waited.

After several minutes, a reply came. "Yes."

"This is Trystin."

"Trystin?"

"The same. You know, your son? The major. I got promoted. The one who built the stone wall holding the sage?"

"I'm sorry. I was away from the office." There was a buzz. "Make sure the gates are locked after you come in."

"I will." Trystin frowned, but after he stepped through he closed the gates and checked them. The gates had never been locked in his lifetime, not that he knew.

The marigolds in the lower garden looked newer, and part of the stone bedding wall had been replaced. Other sections seemed to have been replanted, but with the heavy rain, Trystin wasn't quite sure.

Elsin had the door open, and Trystin scurried inside, dripping.

He looked at the puddles forming around his gear. "I'm sorry about the mess."

"It's good to see you." Elsin stepped forward, and Trystin hugged him, suddenly conscious that his father, always so muscular, was thinner, almost frail.

"Are you all right?" he blurted out.

Elsin offered a faint smile. "As well as can be expected in these times."

"I noticed. I got more than a few dirty looks on the way home—even ran into a Domestic Service officer at the bottom of the hill."

"Jusaki, I'd bet. He's a good man."

"He was friendly, but . . ." Trystin looked around. "Mother?"

"She's . . . not here."

"Isn't it a bit early for her to have left?"

"Let's have some tea. I'd just made a pot. I don't sleep late these days, Trystin." Elsin glanced at the bags on the floor. "Leave them there. They can't hurt the tiles." He padded toward the kitchen.

Trystin followed, a sinking feeling coming over him.

Elsin gestured to one of the chairs at the table in the nook, then extracted a mug from the cupboard. After lifting the tea cozy, he filled the mug and picked up another. Handing one to Trystin, he pulled out the other chair and sank into it.

Trystin took the chair across from his father and waited.

"I suppose . . . I suppose I should have sent you some messages, but I didn't know that they would have gotten there these days, and what could you have done? Except worry, and you didn't need that, not then." Elsin looked at the table. "When I got your message the day before yesterday . . . then there was no way to let you know—"

"What happened? When?"

"Almost four months ago . . . Quiella came to visit . . ."

Trystin vaguely remembered his cousin Quiella as a quiet little blond girl, always into books—she loved the old-fashioned paper books in his father's study.

". . . they went out to go shopping . . . that was the first of the riots—"

"Riots . . . ?"

"Oh, yes . . . we've had several . . . antirev riots . . . it's been a month since the last one."

"Couple of them saw Quiella—that blond hair—she's very beautiful, shy as ever, though." Elsin shook his head. "They overturned the car, tried to drag Quiella away. Your mother keyed in the old combat reflexes and unarmed combat module—she maimed or killed a bunch of them, held them off until the Domestic Service patrols got there." Elsin paused and took another sip of tea. "Her system couldn't take it. She died that night."

"They're supposed to deactivate implants." Trystin could feel his own eyes burning. "They're supposed to—"

"We reactivated about two years ago. It's not that hard if you know systems. We worried about something like this."

The younger man shook his head and stared at the tea. After a long silence he asked, "How's Quiella?"

"All right. She comes to see me every week. She's a sweet child." Elsin took another deep breath. "Courageous in her own way. Don't know as I could come to visit me. She's sweet. It helps, and I tell her that. Selfish old man, I guess."

Trystin got up and walked around the table, putting his hands on his father's shoulders. "No you're not. I'm sorry. I didn't know."

"How could you?"

Trystin squeezed his father's shoulders again before walking over to the window and looking out at the rain falling on the garden. He was afraid to ask the next question, half knowing the answer. Instead, he watched the rain pour down on the pines and the flowers and herbs, the heavy drops beating down the leaves.

Then he looked at the empty place beside his father, and his eyes burned. His mother—she never said that much, just did what had to be done. He swallowed and looked back at the rain. He wanted to hit someone . . . something . . . but that wouldn't do much. After all, a mental voice told him sardonically, isn't that what everyone's doing?

"What else can people do?" he muttered.

"What did you say?" asked his father.

"Nothing. Just arguing with myself." He swallowed and pulled himself together before turning from the window. He might as well get hit all at once.

Elsin took a small sip from the mug, as if waiting fatalistically.

"Salya? Was she . . . at Helconya?" Trystin walked toward his father.

"You knew about Helconya?"

"Only that there was an attack. I never could find out much in the way of details. Even the main admin office on Mara orbit station couldn't tell me . . . about Salya."

"Neither could we. Not until Shinji's cousin returned. All we got—later—was a formal letter—and some medals. And some credits."

Trystin waited.

Elsin looked bleakly toward the window, his eyes focused somewhere else, not on the window, the wall, the rain outside, but some other place in time. "Salya always wanted to build, to create. When she came home, we talked a lot about her work, the technical details, how she engineered the spores." He looked down at the half-empty mug. "I miss her. I miss Nynca."

"Do you know what happened?" Trystin kept his voice soft.

"Not really. Some of them took surface skimmers, atmospheric tugs, and rammed the revvie scouts. That was what saved the station—that and some heroics by a junior major. She died, too. All the . . . most anyway . . . I don't know if Salya took a skimmer. I don't think I'll ever know, and it doesn't matter. I know Shinji did. Some of them . . . they never found. They never found him. They never found her."

Trystin paced back to the window.

The heavy rain continued to tear at the garden, and the clouds seemed darker.

Elsin took a last swallow from his mug, then pushed out

his chair, and trundled toward the teapot. "It's cold here. Haven't felt this cold in a long time."

Trystin turned, watching the slight shuffle in his father's steps, seeing the even-thinner silver hair. "Everything's changed."

"That happens . . ." Elsin put the kettle back on to heat.

"Riots . . . I can't believe it. Here? What's happening?"

Elsin sighed. "What always happens. People are looking for someone to blame. Our heritage comes from two groups who always denied that they were part of the problem. The early ecologists blamed industrialization for environmental degradation even while they continued to purchase all the goods and services produced by industry. And the forerunners of the parashintos always looked down on and isolated strangers. Under pressure, people often revert to their roots, and the Coalition is under a lot of pressure."

Trystin moistened his lips. He'd seen that pressure.

"Prices keep going up, and it's hard to get new equipment, especially electroneural or sophisticated electronics or microtronics. They're talking about conscription to fill support positions in the Service . . ." The older man's words trailed off. "Do you want some more tea?"

"A little, I guess." Trystin turned from the window and the heavy rain. He picked his mug off the table.

"You have to watch out now," Elsin went on. "Always wear your uniform . . . Cambria may not be all that safe for you—especially around the young ones. The older people still believe in restraint, but not the young ones. They just see the losses and cannot understand why the government does nothing."

Trystin nodded. "The uniform means nothing to them. Saw that already." He lifted his mug and held it as his father poured the steaming tea into it.

"It's getting worse. All the politicans are looking for someone to blame, and it's always the revs. 'If it weren't for the greedy Revenants . . .'" Elsin snorted. "The revs are what they've always been—an expansionistic and opportunistic culture with a high birth rate. That's never been the question. We just didn't want to pay the price by stopping them earlier, and we've been an easier target, because we've always tried to stop them, rather than take the fight to them. The Argentis would have started by destroying Wystuh, but we have this horror of total destruction."

Trystin took a cautious sip of his tea, nearly burning his tongue.

"No politician wants to admit either that horror or our unwillingness to take the fight to them. So it's who hates the revs worse now. The Democratic Capitalists almost took the assembly in last month's elections, and Fuseli is pushing for a total conversion to armament production. The Greens have held him off, but they're losing ground. I doubt the new government will last another three months." Elsin shook his head before refilling his mug. "Politics. It doesn't solve anything, and it doesn't bring them back." He looked out at the rain that continued to fall. "Sure as hell doesn't."

"No." Trystin stood shoulder to shoulder with his father, and they watched the clouds and the rain. "No, it doesn't."

48

After a quick swipe of the card through the reader, Trystin slipped off the surtrans. He tried not to wince at the fifteen-cred fare, more than triple the fare the last time. The three other officers in front of him didn't even seem to notice.

He followed them up the wide stone steps to the main Service medical center on Perdya. The rysya and trefil plants in the stone flower boxes beside the steps appeared beaten down from the heavy rain of the past few days, and flower petals were plastered on the edges of the steps. While the day was gray, the clouds were higher and thinner, and no rain had fallen since the night before.

Once inside the med center, he walked straight to the information console.

"Major Desoll, reporting for a follow-up physical."

The civilian technician at the front console stared at him for a moment. "A physical?"

"The Farhkan study."

"What was your name?"

"Desoll. D-E-S-O-L-L."

After a few keystrokes and a quick study of the screen, the technician looked up. "Second floor, all the way to the rear on the south wing. Dr. Kynkara's in charge."

"Thank you."

The civilian did not answer, looking away.

Instead of glaring at her, Trystin walked across the polished stone floor to the wide ramp, passing a commander and a major engaged in a conversation. Neither looked up.

Trystin found his way to the far end of the south wing and another technician at another console.

"Yes, ser?" The dark-haired woman looked up at him, waiting, her slightly slanted eyes skeptical.

"Major Desoll. The Farhkan follow-up study."

"Follow me." She stood and led him down the same side corridor and around the same two corners as he had walked the last time. The same four cubicles and diagnostic consoles waited. Two had open doors. She looked at Trystin. "Run your ID through, ser."

Trystin ran it through the reader, and she tapped several keys on the console keyboard. The console ready light winked green.

"I'm sure you know how this works. After you're done, go to gamma four at the end of the corridor. Wait there for the doctor."

Trystin nodded, not feeling particularly thankful for the cool reception, but the technician was gone. He closed the door, disrobed, and submitted himself to the chilly ministrations of the cold console. After dressing, he walked to the end of the corridor and took a seat next to a dark-haired lieutenant.

The lieutenant glanced at Trystin, then saw the name, rank, and decorations, and looked away, coldly.

"Lieutenant Rifori?"

The lieutenant followed the doctor into the office. Shortly, the doctor left, and the door shut.

"It shouldn't be long, Major." Dr. Kynkara, her short hair graying, paused.

"Thank you." Trystin gave her a brief smile, grateful for the momentary glimpse of humanity. Somehow, he expected coldness in battle and on the perimeter line, but not in a medical center. And not in Cambria.

The doctor entered the office adjoining the one where the interview was taking place and closed the door behind her.

Lieutenant Rifori left within ten minutes, a puzzled look on his face, until he saw Trystin, and his face hardened again before he turned and rapped on the staff office door.

After Rifori left, Dr. Kynkara ushered Trystin into her office.

The alien wore the same uniform/clothing as every Farhkan Trystin had met. Were they all the same? And would he be talking with Rhule Ghere once again or would it be Jhule? How many Farhkans were involved? Was the agenda going to be theft once more?

Trystin inhaled slowly, taking in the vaguely familiar odor, the mixed scents of an unfamiliar flower, a muskiness, and cleanliness.

"Major, this is Rhule Ghere. He is a senior . . . physician . . . in the Farhkan . . . hegemony."

"I've met Dr. Ghere." Vaguely surprised that his voice was so calm, Trystin nodded to Ghere.

The not-quite-human figure wore the same shimmering gray fatigues. The red eyes still peered out from the iron-gray hair and square face, and the wide single-nostril nose flapped with each breath above the protruding crystalline teeth.

"Greetings, Major Desoll."

Again, as they had before, the words scripted through his mind, but Trystin knew somehow that the use of the implant was a fiction, a convenient one for the Farhkans.

"Let me know when you're done," requested the doctor as she left.

"I will." Trystin waited until the door closed and the Farhkan's comm bloc dropped over the room. He settled into the plastic chair opposite Ghere.

"What do you feel about theft these days?" asked the Farhkan.

"I still don't like it. How do you feel about lying? Or is misrepresentation on the nonverbal level not lying?"

Ghere snorted, and Trystin wasn't sure the sound was a laugh.

"You are bright enough to get into trouble, Major."

"You make that sound like a threat, Doctor." Trystin added the next words on a subvocal level through the implant. "Do your mental abilities include the induction of heart attacks or cerebral 'accidents'?"

"I did not mean my words as a threat." Ghere seemed unruffled. "You have thought, as I hoped you might, but you have not thought deeply enough."

"How about answering the question?"

"That is a fair request. Yes, we can talk mind-to-mind, but not to everyone of your species. The implant is symptomatic of ability. That is, it is difficult to convey more than simple thoughts to those who do not have the ability to mentally organize thoughts before speaking them. Thus . . ."

Trystin nodded. Ghere's thoughts/words made sense, but whether they were fully accurate was another question.

". . . and we cannot physically affect another entity directly by mental means . . ."

Directly? That bothered Trystin, although he couldn't immediately figure out an indirect means. "How about indirectly?"

"No more than you can with spoken words." A silent laugh followed. "Now, you might do me the honor of responding to my request about your feelings on theft."

"Theft isn't simple. It sounds simple, but it's not. If I waste people's time with endless chatter, am I stealing their time? How do I know? I'd have to guess whether they wanted to talk or they didn't. If I steal food to live, it is theft, but is it so immoral if those I steal from have plenty?"

"You still do not wish to admit you are a thief?"

Trystin shrugged. "You want a simple answer to a question that isn't simple."

"Is not a failure to answer a question a form of lying?"

Trystin felt what he thought had to be amusement, and he answered. "Not if you don't know the answer. Perhaps I should tell you that I don't know if I am a thief."

"You steal, or you do not."

"When you can give me a definition of theft, then I'll think about answering the question."

"That is not the objective. In your own terms, are you a thief?"

Trystin paused. "The simple answer is no."

"You should think about whether it is the correct answer." After a mental silence, Ghere added, "Is there a correct answer? Is your correct answer good for another being?"

"Probably not, but I also don't want to live in a society where people are free to steal everything under the sun."

"So some theft is acceptable? You do not believe all theft is unacceptable?"

Trystin's forehead felt damp. The questions were simple enough, but a lot more was going on than trying to answer questions. A lot more, and he could feel the anger building inside him. Everywhere he looked, something was hidden, as if everyone—except his father—had something to gain by concealment. And everyone was judging.

"Is some lying acceptable?" asked Ghere, interrupting Trystin's thoughts.

"That depends on what you mean by lying. And by acceptable."

"It is strange. You humans pride yourself on beliefs and values that you claim are absolute, and then you refuse to accept the judgments you have created by those values."

"That gives you the right to judge us?" snapped Trystin.

"I have not ever made such a claim. I have asked you to judge yourself, and you have refused."

"And if I had? If I had said I were a thief . . . then what?"

The snort that seemed like laughter followed. "Then I would have asked you how you could be a thief when you pay for what you use."

"Then why did you bother? You weren't going to accept any answer I gave." Trystin could feel the anger building, anger fueled as much by the cold reception in the med center as by the Farhkan game-playing.

"Because understanding what cannot be answered or resolved is the beginning of wisdom."

"Why do you care about our wisdom? What is your agenda? Why do you subject me . . . and presumably others . . . to unanswerable questions?"

"We do live in the same galaxy, and your species is somewhat . . . aggressive."

"And you're not? You haven't destroyed human ships? Don't make me laugh."

"I would not try that." Ghere paused. "We only destroyed those ships that attempted to attack us, to commit theft, if you will."

"You don't like theft. You've made that clear. So why do you bother with us poor peons of the galaxy? Why not just wipe us out? Get rid of the local vermin?"

"That poses a difficulty. Several." Again, the Farhkan paused. "Such an attempt would not be wise."

"You couldn't do it, is that it? So you'd rather figure out how we work enough to destroy us from within?"

The Farhkan laugh followed. "If we must . . . we will . . . accomplish such destruction . . . but it would be futile. A fool's victory, and the price would be as high for us as for you—as you may see someday."

Trystin sat in the chair. The cold certainty behind Ghere's words chilled his anger. Yet how could destroying humanity also destroy the Farhkans?

Ghere offered nothing.

"All right. I'll bite. You've got the technology to destroy us, but it's so terrible that you'll destroy a chunk of the galaxy too, and you with it?"

"No." This time the laugh was bitter. "The galaxy would *appear* almost unchanged. I choose not to answer that question. That answer you must find."

"Me? You have all the answers. You can say you won't answer, and leave me hanging. I'm just a poor pawn in a game I don't understand."

"Hardly a pawn, Major. And you will understand the game, as you put it. You will . . . if you value your heritage and race."

Trystin swallowed, biting back the anger.

The Farhkan waited a moment, then added, "I would like you to memorize something for future reference. You may find it useful."

"Wait a minute!" Trystin protested. "Useful? Just like that? You threaten me and all humanity, and then you just tell me to memorize something. And what about theft? Or lying? Was that all a subterfuge?" He didn't like the way the Farhkan brought up things and just stopped. Or the incredible threat he'd delivered. Just forget it? How could he?

"All of it is woven together. You—or another human— must discover the pattern and act."

"What if I won't play this game?"

Trystin received the impression of a shrug. "You need to decide. I am not placing judgments upon you. I am not threatening you. It may seem that way. It is not so. I do not lie. But I am a thief, as you may discover. I am not proud of that." Ghere snorted again.

Trystin wanted to hold his head, which had begun to ache. Instead, he just sat there, seething.

"Listen," commanded Ghere. "The key to the temple is. . . ." What followed the words was a series of equations that scripted into Trystin's mind.

"Why?" Trystin asked.

"Please . . ." requested the Farhkan with a mental force-fulness that was more command than request, yet a force-fulness concealing something else.

"You'll have to repeat those," Trystin mumbled. His head throbbed. It took four repetitions before he was certain that he had the phrases in mind, and he had to key them into his implant memory.

"Why do you want me to memorize these?"

"You may find them useful. At least one of you may. It may be you."

"One of us?"

"Yes. One of you. If it is not you, consider yourself fortunate. If it is . . . you are better prepared than most, but you will pay an even higher price. These keys were . . . difficult . . . to obtain." The Farhkan stood.

"Wait a minute!" Trystin stood as his voice climbed. "In all these interviews, you prod me, and you probe. You threaten all humans, and you make me uncomfortable, and then you just drop things. What's the purpose?"

"I do not threaten. I state what is, Major. The goal is to give you—and all those we interview—a way of looking at life that may allow your species to survive. I am not your enemy. I am your patron. Remember that I am your patron."

"That still sounds like a threat."

"We do not make threats, Major. Threats do not work, and they are bad policy. We offer help. You can take it or not take it."

"Why me?"

"Because those members of your species with great power and position are more interested in personal power than species survival."

"Great. Why are you bothering to tell me?"

"Who would you tell? Also"—Trystin gained a sense of something like sadness—"you could learn enough, if you are unfortunate enough." Ghere stood and turned. "Good day, Major."

"Good day, Doctor."

Trystin felt like grabbing the Farhkan and shaking him, but did not. He could not, because the Farhkan suddenly walked out the rear door.

Even through his headache, Trystin could feel a sense of sadness radiating from the alien. Sadness? Why?

When no answers immediately struck him, not that he thought they would, he opened the front door and went for Dr. Kynkara. His head still throbbed, and he wanted to kick people, or throw them down stairs. Or something!

49

 "How was the physical?" asked Elsin as Trystin walked into the kitchen.

"The physical was fine, but the interview with the Farhkan . . ." Trystin slipped off the beret and tucked it into his belt. "Shit . . ."

"Do you want to talk about it?" Elsin paused. "Something to drink?"

"Do you have any juice?"

"Just mixed vegetable and sour apple."

Trystin shivered. "Any iced tea?"

"That's what I'm having."

"Make that two."

Elsin poured a second tumbler and handed it to Trystin. "The mint's in the holder there."

Trystin crushed a sprig into the tea and settled into the second chair at the kitchen table. The whirr of wings drifted through the open window, and he watched as a male heliobird hovered for a moment above the hedge. "They're beautiful."

Elsin nodded, waiting.

Trystin watched until the heliobird whirred toward the pines and out of sight. "There was this Farhkan. He's interviewed me several times, and he seems to be more interested in my ethics than anything else. He's always pressing me to admit I'm a thief."

"Aren't we all?" Elsin lifted his tumbler.

"I suppose so. He said he was, and that he found it hard

to accept. I've kept refusing to admit it in blanket terms. That bothers me. Finally, I asked him what he would have done if I'd admitted it." Trystin took a swallow of the cold tea before continuing. "You know what he said? He said that he would have questioned whether I really was a thief. Then he ended up with something about humans insisting on absolutes when we refused to apply those absolute values to ourselves."

"That's certainly true enough."

"But why does any of this matter to a Farhkan?"

"Maybe they've never had experience with hypocrisy on such a vast scale." Elsin laughed.

"I don't think that's it." Trystin took another deep swallow of the tea. "He's been hammering on me to declare an absolute, but then he'd hammer on me not to."

"We like to make things absolute, but that doesn't mean they are," observed Elsin.

"But why would an alien care? He said—not in so many words—that they'd have to destroy humanity, and that would destroy them, but that I'd have to find out why. And he said that the Coalition's senior officers were too corrupt, or too in love with personal power, to learn what junior officers could. And, then, at the end, he said that I might learn enough if I were unfortunate. Not fortunate—unfortunate. What in hell would a frigging alien care?"

"We do live in the same galaxy. Perhaps they're worried about what we might do to the neighborhood."

"That's what he said, but it seems to me they should worry more about the revs." Trystin cupped his hands around the glass for a moment. "And he kept saying that he wasn't making threats."

"Maybe he wasn't," Elsin said. "If you know something will happen, and you say so . . . is that a threat?"

Trystin shivered and rubbed his forehead. "But he never said anything about the revs. They're more of a threat than we are. Aren't they concerned? It doesn't make sense. Don't they care?"

"They probably do, but why would they tell you?"

"That's true." Trystin took another swallow of tea. "But

what about being unfortunate? That's like a curse."

"Wisdom is a curse, Trystin, and it's usually bought with pain and suffering. Your alien seems rather perceptive."

"Maybe . . . but figure this. That wasn't all." Trystin forced a laugh. "He's basically told me that his people might have to destroy us—and implied that it wouldn't be any problem at all technically—that it wouldn't change the universe in the slightest—and then he asks me to memorize a bunch of stuff. Figure that."

"Oh? I can't say I like where they're pointing you."

"Me, neither," Trystin said, taking a deep swallow of the cold tea.

"What were you supposed to memorize?"

"He told me that the key to the temple was a series of equations, and he insisted that I memorize them."

"That is odd." Elsin frowned. "Do you still remember—"

"Of course. I also keyed them into my implant."

"Do you want to analyze them?"

Trystin pursed his lips, thinking about security. Then he shook his head. No one had said that what the Farhkans told him was classified, and, besides, his father was more trustworthy than most officers, a lot more if the Farhkan were right. "I think I need all the help I can get."

"Why did you shake your head?"

"The strangeness of the whole thing." He didn't even want to mention security to his father.

Elsin stood. "Shall we? I have to use more antiquated equipment."

Trystin chuckled as he rose and followed, carrying his tea. The console in the office was already on. Trystin wondered if it were ever off anymore, now that his father was alone.

"You'll have to use the keyboard. I don't have any direct interface equipment."

After setting his tea on the side table, Trystin sat down in the high-backed blue leather chair and used the keyboard and keys, slowly coding the memorized lines onto the screen.

They both studied the lines of code.

"I can tell you what it looks like—it's the operating protocol for something. I've never seen quite that construction, but here"—Elsin pointed at the screen—"that's an entry key."

"What does it open? How would you use it?"

Elsin studied the equation for a time. "It looks like a simplified protocol for a complex system, and it has to be a human system."

"Why?"

Elsin laughed. "The antique anglo, for one. Second, because I understand at least some of the terms, and while it is possible that an alien system would use another species' phrase for security, it's more than a little unlikely that an alien system would be that transparent or use our symbols."

Trystin stood and offered the console seat to his father, who settled into the chair. For a time, Elsin just sat, apparently concentrating on the codes. Trystin reclaimed his tea and took a sip.

Finally, the older man's fingers blurred across the keyboard, until a separate set of symbols appeared below the lines Trystin had entered.

Trystin blinked. "All right. Now what?"

"I'm guessing, but this section looks like the key itself, and these are merely parameters for system frequencies and band width. Now that's a guess, but I'd present this part"—his hand stretched toward the bracketed plain-language phrase—"just like you do a Service protocol. As I told you, it looks like a human system, and the words are human, almost archaic, somehow . . . but that could be a translation or a transliteration. I wouldn't know for sure."

"What's the stuff you put below?"

"My approximation of an override code. That's even more of a speculation, but the Farhkans don't play jokes. You were given this for a reason, and you probably won't have time for heavy analysis if you need to use it. Things don't work that way, I've discovered. Anticipation generally is worth several tonnes of reaction."

Trystin nodded, his thoughts going to Ulteena Freyer with the word "anticipation." For some reason, he recalled her waiting for him, while her ship waited for her. He should have seen it before she had finally told him.

"Trystin? Trystin?"

"Oh, sorry. I was thinking about anticipation—about someone."

"She must be something."

Trystin grinned, half sheepishly. "She is. But she's there, not here, and I was thinking about how she avoided much trouble by anticipating things. She's the CO of the *Mishima* now." He finished the tea and set the glass on the side table, then he stepped up to the screen. "You'd better explain this."

Elsin coughed. "I'm almost embarrassed to. I'm only guessing, but the layout is pretty standard—so standard it's almost antique. All right, now this is based on the assumption that . . ."

Trystin listened, trying to link in all the explanations, and burning the potential override code into his thoughts and his implant memory, as Elsin outlined the logic and the rationale.

When they were done, Trystin wiped his forehead. He hadn't realized he was sweating. "I need more tea."

"There's not much more I can tell you. It's filed in your directory if you want to review it again before you have to go."

"Good." Trystin's head ached, again, and, Farhkan denial or not, he felt like a pawn on the ancient board in the great room. How long had this been going on? Why him? Or were the Farhkans playing the same game with a bunch of interview subjects? And why did the Service let them? Was the situation with the revs that bad? He shivered again.

"Trystin?" asked his father.

"Just thinking . . . trying to make sense of things."

"Let it settle in. You've got a few days, don't you?"

"A few."

His father cleared his throat. "Did you tell anyone about this . . . key?"

"No. I didn't have a chance. You're suggesting it might not be a good idea?"

"I don't know . . . but with what the Farhkans said about senior officers . . ."

Trystin nodded. That presented another problem. Did he have a duty to report it? And what was he reporting? Would he just look foolish? Would he jeopardize the technology the Coalition was receiving?

He shook his head as they walked back to the kitchen, where Trystin refilled the glass and crushed more mint into the tea. He took a deep swallow. Settling in or not, the questions wouldn't stop. "Have any ideas why the Farhkans wanted me to have this . . . key or whatever it is?"

Elsin shrugged, then rubbed his silvery hair. "Your mother probably could have told you more, but . . . what I do know is that the Farhkans don't lie. I doubt they're more ethical—the one admitted that he was a thief—but they don't lie. So it's a key to something. I just don't know what."

"Neither do I." Trystin took another swallow, almost a gulp, of the tea. "Why—how—would they get access to a human system?"

"He said he was a thief." Elsin laughed.

Trystin swallowed. The interviews were more than psychological evaluations. But what more? And why? "What's their purpose? The Farhkans, I mean? Why me?"

"I don't know what the Farhkans are doing. Several years ago, there was a rumor that they were working with their own version of the Genome Project. That died away."

Trystin moistened his lips. The initial Human Genome Project had been one of the factors leading to the Great Die-off, when the neo-Mahmets, the Revenants, the Eco-Techs, and the Argentis had united in their assaults on Newton and old Earth. Although rumors had persisted for centuries that some of the Immortals had survived, Trystin doubted it. Over time, accidents alone would have done them in, and any routine gene trace would show the genetic modifications.

"They are aliens, Trystin. Aliens with alien motivations, no matter how much they seem human, no matter how much we try to steal or manipulate their knowledge and skills from them. Sometimes, I think they must sit back and laugh at our obviousness."

"So why do they help us?"

"Why do we help the poor? Or save certain environments or species?"

"Only those that take our fancy," pointed out Trystin.

"Maybe we take their fancy." Elsin shrugged.

Trystin refilled his glass again, wiping his forehead and wondering why he was so thirsty.

After a time, Elsin spoke. "By the way, I've transferred the title to the property here to you . . . it's in a trust that you can revoke or modify. The trust provides for maintenance, taxes, and the rest in case anything happens to me while you're unable to be contacted." Elsin delivered the words matter-of-factly, as if they had been rehearsed.

"Why? You're in great shape."

"Property registered to a Service major with a distinguished career is far less likely to be targeted for miscellaneous legal ploys." Elsin's voice was dry. "Besides, I won't live forever, and if you translate the wrong way, I could live another fifty years and still not see you. It's better to handle these things when you can. Anticipation, remember?" He laughed, but there was an edge to that laughter.

"Oh . . . Father." Trystin could feel the lump in his throat.

"You still have that investment trust? With the Pilot's Trust?"

Trystin nodded. "Last time I checked, it had built to over fifty thousand creds."

"And it has arrangements for paying taxes? That's the latest bureaucratic ploy. You look like a rev, and you're late or somehow deficient in taxes, and the revenue service is all over you."

"It does, but maybe we should go over it before I leave."

"Might as well." Elsin nodded. "Make sure it has the maximum statutory length—that's a hundred years now. The longest translation error documented, plus twenty years. If anything happens to me, everything will be handled by your trust. That should ensure that everything will be here for you."

Trystin looked down for a moment, then took another long swallow of the tea, his eyes going to the window where a female heliobird paused before darting toward the upper flower beds. "I miss the gardens."

"They do grow on you. They've been a comfort, and, someday, I hope you'll find them so."

Trystin nodded. He reached out with his left hand and covered his father's right hand for a moment. They continued to look at the greenery beyond the window.

50

 Service Command Headquarters occupied two three-story buildings set in three gardens—one garden between the two buildings and one on each side—all three joining in a series of low flower beds in front of the east-facing buildings. SERCOM was the fourth stop on the number three surtrans route from the West-Break station in Perdya.

Trystin walked along the covered pale green marble walkway, lugging his gear, and glancing between the pillars at the flowers. He recognized most, but not all. A steady flow of uniformed personnel, usually in ones or twos, traversed the walkway. Just before the flower beds that linked all three gardens, the covered walkway split—one section heading to the right building, the other to the left.

Trystin followed the arrow under which read—among others—Personnel and Detailing and continued to the left building.

As he entered the structure, he could sense the energy and probes of the security net. He paused for a moment, wondering if the Farhkan protocol was for Headquarters, then shook his head. The Service security system was a closed system. Whatever protocol, it had would have to be used inside the control center or the console that held the controls—which certainly made sense.

Most high-security installations were closed weave, rather than the modified open-weave systems used on ships or perimeter stations. Implants were only good either almost touching a ship or inside it, and since space combat didn't involve close proximity, the modified system was perfectly secure, especially since the revs didn't use implant technology. Trystin's implant could theoretically, if he had the protocols, access and control any truly openweave system. He shook his head. Of course, most openweave systems guarded their protocols dearly.

He crossed the atriumlike space, with the windows open to the gardens, and paused by one of the information consoles, setting down his gear. "Major Trystin Desoll." He handed across his ID and a copy of his orders. "Reporting for further assignment."

"Yes, ser. Let me check." The dark-haired tech at the front console took in Trystin, studied his uniform, the decorations, and turned her head to the tech at the next console. "Has to be Marshal Fertuna's staff."

"Intelligence? Good bet." The other tech studied Trystin as the fingers of the first flicked across the console keyboard.

"Yes, ser. You're to report to Marshal Fertuna. That's Intelligence—I Section. His office is on the third level of the north building. Just take the cross-garden walkway. It's easier than going back out the front. If you're carrying any weapons or energy implants, check with the tech at the console *outside* his office. Otherwise, just go in. All right?" She offered a pleasant professional smile as she returned his ID and orders. "They'll be expecting you."

"Thank you." Trystin returned the smile, keeping it plastered in place even after he caught the words "poor rev bait."

Even outside the Intelligence office, with its fractionally thicker walls, and stepped-up system net, there was no reference to Marshal Fertuna, just a small sign that said "I Section"—that and a bored-looking senior tech seated at a console in the hall outside.

Trystin nodded.

"Anything to declare, ser?" The technician looked at Trystin's bags.

"Nothing but normal pilot implants. Flight armor and personal effects."

"They'll clear."

The scanners buzzed through the implant, not pleasantly, as Trystin stepped into the office proper.

Another technician gestured from a corner console. "Major Desoll?"

"Yes." Trystin headed toward him.

"You're fortunate. Commander Delapp is waiting for you." The technician's black eyes studied Trystin quickly. "You can leave your gear here, ser, right over there."

Trystin shrugged and set the gear on the stand clearly provided for the purpose, removing the thin case that held his orders and records. He had no doubts that his gear would be scanned again—or, at least, that it could be.

"This way, ser."

Commander Delapp had an office not much larger than the mess on the *Willis*, but most of the back wall was a window overlooking the garden below.

The gray-haired commander stepped forward and extended her hand and a warm smile. "Major Desoll, I'm Katellie Delapp."

"Trystin Desoll, Commander." He took her hand and gave a slight bow.

"Please have a seat." The commander settled behind the console.

Trystin took the wooden captain's chair.

"Major, your CO recommends you highly. And your discretion." The white-haired commander behind the console waited, bright blue eyes fixed on him. "That's unusual in itself. Commander Sasaki is rather cautious. Both the commander and the Pilot Training Command also commend your piloting skill. And you are acceptable to the Farhkans."

"Yes, ser?" Trystin didn't like the last statement at all. "What do the Farhkans have to do with it?"

"Cautious, aren't you? That's good. You'll need to be cautious. We'd like to send you into Revenant territory."

"The Farhkans?" Trystin asked.

"It makes matters easier. You'll find that out later."

He could tell she wasn't about to say more about the Farhkans, and that somehow strengthened his own determination not to mention the Farhkan key. It was childish, but if the Service wanted to keep secrets, then so could he. "You need pilot scouts for the rev perimeter systems?"

"No, not scouts. We're talking about two-overlay missions."

Trystin contained the wince he felt internally. "Two overlay?"

"You wouldn't know the term. We'll load your implant with two identities you can call up for reference."

"I'm a pilot, not an intelligence agent."

"A good one." The commander's eyes caught his. "Do you want to spend the next twenty years somewhere like Parvati outer orbit control?"

"Is that a threat?" Trystin could feel the anger building. More damned threats!

"No." The commander's voice was calm. "You're not stupid. Do you see a pattern in the Revenant attacks?"

"There are a lot more of them."

"There are even more coming. We can't match them in terms of personnel and raw resources, and we don't want to go into the planet-busting business for pretty much the same reason. That's why you're here. That's why every distinguished junior officer who fits the rev physical profile and the psychological profile has been in this office, or will be."

Trystin took a deep breath.

"You fit the profile of the standard Revenant, close enough that we can match their gross gene coding, inspacing screen. Blue-eyed blonds aren't exactly common here in the Coalition."

That Trystin knew all too well.

"Now . . . you can turn us down, and some do, and, believe it or not, nothing bad will happen. At least nothing that wouldn't happen anyway. You'd probably get your own cruiser for a half tour in either Safrya, Helconya, or Parvati, and then a full tour as a heavy cruiser CO in one of the hot systems." Commander Delapp shrugged. "After that, you'd get a tour at the Pilot Training Command, and then either retirement or promotion to the staff level— something like that. We can't afford to waste talent over skin or hair color, no matter what some hotheads in Cambria think."

While he wasn't sure he totally believed the commander, Trystin understood the numbers and the situation. Twenty- to fifty-percent attrition over another two tours wasn't exactly harmless. On the other hand, intelligence missions into revvie territory didn't exactly seem harmless, either. As for resignation . . . he shook his head. Stupid as it might seem, especially after Salya, he had to do something, and he didn't like quitting, which was probably something else the Intelligence types had already figured out. Why was everyone pushing him? Or was it so desperate that they were pushing everyone?

"Your profile says you're not the money type, but Intelligence work carries double hazard pay—for the rest of your Service career—and the double hazard pay is calculated as part of your base pay for retirement purposes."

"Very safe line of work, I can see," said Trystin dryly.

"We're just more honest than the Pilot Training branch," countered the commander with a faint smile. "Any *general* questions?"

"Why do I need the Farhkan approval?"

"You don't. We do. I can't tell you now, but I can guarantee absolutely that if you decide to accept an Intelligence assignment, you will know before you undertake that assignment."

"You implied that this was a one-time shot. What's to keep it from being either terminal or recurring?"

"The Revenant security systems. We can get you in once—guaranteed—and out. Too many transits of the system get flagged. Revenants don't travel that much between systems. We don't either, when you think about it. To create an identity that allows those kinds of transits brings up a level of scrutiny that's hard to pass."

Trystin frowned. "What are the odds?"

"Almost exactly the same as the two tours you have in front of you."

In short . . . not very good, but nothing looked very good. "Why me right now?"

"You were available. Personnel is rotating officers after six troid missions on the same ship, or as soon as possible for officers over that. It's caused some problems, but survival rates drop too quickly after six."

"What will happen to me if I say no?"

"A month at command school, mostly to give you a break. You don't really need anything but the brushup on advanced Revenant tactics. Then another few weeks home leave, and then a frigate in Helconya or Safyra."

Trystin frowned. What difference would he make, killing more Revenants or busting a few more troids? Then, what difference would he make chasing information in the revvie systems? At times, it all seemed futile. He cleared his throat as the commander waited, and finally asked, "Will what you want me to do in the Revenant systems really make a difference?"

"I don't know. All I can honestly say is that I don't think the answer lies in force of arms."

Trystin nodded slowly and spread his hands. "You've convinced me. Now what?"

"You don't need to lie, Major," answered Katellie Delapp. "I doubt I've convinced you in the slightest. You just don't see any real options."

Trystin had to force a grin, but it wasn't too hard. "You've got me."

"The situation has us all. Anyway . . . you go back to school in Yuintah. Actually, it's an enclave in the hills there surrounded by the South Continent's Service reservation."

Trystin frowned, not recalling such a reservation on Perdya's southern continent.

"It's there, Major. And I'm not reading minds. All of you get the same look. It's much easier to hide something on a well-inhabited planet than in the middle of nowhere." She paused. "Are you ready to start?"

"Yes, especially since I don't have any options."

"Good." She tapped something into the console and stood. "Once you leave the building, you won't see anyone besides Service personnel, Farhkans, or Revenants until you finish the job."

Or until he was dead, Trystin added mentally. It was wonderful to be without realistic options, just wonderful.

"Tiedrol will escort you to the atmospheric shuttle. Good luck, Major." She smiled as the tech opened the door. Trystin's gear was racked on the small cart.

"Thank you." He bowed to the commander before he left, wondering just what he had let himself in for, and, for all his thoughts of duty and Salya, why?

He snorted. What were his choices? Another tour on system patrols, wondering if he could figure out another series of impossible ship contortions necessary for survival, punctuated with nightmares and boredom between disasters? Insanity, spending the rest of a short life in a padded cell? Or a reluctant Intelligence agent?

As he followed the cart down the corridor toward the lift shaft, he repressed a laugh. He'd wanted to do more than sit on a perimeter station and wait for revs. He'd wanted to do more than patrol an outer-system belt waiting for endless lines of revs. Now, he was being pushed into doing more, and he didn't like it.

"Ser?" asked Tiedrol in response to the half laugh, half snort.

"Nothing. Just thinking about getting what you wish for." He shook his head.

51

 Trystin paused for a moment beside the double doors of the building that looked like a school and studied the small town that lay below the gentle hillside, noting the extra-wide streets and the low and sprawling houses that all seemed to have central courtyards. In the exact center of the town was a wide building with a single glittering spire.

The man who had introduced himself as Brother Khalid when Trystin had stepped off the atmospheric shuttle waited. In the white square-collared coat and trousers and the open-necked large-collared white shirt, Brother Khalid seemed cool, despite the warm winter sun of the near-tropical locale. "Ready, Brother?"

Trystin tried not to wince at the religious salutation. "Yes, Brother Khalid."

"Good."

They stepped inside. Trystin followed the sandy-haired and tanned Khalid down a corridor and past several classrooms. In one, with an open door, sat a half-dozen men and women dressed in white. None looked up as they passed.

Khalid led Trystin into a small office without windows and closed the door. "Sit down."

Trystin sat.

"First, the technical details. Your personal gear is stored for your return. You can take nothing that could be traced to the Coalition. When we leave here, we'll go to the tailor shop in the back. Your clothes should be ready for you, and you'll be instructed in their wearing, including the garments. *Everything* you're wearing now will be stored for your return. Understood?"

"Yes, Brother Khalid."

"Good. Now . . . as for your mission . . . forget about it. You have one. You'll be briefed when you're ready. Your job now is to assimilate an entire lifetime of Revenant culture in less than two months. It's called total immersion. After the tailor shop, you'll get your first overlay, through your implant. It will give you the basics, including a grammatical update. We really don't have time to do this as well as we'd like, but we'll immerse you until you *feel* the Revenant culture, and we'll keep it up.

"From this point on, you are Deacon Wyllum Hyriss. The familiar is Brother Hyriss. You are of the returned. You will address anyone you meet in New Harmony as 'Sister' or 'Brother,' except as you will learn for more distinguished personages.

"Inside or outside this building, you are Brother Hyriss. You will speak modern Revenant. Your day is structured as though the sessions here are your job—and the rest of the time, you live and react in New Harmony. You will be living in the Cloisters—that's where newly returned missionaries live until they get married to their first wife—and none of them live there more than three months, but obviously that won't be a problem here.

"You are expected to use every facility in the town, especially the stosque—"

"Stosque?"

"It's the everyday church, if you will, as opposed to the Temple. You'll get more on that in the religion sessions. You need to become familiar with all the buildings and to use them, and to converse as any Revenant would. You will even learn to drive a petroleum-powered vehicle. Yes, they still use them. The entire town is scanned, and your every movement will be watched—and every day for the first two weeks, you will be debriefed here on the previous day's successes and failures.

"In the future, you may be assigned to a job in the town as background for your mission. You may not. It just depends." Khalid waited.

"What do we study here?"

"The only non-Revenant material will be your weapons class, where you will learn to build several weapons from common components available on Revenant worlds."

"Weapons?"

"You might have to defend yourself—or more. That depends on your mission, and, no, I don't know yours. But you won't be allowed to bring weapons into whatever Revenant system is your destination. So you must know how to make them if the need arises."

Trystin frowned. Weapons?

"Everything else will be Revenant cultural materials—from the *Book of Toren* to church procedures and protocols—and you will go to church every Sunday and to scripture study group on Wednesday nights."

"Wednesday?"

"Threeday. The day names—they use a variant on the old Earth nomenclature and a seven-day week and irregular months—will be in your first overlay."

"This seems . . . rather elaborate. . . ."

Khalid shook his head, almost sadly. "Most of those who are discovered by the Revenants give themselves away. The culture is structured, quietly xenophobic, and comprised of elaborate, sophisticated, and interlocking rituals. So is the Ecofreak culture. Ecofreaks—that's right—Ecofreaks don't recognize that. Most cultures don't. They only recognize outsiders because they don't seem to fit. Our job is to make you fit. Is that clear?"

Trystin nodded. It was all too clear, but the weapons bit nagged at him.

"Let's go, Brother Hyriss."

"After you, Brother Khalid."

52

Trystin blotted his forehead with the large white handkerchief, absently folding it and replacing it in his jacket hip pocket, thankful for the late-afternoon hill breeze as he walked into the bookstore that featured the hard-covered paper books relegated mainly to collectors on Perdya.

The coolness of the store was refreshing as Trystin stepped toward the section labeled "History."

"There's a new one in, Brother, that you might like," called Imam, the white-haired patriarch who operated the store.

"What might that be?"

Imam bustled from behind the counter that held the accounting console and almost right up to Trystin. "Here!" He pointed to the book on the "New Releases" shelf.

"*Orum's Way*," Trystin read aloud. "How the Battle for the First Temple Was Won." He wondered if the book were merely a rehash of the *Book of Toren* or if it would provide some new insights.

"Good story, and better, it's true. All about Toren's struggle to clear the mount and make it a place for the Lord and the faithful. You know, the old militarists wanted to put a military base there."

"Militarists?" asked Trystin innocently, recognizing the trap, if belatedly.

"That's what they called the people who fought wars for money back in the black centuries after the Die-off—sort of like the Ecofreaks' Service. 'Cept the Ecofreaks won't admit they fight for money."

"That's why they can't withstand the missions of the faithful," Trystin said matter-of-factly.

"Could be, Brother. You'd know better than I, having returned more recently."

"Some things don't change." Trystin studied the book. "That's for sure."

"You think this would be interesting."

"A lot of people are reading it."

Trystin repressed a shrug, then nodded. "You've convinced me, Brother Imam."

"A wise fellow you are." Imam walked back to the console and slipped behind it.

Trystin, no longer fumbling with the separate plastic credit strip or the paper money used for smaller transactions, slid the strip and the book across the counter to Imam.

"Peace be with you, Brother."

"And with you," Trystin answered as he tucked the book under his arm.

Outside the bookstore, he paused as another man in white gestured.

"Have you seen Sister Angelica, Brother Hyriss?" asked Brother Munson.

"She wasn't in the bookstore, Brother. I haven't seen her this afternoon. Could she be up at Circle in the stosque?"

"I don't know. If you should run across her, I'd appreciate it if you would tell her that Brother Khalid is looking for her."

"I will. Peace be with you."

"And you."

Trystin walked across the wide street to the confectionery shop—all the Revenants liked sweets, of all sorts.

"You want to try the lime balls, Brother Hyriss?" asked the sister behind the counter.

"Too tart, Sister."

"No Ecofreak there," laughed the older man from the back door. "They love fruity tarts, the fruitier the better."

Trystin laughed, trying to enjoy the bad pun. "I prefer my confectioneries sweeter, not sickeningly sweet, but honestly sweet."

"Spoken like a true returned, but how long will he be true?" The sister glanced at the older man.

"Get the man his sweets, sweet."

"You, too? All you men like your sweets."

Trystin grinned as the sister turned to him.

53

 "Brother Hyriss, please come forward," requested the instructor identified only as Brother Suledin.

"You are from Nephi, and you are on Orum, somewhere in Wystuh."

Trystin stepped into the space in front of the chairs, not knowing what scene might unfold.

"Brother Hyriss, I understand you come from Nephi. Is that not rather familiar to the Ecofreak systems?"

"I am from Nephi, Brother," acknowledged Trystin with a smile he hoped was open, "and blessed that the Lord and the Prophet have chosen to serve as our shield."

"To be so familiar with the abominations of the Lord must trouble you."

"The Lord has shielded us from untoward familiarity, as you have indeed recognized."

"I would say that familiarity might become you, Brother Hyriss," said Brother Suledin smoothly.

Trystin managed to continue smiling as he replied, "The Lord knows what is, and when one insists on such familiarity, then the beholder may harbor even greater familiarity."

Suledin nodded and turned away from Trystin. "Sister Susanna? You have just arrived in Midinha, and your clothes are wrinkled."

Sister Susanna took Trystin's place.

Trystin's hand moved as if to begin to wipe his forehead.

"Brother Hyriss, did I upset you? Are you too warm? Perhaps there is indeed some familiarity with abominations."

Trystin forced another smile. Did Brother Suledin have eyes in the back of his head? "I am from Nephi, and Nephi is cooler than Wystuh, much cooler. Perhaps you could come to visit sometime."

Without pausing, his point made, Brother Suledin turned back to Sister Angelica. "Sister, are you headed for a nunnery?"

Trystin held in a wince at the insult.

Sister Susanna turned and fixed her eyes directly on Suledin. "Brother, your concern is most welcome, and seemly, and even brotherly, and I will commend your concerns to my husband." She offered a radiant smile.

"Debrief," said Brother Suledin.

All that meant was that he could be objective, Trystin reflected. They still had to stay in character, politely smiling.

"Overt aggression is not expressed, and, if expressed, not allowed to persist. All insults are veiled, as in the reference to abominations with Brother Hyriss—except that insults to third parties not present, such as Ecofreaks or abominations, are allowed, often with puns or other tasteless allusions. This is a highly repressed and stylized culture. Every action is observed and tallied against a social norm. You are *never* in a position when someone is not observing you. You are expected to respond, as would any innocent being, but you must respond in the same style, with veiled allusions.

"Tolerance within the norms is high, but once anyone exceeds those norms, they effectively vanish. Remember one other thing we've been drilling into you. The Revenants seldom lie. They may avoid disclosing or revealing something, but if something is said, you can usually bank on it being true. That's why they punish those who exceed the norms so stringently. Now, they don't call it punishment. In polite terms, they go on a mission for the Prophet, which can be anything from asteroid mining with inadequate equipment to being dumped on a barely habitable planet undergoing final planoforming. No one is exempt, and that is why the system works." He paused. "Debrief ended."

Silence hung over the classroom for a moment.

"Good day to you all, Brothers and Sisters."

"Good day, Brother Suledin."

Trystin did not try to wipe his damp forehead again, at least not inside or in the shade.

54

As Trystin stepped out of the front foyer of the Cloisters, Brother Khalid smiled.

"Brother Khalid."

"Brother Hyriss. The time has arrived for your call to greater service."

"It will take a minute to pack." Certainly not much more, reflected Trystin.

"I will wait."

Trystin nodded and returned to the three-meter-square bachelor quarters, containing a narrow bed, a chest, and a wardrobe. No wonder most of the returned were in a hurry to get married. Being married—he'd really never thought about it. Who would he marry? The only two women who had come even close to understanding him were his mother and Salya. He frowned—and maybe Ulteena. But who knew if she'd even survived the latest round of troid onslaughts, although, if anyone could, she could. He hoped she had, but when he would ever . . . if he would ever . . .

Forcing his mind back to the mundane matter of packing, he pulled out the fabric traveling bag of the returned and opened it. First came the undergarments from the chest, white and longer than he would have preferred, then the two nightshirts, also white, and the white dress belt with the stylized bronze eagle with the lightning bolt that was the symbol of the returned. From the wardrobe came toiletries, including the antique bladed razor and the tube of white leather polish, and white shirts and the second and third white suit.

He put the white dress boots in the side pocket, along with the thick white socks. At least the everyday boots were black.

Once finished packing, including the *Book of Toren* that he had read at least twice completely and still didn't feel he knew well enough, he snapped the bag shut and adjusted the shoulder harness before leaving the empty room.

"You look ready to travel, Brother Hyriss," observed Khalid.

"As the Lord and the Prophet will."

They walked across the street, past the stosque and into the center of New Harmony toward the school building on the far side.

"Some sweets, Brother Hyriss?" called Sister Andrews through the open door of the confectionery store.

"Not today, Sister."

"Nice intonation," said Khalid.

Trystin didn't fall for it. "Sister Andrews does have a nice voice."

Khalid nodded. "Many sisters do. Most are truly good people."

Trystin concealed a frown, but wondered what Khalid's motives might be. "The Lord inspires them."

"That he does, Brother Hyriss, and best you not forget that. All in the Lord's mansions strive to do good, and that is their grace and their failure."

All? wondered Trystin. Did Khalid really believe that? And if he didn't, wasn't he even more hypocritical than most of the Service?

Trystin kept walking, and Khalid offered no other observations. When they reached the school building Khalid led Trystin to the back section. They stopped outside a closed door.

"This is as far as I go, Brother Hyriss. Peace be with you."

"And with you."

Trystin opened the door and stepped inside, closing it behind him.

A white-haired man in the uniform of a senior commander sat behind the desk in the windowless office. His uniform bore no name and no decorations. Idly, Trystin wondered how the commander had reached the office unobserved.

"Sit down, Brother Hyriss."

Trystin sat and set the fabric bag beside the chair, his eyes remaining on the commander.

"Careful, aren't you? That's good. You'll need to be. You're going to the Jerush system."

"Orum?" Trystin was tired of the intelligence types telling him he needed to be cautious. They weren't being asked to stick their necks out.

"As a matter of fact, you're going to Wystuh itself. After you get your second overlay and your mission profile, of course."

Trystin contained the wince he felt. More overlays?

"You'll get the full details with the profile. Your mission is simple enough. You're a Revenant courier pilot of a ship owned by an independent trading firm out of the Hyndji systems—those are the only outsider ships the Revenants allow to enter Revenant systems, and only the outlying systems at that. You'll bring the courier, carrying legitimate Hyndji microtronics and designs, into Braha. Braha is one of the recently opened outlying systems where security isn't quite as tight. From there, you'll travel commercial to Orum, and then to Wystuh itself. Your job is to attack the High Council of Bishops, and to remove, with extreme prejudice, Administrative Fleet Commander and Archbishop Jynckla. Any questions? You don't have to be in character. Double debrief alpha."

For a moment, Trystin said nothing. He should have

seen it from the beginning, especially with the weapons-creation training. Of course he wouldn't be sent just to gather information. He wanted to pound his head for not seeing the obvious. Except he hadn't really wanted to see it, had he?

"Why?"

"You don't like the idea of assassination, do you? Almost none of you do." The commander offered a cold smile. "One afternoon on Mara, on a single afternoon, you slaughtered nearly one hundred revs. You've destroyed thousands on system patrols, but an assassination of one man that might shorten the war and save untold thousands . . . that bothers you."

"It doesn't quite seem the same." Trystin kept his voice level.

"Dead is dead, Brother Hyriss. We're not ordering you to kill children, or pregnant women. We're ordering you to remove a military figure during a war. You think that the admirals who order all those revs into battle ought to be exempt from danger?"

The commander had a point, but Trystin still asked, "What will the assassination of one admiral do?"

"That's a matter of strategy." The commander offered a second cold smile. "However, in general terms, we need to make an example. To show the Revenants that we can strike them anywhere, that their patriarchs aren't exempt from the consequences of their decisions."

"There's no better way to do this? Than someone like me?"

The white-haired man shook his head. "The social and indoctrination codes are so effective that we couldn't buy a traitor—not one we could trust—with half a system's wealth. Besides, that's not the point. The point is to show that we can neutralize anyone. That takes someone who has a range of talents and also technical skills. Why do you suppose you've gotten training in building a crude weapons laser from common electronic parts? You can't exactly cart weapons through security. Also, very few Revenant women have technical skills."

"And you don't have any male agents in place in Wystuh? That's hard to believe."

"Oh, we do. But now isn't the time, and this kind of operation isn't designed—"

"In other words, you've got deep agents placed as serial wives or as returned technicians, and they're fine for more subtle operations, but you don't trust them with something like this."

"It's not a question of trust. We can't get them permanently established on Orum," admitted the commander.

"And I can? That's hard to believe. Or is it that you can't turn them into killers?" An edge of anger seeped into Trystin's voice, an edge he regretted and tried to damp.

"You'd rather go back to commanding a corvette in Parvati system? We could send you back—right now. Do you want that?"

"No." That was an absolute death sentence, especially stated the way the commander had. "But why do you have to use a novice agent?"

The commander shrugged. "As you have doubtless been instructed, much of the Revenant culture is nonverbal, and the Revenants have a clear sense of who belongs and who does not. The best way I can explain is that the so-called returned—those military missionaries who have survived—have a certain look, an aura, that seems to have been created by facing death and deep space. The only people we have that match that are Service pilots, and not all of them. You do. Do you have any idea what it takes to find someone who has Revenant-compatible genes, a Revenant appearance, deep-space aura, intelligence, and ability to learn a new culture without fragmenting?"

"That makes more sense. But if there are so few of us, how can we create the impression of being able to strike anywhere?"

"That will be explained more in your profile, but the basic point is that people react to impressions, not numbers of incidents. Do you have any more questions?" The commander's voice implied that Trystin had already asked too many questions.

"No, ser." He wasn't going to get any real answers, and there was no point in asking questions that wouldn't get answered. He pushed back the seething anger—anger at his own naïveté and at the calculated blackmail used to get him to agree to the mission. The choice was too simple: take the mission and probably die or not take it and certainly die.

"There is one last thing . . . stay away from the Temples. They have defenses that seem to incinerate all non-Revenants as they pass through the gates. That's another reason why we can't put permanent male agents on Orum."

"Lasers, obviously." Trystin noted to himself that such information had not been made available in the cultural briefings—another form of lying and deception.

"Of course. It's not the weaponry, but the recognition patterns. You know the whole ritual for entering the Temple the first time. No one who doesn't go through it gets in except as cinders. It doesn't matter which Temple baptized you, but if you're from another system, you have to present your Temple card. The one you will get *looks* real, but it won't work."

"So why can't we duplicate the card? A closed algorithmic key?"

"Exactly. We've tried. We've tried for fifty years." The commander stood. "Are you ready, Brother Hyriss?"

"As the Lord and His Prophet will." Trystin picked up his fabric bag.

A crooked smile crossed the commander's face. A second door opened in the rear of the room, revealing a ramp downward. Trystin followed the commander down the ramp and along the glow-lamp-lit tunnel to an open doorway.

A technician and what appeared to be a large implant-activation machine waited.

"In the chair, Brother."

Trystin forced himself to be calm as he slipped into the chair, waiting as the helmetlike apparatus was adjusted around his head.

"Good . . . just a tad there . . ."

A faint tingling ran through his implant.

"Sensitive . . . good . . . better take . . ."

Light flared through Trystin's skull, so bright his eyes, even in blackness, watered, and he shivered in the chair.

The profile slipped into place—the trading company, Altus, Limited, and the specific microtronics, the flight schedules, the office manager . . . even the alternate backup identity—thin, but better than nothing in an emergency. The pieces clicked into his mind and his implant.

"One down . . . now . . ."

Another light novaed through Trystin, making the first seem pallid by comparison. His whole body spasmed for a moment, and his eyes felt like knives had been rammed through them.

Then the memories flashed through Trystin's head— the mission to Soharra, and the thin men with veils who opened every door and shut it when they saw his brown square-suit; the holo pictures of the Temple in Wystuh, with the eight four-pointed spires and the angel of the Prophet hovering there in shimmering gold; the cold of the Prophet's asteroid ship, and the small scout that was his, and the triumph of taking Bokara. . . .

"Good take . . ."

Trystin winced, fighting the images, as the tech slowly folded back the apparatus. For a time, he just sat there. Finally, he sat upright and swung his legs around until his boots touched the stone floor.

"Don't fight them," offered the tech, a thin man with a brush mustache. "They'll fade, but you can call on them if you need them."

"And you will need them," added the commander. "Let's go. You can sort it all out on the way."

"Where?"

"To Braha, Brother Hyriss, and the enfolding of the Prophet."

Trystin forced himself to walk erect, although he felt almost crushed by the weight of Brother Hyriss's pseudomemories. The underground corridor seemed to stretch forever, but they walked less than a hundred meters before they reached a small tube-shuttle.

"First seat."

Trystin took the first seat of the dimly lit tubetrain. The doors closed and the shuttle dropped into the tunnel and whispered through the darkness for nearly ten minutes, according to Trystin's implant.

One thing he did understand—sort of—was the need for Farhkan approval, because his return flight, assuming he made it that far, required refueling at the outer Farhkan station. There was also a blunt warning about not crossing the orbit of the sixth planet. But why Farhka? What role were the aliens playing? The questions swirled through him, and the pseudomemories pressed at his entire sense of self.

Why . . . why . . . why . . . ? That was the question that no one was answering.

The shuttle emerged into another underground station, deserted except for two technicians armed with stunners and shockers. Trystin carted himself and his bag up another ramp where he found himself looking out at the atmospheric shuttle port where he had entered training.

"Your orbit shuttle will be here in less than an hour." The commander sank into a chair and pulled out a portable console.

Trystin sat, and called up the mission profile—but try as he could, there was no information on his departure point—or the coordination with the Farhkans. Everything started with his arrival in Braha.

"Where am I headed?" he finally asked.

"To your staging point."

"Why is it necessary to go through Farhka on the return?"

"Even if you are followed, the trail ends there. They don't let revs near their systems. One of the few benefits of cooperating with those gray bastards. That's all, Major." The commander's eyes glazed over as he used his implant to interface with the small console he held.

Standing without answers, Trystin took a deep breath.

He had no real choices, did he? And the commander knew it, the sadistic bastard! Trystin could undertake the mission and defect—and he had no doubts the revs would squeeze his mind dry and kill him. Or he could do the mission and try to survive—and that probably meant surviving Revenants, Farhkans, and the Service . . . if he got that far.

Deep inside, he was even more pleased that he'd never told the Service about his keys to the Temple. Keys to the Temple? He swallowed. To what degree was the entire Service being manipulated by the aliens? Or was he being used to manipulate the Service?

Salya had been right about Farhkan studies and piloting. Oh, how she'd been right. He took another deep breath and began to sort through the pseudomemories.

What else could he do? As Ghere had said, he had to find the answers, and he didn't like it one bit.

55

 Trystin shifted his weight on the hard plastic chair. While the seat wasn't comfortable, at least the gray pilot's shipsuit that had been waiting on the courier was. A second one was folded in his bag. In the commercial world shipsuits were for ship wear, period.

"Where are we? How will I translate out from here?" Trystin asked the major who sat in the tiny mess room with him, watching the single visual screen as the courier eased toward a dark blob in the middle of darkness that appeared to be his destination.

"You don't need to know. The coordinates are in your ship's translation system, and they'll burn out at your first translation."

Trystin nodded. The profile had him returning, via Farhka, to outer orbit control in Chevel, or Safrya, as an alternate. That was why he'd needed Farhkan approval, and that explained some things. If the Farhkans were willing to let Intelligence cover ships' return to their systems, they favored the Coalition in some ways—or they wanted *something* very badly. But what? And why? He still hadn't figured that out.

He could also understand the secrecy about his departure point. He couldn't very well betray what he didn't know, and he really didn't know anything that any Service officer wouldn't know, except that there was a total-immersion system for training spies, and that some spies were assassins.

He didn't know exactly where any of the Intelligence bases were, nor even what officers ran them. He laughed. The Revenants could take him apart and learn very little that they didn't already know. Much simpler than providing suicide devices or organic explosives.

The assassination angle still bothered him. Yet . . . the commander had been right. Trystin's hands were already covered in blood. The assassination of an admiral, while perhaps cowardly, was scarcely terrorism or the murder of an innocent.

The major, who, like all the other Intelligence types outside of Service Headquarters, wore no name badge or decorations, gave him a puzzled glance, but said nothing.

"Need to know. I could spill everything I know, and it wouldn't be of much use to the Revenants."

"We'd prefer you didn't." The major's tone was dry.

"So would I, but you people didn't leave any clues for anyone to use against you."

"I hope not."

The small station looked more like a chunk of rock than a station. In fact, it looked like a Revenant asteroid ship. Trystin and the major waited as the courier was grappled into an interior lock.

"Power changeover."

Instead of full gravity replacing ship gravity, minimal grav did, and Trystin's stomach momentarily lurched upward.

Trystin picked up his fabric bag and followed the major out of the courier—he had never seen the pilot or crew—and into the station, careful not to bound in the low gravity. Only a single tech, wearing armor with a one-way faceplate, remained by the courier.

Once they left the hangar deck, Trystin staggered as he stepped into the corridor and full gravity.

"First stop is the tech shop," announced the major. "They'll do a final fitting on your space armor—it's standard commercial, authentic Hyndji. We could have used Argenti, but the Hyndji is more common and suited to your mission."

One technician waited in the large shop. The armor was laid out on an empty workbench.

Trystin pulled it on slowly, checking each section, particularly the seals and the fittings. Then he picked up the helmet, frowning.

"I know, Brother," said the technician. "Only bad feature about the Hyndji helmets is the field of vision."

After testing the armor, and after the technician made minor adjustments, Trystin took it off and packed it into the carrying case. Then he marched after the silent major toward another hangar lock where a bulbous ship, apparently massing more than a corvette and less than a cruiser, rested in minimal gravity on a flat carriage. Two rails ran under the carriage and toward the lock door.

"It's a standard Revenant trader, manufactured by a Hyndji firm to Revenant standards, with a few slight modifications for our purposes." The major gestured, and another technician, also in nondescript browns, appeared.

"Would you show the brother through his ship?"

"Yes, ser."

The major inclined his head to Trystin. "A pleasure meeting you, Brother, and I wish you well. Take whatever time you need to become familiar with the ship. The technician here will answer any questions you have. When you're ready to launch, just use standard control frequencies and tell them you're ready."

Clearly, Trystin had seen as much of the base as he was going to.

"Food, necessities?"

"The *Paquawrat* is fully stocked."

"Crew?"

"Traders this size run with one pilot. Multiple-pilot safety rules apply only for larger ships with passengers." The major inclined his head.

"Peace be with you," Trystin said.

"And with you."

The technician waited.

"Show me what I need to know." Trystin offered a smile.

"More than I'd be knowing, Brother, but we'll give it a shot. We'll start with the thrusters and translation system."

Trystin followed the technician aft, trying not to bounce much in the low gravity. He watched and listened as the man ran through what was essentially an elaborate pre-flight before they returned to the cockpit, a cockpit with two couches, but with manual controls only before the left-hand seat.

"... standard controls here, and you can switch to manual if you want. The low net's real simple, compared to either Revenant or Coalition standards. You want a full net, just use the command 'FULLNET.' It won't respond except to a Service implant." The technician laughed. "Good thing all the Service implants are all organic or organic density. You won't set off any alarms. Ex-Hyndji military pilots are always doing that."

The technician pulled on his chin. "The specs are on the low net."

"Anything else?"

"One thing." The technician in the nondescript brown coveralls flicked what appeared to be a rivet beside the right-hand screen and a small panel dropped, revealing a single switch. The top position was labeled "B," the bottom "G." "Brother, this is the most important gadget on this scout."

Trystin waited.

"In the blue position, the thrusters are tuned to revvie scale; in the green position to Coalition scale. Don't forget this."

Forgetting that could get Trystin cooked, and he touched the stud, fingering the switch and concentrating on the concept. Finally, he flicked the stud to the lower position. Then he frowned and flicked it back up, but left the panel open.

"That's all I can think of," said the technician. "Except take your time, and review the systems."

"I will."

Trystin escorted the technician back to the ship lock, then closed it after the man stepped onto the hangar deck. He opened the armor's carrying case and stowed the armor in the rack on the back wall of the cockpit, placing the case in the locker underneath. Then he went back to the tiny quarterdeck and took his clothes bag to the minuscule cabin, placing it in the net restraints.

After that he went to the galley, and looked for the samovar. There wasn't one. While the water heated in a pot, he decided to check the cargo bays.

After ten minutes, he stopped, shaking his head. The cargo appeared to be what he'd been briefed that it would be—microtronic components, but all the cases were sealed and stamped with Hyndji break-nots.

He closed the seals to the cargo spaces, and went back to the galley, where, sipping herbal tea, he rehydrated a dehydrated meal. The beef was still dry and too heavy, but his stomach felt better when he returned to the cockpit and plugged into the net.

According to his implant, he'd spent nearly three hours before he felt halfway comfortable with the ship and the systems—although they were similar to and far simpler than either those of a training corvette or of the *Willis*.

Finally, he went through the checklist, as far as he could go in an interior lock.

"Control, this is *Paquawrat*. Ready for departure."

"*Paquawrat*, reduce ship grav to nil."

"Ship grav is nil."

"Opening lock this time. Do not initiate thrusters or attitude jets until instructed."

"Understand no power on thrusters or jets until instructed."

"That's affirmative."

Trystin used the sensors to watch as the outer lock door slid open. Then the carriage on which the *Paquawrat* rested slowly edged the ship toward the darkness of the open lock.

"Electrorepulsion beginning."

Trystin's stomach heaved at the gentle pressure of the directed grav fields, but he kept his attention on the net and the sensors as the trader slowly floated upward from the asteroid station.

Then the lock door closed.

"Hyndji ship *Paquawrat*, you are cleared to proceed."

"Roger, Control." Trystin almost had used "stet" instead of the "roger" used by Revenant pilots. He shook his head as he slowly eased power to the thrusters.

The representative screen showed a dead system—not a single EDI trace. Within minutes, he would have been hard-pressed to relocate the asteroid base.

With a deep breath, he slowly added power until the thrusters were at seventy-five percent, the most any commercial pilot would use, given the massive fuel consumption and stress placed on the fusactor system by higher thrust loads.

As the *Paquawrat* accelerated toward the dust-free translation zone, Trystin continued to range through the ship's networks—high and low—trying to ignore the same nagging question: Just how was an assassination of a senior administrative admiral going to help the Coalition?

How would even several assassinations help stop the endless flow of troid ships and tanks and military missionaries committed to overrunning the Coalition?

Then, again, he reflected ruefully, if the continued comparative military successes of the Coalition hadn't stopped the Revenants, maybe trying anything was better than losing while winning almost every battle.

He frowned. A successful assassination attempt on the enemy's capital planet—how likely was a safe escape? Did the Service really care?

Of course not. He sighed. In the final analysis, what he felt really didn't matter to anyone but himself, and there weren't exactly a bundle of alternatives. If he took the ship and tried to enter non-Coalition space, he'd be branded as either a thief or identified as a Coalition spy, or both—and that probably meant death or the rest of a short life behind some very strong walls.

Besides, he told himself, Jynckla was a revvie military figure, and it was war, and Salya was dead, and she'd been far less military than the rev. So he had to get the job done, and he had to survive—if only to spite them all. But . . . his stomach still twisted.

56

 "Braha Control, this is Hyndji ship *Paquawrat,* commercial code alpha gamma seven five four. Requesting clearance for approach."

"Roger, *Paquawrat.* Request pilot clearance code."

"Braha Control, pilot number is W-H, that is Wood, Heart, five, nine, five, four, two, Quebec. Wood, Heart, five, nine, five, four, two, Quebec."

A pause followed, punctuated with faint static.

"*Paquawrat,* cleared to Beta three this time. Maintain thrust at point zero two or less."

"Roger, Braha Control. Maintaining thrust at point zero two."

Commercial hubs didn't like quick movement around the station—that was clear as Trystin eased the *Paquawrat* around to the beta section and into the old-style, protruded locking dock.

"Control, this is *Paquawrat,* beginning lock approach this time."

"*Paquawrat,* you're cleared. Report full locking."

"Roger, Control."

There was only a slight bump as the ship entered the dock. Trystin got the holdtights magnetized before there was any rebound, and went through the shutdown checklist.

"Braha Control, Hyndji ship *Paquawrat,* locked in place this time, beta three."

"Thanks, three. You're cleared to station power."

"Roger."

Trystin sat in the couch for several seconds, then laughed as he scrambled out. He was the crew.

Once he had completed the power switchover and the pressure check, he triggered the lock.

A woman wearing the uniform of Altus Limited waited at the lock with a clipboard. So did two men in blue shipsuits with white lightning bolts on their sleeves—the Revenant Trade Clearance officers.

Trystin checked the mechanical holdtights first, then the seals on the locking tubes before turning to the woman.

"Inindjy Dotta? I'm Brother Hyriss. I haven't had the opportunity to meet you before."

"I am most pleased to meet you, Brother Hyriss. Pilots such as you make our business possible." Her voice was polite, but no more.

Trystin kept his face calm, knowing that the Hyndji company had been forced to hire Revenant pilots.

"Brother," began the blond and green-eyed officer, "what's the cargo?"

"Assorted microtronics, plus design ensembles, and several proprietary sealed designs commissioned by customers." Trystin had expected it, but he was still glad he'd studied the manifests until he knew almost every item on them.

"What's the status of the seals?"

"They were all clean when I left."

"Do you mind if we come aboard?"

"Of course not, but I believe that Mistress Dotta should accompany us also, since she is the shipper's agent." Trystin gestured to the woman.

"That would be fine."

Trystin opened the cargo spaces easily.

"Now, here are the bundled microtronics. . . ."

The taller agent frowned and looked at him. "Brother Hyriss, you do seem to know this cargo well."

"A pilot who doesn't know his cargo well is all too soon a dead pilot," Trystin returned. "The mass calculations . . ." He shrugged.

"Keep this one, Inindjy," said the second clearance official.

"If we are fortunate . . ." The company official spread her hands.

Trystin stood back as the two looked, scanned with portable equipment, and generally prodded almost everything. They also checked every seal and stamp.

Finally, they returned to where Trystin stood.

"Cargo looks fine, Brother Hyriss. Your card and databloc?"

"They're in the safehold in the cockpit. Just a moment."

The tall man followed Trystin and waited as Trystin retrieved the two encoded plastic oblongs. Then the clearance officer ran both through the portable terminal he held.

Trystin watched the other's eyes for any red reflection, but they showed no reaction except studied boredom when the terminal flashed green.

"You're clear." The officer turned to the woman. "The ship's cleared to unload. A pleasure doing business with you, Inindjy." Then his eyes settled on Trystin. "You taking the ship back out, Brother?"

"Yes, but not for a bit," Trystin answered. "The outrun cargo's not ready."

The shorter official shook his head. "Good work if you can get it. We got to log things in and out every day."

"I'll take that, thank you," said the taller one. "Even commercial pilots don't always make it. Ever see an old one?"

The two officials nodded and walked off the quarter-deck.

"Do you want to sign for the ship now, Mistress Dotta?"

"That would be acceptable." She handed the clipboard to him. The Hyndjis still preferred hard-copy signatures on official documents. "You are due back on the thirtieth of March."

Trystin made the mental translation—roughly the twenty-seventh or eighth of trio—and nodded. If he were in any shape to make it back after undertaking an assassination in the heart of the Revenant capital.

She watched as he reclaimed his bag.

"I'm leaving the armor in place."

"Good. Then you will be back."

"I certainly plan to be, Mistress Dotta."

He watched as she sealed the ship, not that it made any difference to him. With the implant, he could open it without the physical keys. Then he walked up the tube, heading to book passage to Orum.

57

 Trystin shifted his weight in the narrow seat, glad that no one was sitting beside him, then blotted his forehead with the white handkerchief. The transport was hot, and he was even hotter from sitting three hours after translation while the transport maintained modest thrust in-system. Trystin could sense the time-dilation envelope, but the effect was mild, less than an hour over the trip. He still didn't like so many people crammed into a single cabin, like animals in stalls, but that was the way Revenants traveled between systems, probably the only way it was halfway affordable. He'd swallowed at the rate of ten thousand Revenant dollars. Then again, in the Coalition, almost no one traveled between systems, except on Service craft.

The seats were clean, but old, with scratches in the plastic polished over, and the covers on some chairs replaced, while others bore older fabric.

He blotted his forehead again as he sensed the approach of the ship to the orbit station through his implant—the ship's protocols were different, but the overall pattern was familiar enough. One big advantage provided by the implant was the ability to touch and, theoretically, manipulate "open-wave" systems. The Revenants, because they felt the body was a "temple for the Lord," did not use implants. Trystin hoped he could use that advantage.

"You a pilot?" asked the stocky man from the seat across the aisle.

Trystin scanned the other with eyes and implant. "Yes, Brother, fortunate enough to have returned."

"Brother Jymes Harriston."

"Brother Wyllum Hyriss."

"What are you doing being a passenger?"

"I'm a pilot now for a Hyndji trading company. I never got back to Wystuh before I left on my mission. Went from Nephi, and I've got some time between translations." Trystin shrugged.

"The Temple's worth seeing again when you return. I guess you don't realize when you see it all the time."

"I'm looking forward to it." Trystin didn't have to feign that interest.

"Please remain seated until we complete docking. Please remain seated."

"They always say that. It never changes," Harriston remarked. "Can always spot a pilot or a former one. You fellows always get jittery."

Trystin laughed. "I suppose it's because we know what can go wrong."

A gentle *thud* went through the transport, and Trystin winced.

"A little hard?" asked the other, leaning toward Trystin.

"A little."

"You pilots . . ."

"Now that we are docked, please collect your belongings. Then move to the baggage bay behind the rear of the cabin to claim your bags before leaving the transport. Please make sure you have all your belongings."

Trystin nodded politely as he rose, but the other man was gathering some paperbound books, seemingly having forgotten Trystin altogether.

In the middle of the line of two dozen passengers as they filed back toward the lock, Trystin stopped in the baggage bay for only a moment to grab his single bag. Everyone else had two bags, at least. He lifted the bag off the rails, comparing the scratched and tarnished inner rail to the smooth and shiny outer one, clearly a recent replacement. He carried the bag out through the lock, staggering slightly as he stepped from the lower ship gravity to the station gravity. The station gravity was fractionally less than what Trystin was used to—when he had been in gravity. Apparently, the Revenants didn't shift gravity on the ship after docking. Perhaps it caused too many logistical problems. He walked up the locking tube.

The Orum orbit station smelled like every other orbit station Trystin had visited—a mixture of plastic, metal, warm oil, ozone, and people. Some things really didn't change.

At the top of the tube, he waited behind a heavyset older woman with braided hair piled high on her head. When the Soldier of the Lord handed back her card and databloc, Trystin slid his across the flat counter. The officer slipped it into a console, then looked at him.

"Brother Hyriss?"

"Yes, Officer," Trystin responded.

"Would you go through that portal there, ser?" The man pointed to an open doorway.

Trystin could see another Soldier, also blond, standing beside a more elaborate console. "Certainly." He followed the other's directions, knowing that his off-system origin would have flagged him, hoping that they hadn't already pegged him as a spy or assassin.

Don't think assassin, he told himself mentally. What's one rev more or less after all you've done?

When he reached the large console that stood in the alcove, he stopped and waited until the officer finished with the thin man in flowing whites of some sort.

"Next?"

Trystin stepped up and offered card and databloc again.

"Please put your hand there. It's just a formality, but these days, you never know."

Trystin placed his hand on the scanner, and felt the minute prick of the sampler. He also could sense the crude fields of the analyzer as it ran a rough gene-pattern analysis. He tried not to frown at the age of the equipment—obvious from the field fluctuations and the repainted outer cover.

"Good genes. Don't see that kind of stock from the outplanets often."

Then the databloc went into the scanner, and the equipment began to compare the patterns on the card and databloc to those taken by the sampler. The databloc was genuine, as was Wyllum Hyriss. The real Hyriss had died, but not until he'd been on life support long enough to extract memories and genetic codes. The codes in the databloc had been altered to match Trystin's genes, and the probabilities were over ninety-nine point three percent that no irregularities would be detected, except at a Revenant research facility.

Trystin overrode his discomfort and concerns about being that less than one percent probability and waited quietly. He could have manipulated the fields in the equipment, but his tampering would have raised a greater likelihood of detection than doing nothing.

"Good. You're cleared to take the down shuttle, ser. I'm sorry to have bothered you."

"It's certainly not a problem, Officer. I'm appreciative of your effort." And he was, if not exactly in the way described by the words.

"Thank you. Enjoy your stay in Orum. Peace be with you, Brother."

"And with you." Trystin hoisted his bag and walked back to the corridor that led to the lower decks where the shuttles down to Orum waited. Where his less-than-desirable mission waited.

Behind him, he heard, "Next!"

58

 The shuttle screeched as the heavy tires touched the long, straight runway. Trystin could feel the corrections for the crosswind, but the pilot's touch was halfway deft, and the spaceplane slowed, then finally rumbled off the runway and toward the shuttle terminal for Wystuh and Orum's West Continent. The tires bounced slightly on the taxiway, which seemed rougher than the runway.

"Please remain seated until the shuttle comes to a complete stop. Then, and only then, you may claim your bags and depart." Trystin let his head rest against the worn, but clean, fabric of the seat as the spaceplane eased to a stop and the others scurried to get their bags.

He studied the interior of the spaceplane as he waited. While it was clean, and even smelled clean, slightly like a mixture of lavender and pine, there was a tiredness associated with the equipment, the kind of fatigue that became apparent when a ship neared the end of its service life. His implant could detect no interactive system. Did the Revenant shuttles run on manual controls? That was something that hadn't been covered in the mission profile or the training.

After the aisle cleared, he stood and walked to the baggage racks. His fabric bag was the only one left, and he swung the carrying straps over his shoulder.

As Trystin finally walked out of the shuttleway, with his

bag in hand, he could see nearly two dozen people waiting to board another spaceplane that was parked next to where Trystin's shuttle had eased. The outer walls of the terminal were glittering white, although the intensity of that glitter varied slightly. Trystin studied it, and realized that the brighter sections were more recently repaired or refinished. He continued walking toward the center of the terminal.

That there were no security arrangements apparent confirmed for Trystin that the Revenants used the orbit stations as control points.

A technician with an equipment kit and wearing a maroon singlesuit passed Trystin. Ahead of him, a white-haired man and two women greeted a young man in white. One of the women hugged the blond man. All wore white.

Trystin shifted the straps on his bag and stepped around the group, following his implant-provided directions, and the overhead arrows, toward the lower level. The synthetic stone underfoot was immaculately clean, but bore fine cracks in more than a few instances.

A high-speed electric trolley ran between the terminal and central Wystuh, but Trystin was looking for the rental-vehicle section. He found the logo he was seeking in the middle section of the lower level, that of an interlocked *O* and *R,* standing for Orum Rentals. He stepped up to the empty counter, setting down his bag.

"Yes, ser?" The sister behind the counter, scarcely more than eighteen standard years, offered a friendly smile. The free-falling blond hair said that she was unattached, and the blue eyes studied Trystin.

He smiled. "Sister, I'm Brother Hyriss. I sent a request from orbit station."

". . . I told you he'd be a returned bachelor . . . good-looking, too . . . not that many so young . . ."

Trystin couldn't control his flush at the scarcely hidden whisper from the other sister who was seated at the console farther back.

". . . and he's shy, too . . . that's good . . . not an old grouch . . ."

"Ah . . . yes . . . Brother," stumbled the sister at the counter, clearly as discomfited as Trystin was. "Do you want a standard or a luxe?"

"What's the difference? Price and features?"

"In features, not much. The luxe has more room in the back seat and a larger trunk, a little more power, and tinted glass in all the windows."

The other sister snickered with the mention of the tinted glass. Trystin didn't dare to comment as the counter sister flushed.

"The luxe is fifty dollars more a day."

"I'll take the standard." Trystin finally smiled at the other sister. "Even if it doesn't have tinted glass." He handed across the Revenant universal credit strip. "I'd also like a map, if you have one. I wanted to get to Wystuh the long way, through the Dhellicor Gorge."

"It's worth the detour."

"Tell him you'll show him. . . ." hissed the other sister.

The sister at the counter flushed even brighter red. Although the immersion training had tried to convey the pressure for early marriage, being subjected to it in an uncontrolled setting was something else, and Trystin could not only understand, but *feel,* why the returned remained unattached for such short periods.

"Is there anywhere that would be good to stop to eat along the way?" he asked, trying not to let an awkward silence persist.

"Krendsaw's," offered the fair-skinned brunette in the back. "It's just this side of the Gorge."

"That would take you about an hour, if you don't stop at the foresting center," added the blonde, the redness receding from her face. "You're all set, Brother Hyriss." She handed him a key and a folder. "There's your key and the rental agreement. If you need the car for more than the ten days, you can call us here or in Wystuh and let us know. I'm Sister Lewiss, Arkady Lewiss. It shouldn't be a problem." She slid a map across the counter, her hand barely touching his, and only for an instant. "Here's the map."

She leaned forward and used a stylus to point out the green line. "This is the scenic route . . ."

As she explained, Trystin became all too aware of how good she smelled, almost like the delicate roses in the garden at home, how close she was, and how interested she seemed. And how lonely and vulnerable he was.

". . . and this is about where Krendsaw's is. It's a good steak house, but they have everything there. To get to the car, follow the tunnel there to the right and down the ramp. It's in space A-five."

Trystin offered a broader smile. "Thank you *very* much, Sister Lewiss. Peace be with you."

In some ways, he wished he could have taken her up, but it wouldn't have been fair to her, and, Revenant or not, she was still a person. More important, unfortunately, spending time with her would have been an invitation to blow his cover immediately.

As he picked up the bag and walked away, he increased his hearing, partly from curiosity and partly from ego.

". . . he *was* interested, Arkady . . . could tell . . ."

". . . seemed nicer than a lot of the returned . . ."

". . . was returned all right . . . see it in the eyes . . ."

Trystin nodded and turned down the ramp to the tunnel, which he followed to the underground parking area and the space with the blue sign that proclaimed A-5.

The standard car was a four-wheeled, petroleum-fueled, manually driven vehicle, and Trystin was most grateful for the indoctrination provided by Brother Khalid. Otherwise, he would have spent a lot of time fumbling before he'd figured it out, and the locals could have begun to ask embarrassing questions.

Instead, he tucked the bag in the cargo space in the rear, opened by a button on the trunk. There was no lock. In fact, the car had no locks at all, only an ignition key, and Trystin knew that was just as a safety precaution against young children.

The internal-combustion engine turned over easily, and Trystin slipped off the brake and shifted, wishing he'd practiced more, but glad that everything worked.

The drive from the parking area led to a larger road that Trystin followed until he reached the highway with the green "S" emblem, where he turned south, paralleling the main shuttle runway. Only a few vehicles were on the southern road, moving at high rates of speed for manually controlled vehicles.

As a small white car roared around him, barely avoiding another oncoming car, Trystin felt like wiping his forehead. Instead, he concentrated on driving and increasing his own speed.

Almost from his peripheral vision, he could tell that sections of the shuttleport runway had been replaced with new ferrocrete, but others seemed to be overdue for replacement.

Continuing south, still recalling the scent of roses, he shook his head, understanding in his guts as well as in his head something he already knew. With girls like that, no wonder there were so damned many Revenants!

59

 From the plateau where the shuttleport squatted, Trystin continued southward on the scenic road, which wound downward into a valley filled with trees—slender pines, all the same, all planted in rows. Despite the warmth, Trystin kept the window down and the cooler off. The dusty air smelled better than the recycled gas used as a facsimile of breathable air for pilots.

KKhhhchewww!

He rubbed his nose. Perhaps he wasn't as used to natural contaminants as he had once been.

KKkhhchewwww . . .

His nose began to run, and he fished out the big handkerchief, using it as necessary as the car whistled along the road seemingly cut between the pines, pines so identical that they might have been cloned.

Heber Valley Lumber—Trees for Today and Tomorrow
Foresting Center Ahead

Trystin looked from the blue-trimmed white sign to the rows of identical trees—silval monoculture, yet another practice contributing to the Great Die-off on old Earth. Hadn't the Revenants learned anything?

Abruptly, less than a kay beyond the sign, the trees stopped, and a circular building, painted green, stood a hundred meters back from the road. The parking lot held but a few vehicles, and as he sped past, Trystin noted the small sign that identified the Foresting Center.

Beyond the center, the pines continued for several more kays, before another sign appeared—Beth-El. With the sign came the houses, hundreds of houses, each set squarely in a small patch of green. Farther back from the road was the glittering spire of the stosque.

A few minutes later, Trystin was past the houses of Beth-El, and the road began to climb toward a notch in the red rocky slopes of the southern hills. After several kays more, he passed another town, with a stosque and school and a good three hundred houses that he could see. Before long, he went through yet another town, and then another. The trees tended to disguise how many small towns filled the valley.

Krendsaw's was located at a crossroads where the main north-south cargoway crossed the scenic route. Trystin turned into the parking area—nearly empty and flanked by pines of a different type with squat trunks and spreading branches. He checked the time, almost an hour before local noon, then closed the car door. He took the ferro-crete walkway patterned to look like flagstone to the steps and up onto a covered and shaded portico.

"One, Brother?" The young woman standing in the archway smiled at Trystin, her eyes only slightly below his, perfect white teeth flashing for a moment, light brown hair falling freely from a hairband positioned across the top of her head—running almost from ear to ear.

"Please, Sister."

"Would the inside garden be all right?"

"That would be fine."

"Most of the returned like it." She smiled, her eyes dropping to his left hand to see if he were already married.

Trystin nodded, trying to keep a straight face. He'd been warned about the tendency of the sisters to try to be the first wife—the one who set the household rules. But warnings didn't convey how attractive most of the sisters seemed to be, and how tall compared to most Eco-Tech women.

"If you would come this way . . ."

They went through another archway into the courtyard, where a dozen tables were set on the ceramic tiles under two overarching trees that shaded most of the space. Two tables were occupied, one by two older men, and the other by a woman who seemed to be reading while she sipped a clear beverage.

A circular fountain in the center of the courtyard sprayed a thin column of water that fell back in a thin mist which cooled the space. Trystin could feel the itching in his nose subsiding even before he took the seat at the small glass-topped table facing the fountain.

"You're just back, aren't you?" The hostess handed him the menu.

"How did you know?"

"Your nose. It's red." She gave a musical laugh. "It takes a while to get used to the tree pollen around here. The specials are at the top there." She paused. "I'm Sister Megan Barunis. I hope you enjoy your meal."

"I'm sure I will, Sister." Trystin offered as warm a smile as he dared, and less than he would have offered in a less dangerous setting, getting another smile in return before the hostess left.

The top special on the menu was pine chicken with piñon nuts and new Idaho potatoes, whatever variety of potatoes Idaho were. The other special sounded even more problematical—sautéed mushwursts over blue maize pasta.

The menu featured meat—mutton, steak, carbo, beefalo—in large portions ranging up to half a kilogram. Trystin couldn't imagine eating that much meat at one setting—or the ecological impact raising that many herd animals would have.

As he pondered, another sister appeared, dressed in a long blue-checked uniform that was not totally becoming to her fair, freckled face. Like the hostess, she wore her hair flowing free, and her left hand, almost flaunted, was free of rings.

She bent forward to pour his water, standing closer to him and the table than was absolutely necessary, and the long bright-red hair—not the mahogany-red of Perdya—cascaded against the side of his face, bringing the scent of flowers.

"I'm sorry, Brother."

"You don't sound totally sorry, Sister." Trystin grinned and folded the menu.

"Oh, but I am, Brother." She winked, then went on. "I'm Sister Ali Khoures, and I'll be your waitress today. Have you looked at the specials?"

"How is the chicken?"

"Very good. The mushwursts are good, but most returnees find the texture too suggestive of—"

"I'll take the chicken," Trystin said hurriedly.

Sister Khoures laughed. "What would you like to drink?"

"The limeade."

"That goes well with the chicken. Most people order anise tea." The waitress shook her head, and the long red hair rippled.

Trystin took a deep breath quietly, trying to push back the faint hint of summer flowers.

"I'll bring the muffins and your limeade right away."

"Thank you."

On the other side of the fountain, the older woman continued to read, and the two men in white suits ate and talked quietly.

Trystin studied the garden—really more a set of brick-walled flower beds that followed the courtyard walls and surrounded the eating area, except for the four passages into the main building. Wide windows allowed diners in the building to look over the flowers—mainly marigolds and a bright red flower Trystin didn't recognize—into the courtyard garden.

He took several slow and deep breaths. He was supposed to be thinking about his "removal" of Admiral/Archbishop Jynckla. Instead, he was getting distracted by very attractive young women who actually found him desirable, rather than glaring at him for his looks. Would they find him all that desirable if they knew who he really was? That thought sobered him.

He took a deep breath, thinking about his main problem. Just how was killing one admiral going to help the Coalition? Supposedly, people older and wiser than he had it figured, but he could tell that the Revenants weren't exactly monsters—they were human beings with human reactions, and Trystin doubted that the assassination of Marshal Warlock or any other marshal on the streets of Cambria would have much effect on the Coalition. So why would the assassination of Admiral Jynckla have much impact on the Revenants? Was the admiral a strategic genius or something? Or were the Coalition strategists getting so desperate that they'd become willing to try anything?

Those were things he didn't know, but, in the end, he'd have to act without knowing. And after acting, he'd have to escape, probably with an entire planet looking for him. The best assassination would be one that no one knew was an assassination—but the Service wanted one with impact, to deliver a message. He tried not to sigh.

"Are you all right?" asked Sister Khoures. "You looked . . . so far away."

"We can't always escape our past," Trystin answered ambiguously. That was safe enough and in character, besides being true.

"I'm sorry." She paused. "Here are your muffins and your limeade." Her hand somehow brushed Trystin's after she set the plate and glass on the table.

"Thank you." Trystin nodded, and received a smile before she turned and left.

The hostess led two other young women, both unattached sisters from the hairbands, into the courtyard. Trystin sipped the limeade and watched as the taller and sharp-nosed blonde leaned toward the hostess and whispered something. Trystin flicked up his hearing to the limit.

". . . how about the table there, next to the flowers?"

"As you wish, Sisters."

"Thank you."

The hostess, walking more stiffly than Trystin recalled, led the pair to the table for two nearest his table. "Enjoy your meal," she said politely.

"I'm certain we will," responded the thin blonde.

The sandy-haired and stockier sister smiled at Trystin.

Trystin ignored the smile and took another sip of limeade. While he knew he wasn't ugly, the attention was disconcerting, in its own way as disconcerting as the negative attention he had received in Cambria on his last home leave. Was attraction and repulsion all a matter of appearances? Or preconceptions? He hadn't changed, but the students—boys and girls—in Cambria had disliked his rev looks—and had wanted to kill poor blond Quiella, while women he scarcely knew on Orum were almost panting after him.

He broke open one of the still-steaming muffins and spread a touch of butter on it—at least he thought it was butter. After eating the entire sweet muffin, filled with dark berries, in three bites, he took another sip of the limeade. The slight headache he hadn't realized he had began to fade.

". . . handsome . . . not wearing a ring . . ."

". . . with one like that . . . take being number two . . ."

". . . eats like a returned . . . like he'll never taste another good meal . . ."

". . . make sure he got good meals . . ."

Trystin cut back his hearing to normal. He was beginning to discover that hearing too much was sometimes worse than hearing too little.

The hostess escorted in another party, settling the two women and the man with salt-and-pepper hair at the larger table next to Trystin. "Enjoy your meal, Brother and Sisters."

The man nodded curtly at the hostess, and Sister Barunis, dismissed, turned and paused at the edge of Trystin's table. "The berry muffins are usually very good."

"Very good," Trystin agreed. "Is there anything else you'd recommend? I ordered the pine chicken."

"I saw that in the kitchen. It smelled wonderful. If you like desserts, you might try the Saints' chocolate silk pie."

"We'll have to see."

"I imagine you'll find room." The hostess's tone was dry. Trystin grinned. "Probably."

"Tell me how you like it." This time her hand brushed his shoulder as she left.

"I will."

With another radiant smile, she headed back to the front entrance.

Trystin didn't need stepped-up hearing to catch the displeasure from the two women at the adjoining table. He could feel the glare.

"Here's your chicken." Sister Khoures slipped the plate in front of Trystin with a low half-bow that brought her cheek practically beside his.

"Smells good." Trystin caught the pleasant mixed scents of the spiced chicken, flower perfume, and clean woman.

"It should. I told Sister Jerrlyn to give you a good one."

"I appreciate the kindness."

Sister Khoures waited for a moment, then flashed a smile and left.

Trystin wanted to wipe his forehead. Instead, he picked up the knife, absently noting that Sister Barunis had escorted a party of four—a man with three women, presumably his wives—to another large table. Although the man was white-haired, with a heavily lined face, none of the women seemed much older than Trystin, and two were noticeably pregnant.

Trystin slowly sliced a bit of the tender chicken and ate it. The pine taste was faint, and overshadowed by rich brown sauce and complemented by the semicrunchy nut morsels. The Idaho potatoes were just round white peeled potatoes, and the sauce helped them considerably. The greenery was bitter, but he chewed it thoroughly as well.

One of the pregnant women kept studying him, as did the thin-faced blonde at the nearby table.

When he had finished the plate, somewhat surprised that there was nothing left, he sat back—but not for long.

"Would you like some dessert?"

"I've heard about the Saints' chocolate silk pie . . . what else is that good?"

"If you like really tart and sweet things"—Sister Khoures glanced toward the entrance where Sister Barunis presumably was waiting for other customers—"there's the lime crumble pie. We also have fruit tarts, ice cream, and a lemon custard."

"I'll have the chocolate silk pie."

"It is good."

As the waitress left, Trystin reconsidered the benefits of being a patriarch. Up to six wives chosen from among young women like Sister Khoures or Sister Barunis? Or the two who watched his every bite from the nearby table?

"Your pie, Brother." The slice she presented was almost a quarter of a good-sized pie.

"Thank you."

Her hair, and her hand, brushed his shoulder as she left to attend to the party of four.

Trystin finished the silky chocolate of the pie, and the golden pastry crust, in measured bites, half marveling that he had eaten it all without feeling totally gorged.

He sat back and sipped his water.

"Will there be anything more?"

"No, thank you."

She set the antique lunch check on the glass of the table.

"Thank you, Brother." Her steps away from the table were precise and professional.

He studied the bill, and the careful script that said, "Thank you, Sister Ali Khoures."

After using some of the paper bills for a gratuity—Brother Khalid had been firm about that—Trystin took the check to the hostess's station, and Sister Barunis.

"Was everything all right?"

"Excellent, Sister. Excellent. Especially the pie." Trystin handed her the credit strip, which she ran through the reader and handed back to him.

"You could call me Sister Megan, at least." Again, the warm smile followed, with a hint of something else, almost a sadness, that bothered Trystin, though he couldn't identify it, even with stepped-up hearing.

"I'm Brother Wyllum Hyriss. I appreciate your hospitality and kindness."

"What are you doing on Orum?"

"Sightseeing. I took a job as a pilot for a Hyndji trading company, and I've never been to Orum and to the Temple. Friends told me that I should see the Gorge on the way."

"Your friends were right."

"Is there anything else I should see?"

"You ought to stop at some of the overlooks. Don't just look at the Gorge from the road. You can't see the way the sun hits the crystals if you don't leave the car."

"Thank you."

"It was good to meet you, Brother Hyriss. I hope we'll see you here again." She extended a card bearing the restaurant's logo. "Just call me if you need reservations . . . or anything I can help with."

Trystin took it, avoiding a smile at the scripted "Megan Barunis, hostess," and slipping it into his jacket pocket.

"You never know," he said softly, trying not to invite or discourage her. "I'm on my way to see the Temple. After that, my plans aren't settled." He smiled again and turned, feeling her eyes on his back all the way down the steps and out into the parking area, now half full.

The car started easily, and Trystin pulled it up to the edge of the highway. He wanted to wipe his forehead, but didn't, recalling his sessions with Brother Khalid.

Whhsttt! Whhsttt! The Revenant-driven cars whipped by the restaurant's parking lot like so many high-speed torps. Trystin wasn't sure that most torps didn't have more guidance.

Another car pulled up behind him. Then another.

Finally, he pressed the accelerator to the floor.

Screeeechhh!

The combination of the heavy foot and the internal-combustion engine succeeded in getting him back on the road south, even if one of the other southbound cars whistled by him as he was still accelerating. Was guiding vehicles on Revenant planets akin to suicidal military missions? Or suicidal Intelligence missions?

The road, clearly cut by laser, began a continuous climb almost as soon as Trystin had left the restaurant. Scrub cedars and cacti dotted the pink and rocky hillside soil. While the cacti, and there were at least three different varieties, seemed to grow randomly, the older cedars seemed to be approximately the same size and placed in what seemed to be a grid pattern. The original planoforming plantings?

Taking Sister Barunis's advice to heart, he dutifully stopped at the first overlook. There were no signs, and all he could see was the valley he had just left, with trees and towns, and trees and towns.

He moistened his dry lips and tried to count the squares in the trees that seemed to be towns. There were more than thirty. How many more he didn't know, because even with enhanced vision, the angle got so flat for the northern end of the valley that the cleared spaces seemed to blur together near the base of the shuttleport's plateau.

Still . . . thirty towns of a thousand people . . . in just one valley. The valley could have had almost as many people as half of Cambria. Still . . . there was a certain . . . openness . . . a stark beauty . . . to the mountain-framed expanse of trees that was moving.

He walked back to the car.

Another five kays uphill where the road leveled out, he passed a sign—Dhellicor Gorge—but the road just continued to wind through hillsides of pink soil, cacti, and scrub cedars.

After another five kays of driving, the hillside on the left side of the road dropped away into a narrow gorge—less than half a kay across, and deep enough that Trystin could see from the road that the lower walls were in shadow.

Trystin pulled off the highway at the first overlook, marked by a sign stating, appropriately, Overlook #1. There he stopped the petroleum-powered car a good twenty meters short of the edge of the lookout. After setting the brake, he walked across a strip of grass and weeds to the blued-steel railing that separated the hard red-clay parking area from the cliff edge.

He caught his breath.

Below the railing, the ground dropped into a canyon of fluted red-crystal walls that fell a good two kays to a ribbon of silver water winding westward through the canyon. The Gorge walls widened somewhat under the overlook, as if the rock about two hundred meters below the railing were softer, leaving a shadowed patch on the south side of the Gorge, across from Trystin. The early afternoon sun played on the crystals jutting from the rock beneath the overlook, and rainbows and shafts of red light speared into the thin canyon shadows on the other side, as well as down to the narrow river. The facets of light did not blind, but almost interwove into a pattern that changed minute to minute, but so gradually as to defy a description of the changes.

For a long time, Trystin watched the lights playing on the rocks, and the shifts in the reflected silver of the river far below.

The rocks seemed sharper even than those below the Cliffs of the Palien Sea, and starker, without the greenery that enfolded the cliff tops on Perdya. On Orum, the pink-red soil appeared more barren, despite the scattered scrub cedars.

Finally, he turned and started toward his car. Beauty or not, he had a mission he continued to dread. As he walked from the overlook, another car, white, turned into the lookout, but instead of parking well short of the railing, stopped and parked no more than a half-meter from the blued steel.

A man and three women got out. All three women wore skirts to mid-knee and high-necked blouses with sleeves below their elbows. All three were blondes of varying shades, and each had her uncovered hair braided in some intricate fashion, although none of the hairstyles were exactly alike. The tallest woman was pregnant.

The driver was a trim but white-haired man with a slight tan, also wearing a long-sleeved, if light, collared shirt. "See, girls! Best view on Orum! Look at the way those crystals sparkle when the light hits 'em."

Trystin nodded politely as he stepped toward his car.

". . . bet he's recently returned . . . eyes look like deep space . . ."

"He'll be looking for some of the sisters." The man laughed. "Unless they find him first."

". . . poor girls . . ."

"Poor fellow. Now . . . look at the light there! Ever see anything like that?"

Trystin stopped at five other overlooks. Long before his last stop, he understood and felt the appeal of the Gorge. Although each overlook framed a scene similar to the first, showing light, stone walls, and a river far below, each was subtly different, with different shades of the crystalline light that varied from moment to moment, never quite the same. Like the Cliffs of home, the Gorge was unique. Also like the Cliffs, the beauty of the Gorge seemed relatively unappreciated. Still . . . some, like Sister Megan Barunis, appreciated that beauty.

With the stops, it took him nearly three hours before he passed the blue-trimmed and -lettered white sign that marked the end of the Gorge.

As he drove down the laser-melted and textured road, winding along the hillside, his eyes kept straying out to the valley, New Harmony Valley according to the map within his brain. The wide checkerboards of green and brown fields, occasionally interspersed with stands of trees, stretched to the distant line of mountains to the south, nearly as far as Trystin could see, even with boosted vision.

A heavy truck growled up the road on the other side, a thin line of smoke streaming from the exhausts above the wide red cab. The trucker smiled and waved at Trystin.

Trystin returned the friendly gesture, wondering at the possible hypocrisy of an assassin being friendly. Then, soldiers were allowed to kill and be friendly. Maybe arbitrarily deciding that some places should be free from war and that other places were slaughtering grounds was just as hypocritical. Would the people in Cambria be so eager to kill if the war raged across Perdya itself? He shivered. Or would they be even more thirsty for the blood of the Revenants? How could what he did matter? Could he make it matter? Should he try? Could he not try?

Soon, the road flattened as he drove through the middle of the valley, passing irrigated fields on each side of the road, driving and thinking about Wystuh and Admiral Jynckla.

He sniffed. The acrid odor of animal manure inundated the car, getting stronger with each meter traveled. The fields gave way to fences, and within the fenced areas were hundreds, thousands of animals—brown-coated, shaggy, four-legged animals—beefaloes.

Ahead, in the distance, were smokestacks, tall gray stacks rising into the pale sky. While only a thin grayish haze came from the stacks, the distortion told Trystin that the almost colorless air emissions were hot indeed to be visible kays away.

The stock- or feedyards stretched more than four kays. Then, abruptly, the fences were followed by a high wall beside the road, painted or coated with a white so bright that it sparkled in the sun.

Kashmir Meroni Township read the sun-faded sign. Through the gaps in the wall, Trystin glimpsed the town itself. The houses were neat, if smaller than those he had seen earlier, and the yards displayed trimmed lawns and gardens. But the windows seemed smaller, and the walls thicker, and certainly the location, between the vast stock-yards to the east and the industrial facilities ahead, would not have been where Trystin would have chosen to live.

A woman and two children walked along the other side of the road, facing toward Trystin. As he passed the three, he realized that their skins were dark, far darker than even the darkest of the Coalition populations.

One hand fingered his chin, as he thought about the small-windowed small houses between the stockyards and what seemed like kay upon kay of industrial facilities fill-ing the west end of New Harmony Valley. He also had not seen the spire of a stosque.

He sniffed the air again, as the odor of manure was sup-plemented by an oily smell, like solvents. In the rearview mirror, the three figures dwindled as he drove toward his own private day of judgment, trying to sort out warm and friendly women, dying cruisers with their metal guts and crews vaporized across the cold of space, cold-smiling commanders, and iron-gray Farhkans.

He kept driving.

60

Trystin's stomach grumbled. While it had only been a little over four hours since he'd eaten at Krend-saw's, his meals before that had been uneven, and mostly dried or otherwise preserved.

The sign at the edge of the town read Dalowan, a place small enough that it was a red dot and a name on the map he'd been given by Sister Arkady Lewiss. She'd certainly been careful to let him know her full name, as had Sister Megan Barunis and Sister Ali Khoures. He could almost feel the card in his jacket pocket, and he smiled. For some reason, he couldn't see such forwardness in Ulteena, even when she had been younger, especially after seeing what it had cost her to admit she cared about him. Were younger women just more forward in the Revenant systems? Or had he been sheltered somehow?

He slowed the car, as he passed a park, then a school building. Ahead he could see the single glittering spire of the local stosque.

His stomach growled again.

Ahead were several buildings. He stopped at the sign proclaiming R.P.'s, a small building with faded tan plaster walls and three enormous cacti planted in front of the building. The entrance was framed by two man-high red boulders. Only three vehicles sat in the parking area. On the far side of the parking area was a confectionery store—Dalowan Confectioneries.

Trystin grinned. Maybe he'd stop there after he ate—for some lime balls.

A round-faced older woman with hair braided and piled on top of her head greeted Trystin as he stepped into R.P.'s. "A late lunch, Brother?"

"Or an early dinner," Trystin laughed. "I'm not quite sure which."

"This way." She led Trystin to a corner booth, made of dark-varnished and smoothed planks, handing him the menu after he eased himself into the left side where he could see all ten tables that comprised the dining area. "The only special left is the smothered meat loaf, but everything else on the menu is available."

"What would you recommend . . . besides the meat loaf?"

That got a laugh. "None of you returned like meat loaf. I just can't imagine why. Well . . . the chicken tortelada is good, and so is the fried beefalo steak."

Meat and more meat—Trystin still couldn't imagine ingesting that much protein at a sitting. "I'll try the tortelada, with limeade."

"You'll like it. I'll get your limeade." She returned with

the limeade almost immediately, and then went through a swinging door in the back of the dining area.

As Trystin sipped the limeade, his eyes surveyed the room. Two older women with braided hair and wearing the prevalent checked dresses sat at a table under the high window by the front wall. They talked quietly, occasionally sipping from mugs before them—chocolate, probably. In the front corner booth was a middle-aged couple—just a man and a woman.

Trystin took another sip from the limeade. According to the map and his implant calculations, he was only about two hours from the outskirts of Wystuh. Once there, he'd have to round up the electronics supplies he needed. Weapons were not exactly something you carried through multiple security checks. He pursed his lips. He still didn't know how killing one admiral was going to help the Coalition, but he also knew that not killing Jynckla would eventually create a large problem for one Trystin Desoll, perhaps a fatal one.

Was there any other way? So far, he didn't see one, not that would leave him free and alive. Was there any way to do something that would stop the war? He didn't know that, either. It had been simpler to be a pilot, and much simpler to be a perimeter officer, but he'd wanted to do more than react. Now he had at least some choice, and he hadn't the faintest idea of how to exercise it!

He took another sip of limeade and waited for the tortelada. His stomach growled again.

The rationale for assassination was clear enough—to plant the idea that the Coalition could strike anywhere. But Trystin wasn't convinced it would work. He shook his head. Here he was on the home planet of the enemy on a mission he wasn't convinced would work, and without any better ideas. And he knew that too much thinking was a recipe for disaster—which made it all the worse.

He finished the limeade with a gulp.

"Would you like another?" asked the waitress as she saw the empty glass.

"Please, Sister."

As she returned with another limeade, she asked, "Are you headed to Wystuh?"

"Yes. I was sightseeing—the Gorge."

"It's something, the Gorge is. Makes you wonder sometimes. Takes your worries away, too."

Trystin nodded. "It is beautiful, never even the same from moment to moment."

"It didn't seem to take yours away, Brother."

"Probably not, but it is spectacular."

"Remember . . . leave your worries to the Lord. He's the only one big enough to hold them."

"Unless He's the one who created them, Sister." Trystin forced a laugh to cover his excessive openness. "Discovering His will and then doing it isn't always easy."

"He didn't put us here for it to be easy." She patted his shoulder in a motherly way. "You're young, and you're returned. Be thankful for that. You'll find a way."

"Yes, Mother . . ." Trystin grinned.

She returned the grin with a smile, then turned to the door as a single man in a pale blue uniform entered.

"Jonathan! Would you like some punch?"

"Anything cold, Sister Evlyn. Anything cold." The burly peace officer, the first Trystin had seen, sank into the chair next to the credit-strip console.

". . . it's not the same . . ."

The whispered words drifted to Trystin, who, more curious than anything, turned up his hearing to listen to the couple—odd because most families seemed to consist of an older husband and several younger wives.

"What do you want from me?" the older man asked, in an exasperated fashion. "Do you expect the Lord to send another Prophet just for you, Llamora? Do you expect the Prophet to proclaim that the Ecofreaks will stop their abominations and that Joshua will be spirited home?"

"No . . . I just want him to live in peace. Why can't they let us live in peace? Why must we lose so many?"

"Many return." The older man paused. "That fellow across the room's a returnee."

Trystin did not look in their direction. The words about

"another Prophet" skittered through his thoughts. What good would another prophet do? The last one had been bad enough from the Eco-Tech perspective.

"He's not Joshua."

"He's someone's Joshua."

"They're lucky. You still haven't told me why they won't let us live in peace."

"Because they won't. It's more likely Toren himself will return than the Ecofreaks will change. Now, stop sniveling. You don't think I don't know. I was there, dear. Don't forget that. I saw those dark men who moved like machines, always smiling, never—"

"I know, Ed. I know . . . but it's hard. It's hard."

Trystin shook his head. It was hard on both sides, but the damned Revenants had a choice. He wasn't sure the Eco-Techs did. He frowned, wondering if he were just rationalizing.

"Here you are."

The platter held not only the massive chicken tortelada, but a heaping portion of rice and a dark congealed mass covered with cheese, presumably the refried beans.

"I think there might be enough here," Trystin observed.

"Don't want it said that anyone'd go hungry here."

"There's no danger of that."

The waitress/hostess walked over and talked to the peace officer, mainly about the weather, as Trystin slowly worked his way through the enormous meal. The older couple left about the time he gave up on the beans and pushed the plate slightly back.

"Would you like some dessert?"

Trystin looked at the plate and then at Sister Evlyn. "I'm not going away hungry."

"That'll be ten and a quarter, and I'll take you up there at the counter anytime." She went back to talk to the officer, who gulped the last swallow of something from a glass and stood.

"Thanks, Sister Evlyn. Tell Jock I stopped by."

Trystin waited until the door closed. He left several paper bills on the table and stepped up to the console, proffering the strip, which she ran through the reader.

"Glad you liked the tortelada. I couldn't eat half what you ate." She scanned the reader. "Hyriss. Any relation to Sammel Hyriss here?"

"Not that I know, but probably some distant relation. I'm from Nephi originally."

"I think his folks came from out that way." She smiled. "Remember what I told you, Brother Hyriss."

"And I will find a way?"

"That's right."

He took the strip. "Peace be with you, Sister."

"And with you."

Once outside, Trystin walked across the paved parking area to the confectionery store.

Two young women—girls—stood behind the counter. He glanced at the display case and then at the redhead.

"I'd like a half-pound of the lime balls."

The redhead flushed, and the other girl giggled. Then the smaller blonde held a sack while the redhead used the scoop to dish out the lime balls, which hit the metal pan of the scale—*clank . . . clank . . . clank. . . .*

"One and a quarter, ser."

The "ser" was a giveaway that neither girl was of marriageable age.

"Here you go." He handed across the change and took the bag.

As he headed for the open door, he could hear the whispers.

". . . should have called him 'Brother,' Merryn. It's only a month, and he wouldn't know . . . he's handsome . . . no rings . . ."

". . . wouldn't do any good . . ."

Trystin stepped out of the confectionery store, shaking his head, and paused under the overhanging porch for a moment. He took one of the lime balls and popped it in his mouth quickly before the lime melted on his fingers. The last thing he wanted was candy on the white coat—although the white fabric had been treated, as had all whites worn by the Revenants, to resist and repel stains.

To his right was the road he had followed from the Dhellicor Gorge, stretching up the gentle slope that led to the high plateau. Less than a kay south, the houses of Dalowan stopped, and modified cedar trees covered the pinkish soil. The houses were all finished, on the outside, in stucco or cementlike plaster, and all were colored in pale pastels.

With the faint screech, Trystin turned. One of the petroleum-burning cars skidded around the corner, and the driver, half engaged in talking to the young woman beside him, did not seem to be watching the street. A small blond girl and her older brother were crossing the wide street to the confectionery store. Several women and a man stood beside a long six-doored car talking. One pregnant sister watched the children.

Trystin dropped the candy, and vaulted the low railing, kicking himself into his high metabolic rates and stepped-up reflexes. As he ran, he calculated the angles.

"Georgia! Run!" The boy tried to drag his sister, but she resisted, instinctively.

"No!" screamed the mother.

Sccccreeeee . . . The driver tried to stop, and the car seemed to move broadside as Trystin swooped and grabbed both children. He felt a glancing blow on his hip, and saw the horrified expression on the young driver's face. The youth couldn't have reached the local equivalent of his eighteenth birthday.

Trystin, breathing deeply, dropped his metabolism to normal, even as he set down the children. Why had he done it? The last thing he needed was to do something to attract attention.

"Georgia! Dahn! Are you all right?" The sandy-haired and pregnant sister had her arms around the two almost before Trystin had straightened up.

"Brother, I don't know how to thank you. If it hadn't been for you . . ." stammered the man, blond with streaks of white in his hair, a slight paunch, and a tanned face.

The driver had stopped the car—or the raised stone

curb behind the long car had—and he stood, whiter than Trystin's coat, beside it.

"Children, you must watch and look both ways. Please watch."

"... wanted to get there first ... Dahn always does ..." protested the girl.

Dahn just stared at the pavement.

"... don't know how you did it ..." the father stammered.

"I was just in the right place," Trystin said, his thoughts trying to find a way out of the mess.

"... but how ... how ..."

"Just thank the brother and the Lord," murmured the mother.

"... how ..." The father appeared dazed.

Trystin touched his shoulder. "Be thankful. I am." Then he walked over to the youthful driver, who was still shaking. "You're fortunate you didn't kill them."

The driver kept shaking.

"Next time, the Lord might not be watching." Trystin patted him on the shoulder, deciding to rely on theology. "That's your miracle."

"He could have killed them!" The father stepped up to Trystin.

"He didn't, and I suspect he's gotten the Lord's message." Trystin gestured at the driver, who slumped against the fender of the car, shivering.

"You some kind of nut, Brother?"

Probably, thought Trystin to himself, but he turned and looked at the father. "Do I look like a nut? Didn't I save your children? I am what I am." He smiled pleasantly. "Now ... I have a journey to make."

"Where are you going?"

"To Wystuh."

"To the Temple?"

Trystin saw the burly officer walking toward them. He wanted to leave, but it was looking too late already. He swallowed a sigh. Would more blatant theology work? He could try.

"Are you going to the Temple?"

"Yes," he lied, to stop the interrogation, since he had no desire to be incinerated in the middle of Wystuh.

"And after that?" ·

"Where the Lord wills." He offered a smile, and bent down slightly to face the little girl, Georgia. "Please be careful, Georgia."

"I didn't have to be careful. You saved me. The Lord sent you to save me."

"I was here, but I won't always be here. We have to save ourselves. He only points the way." Trystin straightened, hoping he hadn't bent theology too much, hoping that his recollections from his study of the *Book of Toren* were accurate enough.

"Thank you," said the mother.

"Just keep her safe," Trystin suggested. "I need to go."

Behind him, the officer in blue said to the driver, "You stay right here, Billy Bardman. After something like this, you just might be getting your mission call early."

If possible, the youth turned even whiter, and shook even more. Trystin suppressed a frown as the officer in blue approached him.

"I'm Brother Smithson. Jon Smithson." The tall man in the official blue jacket extended his hand.

Trystin took the beefy hand and shook it. "Brother Hyriss. Wyllum Hyriss."

"That was something you did. Never seen a man move so fast."

Trystin forced himself to relax, as if what he had done were commonplace. "Guess you move quickly when you have to."

"You headed to Wystuh?"

Trystin nodded.

"Well . . . thanks again, Brother. The Lord be with you."

"And with you."

Trystin walked back to the car, stopping by the porch of the confectionery store to reclaim the bag of lime balls. What had the officer meant by the reference to the early mission call? Had that been what Peter Warlock had meant

by internal social controls against violence? The reference
had certainly stunned the young man.

As he headed to his car, he tried not to frown. He'd already said too many of the wrong things, little things, and
now he'd aroused a local peace officer's curiosity. He'd
made himself memorable, far too memorable, in saving the
children, and the Revenants doted on small children—
and he hadn't even reached Wystuh.

Brother Khalid would have had far too much to say
about his actions, far too much.

He refrained from wiping his forehead as he drove toward Wystuh. He had to wonder if Headquarters had any
idea how bad an idea it had been to send him. It was one
thing to do a job, a straightforward mission like holding
a perimeter station or defending a system, and to do it well
when you didn't have that much time to think or get to see
those you killed up close. It was another to assign a murder and give him the time to think about it. Or to see children and not have the cold-blooded sense to let them die
in order to avoid unwanted attention.

He shook his head. Jynckla he could still handle. Admirals weren't above the carnage they created. But he
couldn't let children die . . . and that might be his failure.
He took a deep breath.

61

 Trystin noted the air pollution long before he
reached the outskirts of Wystuh—a brownish haze
hanging over the big saucerlike depression that held
Wystuh and the rings of outlying communities. Although
Promised Valley's geography was the principal reason for
Wystuh's status as the first settlement, the depression and
uniform surrounding hills that had speeded the early

planoforming were also immensely helpful in creating inversions and concentrating industrial by-products, especially since the Revenants clearly did not plan out the total ecological impacts of their industrialization.

The scenic highway widened into a divided motorway separated from what appeared to be industrial parks by high white walls. Trystin damped the intensity of his vision again—Wystuh *glittered*. White light seemed to pour at him from every direction as he entered the city proper.

Seventh Octagon read the sign for the first turnoff.

Trystin kept driving, watching the other vehicles carefully. The petrol cars were far more fragile than spacecraft, and the relative motions in close proximity seemed potentially more deadly. He was aiming for the road hotels off the Second Octagon—the ones that catered to Temple visitors.

Several of the road hotels on the Second Octagon were filled, and Trystin finally pulled into a smaller one—Promise Inn—on the north side of Wystuh. As he got out of the car, he glanced southward. Over the low trees loomed the eight spires of the Temple. He paused.

"Sort of gets you, doesn't it, Brother?"

Trystin turned. A white-haired man in a coat of pale blue, so pale that it was almost white, stood beside a four-doored blue car three meters away.

"You don't realize . . ."

"No, you don't. First time in Wystuh, Brother?"

"Yes, Brother," Trystin answered.

"It's always good to see one of the returned coming to give thanks to the Lord and the Prophet. Where're you from originally?"

"Nephi."

"Pilot, aren't you?" The white-haired man stepped toward Trystin.

"How'd you know, Brother?" Trystin asked.

"It's not hard. Most of the returned are pilots these days, and all of you have an air. It's hard to explain," laughed the older man, "but I know it when I see it." He held out a hand. "Brother Carson Orr."

"Brother Wyllum Hyriss."

"I'd guess half of Nephi must be named Hyriss."

Trystin shrugged. "What can I say?"

"It's not your fault. You didn't pick the name."

"No. That's certainly true."

The other man looked at his wrist. "I'm going to be late, but I'll probably be seeing you around." He slipped into the car.

After Brother Orr drove off, Trystin walked across to the office. Inside the glass-walled space, less than five meters square, a gray-haired woman stood behind the counter.

"I was wondering if you might have a room for the next week or so?"

"For how many, Brother?" The badge just below the shoulder of the subdued dark-checked dress read Sister Myra. The braided hair and gold band on her left hand confirmed her status.

"Just for me."

"Giving thanks?"

"And coming to see Wystuh."

"For one or a couple, that's not a problem. A family with two or three wives and children—those suites are all taken. Let's see. You want to be up or down?"

"Whichever is quieter," Trystin answered honestly.

"Probably the one near the middle on the first floor. It will run you thirty a night or one ninety a week."

Trystin paused, knowing that would probably be expected, even for a returned missionary.

"We're less than most, Brother . . ."

"Hyriss," he supplied. Then he shrugged and smiled. "It'll be a long time before I'm here again."

"You never know. The Lord works in mysterious ways."

"His will be done," Trystin responded with the accepted response and pulled out the credit strip. His hand brushed the hip that was beginning to ache from what he knew would be a bad bruise.

"Credit strip—you have a job already?"

"I'm a cargo pilot."

As she ran the strip through the reader, Sister Myra

shook her head. "You couldn't get me up there." She handed him back the strip and a plastic oblong. "Here's your door-reader. Your room is 117. The juice in the cooler comes with the room. So drink what you want. The restaurant opens at six in the morning and closes at eleven."

"Thank you."

Trystin smiled and walked back to the car, listening with extended hearing as the sister turned to the other woman who had entered.

". . . he looks sad behind the smile . . ."

". . . wouldn't you be with what he's seen?"

". . . almost too handsome . . ."

Too handsome? That was hard to believe, especially on a planet of generally especially handsome people. And thinking about what he'd seen? Most Eco-Techs wouldn't have said the Revenants thought about the privations of their military missions.

He pulled the car up in front of 117 and brought in his bag, setting it on the luggage rack, then opening it and hanging out the other suits. He took off his own coat and hung it up, before pulling out the halfway well-thumbed *Book of Toren* he'd received so many light-years away. He set the book on the table and studied the room.

The videolink console—manual style—appeared to have only a handful of channel selections. He flicked it on, and the holos came up around him slowly, with a slight fuzziness. The surround-sound was also somewhat distorted, possibly by the age of the console.

"The *Wystuh Evening News* is brought to you by Bayliss . . ." The image of a green package of something was thrust almost to Trystin's nose.

Trystin flicked to another channel.

"*Know Your Scripture*—the Quiz Show of the Book!"

He flicked again and got what appeared to be some sort of drama, where tall figures in combat suits with lightning bolts assaulted and overwhelmed short figures in black suits. He seemed to be carried along with the missionary troops. With a sigh, he tried another selection.

The volume of the music stunned him.

". . . listen to the Prophet! Listen to the Prophet, yeah, yeah, yeah . . ."

He flicked again.

". . . if you want to order this genuine replica of Nephi's urn—"

Trystin flicked off the videolink. The words were different, and the selections fewer and more religious, but the quality similar to what was broadcast in Cambria—unfortunately.

He picked up the *Book of Toren* and sat down, flipping through the pages, then stopping, recognizing the passage, absently surprised that he had.

". . . for no man who commits his soul unto the Lord can fail in His sight, for the Lord is generous . . ."

Trystin frowned. Generous? He flipped to another section.

". . . do not say, better my cousin than my neighbor, for all men and women are cousins in the sight of the Lord, and all are neighbors . . ."

Trystin wiped his forehead. As his continued studies of Revenant materials kept demonstrating, consistency definitely wasn't a part of the theology. How could the Revenants believe what he had just read, and then make war on the Coalition? Did religion allow a greater inconsistency between internal and external actions? Could he somehow exploit that?

He shifted his weight in the old chair, and his hip throbbed.

Could he use the business about neighbors? How? What did it have to do with an assassination? Somehow, somehow, he had to come up with a way to carry out his mission that made it more than a mere assassination. An assassination wouldn't be enough. That he knew already.

Once more, he blotted his forehead, before flipping the pages of the *Book of Toren,* seeking another scriptural passage. He needed some sort of inspiration—and a way to escape in one piece.

62

As he sat with the once-hot cider in front of him, looking at an empty plate that had held a stack of pancakes he'd never thought he'd finish, Trystin glanced through the window to the corner of the Promise Inn and then to the spires of the Temple beyond the trees.

The Temple—always the Temple—that was already clear enough.

What was it that the revvie officer had said so long ago—back on Mara? Something about while he believed, nothing could change his mind. Trystin nodded to himself. That meant that the belief structure of the Revenants had to be either changed or destroyed. And how could he do that?

He took a sip of the lukewarm cider, and looked back at the Temple spires. He didn't know how to change a belief structure—but he'd better figure out how, and fast. Otherwise, he was stuck carrying out a meaningless mission with a slim chance of survival.

With a shrug, he stood up. In the meantime, he'd better continue on with the preplanned mission, until he could come up with something better. He just hoped he could.

After paying for the breakfast, Trystin settled into the car and began his shopping trip, although he wasn't shopping for quite the same reason other returned missionaries might be. They missed the luxuries and were setting up households or giving presents. Trystin was looking for components convertible to weapons. The problem with passing Revenant screening was that he would have to build what he needed from other components, preferably commonly available items. While that wasn't a technical problem, it took time. Then again, he could use that time to try to come up with more than an assassination.

As he drove down West Kingdom Avenue, Trystin was again glad the implant gave him the ability to darken his vision, because Wystuh glittered—glittered with a white-ness that penetrated everything. Every building was white or off-white, and with the yellow-white sunlight of Jerush burning through the pale blue sky, even the shadows cast by the sun were filled with reflected light. At the same time, he could not help but notice something else. While everything was clean, spotless, there were no new buildings under construction. He did not see one—historic preservation or something?

Entertainment Microtronics Center—that was what the sign read, but Trystin drove by the store twice before he located the parking area, and pulled the rented car into it.

"Could I help you, Brother?" asked the white-haired manager almost as Trystin stepped into the store. All the older men in supervisory positions everywhere seemed to be white-haired. Was being white-haired something that went with being a patriarch?

"Yes, except"—he forced a rueful grin—"I am a little out of touch."

The older man took in Trystin, looked him squarely in the eyes for an instant, and then offered a smile in return. "I can see that. Well . . . let me show you what we have here." He gestured toward a compact black unit with a blank and smooth front, flanked by two speakers.

"The basic audio system is a laser-read, digitally produced sound. The central system is pretty standard . . . how good the sound is depends more on the output speakers than on the processing unit . . ."

Trystin knew what he wanted, but nodded as the salesman took him through the units.

He finally settled on the basic unit, plus a small repair kit. After the salesman accepted the credit strip and entered the transaction, he helped Trystin load the equipment in the rear seat of the rented car.

"Thank you, Brother Hyriss, for choosing us. Thank you."

"Thank you, Brother Gerstin. I put myself in the hands of the Lord, and this is where I found myself. Peace be with you."

"And with you."

Trystin couldn't help but wonder at the other's effusiveness, as if the salesman hadn't seen a real customer in months.

As he drove, his thoughts kept returning to the Revenant officer on Mara and his words—"while I believe." What could stop that kind of faith? Could anything? Trystin finally smiled a crooked smile. Why fight that blind faith? Why not use it? He still didn't know how, but he nodded to himself.

His next stop was a small industrial-supply house on the outskirts of Wystuh. Despite Wystuh's reputation for nonexistent crime, he wondered how safe the area was as he parked the car in front of the low building whose white walls were almost gray. While not streaked with grime, the walls had been washed enough without recoating to convey the impression of dirt.

"Help you, Brother?" The greeting was rough, almost dismissive, and the heavyset man looked almost contemptuously at Trystin's immaculate white suit.

"I'm looking for a replacement sonic unit on a Rubeck cleaner, model 786."

"Hmmm . . . 786 Rubeck . . . sure that's what you want? Lotta wasted power there."

"If you need to fix a 786 . . ." Trystin said.

"Yeah, you need a 786. Let me see."

Trystin walked over to the hard-copy catalog lying on the counter, and began to thumb through it, noting parts and components.

Thump!

"Here. Lucky. Had two even."

"You also have this Remmer wave guide?" Trystin pointed.

"Nah . . . piece of junk. Anything that'll fit can also take a Murrite."

"Could I take a look at the Murrite?"

"Sure. Carry a lot of those. Good for cleaners, just about anything. They say even the missionary forces use them— not like we do, though. Wouldn't know. Spent my time on Josephat."

Trystin whistled. Josephat was a mining asteroid. The man had to be tough.

"Only one who returned. Something, anyway. Just a second."

Thump! The Murrite looked better than the Remmer.

"Looks a lot sturdier."

"Easier to adjust, too."

"How much?"

"Three hundred for the sonic unit and seventy-three for the guide."

"The last thing I need is the Wembley powerpack."

"You need that much power?"

"It's a long story . . ."

"Cost you more than the rest."

"That's fine."

The burly man left and returned with a flat box that he set next to the others.

"Credit strip?" Trystin asked.

"Sure. We take anything that converts to dollars. Lot of business lately. Folks doing more repairs. Don't see how some of the places selling new stuff stay in business."

Trystin handed over the strip.

"What's a God-fearing returnee like you doing here?"

Trystin laughed, thinking about faith. "I don't need to fear the Lord, just men. I'm like everyone else, doing what has to be done."

"Good point, Brother. Didn't need to fear the Lord on Josephat either, just the idiots who thought they knew His will." He handed back the credit strip.

"Yes." Trystin nodded, searching for a proper reply. "The Lord will make His will known in His own way." He picked up the strip and pocketed it and then stacked the smaller box on the larger. "Peace be with you."

"You, too," grunted the big man, scratching his head.

After loading the gear in the car, Trystin decided to return to the Promise Inn before completing his rounds. He was getting a feel for what he wanted to do—somehow separating the Lord from those who thought they knew His will was a first step.

"Rather presumptuous, aren't you?" he murmured to himself, not answering the question as he eased the car into a space within a few meters of his door at the Promise Inn.

Trystin carried the first box of console components into his room and returned for the smaller boxes, and the tool kit.

"Brother Hyriss? Do you need any help?" The older gray-haired sister had walked out to the car from the office.

"No, thank you, Sister . . . I'm sorry, I don't remember your name."

"I'm Sister Myra."

Trystin nodded. Married women used their first names. "No, I just had two loads."

"That'd be a lot to pay to send back to Nephi."

He laughed. "No, this is for here."

"Be visiting friends?"

"Old and new. But aren't all of us children and friends under the Lord and the Prophet?" The phrasing suggested another small step in implying that the current Revenant leadership wasn't exactly infallible.

"Children and friends . . . that'd be an odd way of putting it."

Trystin smiled instead of answering directly. "He is our Father. And all who share His bounty should be friends. So . . ." He spread his hands to continue the implication. So far, Trystin knew he was on sound theological ground, if feeling hypocritical, considering the uses he had for the equipment.

"Perhaps you should take up a calling in communicating for the Lord, Brother Hyriss. You have the gift." Sister Myra bobbed her gray head sagely.

"I'm afraid that's far above me. When you have seen the endless stars in His mansions, then you realize how mighty is all creation—" Trystin broke off and smiled sheepishly.

Trying to straddle the line of the devout and the returned and not sounding overblown was hard, even with the briefings. He sounded so pompous, so full of bullshit. "I guess I get carried away."

"Have you seen the . . . other peoples?"

"The Ecofreaks?" Trystin had been told to expect the question. "Yes. At least, I have seen their ships and their bodies."

Sister Myra glanced over her shoulder. "Are they small and dark, with deep eyes and foul words?"

Trystin pulled at his chin. "Some are. Some are tall and fair."

"They say some are golems, more machine than person."

"That I would not know. They looked like people, and they died like people." Trystin paused, knowing he was treading on delicate ground. "Some fought bravely, and some did not." He shrugged and turned to lift the second box.

Sister Myra followed him. "You look like Colin, a little, except he is younger, and his Farewell was last year."

"I will pray for the success of his mission and his return." Trystin set the box just inside the door to the room. Sister Myra remained outside, apparently cool in the heat of the blinding sun.

Trystin wiped his forehead.

"You're like many from Nephi. It's cooler there."

Trystin nodded.

"He was my only boy."

What could he say? That it was damned unlikely young Colin would return? Trystin shifted his weight from one boot to the other. Finally, he said softly, "I wish I could see the future and tell you what might be, but, as we know, that remains to the Lord. We just have to persevere in doing His will."

"He was tall, like you, and his smile was a lot like yours."

"There isn't anyone like your son, Sister Myra, and I share your prayer that the Lord will keep and preserve him." Except even the old Christian god had only raised one son from the dead.

"Do you think it will end?"

"All things end."

"Soon, I meant." Sister Myra paused and added, "The Prophet said that one day he would return, and we would all dwell in peace."

Everything he said was getting him in deeper water. He pursed his lips before answering. "I'm no tactician, and, as you can see, I am what I am. I've seen what I've seen, and I have seen people who should live, somehow, as brothers and sisters, killing each other." Trystin paused, deciding he couldn't quite be so blunt. "The fighting should end. The Lord has said to bring His word to those who do not believe, and, as a simple man, I cannot see how someone who is dead can hear the word of the Lord. Even the Prophet wrote 'do not say, better my cousin than my neighbor, for all men and women are neighbors in the eyes of the Lord.' "

"Will they stop if we stop? You say that it should end, but will it? In time for Colin and others to return?" asked Sister Myra.

"I don't know. That is something that the Lord will make known." Trystin still hadn't figured out how to make such a will of the Lord known, or how far he could go in planting the germs of his ideas without being denounced as a heretic. As he spoke he wondered why he insisted on opening his mouth, on going beyond the letter of his mission when he hadn't even accomplished his assignment yet—or figured out how he was going to change it to do what he wanted. But so long as people like Sister Myra felt the way they did, completing his original mission would do nothing. Even a hundred missions like his would do nothing. So he added a few more damning words, hoping he could build on them. "All I can do is what I can, and what the Lord asks."

"That is a great deal, Brother Hyriss." Sister Myra nodded. "I wish you well." Her heavy shoes clicked on the concrete as she walked back to the office.

Trystin stepped into the room and closed the door. He wiped his forehead. He had more than a little work to do,

both in constructing the laser and in trying to figure out
how to complete his own plans for using the blind faith of
the Revenants, damned fool that he was getting to be. But,
damn it, the Revenants were people, too. Ulteena would
have understood. So would his parents. He shrugged. Then
there were people like the Park policeman at the Cliffs and
the fanatical revvie officer who would have fought forever—the kind of people who refused to look beyond their
narrow prejudices. And there were all too many of those
on both sides.

He looked at the *Book of Toren* on the table, hoping he
could find answers between the lines of the scriptures. He
wasn't going to find answers in the words themselves.

He smiled. Or was he? Another prophet . . . a son and
a temple raised in three days . . . and who would kill someone who was already dead? If he could put those together
correctly with the Service-required assassination . . . then
maybe he could shake the Revenants' faith.

He lifted the *Book of Toren* and began to flip through
the pages. The laser could wait a few minutes.

63

 Trystin's eyes drifted from the thin sheaf of papers
on the side table to the three sections of equipment
on the bed—essentially a handgunlike laser pro-
jector, a cable, and a flat powerpak that could be worn
under his clothes. He could have assembled the components into a relatively standard laser far more quickly, but
his tentative plan required a laser with a wider focus, something that would create what amounted to a pillar of flame
rather than a large surgical hole through a body. After all,
hadn't every deity in existence used a pillar of fire at some
point or another?

After three days of driving around Wystuh and studying the general layout of the city—in between building the device on the bed and assembling the scriptural background represented by the slim stack of papers on the table, he still had to complete his planning. He was operating backward, figuring the theological support and the necessary weapons configuration before establishing whether he could even pull his own plan off, if he could even call it a plan.

Making Jynckla a victim of the Lord—or a sacrifice— laughable, except it was better than a meaningless assassination linked to the Coalition, better than the meaningless death of another soldier. Somehow . . . in some way, it had to be tied more closely to the faith of the Revenants, but he wasn't making that much headway.

After a last look at the equipment, he split the pieces apart, putting the handgun section in the printed paper catalog he'd picked up and hollowed out, the cable in one pocket of the clothing bag, and the powerpak in the bottom of the main section. The catalog itself went under the *Book of Toren* on the side table.

Then he picked up the single remaining large box, into which he had packed all the leftovers, and carted it out to the car, where he placed it in the rear seat.

With a deep breath, he got in and started the car, pulling it out of the lot and heading in toward the Temple. The Temple was the center of the faith, and maybe seeing it up close would help his scattered thoughts. Maybe that was why he'd avoided it, because he was afraid seeing it would show him how stupid his half-formed plan was.

Wystuh was a city based on an octagonal grid—that had been the vision of the cities of the Promised Lands since the first prophets of the Lord had settled the Jerush system.

Trystin parked the car just inside the First Octagon and walked up East Temple Avenue. Across the avenue was a long building constructed of large white stones. The dark-framed marquee bore the words "Tonight! Ballem Michel—the Seer of Music." Wondering what a seer of music might be, Trystin walked slowly toward the Temple Square, the center of Wystuh.

The faint breeze that whispered around him was not enough to cool him, and he took out the handkerchief and blotted his forehead quickly as he walked, hoping no one saw. Beside him were low buildings, none more than four stories, containing shops. Several storefronts were empty, but even the empty ones looked immaculately clean.

The wide avenue carried what seemed to be light traffic—occasional trucks, regular electrobuses, and personal cars. Trystin sniffed. The faint odor of burned hydrocarbons permeated the atmosphere, along with something that smelled like popcorn.

It was popcorn. As he passed the next cross street, he could see a cart and a vendor selling bags of the stuff. A mother handed her daughter a bag, and the two walked hand in hand down the glitter-white sidewalk away from Trystin.

After walking another block, he stopped opposite the square, studying the white walls and eight spires of the Temple that rose over a hundred meters into the blue-pink sky. The Temple's northwest spire bore the laser-imposed image of the Angel of the Prophet.

Surrounding the Temple were the eight Arks of the Revealed—each over fifty meters tall. Each Ark was really a building sacred to some divine aspect of the Prophet—the Ark of Teaching, the Ark of Healing, the Ark of Technology, the Ark of Ministry, the Ark of Music, the Ark of the Family, the Ark of the Producing Land, and the Ark of the Producing Waters.

At the corner, with a casual look at the Fountain of Life, its eight jets forming a single column of water over thirty meters high, Trystin crossed the street and entered the octagonal section of land that held the Temple and the eight Arks.

Even before he neared the Temple gates, he could sense the energies and the hidden systems that most Revenants would have denied ever existed. As he stepped within meters of the closed gates, he reached out with his implant, ever so gently, to scan the systems—and almost froze where he stood.

His false identity, superficial memories, and basic Revenant gene patterns would not be enough. The data net and systems that lay behind the shimmering white walls, while not as powerful as most Coalition systems, were certainly powerful enough to hold the absolute identity of every true Revenant admitted to the Temple, and the energies held there were certainly enough to incinerate him. But the system was an open-weave operation—that he could tell, and he might be able to tap it from outside.

His lips pursed, he let his eyes flick to the schedule board. "11:00 A.M., Thursday. Ceremony of Remembrance." Underneath the board was a screen, and Trystin stepped up to view the information scrolling there.

After a time, he nodded. Certainly, all the high Revenant military mission officials would be there, since the ceremony was to honor the missionaries sent to remove the abominations of the Lord. If he could enter the Temple ... he thought about the warnings and the force of the systems less than meters away and repressed a shiver.

Instead he stepped toward the Temple walls, not close enough to touch them, but close enough to see what more he could sense with his implant.

The system was in standdown, or partial standdown. Somehow, he needed a key to the Temple's systems. A key to the Temple? He swallowed. Did he have the actual protocol? Had the Farhkans stolen it, just to give it to him? And why? Because no Farhkan could ever approach the Temples?

The key raised a few other questions—like why he'd never told the Service. Was it just his stubbornness? Or some subconscious suggestion by the Farhkans? Trystin shivered.

Did the Service know? They couldn't. They would have taken him apart like a broken timepiece to get something they thought was a key to the Revenant Temples. Had he repressed the key—and letting anyone besides his father know—because he unconsciously knew what the Service would have done?

Was there any doubt? Was deep space cold?

Slowly, after swallowing and taking a deep breath, he called up the protocol that the Farhkan had given him, as well as the override command line his father had designed. He concentrated, trying to match them, but, while they seemed at least vaguely similar, there was no real way to tell unless the systems were in full use. The open-weave receptors were shut down, and the main Temple doors were closed at the moment.

Trystin stood there for a time, but without either success or failure.

Did he have enough faith to walk through those gates when they were operational? This time he did shudder. He had two days to decide. Were they enough? Were they too much?

Faith? What did the Revenants know about faith?

"Brother? Are you all right?" A young sister stood in front of Trystin, wearing the blue sash of a Temple Guide.

He shook his head. "Yes, I mean, Sister."

"It is overwhelming sometimes. Even I look up there and get the chills." She smiled, only a friendly smile, and Trystin momentarily wanted to hug her. "You haven't been here before, have you?"

"No. This is my first visit to the Temple."

"I hope it won't be the last."

"That's not my decision, but the Lord's." Trystin offered a smile. After what he'd just been through, that was about how he felt.

"It makes you feel that way, but you'll get over it."

"Thank you, Sister. May your faith always so comfort you." He hoped he could find enough faith to do what looked to be necessary. Still, there might be a way out. He needed to check the Ministry of Missions, more closely than he'd been able to do from the car.

"May yours be of comfort also," she answered before turning to another visitor to the Temple Square.

Trystin slowly walked around the Square, taking in the

eight Arks that surrounded the Temple, studying their apparent exits and entrances, and using his implant and his hearing to trace what seemed to be underground passages from the Arks to the Temple itself.

Finally, after walking around the Temple for over an hour, he started down East Kingdom Avenue, toward the Ministry of Missions, where Jynckla had his office. Even East Kingdom Avenue, while almost dust-free, had patches in the bright white pavement.

He walked by the Ministry of Missions, neither hurrying nor dawdling. The entrance to the heavy-walled, four-story Ministry building was definitely, if unobtrusively, guarded and the heavy lasers concealed there were even more obvious than those hidden in the Temple gates. The two doormen were also heavily armed, although Trystin could have taken care of them. He just couldn't have taken care of the lasers.

That almost mandated an effort to enter the Temple.

He walked back to the car without retracing his steps past the Ministry. He still needed to find a place to dump the leftover electronics. He needed to think some more, a lot more, about the application and conversion and uses of faith. And about his faith in the Farhkans and his father.

He tried not to shiver as he started the internal-combustion engine, repressing thoughts about how to counterfeit a prophet without becoming a martyr—or a statistic.

64

 The crowds hurried toward the Temple, flooding past the eight Arks and the Fountain of Life, and Trystin tried to remain inconspicuous as he walked toward the Temple, equipment strapped in place under the white coat.

Following two young women in long white outfits, he stepped toward the gate, ignoring the glance of the uniformed Soldier of the Lord standing in the alcove.

"Abomination! Abomination of the Lord!" The words rang out through the entire Square. Revenants of all ages turned toward the Temple gates.

Trystin looked around with the others, although his heart was pounding and his body was cloaked in instant cold sweat.

"Abomination of the Lord!"

The Soldier of the Lord, hard-eyed, turned toward Trystin, but before he could act, a lance of light flared from the Temple gates toward Trystin—burning, BURNING, *BURNING!!!!*

Trystin sat bolt upright in bed. His arms twitched, and a faint burning ran through his whole body. He forced himself to take a deep breath, then another, and a third, but he kept shuddering.

He wiped his forehead on the counterpane.

Finally, he got up, and soft light flooded the room. It was only slightly after midnight, and he walked into the fresher, where he splashed cold water on his face.

He shivered again.

Clearly, his subconscious was telling him that trying to walk into the Temple was suicidal, not to mention foolish, ill-considered, and just plain stupid.

But the problem he faced was that turning Jynckla into an example of the Lord for perpetuating slaughter wouldn't have the impact he needed if it didn't happen in the Temple itself. And he couldn't "disappear" in the streets the way he could behind a flash of light in the Temple.

His other problem was that he didn't know how open the Temple's net really was. Still . . .

He splashed his face again, trying to cool his flushed skin.

He could just try to enter the Temple, not too obviously,

and feel out the systems. If his efforts didn't work, he could just slip away and try something else. No one knew him, not really.

He took a deep breath and used a towel to blot away the water.

Why nightmares? He didn't recall having had many nightmares until the last few years. He hadn't even had nightmares when he'd been on the Maran perimeter. He'd only had nightmares when he'd started to think about the war, really think, and to understand that he could die, that he could be killed. Was that why those who ran societies liked their soldiers young? So they didn't have the age or the experience to think about the stupidities of the wars they fought—or might fight? He tried to laugh, but couldn't.

His face still damp, he began to walk around the room in the darkness, breathing deeply. The burning that ran in lines throughout his body slowly faded, but did not quite disappear, continuing to tingle through all his nerves.

After taking another drink of water, and breathing deeply for several minutes longer, he ran through a short set of stretching exercises, trying to work out the muscular knots created by the nightmare.

Then he washed his face again, turned off the lights, and climbed into bed. But he lay for a long time, looking into the darkness.

65

 After completing another drive around central Wystuh, and the Temple area, Trystin slipped the car into the space in front of his room. All the spaces near the ends of the building—and the staircases— were taken. He stepped from the coolness of the car into the heat, but did not wipe his forehead as he walked toward the room.

Once inside, he checked the space, visually, and with implant-enhanced senses, but he could find no trace that anyone had been there, not that he was any expert. The walls that had been carefully painted and repainted looked the same, as did the well-scrubbed carpet that was beginning to fray near the door.

He washed his hands and face, blotted some smudges off the white coat, and stepped back into the late-afternoon heat. He walked by the office, and the sister who had checked him into the room lifted a hand and waved. He smiled and waved back.

Only a handful of tables were taken in the small restaurant adjoining the Promise Inn.

"One, Brother?" asked the gray-haired hostess.

"Please." Trystin followed her to a small table for two along the wall. A pale green cloth covered the table, and the two napkins also appeared to be of real cotton or linen.

"The special is beefalo stew with noodles and greens. That comes with dessert, and a drink, and it's seven and a quarter."

"Thank you."

"A pleasure, Brother." The hostess smiled and left Trystin.

His stomach rumbled, and he glanced quickly at the menu. Although the food was heavy, the Revenants did serve good cooking—everywhere he had eaten so far.

"Have you decided, ser?" The waitress was also an older sister, wearing rings and braided hair, and not a checked dress, but a gold-colored tunic and long matching trousers.

"I'll have the stew special, with limeade." He wished he could get tea, but real tea and cafe were forbidden on the Revenant worlds, and anise tea tasted like weak liquid candy.

"I'll bring the limeade right away."

A single older man sat at the table by the door, hands cupped around a glass, eyes staring into space. The corner table held four women, all wearing what seemed to be matching dresses and conversing animatedly.

". . . Heber's Farewell—that was something . . ."

". . . going to be a pilot, not just a plain missionary . . ."

". . . missionary's a missionary . . . equal in the sight of the Lord . . ."

"You ask me . . . doesn't matter . . ."

"Sarah's daughter . . . her Farewell . . ."

". . . doesn't seem right, her wanting to be an Angel . . . such a sweet child she was . . ."

". . . strong-willed, though . . . that's what Becki told me . . ."

Trystin nodded to himself. He had the feeling that overtly strong-willed women got a lot of mission calls.

"Here you are."

"Thank you." Trystin ignored the growling in his stomach and took a sip of the limeade, waiting for his beefalo stew to arrive.

"Brother Hyriss!" Carson Orr walked straight across the room toward Trystin's table with a broad smile.

"Brother Orr." Trystin stood. Orr's appearance wasn't exactly coincidence. "What a coincidence."

"Would you mind if I joined you for a moment? Just for some lemonade. I'll have to be going shortly."

"Of course not."

The older waitress, silvered golden hair braided neatly, stopped. "Will you be having dinner, Brother?"

"No. I'd like some lemonade, though." When she left, Orr turned his pale blue eyes on Trystin. "How are you finding Wystuh?"

"In some ways, it's as I thought it would be. In others, different." Trystin took a small sip of limeade.

"I can imagine that. No place you haven't been is the way you expect." Orr smiled. "How are you finding the people?"

"Like most places . . . friendly. Sometimes, very friendly."

"The unmarried sisters?"

Trystin blushed. He had been more than careful to avoid them.

"Young returnee like you, you ought to be thinking about settling down. You think you have all the time in the world, but life's not always like that."

"I've already discovered that. The Lord has His own plans for us, not exactly what we might have intended." That was certainly true enough, reflected Trystin, and he might as well keep building the background for his plan and his escape.

Orr gave Trystin the faintest of quizzical looks.

Trystin waited calmly.

"I heard from an old friend. You might have met him. Jon Smithson."

Trystin raised his eyebrows. His guts twisted. Did he run, or play it out? Did they really know, or was it all cat and mouse? How much time did he have? Or did they think he might lead them to others? "I might have."

"Big beefy fellow. He works in Dalowan—small town south of Wystuh."

"Is he a peace officer?" Trystin asked with a hint of curiosity.

"I see you recall him."

"I only met him once. Very briefly."

"He said you saved some children."

Trystin forced a short laugh. "I did what had to be done." He'd known that saving the two might come back to haunt him, but he hadn't thought it would happen quite so quickly.

"Most folks wouldn't know how to react quick enough."

"I am a pilot, and that's something we're trained in."

"So I'm told."

The waitress set a tall glass by Orr.

"Thank you, Sister." Orr turned back to Trystin. "You fought the golems, Brother Hyriss. Are they machines, or are they human?" softly asked the white-haired man in the pale blue jacket, a blue so pale it was nearly white, so pale that probably only Trystin's enhanced vision could spot the difference.

"I don't know," Trystin answered slowly, trying to answer as a returned missionary, a thoughtful one, might. "The Prophet, bless his name, spoke of abominations, and there are abominations throughout the mansions of heaven."

"I'd call that a safe answer, and it's true enough. Yet . . ." The other shook his head. "The Prophet said that the Lord works in mysterious ways." He shrugged. "He said that we can't always fathom His ways 'cause His ways are not our ways. Me . . . I've found that learning the ways of men is a mite bit easier."

"That's certainly true." Trystin tried to remain composed, faintly amused at Orr's folksy tone, but knowing it concealed a sharp mind.

"This fellow appears from nowhere, and he looks like a brother. He talks like a brother, and he knows what a brother should know. And by the Prophet's tongue, his eyes even have that faraway look in them. Heck, I've seen enough of the returned to know you can't counterfeit that. Does that make him a brother?"

"It would seem so." Trystin continued to smile, still amused in spite of himself, in spite of the situation, in spite of the sweat that ran down his back.

"That's what I said to myself. I told Jon that, too. And, you know, without a thought for your own safety, you rescued two children you didn't even know. That's certainly the act of a good brother."

"One does what has to be done." Trystin didn't miss Orr's deliberate switch from the impersonal to the personal.

"I've got a problem, Brother Hyriss, a real problem. Maybe you could help me out. I'm not sure, not real sure, but from what Jon said, you moved faster than even a top pilot, and that bothers me. Now, I know it shouldn't. You saved those kids." Orr pushed his white hair back off his forehead. "But it does. If you were a golem, one of those reflex-enhanced Ecofreaks, you wouldn't have saved the kids." He shook his head. "But . . . if you weren't . . . strange . . . somehow . . . you couldn't have done it."

Trystin had to talk his way out of it. He needed time, and if he went into a Revenant medical facility for tests, he wasn't likely to emerge—not as a whole and sane individual.

"Strange? Is it so strange that I wanted to save a child? Does a name mean that something is so?" Trystin picked up the knife. "I could call this a lily, but does calling it a lily make it one?" He set the knife down and picked up his glass, looking at the limeade for a moment. "What one believes makes all the difference." Again, he wished the drink were tea rather than limeade. He carefully sipped some until the greenish liquid filled only half the crystal, then lifted the glass. "Is it half full or half empty?"

"That's an old riddle, but I'm not sure I take your meaning." Orr squinted at Trystin.

Trystin forced a shrug, although he felt as though he were walking on the edge of a cliff. "True enough. But one man could look at the glass and say it was half full, another, half empty. Both would be observing a truth." He almost nodded as he lifted the glass and swallowed the last of the limeade in a long, long swallow before setting it down. "Now . . is the glass full or empty?"

"Most folks would say it was empty." Orr grinned. "I get the feeling you're not most folks, Brother Hyriss."

"You've seen through me," admitted Trystin. "The glass is full. Full of air. We live in the open air, and we don't see the air, but we need it. So which is worth more—the glass full of liquid or the glass full of air?"

"You're a tricky fellow." Orr shook his head ruefully. "Almost makes me think of the way the dark ones speak and write."

Trystin felt as though he had stepped off the edge of the cliff and that it was only a matter of time before he smashed far below. Instead of bolting or even wiping his forehead against the sudden heat he felt, he nodded. "I know that, Brother, and arguments are only words. Logic doesn't mean truth." He frowned, and he didn't have to force the gesture. "But an elder in the dark of airless heaven who needs another minute to complete his mission may have more need of the glass of air than the liquid."

"I've always believed that the Lord provides."

"Indeed He does," answered Trystin. "He provides, and we must use what He provides. But is what we see what He sees? Is a label a measure of what is? Or should one judge by actions rather than by labels?"

Orr laughed and pushed back his chair. "You make interesting points, Brother Hyriss. Most interesting. Will you be attending the Ceremony of Remembrance at the Temple tomorrow?"

"I had planned to." Trystin managed to nod, even as he realized he was being pushed into implementing his half-assed plan whether he wanted to or not. He didn't sense Orr was lying, and that meant he had until tomorrow, but not any longer.

"I'll look forward to seeing you there." The older man stood. "It's time for me to head home. The wives are already probably more than a little irritated. Peace be with you."

"And with you."

Trystin waited for the waitress and the stew. Was he being a damned fool in not disappearing? Could he trust Orr's implied promise? If he couldn't, how could he disappear? The Service had been right. The whole world was an intelligence network. It seemed, just because he'd saved the children, that Orr was giving him a chance—of sorts. Was he telling Trystin to disappear? Or hoping that Trystin could enter the Temple without being incinerated?

Trystin didn't know. What was also clear to him was that the only way he'd get off Orum was if they thought he were dead, and most times, dead men didn't go anywhere.

This time was going to be the exception—he hoped—at least if they let him play it out his way. If his keys worked . . . if his alternative identity worked for a bit . . . if his theology was correct . . . if . . .

He took a deep breath. After dinner he had more memorizing to do—the whole stack of papers he'd written out. The last thing he needed was to forget his lines in the middle of the Temple—assuming he got that far. The Service

would get its assassination, and so would the Revenants.
He hoped he could deliver even more. He had to. He also
hoped he didn't have another nightmare—sleeping or
awake—but that was probably asking too much.

He hoped, again, he was reading Orr correctly, and that
Brother Khalid had been right about the Revenants seldom lying.

66

 Through the night, every sound, every rustle
seemed magnified, but no one pounded on the door
to his room, and in time, Trystin slept, if not nearly
so well as he would have wished, with the words and
phrases he had committed to memory running through his
mind. He tried not to dwell on the shakiness of what he
planned—or the suspicions that somehow he'd been programmed to do it by Rhule Ghere.

In a way, neither mattered, now that Orr had effectively
unmasked him. He had one chance, and that was it. So he
slept and woke, slept and woke.

He struggled through an early breakfast—without any
appearances by Brother Carson Orr—and the words and
phrases he had committed to memory still ran through his
thoughts, and kept recurring as he gathered himself and
his equipment together.

At ten-thirty, Trystin parked the car on the street, two
blocks off the square. The fabric clothes bag was out of
sight in the trunk, although he had not officially checked
out of the Promise Inn. After parking, he got out and
walked toward the Temple. He was early, early enough so
that if matters went as planned, which they probably
wouldn't, he wouldn't be at the very back of the Temple.
The ten-meter-wide sidewalks allowed quick movement

and understated the large number of white-clad Revenants headed toward the Temple. Then again, he looked like any other white-clad Revenant, except he had certain equipment fastened in, around, and under what he wore. Like most of the men, around his neck was the brown sash of the returned missionary. Unlike most, he wore the gold stripe signifying service in the Fleet of the Faithful. His hip still twinged from the bruise received in his rescue of the two children, and he still wasn't sure whether the rescue had bought him time or brought him to the attention of the Revenants sooner than necessary—or both.

Ahead of him walked a gray-haired patriarch accompanied by three sisters, all three sisters with the elaborate swirled braids that seemed the norm, and all in long white dresses. To his left were two sisters walking side by side, although they wore long white trousers and long white jackets.

Trystin listened, hoping behind the faint smile on his face that his redesigned mission would shake up the almost blind faith of the Revenants. It probably wouldn't, but he had to try, and at least he should be able to accomplish the letter of the mission.

". . . always like the Farewell celebration for the missions . . ."

". . . told you that those girls needed more time at the lower school . . ."

". . . going on twenty years . . . Clyde should be returning soon . . ."

". . . won't look much older, they say . . ."

". . . hard to have a returnee not much older than the eldest wife's grandchildren . . ."

The flow of Revenants swept across the avenue into the square, and Trystin kept pace, turning his implant up full, ignoring the faint burning buzzing that invaded his whole nervous system. He was going to need the implant's full capacity, and that might not be enough.

The Temple gates were flung wide—all eight of the massive gates—each one opposite an Ark. Beside each gate was a pair of uniformed Soldiers of the Lord, but none bore obvious weapons in their dress white uniforms, trimmed with brass gleaming like burnished gold.

Trystin turned toward the gate opposite the Ark of Producing Waters, almost feeling immersed in the flood of quiet conversations.

"... Jayne says they're going to name her son after some old composer ..."

"... add another room to the house once he marries Sister Mergen ..."

"All the high admirals will be here ..."

"... just people of the Lord like us ..."

"... wish we didn't have to come, Mother ..."

Trystin forced a pleasant smile on his face as he looked up at the white shimmering walls of the Temple. Even from fifty meters away, he could sense the energy flows in and around the massively towering snow-white stone structure. He reached out with the implant.

"Brother Hyriss!"

Trystin turned. There stood Carson Orr, walking toward him with a broad smile.

"Brother Orr." Trystin extended a hand.

"Brother Hyriss ... I wondered if you would be here. Some returnees from the far lands find the Temple so overwhelming that they don't make it through the gates." Orr slipped into step beside him. "Like I said, though, you're not most folks."

"The Lord has called me." Now Trystin was definitely committed, and he resolved that his language had better match his actions, since he had no other options but to make his burnt offerings to the Prophet, so to speak. In the process, the Coalition would get its neutralization—if he had guessed right. If not, he was dead, one way or another.

If successful, whether he would plant enough doubts with the faithful was another question.

"In what way, Brother Hyriss?"

Trystin used his implant systems to scan, as he could, Orr, but the man radiated no energies, and carried no energy weapons. Somehow, Trystin doubted that Orr carried something like a slug thrower, which meant that Orr was either relying on the gates to take care of Trystin—or something else. Or Trystin would simply be scooped up and taken care of after the ceremony, so that the Revenants could figure out how he entered the Temple.

"Each man is called in his own way, Brother," Trystin temporized, not wanting to reveal too much until he was actually inside the Temple, where he doubted that the Revenants would try to drag him away.

"Perhaps, but few of the returned are called again." Orr's eyes glanced to the right, and Trystin followed them, catching a glimpse of nearly a dozen white-clad men standing at the edge of the swirling flow of worshipers.

Trystin repressed a grin, then didn't have to make the effort. Even before he walked up to the Temple gates, the gates that pulsed with forces and the hidden systems that most Revenants never knew existed, Trystin knew that all the effort of the Eco-Tech science, false identity and all, even his basically Revenant gene patterns, would not be enough. Behind the shimmering white walls lay a system powerful enough to reveal him as the fraud he was . . . unless his risky scheme worked.

He'd been warned about the chance of being incinerated on the spot, but somehow it seemed more immediate, much more immediate, especially with Orr at his elbow. If he broke and ran, he didn't have much hope either—not that weapons were that much in evidence, even with the white-clad Soldiers of the Lord. But Carson Orr had his forces out and deployed, and even with full augmentation, Trystin wasn't going to win any contests of force—not for long. Besides, the fact that Orr was accompanying him and that the reinforcements were standing back might give him opportunity enough.

"I have returned." That was enough, and ambiguous enough. But he was sweating, despite the breeze that kept those around him cool.

Orr glanced sideways at him. "You look disturbed."

Trystin definitely needed a key to the Temple. He swallowed. At this point, he could only hope he had the actual

protocol. Otherwise he was dead, far sooner than he
needed to be.

"What must be must be." Trystin looked at Orr. "Do not
deny me what must be." He hoped he had the rhetoric
close enough. If he were right, every word he said in the
Temple would be recalled and studied.

Orr's brow crinkled, and his eyes darted back toward his
troops—associates, whatever they might be, then back to
Trystin.

As they approached the gates, Trystin stumbled and
brushed the wall, staggering.

"Are you all right, Brother Hyriss?"

"I think I tripped on something." Trystin stopped and
massaged his leg, casting his implant toward the net that
began a few meters before him. The mass of data was
enormous, and he staggered, again, wiping his forehead as
he straightened. What part of the key?

His father's explanation surfaced—"just like a Service
protocol"—and he projected the key toward the net.

"WELCOME, SON OF THE PROPHET!"

The unseen and unheard greeting rolled through him,
and he picked up the response, lying behind the greeting
as if in plain view, and projected it back, both vocally and
through the implant. "I greet the Souls of the Eternal and
the Revelations of the Book."

Beside him, Orr swallowed, hard and visibly. "Seems like
I said, maybe, just maybe, you're not what you seem. At
times . . . it sure is hard to figure how the Lord works."

Trystin stepped into the stone arch of the gate and the
energies that swirled around and through it, using his key
to the huge open-weave system to override the weapons
and energy detectors. His thoughts raced along the command paths, trying to analyze the checkpoints as he kept
walking . . . and sweating.

Orr kept close beside him.

"As you may behold," Trystin replied. "The Lord is the
Lord, and none may deny Him or His works." Now was
not the time to be cautious, because, one way or the other,
he was committed.

He could sense the confusion from the main system network as a series of interrogatories flooded the system, but, with the override control he and his father had developed, he shunted them aside, touching the short-range improvised laser grip in his pocket. A slug thrower or a standard laser would have been far easier—he could have just bought a hunting weapon—but it wouldn't do what he had in mind.

A crooked smile crossed his face as he recalled the mission profile—the idea of keeping it simple. He almost laughed. Despite all the rhetoric about the need to keep things simple, simplicity usually didn't get the job done, not in complex societies.

Of course, there would be hell to pay, whether he succeeded or failed, but he only had to worry about it if he succeeded. And, as Brother Orr's presence had shown, he couldn't have succeeded with the Coalition's straight assassination—not and had any chance to escape.

Then, as he had come to realize over the past few days, he doubted that he'd ever been intended to escape. Officers who looked like Revenants were getting to be embarrassments in the Coalition, unless they died gloriously. He'd see what he could do about that.

The next set of arches contained the ultrasonic cleaners that vibrated dust and dirt loose from clothes, as well as the gentle suction that whisked away all remnants of uncleanliness.

From what Trystin recalled, in the old days of Deseretism, all entrants to the Temple actually changed all their clothes, and the neo-Mahmets had left their shoes outside the mosques. Technology had simplified those aspects, at least.

". . . *what will be will be . . .*" subvocalized Orr.

"And it will be the will of the Lord," Trystin added, as he picked up Orr's words.

"You are a surprising fellow," Orr said after a quick swallow.

"Surely you do not doubt the Lord and the sanctity of the Temple?" Trystin asked, as they continued past the second arch and into the vaulting antechamber to the Temple proper. His words were both for Orr and the recorders that monitored the Temple.

"... *not His will, but yours ...*" Orr said subvocally.

Trystin would have agreed, but his plans didn't include admitting frailty at the moment, only planting more seeds for what he had planned, for his efforts to shake the entire faith of the Revenants. "His will be done."

Orr's eyes glanced toward the right portal.

"Through the left portal, Brother Orr." Trystin kept his head high, as would any returnee, proud to be able to bring thanks to his Lord.

"Many returnees would prefer the right."

"I stand on the left hand of the Lord." Especially since your statement tells me that you have some support arrangements on the right, Trystin reflected.

They slipped through another curtain of unseen energies and into the Temple proper, the white stone columns rising into an arch nearly fifty meters above the rows of straight-backed white pews.

Trystin's eyes flicked across the Temple interior, and he jumped his reflexes and reactions a notch, as he tried to determine the location of the admirals and the bishops and archbishops and caliphs.

The information clicked into place as his eyes scanned the front of the Temple.

Trystin headed toward the left side of the center section, stopping beside a place almost on the wide side aisle. He stepped back. "After you, Brother Orr."

Orr looked at the aisle seat. "I was thinking I'd defer to you, Brother Hyriss, seeing as how you're more recently returned."

Trystin smiled. "After you, Brother. For you are honored and should sit on the right hand. Remember that in times to come." He didn't think that Orr would see the implied command exactly as an honor.

As he spoke, Trystin's commands, through his pilot implant, finally managed to unravel the open-weave channels enough to reach the control center. He ignored the sweat running down his back.

The older man paled for the first time. *". . . Lord help me . . ."*

"He will. For is it not written that the work of the Lord is the work of all faithful souls?"

"I'm having a mite bit of trouble determining who's a faithful soul at the moment." Orr's folksiness seemed forced.

"Do not presume to know me, or the ways of the Lord," Trystin said quietly, but not quietly enough, for a sister in the pew in front glanced back at them.

The whispers died away, to be replaced with music.

Trystin didn't know if he were really ready, but he kept his implant merged with the Temple's open-weave system, ready to override the system, even as he continued to trace out the basic controls for lighting and the decorative lasers and sparklebeams.

The music swelled from the organ, augmented by underlying subsonics, designed to instill the feeling of awe.

Orr shifted his weight, and Trystin tried not to, even as his efforts with his implant sent another round of prickling and burning through his system. He had the feeling he was operating at the edge of his capabilities, as if he had much choice with Orr standing beside him and presumably knowing Trystin was a Coalition agent, albeit a strange one.

As the organ died away, a figure in white, enhanced by the sparklebeam that enshrouded him, stepped into the podium on the right front side of the Temple. He raised his hands, then lowered them as he began to speak. "We are gathered here in the name of the Lord, and of His Prophet, to celebrate and commemorate the sacrifice and the accomplishments of His missionaries, to consecrate ourselves, our souls and bodies, to the end that His work and the teachings of His Prophet shall not perish but ring through all the mansions of the Lord's domain. . . ."

Trystin let the bioimplants do their work, letting his eyes scan the row of archbishops to the side and below the

Revelator's podium, until the pictures matched, and he identified Archbishop Jynckla.

"Let us pray . . . O Eternal Father, creator of bountiful worlds and endless heavens, maker of all things visible and invisible . . ."

Trystin's mind continued to work, running through the Temple's net system until he had the overrides well in hand, including the locks on the control systems—someone had designed the system to be able to lock out the technicians in the upper booths . . . and Trystin was going to use that ability.

Orr shifted his weight as he stood beside Trystin, head bowed.

". . . determiner of all that can be determined . . . knower of all that can be known. . . . Grant us Thy peace."

"Amen."

After the prayer, the Revenants sat down, and Trystin followed their example.

"The Revelator of the Prophet!"

A series of trumpet notes, cascading from nowhere, filled the Temple, and the unheard subsonics rumbled and created more awe.

Just as the Revelator rose, so did Trystin, setting his hand on Orr's shoulder, and whispering. "Be of good courage, and deny me not, for what will be is the will of the Lord."

Orr clutched at Trystin, but Trystin slipped from the older man's grasp with the speed of enhanced reflexes and metabolism.

Calling on the laser sparklelight to surround him, to give him the aura of a saint, he walked up the aisle. He also locked out the speaker to the podium where the Revelator stood.

". . . oh . . ."

". . . not in the program . . ."

Forcing himself to carry himself as a stately figure, not quite ponderously, he walked the ten meters to the base of what he would have termed a sanctuary, then ascended the two steps. A faint murmur ran through the faithful as he turned, ignoring the Revelator at the podium.

"You have called upon the Lord, knower of all that can be known. Do you not think that He knows those among you who have profaned His will? You have called upon the Lord the creator. Do you not think that if they cast down this Temple, the Lord would rebuild it, almost before your eyes?" Trystin wasn't above using the hidden amplifiers to boost his voice, or jacking up the subsonic overtones. He just hoped his memory would hold all that he had planned and memorized. He was also, belatedly, very glad he had reread Chaplain Matsugi's handout after Commander Folsom's long-ago tongue-lashing . . . and that he had been required to bring a *Book of Toren* with him—necessary for the details behind his speeches.

A whispering began to fill the Temple, and Trystin boosted his voice to almost booming power.

"Once was a son of God betrayed, and once was a prophet betrayed, and yet in the years in which we live another has been betrayed . . . betrayed by hatred and betrayed by another false god. Our God is a God of love, and He has stood by us while we have followed hatred and destruction, for He is a God of love. He has stood by us while we have hunted down our fellows . . ."

". . . heresy . . ."

". . . get the controls . . ."

". . . they're locked . . ."

Trystin kept a straight face even as he could hear the priests muttering, then he turned and pointed at the two behind the Revelator.

"You have betrayed the Prophet, and the son of God and man, who sits at the right hand of the Father." As he spoke, he tweaked the controls, and the red-light laser flared across the two, illuminating them, but not harming either. "For lo, another will come to sit at the left hand of the Father."

Luckily, juggling the multiple controls mentally was not nearly so difficult as juggling the inputs on a translation ship, but how the results of his juggling would impact the Revenant beliefs—that would be another question.

Trystin turned toward Archbishop Jynckla, and another cone of sparklelight surrounded the white-haired archbishop with the tanned face and kindly smile. "You have been guilty of hatred and hypocrisy—even so, the Lord will take you unto Him."

The desperate mutterings and adjustments from the control booth simmered through him, and he tried to put them out of mind, even as he held to the control locks.

". . . madman . . ."

". . . Kersowin and Jynckla . . . have your heads . . ."

Trystin, under the cover of the sparklelight, removed and powered the laser handpiece and grip, then raised his hands, directing the sparklelaser focus around him so that he shimmered and shone.

"The Lord has offered you love, and you have rejected that love. The Lord has asked you to love thy neighbor as thyself, and you have not. How can you bring the word of the Lord to your neighbor when you kill that neighbor before you come close enough to speak? How can you kill and speak of love in the name of your Lord? Yet, in the name of the Lord will I love you as I love myself—so I can do no less for me than for you."

As he spoke, he pointed the small, comparatively widefocused laser on Jynckla, and with a precision only possible through the implant and enhanced reflexes, swept it down the white-clothed figure, raising a shower of sparks and ashes. In little more than instants, the flames rose from the antique wooden box where the archbishop had been sitting.

Trystin didn't let himself feel any relief. The trickiest part was yet to come—portraying himself as prophet and sacrifice . . . and escaping it.

Trystin turned back to the stunned congregation, continuing with his prepared text and boosted speech.

"You know the Lord, and the Lord knows you in your hearts. Judge not, lest you be judged, and yet, I say unto you, even as He will raise this Temple in less than three days, yes, even in the quickness of time, will He also give me for you, for someone must speak for you. You who would not speak for love. For you, someone must speak. For you, someone must offer forgiveness. Someone must atone for you—both now and in the fullness of time."

Someone had to do something—that he knew, but he still fought the sense of hypocrisy all the way through the words. With the last syllable, Trystin triggered his reflexes into high speed and called in both the light cloak, and the projections. He stepped back behind the cloak of blinding light, and pointed the laser at the golden carpet, letting the smoke and fire grow, while the projections showed only flame.

Light flared through the Temple, light so brilliant that all the Revenants blinked, and their eyes watered. As they blinked and as they wept in spite of themselves, a figure in white blazed into smoke right on the steps between the podiums. That tall figure seemed to grow, to glimmer with golden light. Then it crumpled and vanished into trails of smoke, leaving only a burned circular space and ashes drifting through the air.

At the same time, Trystin filled the Temple with the deepest of the subsonics, then slipped through the back door into a sort of robing room, even as the lights dimmed, and those in the Temple rubbed their eyes again.

His hands were reddened, lightly burned, because the sparklelaser generated heat when it hit metal, and they hurt. Still . . . unless someone had smuggled high-tech recording equipment into the Temple, the Revenant worshipers should have been left with the lasting impression that one Brother Hyriss had offered himself as a sacrifice for them. With luck, Orr and the others would not be looking for a dead man.

With luck . . . but Trystin wasn't sure he could count on that, and he still had to get out of the Temple and off Orum, plus make some appearances as he departed—safe appearances ahead of the desperate dragnet that would be after him.

He dropped his reflexes down to one notch above normal, ignoring the pounding headache he already had developed, and used the Temple system to scan the area. No one was around, although he could sense the continuing efforts of the system technicians to unlock the Temple system.

He ran along the empty corridor and around two corners, to the staircase the system said was there. He bounded down three flights, moving as fast as he could to exceed the expectations of normal human ability. He'd pay later, but for now, he needed speed.

He made it to the ventilation and power-access tunnel that led under the square of the Ark of Healing even before the system registered the opening of the doors to the Temple.

He nodded and began to run along the catwalk. Unfortunately, the easy part was over, he feared, trying to breathe deeply and easily to force more oxygen into his system.

The access tunnel led into the maintenance room in the base of the Ark of Healing—an empty room, although he could sense voices in the adjoining area, presumably support staff of some sort.

". . . just another ceremony . . ."

". . . not so loud . . ."

Trystin smiled, but even that gesture hurt. He wiped his steaming forehead with the big handkerchief and eased his way to the maintenance staircase. Three flights up he broke the lock and stepped out onto the grounds. He was on the far side of the Ark of Healing, not all that far from the edge of the square.

He could see a few white-clad Soldiers of the Lord by the one gate in his field of vision, but they had not left their station in the few moments it took him to leave the square proper.

Walking briskly, he started toward the car, grateful that the streets and sidewalks were not totally empty, even as he could sense the growing roar from the area around the Temple behind him.

From what he could determine, no one was following

him. In a way, that made sense. Traffic was controlled by
access to Orum, and by the Temple. Few outsiders could
escape the orbit-station screens. Anyone who did and who
didn't go to the Temple sooner or later was suspect, and
that assumed they were good enough to avoid raising immediate Revenant suspicions. Since the Temple had the
power to destroy outsiders, sooner or later the culture destroyed all outsiders—without such amenities as extensive
secret police. A few smart officials like Orr were probably
all the Revenants needed.

He rubbed his forehead, which relieved some of the
pressure there, but reminded him of the tenderness of his
lightly burned hands. Sparklelasers did have some energy,
which was why those who used them did not carry metals.

He kept walking.

After covering the two long blocks away from the Temple, he slipped into the car, using his implant to check for
added and explosive circuitry, but found none. He started
the vehicle and pulled out into the sparse traffic, turning
at the first corner. Behind him, he could see people beginning to boil out of the Temple Square area.

He headed down South Kingdom toward the Promise
Inn, detouring at Loyola to stop behind a restaurant with
an outside disposal unit in the alley. The laser and the
powerpak went into the unit, and Trystin darted back to
the car.

While they'd doubtless find the equipment, he didn't
want to carry it, since it was burned out anyway, and if he
were picked up, there was a slight chance they would be
somewhat confused if he didn't have any weapons. That
made him only slightly less of a damned fool.

Wystuh was essentially a weaponless city, and that *might*
help.

Then, again, it might not.

Trystin kept driving, wondering if Orr would believe
his eyes or his feelings. Trystin was afraid the man—too
smart for Trystin's good—would keep looking while everyone else remained in a state of cultural shock.

Still . . . Orr was smart, and high enough in whatever

organization to call his own shots—literally and figuratively.

Trystin nodded to himself and guided the car toward the Promise Inn. Orr would either come alone, or not at all.

67

 When Trystin reached the Promise Inn, he checked the area, but everything looked normal. He parked back around the corner of the building on the far end away from the office, then walked back toward the empty office, passing his former room. In some ways, he wished that Orr or Sister Myra or one of the other wives would return quickly, or he would have to leave, and he really needed a witness or two, one who knew him and who would not be a threat.

After a time, a blue car appeared. Trystin forced a smile, waited, and, after jamming his reflexes, metabolism, and hearing into high, scanned the area. He could sense no one but Orr and no unusual electronics. It might be worth the risk. He walked down the side of the building toward the vacant room he had left earlier. He opened the door and stood outside, waiting.

"Brother Hyriss, I'd sure be pleased if I might have a word." Carson Orr walked toward Trystin, his hands clearly in the open. A slow grin crossed his face. "Two returns in a lifetime . . . that's not something you see often."

Forcing his speech to be normal—so slow, it seemed—Trystin gestured to the door and answered, "People see what they want, not what is."

Without hesitation, Orr stepped inside. Trystin shut the door. Orr wanted something, besides Trystin's head, and that was a start.

The Revenant security officer offered a rueful grin as he

turned to Trystin. "Most folks, now, would take death as permanent. I was right, there, about you not being like most folks."

"I said the Lord would rebuild this Temple." Trystin shrugged.

"I'm not much on Scripture," Orr confessed, "but I recall that someone else said that, and I'm not convinced that you're exactly on the same side as that fellow. But I'd like to give everyone a fair chance."

"I am what I am." Trystin intended to play it out as well as he could, since Orr was clearly trying to convey something—and it wasn't something he wanted to share, since the Revenant had come alone. Trystin's implant and his enhanced senses could find nothing surrounding Orr, except for the small recorder trained on Trystin, and Trystin was going to use that to his own advantage to plant the seeds of doubt.

"Heck, that's almost like you're saying you're another prophet." Orr's tone turned rueful. "Folks like that tend to get locked up, you understand?"

Trystin shook his head slowly. "I claim nothing. All too often men and false gods claim. What matters a claim to the Lord? You have claimed you do the will of the Lord when you slaughter others. They claim the will of their Lord when they slaughter you. An older prophet said to consider the beam in your own eye before the mote in your brother's. The Lord is what the Lord is, and I am what I am."

"You're a young fellow to be a prophet, not a white hair on your head. Now, poor Admiral Jynckla, he looked like a prophet, you might say. Still can't figure out what he did that would have upset the Lord." Orr shrugged. "Or anyone else."

"Those who seek to destroy with fire can themselves be destroyed by fire. Destruction of those who could be brothers and sisters is not a demonstration of love. And the Lord has always been a God of Love."

"I'm not sure . . . what did that accomplish?" Orr's voice turned harder, and his eyes fixed on Trystin. "I don't understand. You can't say that the death of one admiral—"

"I was sent by a higher authority to deliver a message. The Lord does not beg, but He will instruct." Trystin smiled. "Now . . . I have done what I was sent to do, and those who have eyes to see and ears to hear may learn more of the will of the Lord."

"I'm thinking you'd better wait and come with me, young fellow."

"My time has come." Trystin moved, and Orr's hands came up, but far too slowly, as Trystin flashed around behind him, delivering two quick blows that the hidden recorder would not pick up—blows more dangerous than fatal ones if they failed, but the agent, for Orr could be nothing else, crumpled. Trystin needed no more dead bodies. Too many belonged to him already.

Trystin deactivated the recorder, and then laid Orr out on the bed.

For the second time, he left the room.

"Brother Hyriss, is that you?" Sister Myra came out as Trystin glanced toward the office.

He smiled. Step two. "The Temple has been razed, and restored. Remember—the Lord is a God of Love."

The sisters turned and looked at each other.

"But . . . you were burned. We were at the Temple."

Trystin offered what he hoped was a gentle smile. "I am as real as you." He extended an arm. "Is this not flesh?"

Finally, Sister Elena touched his sleeve, and then his hand. "He feels real. His hands are red, as if they were burned and are healing."

"Were your hands burned?" asked Sister Myra.

"You saw the fire, didn't you?" Trystin asked, evading the question. "All men must burn, sooner or later."

"But . . ."

"I have come to do what I was charged with, and now I must return." That was certainly true, and he felt better when he could stick to the literal truth.

Again, the two exchanged glances.

"For a time, I will go as others do, and then I will return

to my place in the Lord's mansions." Again, his words
were mostly true.

"You were destroyed in fire."

"Did I not say that the Lord would rebuild this Temple?" Trystin forced himself to keep the smile in place, although he could feel the burning spreading through his
body.

The first steps were complete in planting the seeds of
doubt about the infallibility of the Revenants' revealed
religion. Perhaps Sister Myra and Sister Elena would help
spread those doubts.

68

 As he crossed the terminal, Trystin avoided the
Orum Rental counter, Sister Arkady Lewiss or not.
The rental car would have just mysteriously re-
turned, and Trystin smiled at the thought.

His smile vanished as he walked and thought about Orr.
He still didn't quite understand the man's game. Orr had
dropped the folksy tone, almost as if to force Trystin into
either disabling him or killing him. Why?

As he pondered, he glanced around casually. There were
advantages to looking average. Trystin passed several other
tall blond men in the terminal as he headed for the interstellar terminal. At least he didn't stick out the way he
would have in Cambria.

His thoughts about Orr would have to wait as he stepped
up to the passage counter, where, not surprisingly, there
was no line. He offered a worried look. "Is there any way
I could get on the Braha ship?"

"They're loading the shuttle now, Brother . . . and with
the clearances . . ."

"I understand. . . ." Trystin let his face hang. "You see

. . . it's my sister's son. I just found out. It's his Farewell, and I only returned myself. . . ."

The sister behind the counter nodded sympathetically.

Trystin slipped the databloc and card onto the counter. "If you could do something . . ."

"I'll try, Brother." She took the databloc that identified him as Brother Stannel Svensen.

Trystin kept his hearing intensified, despite the buzzing and flashes of burning through his system.

"Let him go, Doreen," said an older sister behind the counter. "There's space, and you know the directive we got. . . ."

"Let me flash the shuttle." She picked up the handset. "Shuttle two, we have another passenger for Braha. We can get him there in five."

". . . *five we can handle . . .*" Trystin could hear the tinny voice at the other end.

"Brother Svensen, you're in luck. We need to hurry." She flashed him a smile, handed him back the databloc and credit strip, as well as a folder and a keycard, and slipped from behind the counter, walking almost at a run.

Trystin tucked the folder into his jacket pocket, and kept pace easily as they went up a back set of stairs and along a narrow corridor. He'd been hoping that leaving somewhere might just be easier than entering. So far, so good.

"You're lucky, Brother. The star traffic is down these days, and an extra passenger sometimes means a lot." She opened the staff door to the upper concourse. "There's the shuttle."

"I do want to make this Farewell," Trystin said, another statement with a great deal of literal truth.

"You shouldn't have any problem. Here we are."

Trystin handed the square keycard to the shuttle attendant and ran his second phoney ID through the reader. The light blinked green.

The sister who had helped get him on the shuttle flashed a smile and waved. Trystin smiled back.

"You're cleared, Brother," said the shuttle attendant.

"Please take a seat, any free seat, as quickly as you can. I'll take your bag and stow it." She closed the door behind him and followed him down the shuttleway.

"This the last one, Sister Liza?" asked the junior single-suited pilot just inside the lock.

"He's the one. Gives you fourteen."

"So long as we're over breakpoint. I'll take his gear."

Trystin slipped past the two, amazed in a way that the pilots had no net system and ran the shuttle through purely manual controls.

The interior of the spaceplane smelled clean, the same scent of lavender and pine, and the same tiredness associated with the equipment. The interior was a pale off-green shade, and that meant a different tired spaceplane nearing the end of its service life.

He strapped into the first open seat, a wall seat. There were no ports or windows, and an older white-haired man shifted his weight to let Trystin sit down.

"Please make sure your harnesses are securely fastened."

"They always say that," observed Trystin's seatmate. "You'd have to be a fool not to strap in."

Trystin completed clicking his harness in place.

"You the one they held the shuttle for?"

"I think so. It took me longer to get to the port from Wystuh than I'd planned."

"You drive?"

"Unfortunately."

"I took the trolley. It's much faster."

"You travel this route much?" Trystin asked.

"Not so often as I used to. They keep jacking up the prices. Everything's more expensive. I can remember when you could go out to dinner at a fancy place like the Peaks or Krendsaw's, and all it cost was three dollars for a couple."

Trystin reflected as the shuttle lurched backward from the terminal—he hadn't seen a meal for less than about eight Revenant dollars for one person.

"And it wasn't that long ago."

"You can't do that now," agreed Trystin.

"You can't even come close. I don't know how you younger people will manage. Now that they're allowing six wives . . . it's been hard enough for us, and I was only blessed with four."

A muffled roar rose into a high-pitched whine, and the shuttle began to accelerate down the long runway, the noise drowning out all possibility of normal conversation. The sound burned through Trystin, and he frantically dropped his sensory perceptions to normal, but some of the buzzing and burning remained, enough that a residual burning gnawed at him.

With a deep breath, Trystin leaned back and closed his eyes. Acceleration or not, noise or not, he was exhausted, and most of the noise seemed to die away.

Out of a gray fog a spear of light flashed.

"Abomination of the Lord! . . ." A Soldier of the Lord pointed a laser at Trystin as he tried to scramble from the seat, even as he knew it was a dream.

He tried to shake his head, trying to swim out of the fatigue-induced nightmare, but his head did not want to move. Lances of light bracketed him.

"Doubter . . . how can you doubt the will of the Lord!" His hip burned, and so did his eyes—

"Please remain in your seats until docking is complete. Please remain in your seats until docking is complete."

Trystin jerked fully awake. The words had buzzing overtones that worried him. He was the one having the doubts, not the Revenants, and it shouldn't have been that way. As he shifted his weight, the bruised hip throbbed.

"They always say that," observed Trystin's seatmate.

"Probably because people don't stay in their seats."

"Wasn't like this years ago. People had better manners, and a smile for everyone."

"Why do you think it's changed?" Trystin asked, taking the handkerchief and wiping his forehead.

A soft *clunk* ran through the spaceplane.

"The Ecofreaks. It takes so much energy and so many resources to support the missions there. Look at this shuttle. It's old, like me." The other shrugged. "Something has to change."

"Docking is complete. You may leave the shuttle and claim your bags."

"It's begun to change, Brother," Trystin said. "God is the Lord of Love." He smiled. "If you'll excuse me, I'm on my way to an important Farewell."

"Oh . . . certainly."

"Thank you."

Trystin scurried forward and grabbed the light fabric bag from the racks and rushed through the lock. So far, it looked as though the Revenants hadn't put together his death and resurrection—at least no one but Orr had, and the agent probably hadn't been found yet.

Trystin worried his lip. What had Orr been trying to tell him? Had the agent wanted him to escape? Why? He kept walking.

The Orum orbit station still smelled like a mixture of plastic, metal, warm oil, ozone, and people. Trystin added one more smell—fear—his. He just hoped it weren't as apparent to others as to him as he headed toward the tube slide to the upper level where the Braha transport waited.

At the top of the tube, he waited behind a thin mid-aged sister with heavy gold rings on her fingers. The Soldier of the Lord handed her back her card and databloc, and nodded. "Next."

Trystin put his bag on the belt, and then slid his keycard and ID across the counter. Both went into a console that winked green. The Soldier handed them back to Trystin. "Next."

Trystin walked through the gate and then picked up his bag and headed toward alpha four, where the Braha transport was scheduled to be loading.

About a dozen people walked or sat in the hard plastic chairs along the corridor wall. Trystin was grateful for the station's half-gravity, and for the nap on the shuttle, but he still felt light-headed and hot. Was he getting sick?

He forced himself to concentrate until he sat in one of the vacant plastic chairs, waiting for the announcement to board the shuttle. When he closed his eyes, red flashes seemed to cross the inside of his lids. If he left his eyes open, they burned.

He alternated opening and closing his eyes while he waited for the boarding announcement to come—hoping it would before anyone came looking for him. He half wondered if anyone cared. Then he shook his head. Orr had certainly cared . . . yet he hadn't brought a whole crew of agents with him, and the scene outside the Temple had indicated that Orr certainly could have.

"We are now ready to board the Braha transport. You are limited to three bags. Please carry them with you and give them to the crewman in the baggage section of the transport. Board through the lock marked alpha four. Alpha four for the Braha transport."

Trystin stood and ended up in the middle of the two dozen souls waiting outside the lock tube for the attendant to reread their keycards. Then, with the others, he filed down the lock tube to the transport heading to Braha.

"You're traveling light," observed a man not much older than Trystin.

"Going to a Farewell and then where I've been called."

The other nodded, handed two large bags to the crewman, and walked forward. Trystin handed over his single light bag.

"I wish we got more of these," said the crewman with a smile.

"I wish I had more to put in it," countered Trystin. He turned and walked forward into the cramped passenger compartment. As on the transport he had taken on his way to Orum, the seats were clean, but old, with scratches in the heavy plastic parts polished over.

Trystin sank into a seat and waited, trying to ignore the burning and buzzings that spread from his implant through his entire body, still trying to puzzle out Orr's game . . . and the role the Farhkans had played. It almost seemed as if Orr had wanted him to succeed after the mess in the Temple, yet Orr had been ready to drag him in for interrogation beforehand.

What did the Farhkans get out of it all? One assassination more or less couldn't have concerned Rhule Ghere in the slightest. Yet the Farhkan had claimed he was Trystin's patron, whatever that meant.

Trystin had played prophet for a religion he didn't believe in, helped by an alien who'd stolen the open-weave net keys without ever offering the slightest guidance—except . . . had the Farhkans played with his mind? Could they do that?

He winced, and the buzzing in his head got even worse, and, again, he struggled with pure physical pain, almost a relief after the moral questions.

69

"Can violence and the use of force to effect change upon the universe be left to the young? Do they see what was, what is, and what might yet be? Have they suffered, watched evil fall upon the good, or good upon the evil?

"Or should the burden of violence be left to those who can bear it most lightly—upon those who have closed their minds or their feelings? How then can they understand the suffering that they must inflict?

"Should the burden of force be laid upon the short-lived, who will not see the consequences of their actions? How can they dispense force with compassion if they can escape the knowledge of what they do? . . .

"The greater the force brought to bear, the older and wiser must be the entity who wields it. Wisdom allows sorrow. Age allows experience, and knowledge reinforces wisdom and experience. . . .

"Those who would bear the burden of force must be those who are strong and do not seek it, for those who seek force would misuse it, and those who are weak would shy from what they must do. . . ."

Findings of the Colloquy
[Translated from the Farhkan]
1227 E.N.P.

70

 Ignoring the faint buzzing that had hovered in and around him since well before the translation from the Jerush system to the Braha system, Trystin blotted his forehead with the handkerchief that had become almost as damp as the sodden white shirt under his white suit coat. Sitting more than three hours in the poorly ventilated transport had left all the passengers looking wilted.

He blotted his forehead again, wondering how much longer before the transport would dock at Braha station. A flicker in the ship's system tingled through his implant, and the burning through his nerves intensified fractionally, then dropped. Was that part of the penalty for becoming an assassin, or just an inadvertent by-product? Assassin . . . he still didn't like the term, but he'd done it, and whether Jynckla had been an admiral or not, killing him in the Temple had been different than in a perimeter battle. Trystin just hoped his modifications had made it worth more than a meaningless assassination.

The minute fluctuation in the artificial gravity signified some power change, hopefully the final deceleration into the station. Trystin took a deep breath. Since messages had to be carried between systems, it looked as though he actually had a good chance to escape—unless a fast courier were right behind the transport.

Once more he blotted his face as the ship's net revealed

the approach to the orbit station. He massaged his forehead in an effort to reduce the throbbing in his temples.

The transport shivered with a faint *thump,* and Trystin straightened in his seat.

"We have docked at Braha station. Before leaving your seat, please collect your belongings. Then move to the baggage bay behind the rear of the cabin to claim your bags before leaving the transport. Please make sure you have all your belongings."

Trystin unfastened the harness and eased to his feet, nodding politely at the middle-aged Revenant in the seat across the aisle. He walked stiffly back to the baggage bay, arriving behind two other men. As they took their bags, Trystin grabbed his single bag and lifted it off the rails. He staggered when he went through the lock into full station gravity, but caught himself. His hip throbbed from the sudden lurch.

"Careful there, ser."

"Thank you." Trystin forced himself erect. Pursuit or not, there were limits to how far he could push himself. He needed something to eat, something to drink, or he wasn't going to have the energy to do anything, or the ability to think through anything.

He dragged himself toward the main corridor.

The Eatery wasn't much more than four tables and a counter dispensing rehydrated food and juices, but Trystin didn't care as he leaned against the counter.

"The pasta, please."

"Rough trip, Brother? What do you want to drink?"

"Some limeade and some water. It was hot. It seems like it gets hotter every time."

"That's what a lot of people say. Sit down. I'll call you."

Trystin slumped into a plastic chair at a plastic table bolted to the plastic-covered station deck. In the corridor outside, a string of people walked briskly by, intermittently, some in uniform, others in shipsuits. A few men wore white suits, and a few women wore checked dresses.

"Pasta's ready."

Trystin stood and handed over the credit strip.

"That'll be fifteen."

He winced at the cost, not that it mattered in a way.

"Everything has to come up by shuttle, Brother."

"I know, but—"

"You've got to eat." The counterman smiled sympathetically. "You get to leave. I'm here all the time. This is my off-shift job. Takes two to make ends meet, these days."

"Sorry." Trystin had been hearing that a lot.

"We all do what we have to."

"Right." Trystin juggled the squarish plate and the two plastic tumblers over to the small table and began to eat. The pasta had a consistency somewhere between soggy paper and rubber eggs, with a taste combining the best of each. The sauce tasted like glue flavored with lemonade. Trystin ate it all, and drank all of the bitter limeade and the large glass of water.

The worst of the headache began to subside even before he finished the pasta, but the burning that ran from the implant throughout his body only receded to a tingling. Maybe he just needed rest—and quiet—but it was going to be a while before he got that.

He sat for a few minutes after he finished, but only for a few minutes. Then he picked up his bag and headed for beta three and the *Paquawrat*. The courier/trader was supposed to be waiting. He hoped it was. He was tired, and it probably wouldn't be too long before a courier arrived at the station with a pickup order for Wyllum Hyriss, or anyone looking like him.

He shifted the bag from his right hand to his left and kept walking along the gently curved corridor.

Beta three seemed deserted. The seals across the lock door remained intact. Trystin glanced in both directions and walked straight down to the lock, using the implant to open the ship's lock.

Crack!

The seals splintered as the lock opened partway.

Trystin stepped up to the lock, then paused and turned as a faint vibration, barely sensed above the renewed burning and static from the implant, warned him.

"What are you doing there, Brother?" The Security Guard lumbered toward Trystin, the stun rifle pointed in his general direction.

"Nothing. Came down here to find a friend. . . ." Trystin held up his hands. He should have guessed the Revenants might have had at least a cursory watch on the *Paquawrat*. "I was standing here. I was just standing here. See?" He pointed toward the partly open lock door. "It just opened."

The guard's eyes flicked toward the door.

"Peace be with you." Trystin accelerated and used his speed to rip the rifle out of the guard's hands and to turn it on the guard.

Thrum.

His arms burned as he set the rifle beside the unconscious guard. But he had no time to waste as he cranked open the lock door manually, just wide enough to slip inside. His guts wrenched upward as he left the station gravity and entered the almost null gee of the ship.

He ignored the stale air and his tendency to float away from the lock mechanism, but he didn't know how long before the alarms would bring another set of guards or soldiers running. So he jammed his feet under the hold bar and kept cranking. Then he slammed the manual locks in place and float-stumbled into the cockpit, where he used the remaining power in the accumulators to start the fusactor.

Once the fusactor was running, he put on minimal gravity and hurried back to the lock to release the mechanical holdtights. That left the ship held to the station only through the magnetic holdtights.

He stood behind the pilot's couch and stripped off the still damp and smelly white suit, shirt, and Revenant undergarments, even while he used the implant to begin the departure checklist. After pulling on dry undergarments and a dry shipsuit, he dropped into the pilot's couch and completed the checklist.

His headache had returned—not the best of signs—but he needed the speed and reflexes. He checked the representational screen and the ship's position.

Once everything seemed in the green, he pulsed the station. He might as well try to do it openly. He called up the canned flight profile that outlined the flight from Braha to Alundill.

"Braha Control, this is Hyndji ship *Paquawrat*. Request clearance for departure this time."

"Hyndji ship *Paquawrat,* this is Braha Control. Request flight profile. Interrogative flight profile."

"Braha Control, *Paquawrat,* profile follows." Trystin pulsed the profile to the station control, then demagnetized the holdtights, watching the screens. Even without thrusters, the ship should slowly begin to separate from the station.

"Roger, *Paquawrat*. Request pilot clearance code."

Trystin mentally fumbled with Svenson's pilot code, then answered, "Braha Control, pilot number is S-S, that is Sierra, Sierra, one, four, five, four, two, Cat. Sierra, Sierra, one, four five, four, two, Cat." He wiped his forehead, not liking the pilot number request. While it wasn't that untoward, his briefing materials indicated that number requests were seldom made for outbound vessels, and Svenson was only on file as a backup, which could raise other flags.

"*Paquawrat,* please stand by."

Mental alarms went off, and Trystin gave the attitude jets and the thrusters the faintest of pulses to orient the ship clear of the station and perpendicular to the system's ecliptic.

"Hyndji ship *Paquawrat,* this is Braha Control, do you read? Do you read? Request your intentions this time."

"Braha Control, this is Hyndji ship *Paquawrat*. Awaiting clearance this time. Awaiting clearance this time." Trystin watched the gentle separation from the station, hoping his minimal single-time use of thrusters and jets had gone unnoticed and that he would have adequate clearance before Braha Control realized what he was doing.

"Roger, *Paquawrat*. Request you stand by."

"Roger, Braha Control." Trystin could sense almost twenty meters had opened between the *Paquawrat* and the station.

"*Paquawrat,* request you return to beta three this time."

"Braha Control," stalled Trystin, "Hyndji ship *Paquawrat* berthed at beta three." The separation was now thirty meters and had to be obvious to Braha Control.

"*Paquawrat,* request your immediate return to beta three this time. You are not cleared for departure. I say again. You are not cleared for departure."

"Roger, Braha Control, proceeding with departure this time." Trystin pushed the thrusters up to five percent—close to the safe limit so near the station—and the *Paquawrat* began to accelerate away from the system.

"Hyndji ship *Paquawrat,* return to Braha station immediately. Return to Braha station immediately."

"Braha Control, say again your last. Please say again your last." The trader continued to move away from the station, and Trystin eased in more power, trying to keep the thrust as high as possible without bringing the cutting range of the thrusters close to the station.

"*Paquawrat,* return to Braha station. If you do not return, you will be fired upon. If you do not return, you will be fired upon."

Trystin upped the thrust to thirty percent, waited, and then went to eighty percent. He scanned the screens, especially the EDI indicators, for signs of Revenant warships.

The EDI remained unchanged, and he added full thrust through the implant, again massaging his head at the burning that resulted.

Three minutes passed, then five, and Trystin waited as the *Paquawrat* barreled toward the upper fringe of Braha system perpendicular to the ecliptic. No matter where the Revenant ships were, no matter how fast, they couldn't get an angle on the *Paquawrat.* It would be a stern chase all the way.

Trystin didn't want to think about the translation error he was going to pile up, not at the moment.

Two points of light flared on the EDI—bright blue-white—and dotted tracks flared from off the fifth planet.

"Scouts," he muttered to himself, as he checked their speed. Both were already running at slightly over a hundred-percent normal flank speed.

"Hyndji ship *Paquawrat,* this is Braha Control, do you read? Do you read? This is your last warning. Request you return to Braha station. If you return, you will not be fired upon. I say again, if you return you will not be fired upon."

Great to be so popular, reflected Trystin. Still . . . maybe—just maybe—his plan had worked. There were only two scouts on his tail, and that was standard for an unidentified commercial ship. Then again, they didn't need more than two for an unarmed ship, although they wouldn't have known that the shields were military strength.

His body burned almost continually now—clearly the result of overuse of his implant and high reflex and metabolic rates.

The EDI traces showed the steady closure of the scouts. Trystin checked the dust density. Still too high for translation, but thinning rapidly.

Another ten minutes passed, and the two Revenant ships were closing, even as the *Paquawrat* had begun to warp the time envelope, ever so slightly.

There were no further transmissions from the Revenants, just the steady closure of the two scouts.

Trystin's thoughts seemed crystal clear beyond the pain, yet he *knew* he wasn't thinking clearly. What would happen when he returned? If he returned? He recalculated the closure rates and plotted them against the dust density. Close—it would be close.

Too close. He upped the fusactor to one hundred ten percent and clicked off the time. Basically, he had five minutes at that level before he started to degrade the system, and he should have applied the additional acceleration earlier. The apparent clarity of his thoughts was a definite illusion.

The scouts inched closer on the representational screen;

the dust density edged downward; and the minutes passed.

After four minutes and fifty standard seconds of one-hundred-ten-percent power, Trystin dropped the fusactor output to one-hundred-percent normal rated maximum output.

The rate of closure had grown smaller. Had the Revenants strained their systems too much in the beginning?

If he did make it back, to what could he look forward? Would it be a suicide command in the Parvati system? Or a quiet disappearance? The subject of riots in Cambria every time he stepped outside? Would the Revenants launch some sort of all-out attack? Would he be the scapegoat for it? Had he jabbed at their religion too hard? Or would anyone care? His lips tightened as he thought about the key to the Temple. . . .

The dust density dropped to the point of allowing emergency translation. Trystin checked the ranges. The Revenants were still out of max torp range.

He kept calculating—range versus dust; dust versus range.

"Initiate translation sequence." Trystin pulsed the order to the system.

"Sequence initiating."

As he monitored the power buildup, another thought struck him. There had to be holos of him in the Temple, and the Service would want to know how he'd gotten there. He swallowed, and another spear of pain lanced through his skull. What could he do? Surprisingly, words flashed through his mind, old words. "There's a rumor. If you slew the ship and apply power just as you translate—it increases the translation error severalfold, maybe more."

Trystin applied full power to the thrusters, and thanked Ulteena, knowing he probably wouldn't see her again, or perhaps anyone he had known in the Coalition, and regretting that. He hadn't realized how much he would miss her, how very much. There was a lot he hadn't realized.

His fingers were shaking, and each computation seemed to take longer, and longer. Strings of equations danced along his fingers, and rings of light surrounded everything his eyes rested upon. Every movement of his head burned, and if he turned quickly his booted feet twitched.

Just before he pushed the translation stud, Trystin remembered to touch the false stud and flick the thruster tuning switch. He hoped it wouldn't be that critical with the translation error he was piling up. Then again, he was headed to Farhka, and who knew how they felt about time?

He slewed the *Paquawrat* and triggered translation . . .

. . . and black became white, and white black . . . and for that endless moment the ship was in translation, he was bathed in ecstasy, the pain gone, pleasure running through him with the black light.

Thud!

With the drop into real time, the haze of burning red pain returned—intensified—as the *Paquawrat* thrust through normal space outside Farhka . . . somewhere . . . somewhen.

With the blurriness of his vision, and the stabbing in his skull, focusing on even the representational screen was difficult, but necessary since the *Paquawrat* was high above the ecliptic and on an angled course away from Farhka that he had to correct, without dropping inside the orbit of the sixth planet.

"There . . ." *There . . . there . . . there . . .* His own words echoed inside his skull and ears, and his eyes watered. He closed them and felt as though he were twirling upside down. He opened his eyes, and knives of light stabbed through them.

Silently, slowly, he refocused his attention on the approach course to the outer Farhkan station. The briefing profile had cautioned against going inside the orbit of the sixth planet. At least the outer orbit station showed on the screens, almost like an energy beacon, and he aimed the *Paquawrat* toward that beacon.

Then he leaned back in the couch and tried not to see anything, nor to hear anything. Nor to think—not about the images of Soldiers of the Lord, nor an archbishop whose fault had been to be in the wrong place with the wrong name, nor Quentar who'd thought the only safe Revenant was a dead one, nor James who'd saved his neck more than once with his knowledge and never asked for acknowledgment, nor Ulteena, who'd taught him the value of anticipation and never asked. . . .

The accumulators hiccuped, and the hiccup jolted down his spine. Both feet twitched, and his boots thumped the cockpit floor.

He sighed, and his breath sounded like a hurricane whistling through his body. He tried to tamp down his sensitivity, but nothing happened. His breath still rumbled and whistled, and his feet twitched.

Slowly, he studied the system readouts. He had another two hours of torture before he reached the outer Farhkan station.

The time passed slowly, the red haze swelling and ebbing, his feet occasionally twitching, and each sound slashing at him. With his eyes open, the cockpit light as low as he dared leave it, his eyes burned. If he closed them, he seemed to whirl in space.

Periodically, he checked the ship, his position, and his progress. How much translation error he'd piled up he had no idea, because Farhkan systems didn't provide human-style comparators. He supposed the Farhkans could tell him.

Finally, after almost two hours, he straightened and transmitted. "Farhka Station one, this is Coalition ship *Paquawrat,* code name Holy Roller." Trystin took another deep breath. "Request approach clearance and lock assignment."

"Human ship, this is Farhka. Reason for your porting is what?"

"Request assistance . . . Coalition ship *Paquawrat,* code name Holy Roller, requesting refueling and assistance."

"Have you a patron? Please state the name of your patron."

Patron? What the hell was a patron? *Patron . . . patron . . . patron . . .*

Trystin closed his eyes and wished he had not as the cockpit seemed to whirl around him. Patron?

Ghere! He'd said "patron" twice, emphasizing it. Trystin opened his eyes and said the name slowly. "Rhule Ghere. Dr. Rhule Ghere."

A hissing sound carried through him, a sound with knife edges. Then there was silence. Trystin began to decelerate, calculating his own approach.

Five minutes passed . . . then ten.

"Human pilot, please state your name. Please state your name."

"Trystin Desoll. Trystin Desoll. Major, Coalition Service."

Another hissing rushed through him, knife-edged, and he stepped up the deceleration. His feet twitched, and his jaw developed a tic.

He slowed the ship more, noting the two Farhkan craft that bracketed him, unable to do more than watch, half wondering if even the return flight profile had been a setup to ensure he never got back. Escaped assassins were embarrassments, he suspected, again, too late.

"Human pilot Desoll, you are cleared to dock. Follow the energy beacon. Follow the visual green light. Follow the long audio signal on your emergency frequency."

"Thank you, Farhka. I have the green light. . . ." Trystin winced as the sounds overpowered him, and he waited for them to pass. "I have the beacon."

Edging the ship up to the small lock was agony. Even the signals from the magnetic holdtights slammed through his implant as they locked the ship to the Farhkan station's hull.

Holding on to the edge of the couch, then bracing himself on the bulkhead, he shuffled toward the lock. His fingers trembled, and his arms shivered as he opened the lock.

In the locking port stood four Farhkans. Two trained some sort of heavy weapons on Trystin.

Trystin stepped from the ship, and the heavier gravity clawed at him. He tottered there for a moment, the strange clean and musky smell of Farhkans around him, the strange weapons they did not need pointed at him, when he could scarcely even walk.

He wavered for only a long moment before the darkness reached out of his brain and smote him down.

71

 "Without a deity the universe is uncertain. But, once the deistic faiths have been analyzed, they provide no greater certainty, nor is there any verified evidence that deities per se have improved humanity or its institutions. Certainly, improvements have occurred, but those improvements have been accomplished in purely human fashion. These accomplishments have proved that people can bring greater certainty, greater goodness, greater understanding into the universe, and, while they may have been inspired by faith, those good people have done so without the physical help of a deity.

"Thus, it can be argued that the invention of a deity only serves as a pretext for human beings to believe in a set of values beyond those rooted merely in self. Yet, most societies in history have chastised those individuals who have attempted to acknowledge publicly that need for a set of values beyond those rooted merely in the individual's needs, or that a 'mere' human being could consider and develop such values. Thus, great truths have always been presented in the guise of divinely inspired guidance.

"Yet theologies exist which claim that men and women will be as gods, or equal with god, upon their physical death, and they have proved immensely popular and successful, despite the inherent contradiction. How, logically, can death transfigure a man or woman into a being that much superior to the one who lived on earth? Such a theology avoids the need to admit that individuals can develop and live by a moral code with 'higher' values, as well as the need to admit the effort required in doing so, by providing a deity with the wherewithal to accomplish a theological transmutation almost magically. . . .

"That is the greatest danger in theology and deities— that they create the impression that goodness cannot be created or maintained by mere humans without divine help. This allows all measure of excuses . . . and strange contortions to explain perfectly logical occurrences. . . ."

The Eco-Tech Dialogues
Prologue

72

 In the darkness, angels with knives of fire seared his flesh, peeled back his skull, and flayed him with whips of raw pain. Then they laid him upon an altar under a blazing sun and chuckled . . . chuckled . . . chuckled . . .

In the light, lashes of darkness froze his skin, stabbed through his thoughts, and . . . burned . . . burned . . . burned . . .

In the icy wastes of an unknown storm, he shivered as he burned, trying to explain without words while his words drifted unheard.

In the depths of an unknown ocean, he floated, not breathing, not drowning—just floating—while green-tusked whales hovered around his corpse. . . .

Trystin groaned, amazed that he could speak, and that the sound did not deafen him. Finally, hoping that the cockpit was not too much of a mess—or had he actually reached the Farhkan station?—he opened his eyes.

Nothing spectacular. He half lay, half reclined, in something that looked like a cross between a bed and a long reclining chair. He wore nothing, but a loose sheet was draped over him. The reclining chair/bed rested in a cubicle perhaps three meters on a side.

"Do not be alarmed. Someone will be with you soon." The words scrolled through his head.

Trystin grinned, despite the strange surroundings. For the first time in years, there was no underlying static, no buzzing, no pain associated with the implant. And he felt good. He sat up and let the silky sheet slide back to his waist. He looked thinner, with some loss of muscle mass, but not a lot. That had to be expected from lying around whatever it was that passed for a Farhkan hospital. He hoped it was a Farhkan hospital.

The door irised open, and two Farhkans in shimmering gray fatigues stepped into the room. One carried a square satchellike bag.

"Major Desoll?"

"Yes? You're Rhule Ghere, aren't you?"

"That is correct. This is Ruyalt Dhale. He is . . . a specialist."

"In aliens like me?"

"Yes." There was no humor in the response.

"I'd like to thank you both. I was in pretty bad shape."

"Yes." Ghere looked at Dhale. "You died. Neurosensory breakdown. It is said to be painful."

"I died? I don't feel dead."

"You are very alive." The second Farhkan's "voice" carried a tinge of what Trystin could only have termed humor. "You will be alive for a long time. Please be still for a moment."

Trystin remained still as Dhale opened the satchel and focused an odd-shaped instrument on him, then another, and another.

Finally, Dhale straightened, packed his instruments back into the satchel, looked at Ghere, and departed.

"You may wish to wash before you resume your normal coverings, although I can assure you that you have been kept scrupulously clean." Ghere pointed to a standard-looking door. "Those are human facilities, built for your use."

"Where are we?"

"You have remained on station one. That was more . . . expedient. I will wait outside. The main door will open as you near it."

"My clothes?"

"In the facilities room." Ghere walked out as silently and stolidly as he had walked in.

Trystin eased off the hospital recliner and padded to the facilities room. Hanging on oblong hangers on the wall were undergarments and the gray shipsuit and accessories—all spotlessly clean. There was also a huge gray towel next to a narrow shower.

After using the facilities, Trystin felt his face—clean-shaven. He showered and dressed quickly. Then he went to find Rhule Ghere.

Ghere, sitting in a large loungelike chair in a larger room outside the cubicle where Trystin had awakened, motioned to the other large chair. Trystin sat, feeling somewhat swallowed by the chair, and edged forward in it.

After a long moment of silence, Trystin said, "I don't know where to begin. I'd like to thank you again."

"You may not wish to."

"Why not?"

Ghere shifted his weight. "You died. We repaired you. But we could not repair you as you were. You have been on Farhka station for nearly two of your standard years."

Trystin swallowed. Then he asked, "I piled up some considerable translation error. Do you know how much?"

Ghere gave the impression of a shrug. "Not exactly. We did not know precisely . . ."

"Just generally," Trystin pressed.

"We calculated approximately thirteen of your years."

Fifteen years! Gone. Trystin's mind blanked for a moment, but Ghere continued.

". . . because of your participation in the study, I did

have your medical records. You are as close to what you were as was feasible to create you."

"Create me?"

"You are a partly regrown version of you. Your entire neural system had to be replaced. Your memories were stored and replaced. Some of them may seem hazy at times." Ghere's voice floated through Trystin's thoughts, almost as though unrolling on his mental screen, but more completely and more quickly. "Do you know why we were required to do so much?"

"No." Trystin did not speak, just let the thought flow.

"You should. In order to cope with the pressures of the Revenants' assaults, your people have used biotechnology, nanotechnology, and high technology to allow every officer in your Service to handle neural data loads beyond what one might call your design capacity." The mental equivalent of a chuckle followed. "Most have died young."

"What else could we have done? We don't have all those bodies. Over any length of time, no ecosystem will support that. The Great Die-off proved that, but the Revenants don't want to believe history."

"It is sad. Still . . . you have changed matters greatly . . . as you will find. . . ." Ghere projected a laugh into Trystin's thoughts. "For this we thank you."

"For what?" Trystin's lips tightened. "For being able to mess with my mind? To program me to get into the Revenants' Temple? What the hell else did you do to me?" He paused, then added, "And while you're at it, would you tell me why? Why, for god's sake?"

"You do not believe in god." Again, there was a semblance of a mental chuckle that ended quickly. "We did not program you, or exert any compulsion on you. Such compulsions are . . . unethical. They also do not work, because they restrict the one compelled. Such restrictions create failure."

"Fine. You didn't compel me. You sure set me up."

"We did not make you a pilot. We did not make your choice to become an Intelligence agent—"

"How did you know that?"

"In rebuilding neural systems, one learns much. Only Ruyalt Dhale and I know those things. No one else will know, and we do not lie."

The Farhkans didn't have to, Trystin thought bitterly. "So you gave me the keys to the Temple and asked enough questions to point me in the right direction and watched the fun? How many Service officers in Intelligence did it take before you got me?"

"One hundred and thirty-one officers over twenty years. There were but four who were given the Temple protocols, and you were the only one who could transcend his culture."

"The others?"

"None of them used the keys. They were executed."

Trystin shivered.

"How did you get to Orr?"

"Orr?" Ghere's mental voice revealed puzzlement.

"Never mind. So what was this great thing I was so fortunate to accomplish?"

"We would not use the term 'fortunate.' Would you?" Ghere offered another wry-feeling laugh.

"Sorry. Wrong word. You still didn't say why you did all this. Why did you give us technology? Why did you manipulate me? Why have you been following me around for two decades?"

A long silence followed the question.

Finally, Ghere answered, with long pauses between phrases, as though he had not rehearsed the exact answer, or as though he were groping for a simple way to explain something very complex to a child. At that, Trystin bristled even as he listened.

"Complex technology brings greater use of force. Unless a culture actively resists, force always attracts those less . . . ethical. Technology also allows greater . . . populace growth. Use of machines pushes most intelligences toward more . . . rigid . . . social controls. Rigidity creates greater conflicts, requiring more force. This fuels conflict, and conflicts are first turned toward other cultures."

"So why didn't you just bounce on the Revenants yourselves?"

"We did so," answered Ghere. "But alien intelligences are never accepted as valid, and more and more force would have been required—enough force to destroy the co-race you term Revenants. Force corrupts the user, and we could not afford that degree of corruption."

"Oh . . . you wanted to pawn off the corruption on us, on good old Trystin?"

"You would turn the destiny of your race over to us?" asked Ghere.

Put that way, Trystin didn't like it at all. "So why was I the fortunate one?"

"As I once feared, you have been unfortunate," Ghere admitted bluntly. "For that we are thankful. You have learned from that, and you will learn more. It is best you discover why we are thankful after you return to your people. They will be pleased to see you."

"To lynch me?" What had happened after he'd left the Jerush system? Ghere had kept avoiding an answer to that question.

"No. You are . . . a figure of some . . . note. We do not deceive. We are thieves, Major, but not liars. Now, you must go." There was a finality to Ghere's thought that discouraged further inquiry there.

"You still haven't answered my questions, and you've done something to my implant."

"Once you return to your people, you will know enough to answer your own questions. You no longer need the implant, although it remains in place. We integrated those facilities into your system." Ghere offered a smile. "Your Service will doubtless deactivate the implant at some point, but that will not change you. Not now. Not ever. Also, to ensure that you did regenerate properly, we had to make some other modifications."

"Such as?" Trystin looked at his hands. They looked normal, except his vision seemed preternaturally clear.

"You will age slowly, if at all."

Trystin glanced at Ghere, looking over the calm, square,

and impassive face. "Why did you decide I was worthy of the . . . this blessing?"

"I did not make that decision alone. We . . . all the doctors . . . felt that such a decision would be beneficial . . . and might repay you."

"Repay me? For being an assassin of other humans? For being your tool?"

"You killed many before, to little effect. What you have done this time has been of great benefit."

"To whom? The great Farhkan empire?"

"You need not be so bitter. You have done well, as you will discover, for your own race. You have also helped our understanding of your race greatly, and that will benefit us all."

Trystin took a deep breath, the calm certainty of the Farhkan flooding over him. "Great. You make me sound like I'm worthy of something . . . and you won't tell me what. And you still haven't really answered my questions."

"I cannot answer those questions. You must." Ghere pursed those too-thin lips. "As for worthy . . . yes, you are worthy. In the sense that a doctor is worthy to bear suffering, or an . . . But it is not a blessing. In the closest analogue from Farhkan, the word might translate as 'Kyrsesuffer.' It is better translated as a curse, and those of our people to whom it is offered accept it reluctantly. Some refuse."

"Refuse the gift of never growing old?" Trystin was still angry at the evasions.

Ghere laughed, a sharp bark that even Trystin did not hear as humor. "Refuse the gift of seeing people make the same mistakes generation after generation? Refuse the gift of becoming more and more distant from those around you as you understand the fragility of life, and the joy created by that fragility—a joy that will become more foreign to you with each decade?"

Trystin looked at his hands again.

"As you see more, you will become wiser. As you become wiser, you must risk more and more to persuade others that you are not aloof, that you are not a person apart. And that will cause them both to respect you and fear you. More."

The silence drew out. Finally, Trystin threw another question at the Farhkan. "Why did you keep questioning me about theft?"

"You know the answer. Your species seeks absolutes."

And he did. Theft was not the question. They had badgered Ulteena about mathematics, and others about some aspect of their beliefs—all absolutes. What they had pushed him to see was that life offered no absolutes, no hard truths. While many speculated about that simple observation, the Farhkans had prodded and pushed. Why?

Trystin began to speak, slowly. "The only absolute truth is change, and death is the only way to stop change. Life is a series of judgments on changing situations, and no ideal, no belief fits every solution. Yet humans need to believe in something beyond themselves. Perhaps all intelligences do. If we do not act on higher motivations, then we can justify any action, no matter how horrible, as necessary for our survival. We are endlessly caught between the need for high moral absolutes—which will fail enough that any absolute can be demonstrated as false—and our tendency for individual judgments to degenerate into self-gratifying and unethical narcissism. Trying to force absolutes on others results in death and destruction, yet failing to act beyond one's self also leads to death and destruction, generally a lot sooner."

"That is true, and simple. Yet your species still fails to accept that." Ghere stood. "It is time to go."

"Go? Where?"

"You requested refueling and assistance. We have provided that." Again, the hard humorless bark followed the unspoken words. "Now you must return to your people. Your ship is ready."

Wordlessly, Trystin followed the Farhkan along the wide and nearly empty corridors of the station, a station that felt more ancient, much more ancient than the Temple on

Orum or even the crystal canyons of the Dhellicor Gorge or the seaswept Cliffs of Cambria. How long had the station been there? How old were the Farhkans?

"Old enough to know better, and young enough to hope." The words bore humor and sadness as they ran through his head.

Ghere paused outside the open lock to the *Paquawrat*. "A safe trip to you, Major Desoll."

"Thank you . . . again."

"Do not thank me." Ghere nodded and stood silently.

"All right. I won't. But I appreciate being alive."

"That is good. May it always be so."

After another long silence, Trystin slipped through the open lock. The ship was spotless, certainly not the way he had left it, and held the musky clean odor of Farhkans.

Trystin stepped back, using his implant to close the door as he slipped into the tiny cockpit. Except . . . was it the implant? Could he believe Ghere? Or worse, how could he fail to believe the alien?

After checking through the ship, he strapped into the couch and began the checklist, still amazed at the clarity and speed with which he interfaced with the ship's net. Almost no time seemed to have passed when he pulsed the station.

"Farhka Station, this is Coalition ship *Paquawrat*. Requesting departure instructions."

"Coalition ship *Paquawrat*, this is Farhka. Are you ready to depart?"

Even through the direct-feed, the alienness of the words came through as silver-edged, shining, and impossibly distant.

"Ready to depart." As ready as you are.

Beyond the hull, he could feel the cold light of the stars.

73

As the *Paquawrat* slipped out of translation and dropped into the outskirts of the Chevel system, Trystin scanned the EDI once, then again. After checking the limited number of drives and ships registering, he checked a third time.

Then he fingered his chin for a moment before directing the *Paquawrat* in-system toward Chevel Beta, absently triggered the temporal comparators to determine his specific translation error. Although Ghere had indicated the initial error was on the magnitude of thirteen years, since the Farhkans had no such system, or not one adapted for human use, he had no idea exactly how much translation error he had piled up along the way, in addition to the two years he'd spent being "rebuilt."

He checked the EDI again, but nothing had changed from the first scan. There also seemed to be no EDI activity around Chevel Beta, strange indeed for the principal training facility it had been when he had left. Had there been that much change?

Cling!

With the sound of the comparators, he called up the numbers and swallowed. Both Ghere—and Ulteena—had been right. The time since he had left Braha totaled fifteen years, seven months, five days, thirteen hours, and twenty-one minutes. Slewing a ship at the moment of translation had definitely compounded the translation error. Somehow the numbers seemed more real on the comparator than they had when "spoken" by Ghere.

He did shake his head, more than once, as the *Paquawrat* arrowed into Chevel system. The drives he caught on the EDI were greenish, not blue. So the Coalition still held the system. Had the Revenants been defeated? Or had the war moved elsewhere?

Finally, after another deep breath, he pulsed off his message. "Chevel Control, this is Coalition ship *Paquawrat,* code name Holy Roller one. Holy Roller one."

Only static greeted his effort. He switched to the universal frequency and repeated the message.

"Unidentified craft, say again."

"I say again, this is Coalition ship *Paquawrat,* code name Holy Roller one. Holy Roller one. Estimated translation and envelope error is approximately one five years."

A long period of relative silence followed, punctuated only by static. Finally, an answer came.

"Holy Roller one, request authentication red."

Trystin called up the authentication tables, trying not to sigh, then pulsed off the codes, wondering why there seemed to be such consternation. Yes, he'd had compounded translation error and time out for medical rebuilding, totaling, if the comparators were correct, more than fifteen years, but a fifteen-year error wasn't exactly unheard of for Intelligence missions with multiple translations, especially through rev systems.

"Authentication red follows . . ."

"Holy Roller one . . . cleared to epsilon area, orbit station, Chevel Alpha. Chevel Alpha."

Trystin had caught the surprise in the voice. Why the surprise? Had translation error been eliminated? That was certainly possible. And Chevel Alpha? What had happened at Beta?

He checked the EDI again. The ships in Chevel system were definitely Coalition ships, but there were no traces where Beta had been. None. A Revenant attack?

Finally, Chevel Alpha loomed up even in the short-range screens.

"Chevel Control, this is Holy Roller one, ready to commence approach."

"Holy Roller one, you are cleared to epsilon one. Epsilon one."

"Stet. Commencing approach to epsilon one this time."

The new/improved implant made the approach like glass, and Trystin slid the *Paquawrat* into the lock with barely a measurable impact.

He applied the magnetic holdtights, and pulsed control. "Holy Roller locked at epsilon one. Shutting down this time."

"Cleared to shutdown . . . smooth approach."

"Thank you."

Trystin unstrapped, checked through the ship, and then triggered the lock.

A short black-haired major waited at the lock, with two armed guards behind him.

"Ser!" The major snapped a salute at Trystin.

Trystin, puzzled as he was, returned it, even though he wasn't in uniform, just a shipsuit. He realized he could sense the entire station's net, even read the protocols behind the net. At that he frowned. He didn't recall that kind of clarity before. What else had the Farhkans done to him?

As they cleared the lock tube and entered the main corridor, Trystin tried not to gape. Behind the roped-off area stood at least two dozen service personnel, and Trystin could hear the murmurs without even raising his sensitivity.

". . . tall bastard . . . not in uniform . . ."

". . . fifteen years they say . . . big hero before that . . ."

". . . know who he was?"

"Commander wouldn't say . . ."

The guards glanced at the small crowd, then at Trystin, but the major kept walking, leading Trystin to a private lift shaft. What had they let out about him? A big hero?

"All the way to the top, ser." The major stepped into the polarized-gravity shaft.

Trystin swung on and off after the major.

After exiting the shaft, they walked another thirty meters to a heavy door with the words printed in gold beside it—Station Commander.

"Go on in, ser. You're expected."

The two guards took up positions flanking the door.

"Thank you, Major," Trystin said.

"Yes, ser."

With a look at the door, Trystin slowly touched it and entered.

Standing by the console was a trim commander with dark hair lightly streaked with gray and a young face. "You're God, you know? Or the closest thing to Him."

"God? All I was trying to do was shake some sense into them." Trystin smiled as he studied the trim and still athletic-looking woman. The name on the uniform confirmed what he'd hoped, almost expected. She'd anticipated everything. He wanted to grin, to hug her, but fear and formality held him. Too many years lay between them, and he didn't know if she felt the same way he did, or if she'd found someone else. Fifteen years was a long time for love barely expressed. "God? From a faked death?"

"You underestimated the power of religion. You became the Prophet returned." Ulteena Freyer laughed. "Did you really think they'd give up their faith? Rather than give up their faith, they made your mission part of it—a very important part." She smiled warmly at him. "Please take a seat."

"I was trying to foment a little dissension." He paused. "No, that's too flippant. How about trying to make the system less warlike—injecting a little love?" He snorted. "Through violence, of course, like all religious reformers." He wondered how much Ulteena knew, and how much he should reveal.

"Dissension? They're more unified than ever, these days." She paused. "You did bring more 'love,' as you put it, into their culture, and they are, thanks also to you, more peaceful."

"Me?" Trystin shook his head and sat down beside the low table on which rested a tray containing tea and breads. "That's hard to believe." He moistened his lips. Ghere had said he had done well, but he hadn't wanted to believe the alien. Was that because he couldn't believe anything good could come from a dressed-up assassination? His eyes crossed to Ulteena. She didn't look fifteen years older—a few perhaps, but not fifteen.

"You'd better get used to it. You're part of history now."

Part of history? He looked at the worn carpet on the station floor and then back at Ulteena. Competent as she appeared, he could sense a vulnerability. Strange that he'd never seen it before. "I'm glad to see you survived the *Mishima*. Very glad," he added, afraid to say more.

"So am I. I'm also glad you didn't start in on the commander business, especially since commanders take second seat to prophets these days. Anyway, you're a full commander too, even if you didn't know it."

"A recent promotion?"

"Hardly. Not too recent."

"Why don't you tell me what happened?"

Ulteena Freyer shook her head. "We need to get the formalities out of the way. You tell me what you did and why, first, before . . . Please do . . ." She gestured to the tray. "Feel free to have some. Oh . . ." She rattled off a code.

Trystin smiled. "So you're my debriefing officer?"

"They wanted you to be comfortable, and I'm about the only one left that you knew. That may be why they kept me around. Please have some tea." She settled into the seat across the low table from him.

The only one? Trystin felt very alone, and his eyes rested on Ulteena for a long moment before he spoke. "Thank you. I will." He took a deep breath. "It sounds simple, but it wasn't. I just asked one question—what earthly good a plain assassination of an admiral and archbishop would do. I couldn't see that it would do anything. I also didn't see that returning without doing something would be terribly good for my health, especially with my heritage."

Ulteena nodded.

"So . . ." Trystin talked for a good ten minutes. He attributed his success in "partially" subverting the Temple system to training from his father, trying to avoid blatant lies. He only mentioned the Farhkans as his medical saviors, doubting that the all-too-instinctive human revulsion for the immortals had subsided much in so comparatively few years. "In the end, they patched me up and sent me packing. I never saw more than one room and a long corridor, and a shower. I didn't even know the exact amount of the translation error until I reached Chevel." He spread his hands. "Now . . . what happened?"

"We don't know all of it. Of course, we found out about the business in the Temple, but that wasn't all that hard to find out given your growing importance as a key Revenant religious figure. Then came all the rewriting of Scripture, very extensive, I might add, and we managed to get bootleg holos of you. It took more snooping—years really— to discover that your ship did manage to reach translation, because that was something someone in the rev security operation wanted to keep very quiet. . . ."

Orr, thought Trystin. He wanted me to be the Prophet. The crazy Revenant actually wanted that.

". . . we thought you might be coming back, and we alerted the Farhkans, but no one was certain until the Farhkans sent a courier more than a year ago indicating that you had been injured and required extensive medical care. That was when I got extended and transferred here."

Trystin nodded.

"Thankfully, things have been relatively dull for the past few years."

"What really happened?" Trystin asked again, finally pouring a cup of tea for himself and for Ulteena.

"I told you. You're the Prophet returned."

Trystin shook his head. "It happened, and I tried to plan it out, but once it happens it's still hard to believe that one incident can change a whole religion."

"It can if the theocracy in charge wants it to." Ulteena smiled. "Look. The Revenants—'rev' is out these days, by the way, and we have full diplomatic relations—have in effect said that they've changed, that the Prophet has revealed the new truth, and that's just the way it is. They don't want to know about you, and, with the improvements here, no one in HQ has the slightest interest in upsetting the Revenant leadership. We were hurting too badly, as you know, and so were the Revenants—"

"I saw that. Everything was quietly getting shabby. Too few returnees. Too many patriarchs with younger and younger wives. Young women desperate for any returnee."

"You learned a lot in a short time." Ulteena raised her eyebrows. "As I was saying, the Revenants really wanted a way out of the endless missions. So the appearance of a Prophet of love gave them an out. And they took it. Now they have real live holo shots of your self-sacrifice in the Temple, and interviews with people who saw your already healing hands after 'the Temple was rebuilt.' " Ulteena gave him a wry smile. "Let's see . . . 'another will come to sit at the left hand of the Father.' The one I liked was 'how can you bring the word of the Lord to your neighbor when you kill that neighbor before you come close enough to speak?' "

Trystin groaned.

"I'm glad you thought those words out—or you were truly inspired."

"Mostly I based it on their Scripture, the stuff I had to learn . . . and I plagiarized."

"Inspired plagiarism." Ulteena took a long sip from the cup. "You did look inspiring in that white suit, but I'm glad you didn't wear it here. Are the suits in the ship?"

"Yes. Why?"

"Well . . . we could send them back to Wystuh as genuine relics of the Prophet." She gave a warm, almost impish smile at Trystin's open mouth. "We wouldn't. The suits will vanish. It's better that way. Then Headquarters can breathe a sigh of relief."

"Everything is wonderful now?"

Ulteena snorted. "Nothing is ever wonderful. We granted them the right to send a few hundred peaceful, Book-toting missionaries to the Coalition every year. They agreed to stop sending troids, but we have to let them meet the last ones en route, and so far that's worked all right. We gave them the rights to the Vyncette system, and they're planoforming for all it's worth, and we're selling them technology. There are skirmishes over unclaimed outer systems, and we and they have lost a few ships through 'accidents,' but it's much better than the mess we had before you left. We've also gotten the rights to ship technology to

their home systems, but we have to have Revenant part-
ners. In short, it's an unholy muddled mess—but we're not
destroying each other."

"You look good."

"Remarkably well preserved? Almost nine years of
translation and time-dilation error help." She laughed.

"You don't look even a mere six years older."

"You're gallant, but I read a mirror as well as a screen,
and I don't look nearly so well-preserved as you."

"Farhkan surgery and translation errors." He lifted the
plate of cakes to her. "So what do I do? Disappear?"

"You don't have to. No one knows that Commander
Desoll was the Prophet. I've got your uniforms." She ap-
praised him. "You'll certainly still fit in them. You change
before you leave the office. You take early retirement with
the incredible compound retirement you earned and deserve, and you use that and that trust you set up—we know
everything—to grow flowers, teach, do anything you
want." She shrugged. "And keep your mouth shut."

"Or I disappear?"

"That could happen, but most probably the Coalition
would just brand you as harmless and mentally unhinged
by excessive translation—a poor sad veteran."

"And if I persisted—an institution?"

"Probably . . . but what would be the point? To prove
the hypocrisy of religion when every thinking individual
understands that hypocrisy and when those who don't
think wouldn't ever understand?"

Trystin nodded slowly. Ulteena had always made sense.
"What about you?"

"I grow old in the Service—if they let me."

"Maybe you should retire?"

"Is that a proposition?"

"Right now it's a suggestion. I'm in no shape to make
propositions . . . and I don't know . . . where you . . . I'm
still in shock."

"Good. Formalities first. Always first," she added sardonically. "You need to change into your uniform. I took
the liberty of adding all your combat decorations, plus the

full commander's silver triangles. You'll look impressive. You do have one last job before you head to Cambria."

"What?"

"Just parade around the station in full dress uniform and talk a little about the old days and the Maran battles. If anyone asks you about what you were doing, just smile and shake your head. Add a few words about how high-speed angular translations add up to fifteen years in a hurry. That's it. Then we'll send you home on a fast courier."

"That's it?"

"That's it. Disappointing, isn't it? Your uniform is in the adjoining room. I won't peek." She smiled. "In fact, I'll be out in the corridor laying some groundwork." The commander stood.

So did Trystin, watching as she left, enjoying the sight of her, realizing he had missed her—and not known how much he had. He shook his head slowly, and took a deep breath. So he wasn't done yet?

Would he ever be done? Not if Rhule Ghere was right.

He looked at the door, but Ulteena was gone. Once again, the important things had gotten lost in the details—Ulteena was important, and he hadn't even told her, and, with her reluctance, it was up to him, if she ever let him get close enough.

74

 "Not always will the Lord be at your left hand, or your right. I was here to save a child, but I will not always be with you."

"All are children and friends under the Lord and the Prophet, for the Lord is our Father. And all who share His bounty should be His children. For when one has seen the endless stars in His mansions, then one must realize how mighty is all creation. . . ."

"I am what I am. The Lord has seen what I have seen, and I have seen brothers and sisters killing each other. The Lord has said to bring His word to those who do not believe, yet how can someone who is dead hear the word of the Lord? Even Toren the Prophet wrote 'do not say, better my cousin than my neighbor, for all men and women are neighbors in the eyes of the Lord.' "

"The Lord has His own plans for you and for me; we are to be molded for His use, whether we will or not."

"Does a name mean that it is so? Does calling a knife a lily make it one? Arguments are but words, and the logic of the scholars often bears little truth, only fine structure, like a well-built palace of sin."

"Be of good courage, and deny me not, for what will be is the will of the Lord. Cast down this Temple, and the Lord will rebuild it, almost before your eyes."

"You know the Lord, and the Lord knows you in your hearts. Judge not, lest you be judged, and yet, I say unto you, even as He will raise this Temple in less than three days, yes, even in the quickness of time, will He also give me for you, for someone must speak for you, you who would not speak for love. For you, someone must speak. For you, someone must offer forgiveness. Someone must atone for you—both now and in the fullness of time."

"I am what I am. I claim nothing. All too often men claim. What matters a claim to the Lord? You have claimed you do the will of the Lord when you slaughter others. An older prophet said to consider the beam in your own eye before the mote in your brother's."

"Those who seek to destroy with fire can themselves be destroyed by fire. Destruction of those who could be brothers and sisters is not a demonstration of love. And the Lord has always been a God of Love."

"I was sent to deliver a message. The Lord does not beg, but He will instruct. I have done what I was sent to do, and those who have eyes to see and ears to hear may learn more of the will of the Lord."

"I am as real as you. Is this arm not flesh? You saw the fire, did you not? The ashes, did you not? All men must burn, sooner or later. I have come to do what I was charged with, and now I must return. For a time, I will go as others do, and then I will return to my place in the Lord's mansions."

Most Quoted Excerpts
The Book of the Prophet
(Revised and Annotated)

75

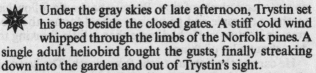 Under the gray skies of late afternoon, Trystin set his bags beside the closed gates. A stiff cold wind whipped through the limbs of the Norfolk pines. A single adult heliobird fought the gusts, finally streaking down into the garden and out of Trystin's sight.

He used the key from the Pilot's Trust to open the wrought-iron gates, wincing at the squeaking of the hinges. Then he picked up the two bags and walked a good dozen paces along the stones covered with the thinnest film of soil.

The sage still remained, if tattered, in the stone bed he had built more years ago than had passed for him. His eyes crossed the gardens, and he looked up the winding walk, pausing to study the bonsai cedar in the circular planter where the walk split around it. The cedar had grown—far too much—even though the limbs were perhaps only twenty centimeters out of place from when he had last visited the house.

But the symmetry was wrong, somehow. Were there still pruning shears in the garden shed? Time to prune? He would have that, too much time to prune and think. He had decided to say more to Ulteena before he had left Chevel Alpha, but she had disappeared, and no one could tell him where. He'd left a note with his address, and a comment that he wasn't below begging.

Now, he wondered if it had been too flippant . . . but it was as though she were embarrassed that she'd ever confessed to caring. He took a deep breath. If the note didn't work, he did have the time and funds to find her—if she were interested in a retired commander and prophet—and he would ask her. He grinned. After all, they were both commanders now.

His eyes dropped to the dull stones of the walk, and the smile disappeared. They had always been polished before, as a family custom, often for disciplinary reasons, but the professional gardeners hired by the Pilot's Trust to take care of the house and grounds didn't polish stones.

Trystin couldn't put it all back the way it should be, not all at once, but he'd certainly have the time. Yes, he was going to have plenty of time. Perhaps he should follow his mother's example and go back to school for another degree—a doctorate. He had more than a little thinking to do—about a lot of things.

He carried the bags up to the front porch. The keycard worked, and the lock clicked. After opening the door, he set the bags on the polished tiles of the hall floor—the inside of the house was clean, lifeless, like a museum.

Leaving the bags, he walked toward the kitchen. His boots clunked.

On the center of the kitchen table was a folder sealed in plastic—the first time Trystin could recall plastic around the house. He rummaged through the drawers to find the scissors, then neatly cut the sealed envelope along the edge. Inside was a short computer-generated note.

17 octem 795
Trystin,
   As we promised, everything will be kept for your return.
   Prophets always do return. That is something

we consultants know, but I must admit I never thought I'd father a great religious figure.

All my work remains in the system, for you to use or dispose of as you see fit. I can tell—implants are good for some things—that my days are limited, and, if you find this, obviously, my diagnosis was correct. I will have the master suite cleared. To come back to that would be asking too much of you, and you need a fresh start, at least in the bedroom.

Enjoy the gardens, and your thoughts, and whoever you find to share them with. Do find someone. I have faith that you can and knowledge enough to insist you should.

I could wax long and sentimental, a weakness of age and frailty, but I will not. You know how I feel. I am proud of you, and I always have been. Our thoughts and love are with you, and may the gardens give you the pleasure they have given me.

The words "love" and "Father" were scrawled under the printed words. Trystin's eyes burned, and he could barely swallow.

He left the folder on the table and walked toward the window, pulling back the shades and sliding open the glass, letting the cool dampness of the late fall slip into the house.

After a moment, he walked down to the office, standing in the archway and looking at the silent systems, the blank screens, and the row of old-fashioned wooden cases that held antique bound paper books even more dated than the cases. For a time, he just looked, then turned.

He did not look into the room that had been Salya's.

The master suite was empty, as his father had written. He shook his head. His father had lived by his word. Trystin only hoped he could manage as well.

The great room seemed unchanged—the old chess table was still in place, and Trystin ran his fingers over the smooth wood. Maybe it did really date back to old Earth. He slid open two more windows, enjoying the damp chill.

A buzz sounded.

Trystin paused, then hurried to the kitchen where he fumbled with the console on the faintly dusty counter. "Yes?"

"This is Ulteena. May I come in?"

Trystin swallowed, then answered, "Of course. The gates are open."

"Thank you."

Even through the speakers, her voice sounded formal, and Trystin found he didn't like that. Then, he had sounded formal. And he liked that thought even less . . . far less.

He hurried out the front door and down the path to find her looking at the bonsai cedar.

"It needs work," he explained.

She turned. "You look so young."

"I don't feel young."

"I shouldn't have come."

Trystin looked at the one woman who had always anticipated everything. He smiled. "Yes you should have. I need you."

She glanced toward the cedar as if she had not heard his words. "I'm glad you kept the house and the garden." Her voice floated more lightly than the faint fall breeze, coming to him with the mixed scents of the last miniature yellow roses of the year, the rysya, and the ancient pines.

Abruptly, she turned to him. "What did you say?"

"I love you, and I need you," he repeated, his eyes blurring again.

"You've never . . ." She shook her head, as if in disbelief.

"I've always . . . I just was afraid . . . because you were always so competent. I told you that, on the outer orbit station, remember?" He let the tears stream down his face, as he saw the matching dampness streak her cheeks. He laughed roughly. "And you were always senior. You didn't let me forget it, that first time."

"That was stupid." Her eyes met his.

"That was a long time ago, and I was always stupid about you. I thought you didn't care."

"I almost didn't come," she insisted. "If you hadn't left the note . . ."

"I would have found you—this time," he answered, taking her hand firmly as they stood in late fall and the long twilight.